MW01133358

They Called Him YESHUA:

The Story of the Young Jesus

How Jesus's
Unrecorded Years
Shaped His Ministry

Donald L. Brake
with Shelly Beach

Archway Publishing books may be ordered through booksellers or by contacting:

Archway Publishing
1663 Liberty Drive
Bloomington, IN 47403
www.archwaypublishing.com
1 (888) 242-5904

ISBN: 978-1-4808-7298-1 (sc)
ISBN: 978-1-4808-7296-7 (hc)
ISBN: 978-1-4808-7297-4 (e)

Library of Congress Control Number: 2019900057

Print information available on the last page.

Archway Publishing rev. date: 02/11/2019

Endorsements

"What are the startling implications if Jesus was never a hypocrite? What if he didn't waste the first thirty years of his life here on earth? With biblical and historical accuracy, insightful sanctified imagination, and brilliant storytelling, Brake and Beach foreshadow what we know with certainty from the New Testament. Get ready for epiphanies aplenty."

—David Sanford, executive editor of four Bibles published by Zondervan and Tyndale House

"I've spent the last two days totally consumed with *They Called Him Yeshua*. It's a wonderful piece of work. I found it a powerful work, providing much food for reflection. I really like the way the authors developed Jesus growing in wisdom as a real human, yet maintaining his divinity all the while. The jealousy and animosity of his siblings is well portrayed, as is his parents' grappling with how to parent this holy child.

"*They Called Him Yeshua* is a true page-turner novel about the first thirty years of Jesus's life on earth. Rich with historical and geographical background of Jesus's early years, *They Called Him Yeshua* recreates the family and community life in which the infant Jesus grew into manhood. Here is a moving portrayal of the early years of the most important person in all of history. While weaving a captivating tale, the authors also provide rich insights into the mystery of God humbling himself and being found in human form to ultimately become our Savior."

—Diana Severance, PhD, Director, Dunham Bible Museum, Houston Baptist University

"This book's richness of historical and cultural detail—especially concerning the dangers of being a Jewish parent under the dark menace of Roman rule—helped me understand in a much deeper way things like the peril of the birth of Jesus and Mary's panic when the child was lost in Jerusalem. With warmth, tenderness, and care, the authors picture poignant details: a young Yeshua saying "I want you to teach me too. I need to understand how you see the world. That is your gift to me." This book is a gift to anyone who loves such a son."

—Dr. Latayne C. Scott, prolific writer, novelist, historian, and award-winning author of *A Conspiracy of Breath*

"Dr. Brake's re-creation of the scenes of Jesus's early years highlights their impact and influences in his ministry. Jesus's lost years are brought to life in an easily read, engaging story."

—Carol Trumbold, retired executive vice president, publishing company

"I became immersed in this story and realized that the license used to fill in the gaps not recorded in scripture based on historical truths. You find yourself living with Mary and Joseph and the families. You fear when the Roman soldiers descend on the residents. Rarely do you find a historical novel in the vein of Brock and Bodie Thoene, but the author has done it. A powerful, eye-opening ride."

—Mike Petersen, Church Ministry Manager, Tyndale House Publishers

"As a rule, I don't read many novels. But when a man of Dr. Don Brake's character and stature chooses to write one, my interest is piqued! *They Called Him Yeshua* has stimulated me to pursue Jesus even more closely.

"The *mind* of a seasoned historian, a biblical linguist, and a cultural analyst, combined with the *heart and soul* of a lifelong humble Jesus follower, has developed in Don Brake a sacred imagination. Don is well qualified to help us look curiously into the early decades of our Savior's earthly life, years where scripture is largely silent.

"In these pages, you are welcomed inside the home of a young son of Israel who is "*growing in wisdom and stature.*" Do step inside. Smell the morning bread baking. Feel the daily tension living in small-town Nazareth where the brutal Roman military is stationed. Reflect on the love, and the fear, and the faith of a family living amid oppressive pain from multiple sources—politics, the economy, and religion. And see the young boy blossom into the grown man who is the Savior of the world and its Deliverer.

"I want to know my Lord more intimately. Don Brake has helped me. Reflecting on some of the pages here, I walked today where Jesus walked."

—Stu Weber, pastor, author, and retired US Army veteran awarded three Bronze Stars as a Green Beret in Vietnam. He is a best-selling author of several Gold Medallion finalist books. *The Tender Warrior* is a twenty-year bestseller.

"Donald Brake conveys his scholarly wisdom and passion for biblical accuracy through a heart-rending story of Joseph, Jesus Christ's earthly father. Through his extensive personal experiences in Israel, Brake writes as a scribe, communicating the scenes as they're happening, yet making readers privy to under currents with powerful ramifications. Yes, this is a novel, but it is also devotional, study, and inspiration to draw us nearer to the One they called, *Yeshua.*"

—Mesu Andrews, Novelist of nine biblical character novels and the 2012 Evangelical Christian Publishers Association Debut Author Book of the Year.

Dedicated to those who made unique
impacts on my life and ministry:

Rev. Ernest Lauderman, pastor, Colchester, Illinois
Ellsworth Platt, businessman, Shelbyville, Illinois
Rev. Richard Marseau, pastor, Waukegan, Illinois
Bob and Helen Crump, missionaries, South America
Jerry and Eileen Mitchell, businessman, friend, Waukegan, Illinois
Dr. Arthur Mercer, teacher, Moody Bible Institute, Chicago, Illinois
Dr. James T. Jeremiah, college president, Cedarville, Ohio
Dr. George Lawlor, teacher, Cedarville, Ohio
Dr. Dwight Pentecost, pastor and teacher, Dallas, Texas
Dr. Charles Ryrie, teacher, rare Bible collector, Dallas, Texas
Dr. Edward Goodrick, colleague, friend, Portland, Oregon
Dr. Timothy Aldrich, colleague, friend, Portland, Oregon
James Monson, biblical geographer and historian, Jerusalem, Israel

* * *

Contents

A Word

Believers, ever curious, long for intimate details about our beloved Savior, or the story behind the story, to understand not just biblical events but also what led to them. Jesus often used past events, cultural stories, and everyday incidents for His parables and sermons.

Make no mistake, the canonical Gospels reveal all the information we *need* to know about the Savior and His plan of redemption. *We need no more.*

They Called Him Yeshua is more than an ordinary fictional account of lives of biblical characters; it also recounts possibilities about what Jesus was like and what He experienced as a divine being voluntarily housed in a human body. This novel creates realistic fictional stories that help us imagine how His family reacted to Jesus as He grew and followed His path from self-awareness to His divine mission on earth.

The reader will find *They Called Him Yeshua* to be honest about the universality of human emotions and the struggles Jesus's family faced. Above all, it is the authors' desire that your love and gratitude may be stirred toward the Creator-God who sacrificed His Son, as a lowly man, to become your Savior.

This novel ends with Jesus's baptism, but the factually accurate, trustworthy, and historical account of Jesus's earthly life begins with the Gospels. The biblical story includes the account of His deity, His miracles, the Christian Manifesto, His divine act of self-sacrifice on the cross, His resurrection, and His promise of an eternity prepared for those who place their trust in Him.

The mystery of the incarnation has been discussed, and debated, as has the excuse for persecution and banishment, throughout the centuries. How can Jesus be both God and man? Was He *always* deity, or did He *become* God at birth, at His baptism, or at His resurrection? Did He have a dual personality? Jesus's life prior to His ministry, as portrayed in this novel, helps unravel some of the mysteries of the incarnation. Jesus received His humanity from the DNA of His mother, Mary, and her parents. He received His deity from the Holy Spirit. Some psychologists believe that full personality and brain function are not completely developed until the age of twenty-five to thirty (the time of His baptism).

As a human, the God-man chose to express Himself *only* through the limitations of the human mind as an infant, an adolescent, and a young adult. Therefore, Jesus acted and behaved as a normal human, but of course precociously and without sin. By the time of His baptism, He had fully developed intellectually, and His personality was complete. His humanity caught up with His divinity, and that gave Him the freedom to fulfill His mission, *but* He was always God-man—that is the mystery of the incarnation.

Though *he was God*, he did not think of equality with God as something to cling to.

Instead, he *gave up his divine privileges*; he took the humble position of a slave and was *born as a human being*. When he appeared in human form, he *humbled himself in obedience to God* and died a criminal's death on a cross. (Philippians 2:6–8, emphasis added)

Jesus changed the course of human history, and His incomparable influence is validated every time we record a date or glance at a calendar. His parting words promised He would return. The world is a better place because of this man they called Yeshua.

What we do see is Jesus, who for a little while was given a position a little lower than the angels; and because he suffered death for us, he is now crowned with glory and honor. (Hebrews 2:9)

Oppression

Times were hard under Roman tyranny. Life marked with fear and oppression replaced the days of Hasmonean independence. Gone were the days of powerful King David and Solomon. The new world order divided society into the weak and helpless struggling against the powerful and coercive. Fear gripped the kingdom of Israel as the heavy hand of Roman oppression placed the Israelites under subjection. Despotism fostered resistance groups like the Zealots and Sicarii, who sought in vain to restore Israel to independence and glory. Their bold rebellion and attacks on their oppressor led to retaliation and escalating hardship.

A Jewish family entered this world in obscurity. Their descendants would change the world forever and one day reinstate the kingdom of Israel under the authority of the Jewish Messiah. Their lives bore witness to the best of humankind and the worst of humankind. Life under authoritarian dictatorship pressed them all into a life of faith in the most adverse conditions.

This is their story.

Act 1

Survival: Birth (ca. 7–4 BC)[1]

(Hebrew Calendar ca. 3754–3757/8)

One
The Thunder of Roman Terror

At the cock's crow, Joseph's eyes flew open. He grabbed his dagger and jerked upright, then relaxed at the sight of the golden aura of dawn on the eastern horizon. The aroma of freshly baked bread drifted across the rooftop, and he moaned and slunk back in a heap on his mat.

Ima's baking—her fail-proof wake-up call.

Through one slitted eye, Joseph glimpsed the amethyst sky crowning Nazareth, still shrouding the dawn. He lowered his gaze to the rooftop sleeping quarters he shared with his brothers.

Nathan and Cleophas still slept. Joseph sighed at their snoring. The two seldom stirred to the sound of the cock's crow. *How fortunate to be younger brothers.* He stretched and rose on one elbow as he watched their chests rise and fall. His brothers seldom enjoyed the carefree sleep of boys since they'd begun men's work in the family's fields. They were growing up—but then, everyone's life had changed since Matthan had left. But the responsibilities of the eldest did not fall on Nathan's and Cleophas's shoulders.

Joseph's stomach twisted with the familiar ache, and he rolled onto his back and stared up at the fading stars. Was Matthan looking at the same sky this morning? Was he safe? His older brother had left home three months ago, and the family had not heard a word from him. Had he joined the rebels? They all suspected he had, even though no one talked about Matthan. Abba Jacob had forbidden the family to even speak Joseph's older brother's name.

Joseph rubbed his stomach to ease the familiar ache. Then he stood and straightened the *simlah* Ima had lovingly sewn to serve as his outer garment and blanket. He stepped over Nathan and crept down the steep stone stairs along the exterior of the family's small row house and walked toward the door into the kitchen as he prayed.

Yahweh, protect my brother. Watch over him, wherever his heart has led him.

The aroma of Ima Naomi's brown bread made his mouth water as he pulled open the rough wooden door, ducked his head, and stepped into the golden glow of burning oil lamps. He blinked for a moment, and familiar shapes emerged in the lamplit haze. Little Miriam and Keturah, one bent over the grinding wheel and the other at the smoking *tannur* along the back wall of the tiny kitchen, were too busy working to see him slip through the door into the kitchen. But Ima Naomi, her round face red from the heat of baking, sensed his presence and turned from the steaming bread she had just pulled from the clay tannur. She greeted Joseph with a peck on the cheek.

"Why so early, my son?" She bustled between rough wood shelves loaded with hand-carved sycamore bowls, dried fruits and vegetables, dates, figs, and assorted grains.

"The flour must be finer, Keturah," she called across the room.

Joseph had learned that Ima could command more people than a Roman centurion and remain calm.

"If you skimp on the grinding, beautiful daughter, the bread will be coarse."

"Yes, Ima."

Joseph caught his sister's shy glance in his direction, and her cheeks blushed a sudden pink. He winked, assuring her of his brotherly delight in her, and she turned back to her grinding. Since Matthan left, Joseph was the oldest, and his little sisters tried desperately to please him. And he wanted to assure them he loved them unconditionally. The girls had captured his heart when they had been born, an easy task after having only men in the house for so many years.

And soon their home would gain another woman. Joseph's thoughts drifted as he stared toward a small room just off the kitchen at the back of the house—a recent addition still under construction.

He felt a playful jostle of his shoulder. Ima had stepped away from her baking at the tannur and stood at his side, her graying, dark, curly hair grazing his shoulder.

"You're thinking about Mary, aren't you?"

Joseph's neck and cheeks grew warm as his sisters giggled.

"How did you know?"

Ima's arm encircled his waist. "When your eyes spark like flint against flint, I can see that Mary is occupying your thoughts, my son."

He kissed her forehead and whispered, "The sparkle of flint against flint is but a shadow of what I feel for her, Ima."

She threw her head back and laughed, lines crinkling around her eyes.

Behind him, on the other side of a woolen curtain in the sleeping chamber Abba and Ima shared, Joseph heard the sounds of Abba waking.

"My wife, have you started the Shavuot celebration without me?"

Abba Jacob shoved aside the curtain and rubbed sleep from his eyes. Tying the cord of his sleeping garment around his generous waist, he stretched his hands overhead with a yawn, his fingertips brushing the straw-plastered ceiling. He was an imposing man, a head taller than most Galileans. Jacob strode across the kitchen and, with a good-natured growl, grabbed Keturah and buried his beard in her neck as she squealed. Joseph smiled as he watched his father's morning antics.

"Enough, Jacob, you'll wake the village." Ima's reprimand came with a smile and a flash of pride. Jacob ben Matthan was known throughout Nazareth as an honorable man and exemplary abba. Joseph guessed that was why it had hurt so when his firstborn had abruptly left the family without explanation.

Abba Jacob released Keturah and leveled a playful look at Ima. "Careful, or you'll be my next victim." In two steps, he closed the distance and kissed Ima. "Good morning, beautiful wife."

Joseph had always admired the love Abba showed Ima Naomi. Men seldom demonstrated their affection for women in public.

I want to love Mary like that—to protect her, show her tenderness, and look at her that way.

A question tugged at Joseph's thoughts. *But will I be a good husband like Abba?*

Joseph was painfully aware that in just twelve short months, his qualities as a husband would be tested.

He cleared his throat. "Abba, since Nathan and Cleophas are such good help in the fields, I wondered if I might I stay home today and work on the bridal chamber."

The levity in the room withered like an unwatered flower in the Galilean sun. Joseph was confident the family loved Mary and was excited about the addition to the family home, but Joseph's absence in the fields created more work for the other men.

The smile faded from Abba Jacob's face, and Joseph's heart sank.

"Farmers must work every hour of daylight. We can't predict Roman raids or tax collectors' demands, or bad weather, so when Yahweh gives us sunshine at harvest, we work. If the Romans ever discover your brother's absence and his connection with ..." Abba's voice broke. He struggled to regain his composure before he continued. "Our fields give us the means to purchase the building supplies needed to construct the bridal chamber. You're the firstborn now, Joseph. The wheat is ripe. I won't apologize for putting you to work."

Abba Jacob stared at Joseph, daring him to argue. Joseph discerned that his abba's words were about more than working—they were about Joseph's future. Abba knew Joseph's passion for carpentry—building furniture, wagons, crafting utensils. But when Matthan deserted the family, Joseph became the eldest, and Abba's inheritance and Matthan's responsibilities had been transferred to him. Joseph had no choice but to give up the carpentry work he loved so he could maintain the land his ancestors had owned since the days of Yehoshua.

Joseph lowered his head. "Abba, I'm honored to work our land. I'll go now and wake Nathan and Cleophas." He turned toward the door.

But before he took his first step, a hand gripped his shoulder. "Thank you, Son."

Joseph nodded but didn't turn around. He couldn't let his father see the disappointment in his eyes. He walked out the door and broke into a run toward the stairs to the rooftop. Leaping two rough-cut steps at a time, he burst onto the rooftop just as the sun cleared the horizon and exploded orange.

"Up, you sluggards!" He poked his brothers with his sandaled foot as they moaned and muttered.

"I can always use the water jug again ..." At those words, they scrambled from their mats and raced toward the stairs. Joseph shook his head and smiled as he followed.

He took his position on a stool at the table and listened to the family banter as he scanned Ima's neatly stacked shelves and baskets full of wheat, barley, dried figs, olives, and raisins. Yahweh had provided abundantly for their family, and a twinge of guilt tugged at Joseph's heart. Many households in Nazareth were struggling to eat and pay Roman taxes. On any day, troops could invade a village and falsely accuse Jews of sheltering members of the resistance. Just last month, their family had hidden on the roof as the earth shook, tables rattled, and thundering hooves broke the predawn silence. Jews who resided in Roman territory fought fear and intimidation as if battling swords and spears.

A trickle of sweat ran down Joseph's back. The month of Sivan had been hot this year. Already the air in the kitchen was stifling. He brushed the back of his hand across his forehead to erase the moisture.

"Perhaps we should get to the fields before the sun gets hotter." Joseph hoped his eagerness to begin the workday would please Abba.

Abba offered a satisfied nod. Ima rose from the table and instructed the girls to fill the waterskins. Joseph's sisters scurried across the room and pulled the waterskins from a peg that protruded from the rear rock wall of the kitchen. Then they slipped out the kitchen door.

"We'll bring the midday meal to the fields early," Ima continued. "You'll need more rest today. It's already growing hot. By midday the heat will be powerful enough to scorch the tail off a rooster."

Joseph laughed. Ima always made him laugh. Just being in her presence made the world more secure, more loving, more beautiful. For a few moments the kitchen hummed with conversation about crops, irrigation, and the price of corn. Soon the girls returned with bulging waterskins and secured them over the men's shoulders with leather straps. Joseph felt an escaping drip trace a course down his back as he watched Abba press a kiss on Ima's forehead.

"Yes, Naomi. I hear y—"

The rumble of horse hooves silenced his voice. The sound grew, rattling the plates and cups on the table. Wordlessly, everyone rushed into the courtyard to scan the southeastern horizon. Joseph took a position beside his father, in front of the rest of the family. In the distance cresting the hill, a flag flew the idolatrous image of Caesar, signifying allegiance to Rome and danger to Jews.

Most *equitatae*—cohorts of thirty men—were attached to the Augustan Regiment stationed in Caesarea, but they avoided flying pagan images because the practice incensed Jews. The soldiers descending on Nazareth cared little about giving offense. Their captain's red cape snapped in the breeze, his battle decorations displayed to those forced to bow to his authority. Joseph turned his head and spit on the ground.

Ima Naomi was clutching his sisters to her side, her face stricken.

"Hide the girls on the rooftop inside the empty grain baskets, Ima. Quickly! Pile our sleeping mats on top. And pray!" Joseph forced his voice to sound calm. He did not want to frighten his sisters.

Before Joseph could form his next thought, Nathan and Cleophas hitched up their tunics and sprinted for the stairs, Ima only steps behind. Joseph imagined what she was thinking: the soldiers mustn't discover there were unspoiled girls in their household.

For a few paralyzing moments, Joseph stood beside his brothers, watching as the streets of Nazareth emptied and every resident sought refuge from the sure and coming nightmare.

"Inside! Now!" Abba shoved his remaining sons toward the door.

They scrambled inside, and Joseph slammed the door. "Should I bolt it, Abba?"

Joseph saw indecision flicker across his father's face—a look Joseph had seldom seen.

"Why? Nothing can keep them out." The defeat in his father's eyes cut Joseph like a blade, and he dropped his gaze to the floor, embarrassed at his father's tone of discouragement.

Abba altered the remains of their meal to look like two fewer family members had been interrupted while eating.

"Hide your sisters' plates."

He grabbed the girls' cups and plunged them in a basket of grain. The sound of snorting steeds told them that the soldiers were drawing nearer. Joseph's heart echoed the sound of pounding hooves as he raced around the room.

"Boys, sit down and don't speak. If the soldiers ask about Matthan, I'll answer."

Naomi's sandals slapped against the floor above, interspersed with people's cries and pounding hooves in nearby streets. Moments later, she raced through the back door, her blue mantle billowing behind her, and took her place at the table beside Abba as she gasped for deep, calming breaths.

Joseph strained his ears, not a second too soon. The sound of voices and the whinny of horses told him that the Romans were reining their Arabian stallions to a halt outside their courtyard gate. He tried to steady his shaking hands as he poured wine mixed with water into everyone's cups.

Please, Yahweh, don't let them find Miriam and Keturah.

The sound of hobnailed sandals pounded the ground in the courtyard—one after another, after another—the entire regiment dismounting and waiting for their captain's command.

"Bring me every male thirteen and older," a voice shouted. "Search every hovel."

Ima's eyes glistened with terror. "Jacob, they *cannot* take our sons!" she whispered.

The captain's voice pounded like a drum in the sweltering heat.

"Take every male to the center of town for interrogation. If they refuse to cooperate, march them to Tiberias in chains."

Joseph swallowed his panic. The threat of the hellish prison made him wonder, *Had Matthan been captured? Was he imprisoned in Tiberias? Or was he safe in Judea with the rebels?*

Terrified shouts and cries for mercy rang out in the distance. Then without warning, the door burst open with a slamming of wood against stone, scattering slivers of board across the rough stone floor. The red-caped captain pushed his way through the small doorway. Muscles taut and exposed in his short-sleeved tunic, he surveyed the family in ominous silence. The red-feathered plume atop his galea made him look taller and more menacing than the other soldiers who crowded into the room behind him.

The captain filled the family's small common chamber more with presence than with size. Six soldiers stood behind him.

"Search everything," he ordered, staring at Abba Jacob with cold, dark eyes.

The soldiers upended baskets and tossed bread into the waste pots. They ground vegetables into the bed mats with the heels of their caligae. Joseph and his family sat motionless and mute at the table—until one soldier flipped it on its side. Two soldiers ruthlessly searched Abba and Ima's sleeping room, which was separated from one wall of the kitchen by a thick curtain. Throughout the ordeal, the captain stood silently near the door, observing. Abba stared back into the officer's determined eyes but never said a word. It was a look Joseph had not seen before. The screams and sobs coming from outside told him that friends and neighbors were enduring worse, or perhaps that worse was yet to come for his family.

"Do you think I enjoy this?" the captain challenged Abba, his eyes angry but his expression unchanged. "We have marched for days to apprehend rebels in the empire because the local garrison couldn't take care of minor uprisings in this armpit of Galilee." He spat the final word and, with one sweeping motion, knocked over a small table, sending Ima's favorite grinding bowl to the floor. It splintered.

Joseph watched his father's face. Abba Jacob didn't flinch, but his wide eyes told Joseph he was preparing to speak.

"I understand that you are a man under authority who uses his authority to reach a necessary end." His tone was as smooth as finely carded wool. "I cannot judge your intent."

The captain's stony expression softened. "My *end* is to destroy Galilean rebels, not your wife's pottery." He noted one of his soldiers starting up the rooftop steps. "Stop!" he shouted. "You are wasting time, idiot. Why would they hide sons on the rooftop when they are keeping three able-bodied sons here in plain sight?"

Joseph felt like laughing and crying at the same time. Relief for his sisters flooded over him, but he knew he and his two brothers would not escape interrogation and perhaps torture, confinement, or forced conscription.

"The three of you, come with me." The captain nodded toward the door and then met Abba's gaze. "If your sons tell me the truth, they may return. If they lie or refuse to cooperate, you will never see them again."

Joseph walked toward the door with his brothers. His last sight as he exited his home under guard was of Ima Naomi falling into Abba's arms, tears of gratitude mixed with terror streaming down her face and darkening the sleeve of her husband's tunic.

She had already lost one son.

As they led him away into the unknown, Joseph remembered words his father had told him when he turned twelve: "The Romans say, 'All revolts begin in Galilee.'"[2] Abba had continued, "They fear us, Joseph. We are mere farmers and shepherds, yet they fear us. Not so much us, but our God.

"Perhaps they're not as stupid as we like to believe."

Two

Joseph's Shackles Broken

The shackles cut deeper into his wrists and ankles with each step. After connecting a chain to a Roman supply wagon, guards dragged Joseph and his brothers to town, where they separated the young men. A soldier led Joseph beneath an open tent, where a guard chained him to a tree. A chair constructed of wood and animals' skins stood in the center of the tent, with a small table to the right and a whip placed in the center. Moments later the captain appeared and settled at the table after ordering Joseph to remain standing.

The truth is my only defense, but I cannot speak a word about Matthan without putting the family at risk.

He swallowed and looked the captain in the eye as the interrogation began.

The captain pummeled him with question after question. What did he and his brothers do, whom did they associate with, and what were their religious practices, political leanings, social connections, and dealings with Jewish rebels? Hours passed.

No sitting.

No food.

No water.

The only break was the burn of the lash across his back.

The sun crept across the sky as Joseph's throat grew parched and his legs weakened. Sometime after the sun reached its highpoint heralding midday, the captain released him—but not before ordering a beating and giving warning that he would return and officially conscript Joseph into the Roman army. Only Joseph's age had spared him this time.

Joseph stood numb and drenched in blood as guards removed the shackles—but not before they beat him mercilessly. He stumbled toward the village well to ease his wounds and to put as much distance between himself and his torturers as he could before they changed their minds. He staggered the few final steps toward the well, his mind blurred from the pain.

The captain ordered that all boys thirteen and over be taken. I am over eighteen and in perfect health, yet they released me. It is a miracle.

He dropped to his knees in the dirt and wept in gratitude.

You alone spared me, mighty Yahweh. It is by Your hand that I still draw breath. All glory and thanks be to Your name. You alone are the hope of Israel. Please, please protect my brothers.

Joseph drew the brown woven sash that secured his simlah from his waist and dipped it into the trough used to water the animals. Over and over he saturated it, wrung it out, and squeezed it over his wounds. His parents and sisters could not see how badly the Romans had beaten him. They worried enough about Matthan.

Just before dusk, Joseph limped into the courtyard of his home and the outstretched arms of Ima and his sisters. His brothers had already returned, released for reasons they would never understand. Abba Jacob had stood near the doorway, bowing and praying.

Later that day, as Joseph helped Ima Naomi and Abba Jacob put right the scattered and broken mess of their home, a neighbor stopped by to share news. Roman forces had taken several young men from Nazareth to Herod's local jail. Joseph was filled with gratitude. His sisters had been spared! And Roman officers had released Nathan, Cleophas, and him from the interrogation in the town square. Life would go on—at least for now.

By evening the rhythm of life had returned, but Joseph was aware that the family would move forward beneath a thinly veiled shroud of safety. Soon after evening fell and Joseph went to bed, he heard sounds below of Abba Jacob drawing Ima Naomi away from her nightly vigil at the open door of the house and into the comfort of his arms.

Once again, Matthan had not returned home. And in the darkness below his rooftop bedroom, Joseph again overheard Ima's muffled sobs.

Three

A Farmer Chooses Carpentry

Sweat fell from the tip of Joseph's nose to a blotch of muddied wood shavings near his feet. He thanked Yahweh for the small carpentry workroom Abba Jacob had allowed him to build behind the house, just steps from the wedding chamber.

Joseph wiped his forehead on the sleeve of his *kethoneth*, then stooped lower over his workbench. He stroked his knife against the wood as he shaped the fragrant limb of a walnut tree into a table leg. He turned and selected a fine sandstone, then massaged the rough leg to a polished silky surface. Closing his eyes, he ran his fingers across the surface to test the texture.

"Perfect."

At the sound of footsteps, he turned. Abba Jacob stood just inside the low door, concern furrowing his brow. Joseph pointed to a cushioned bench fashioned out of multihued local woods, and Abba sat down.

"Joseph, your customers in Nazareth praise you. Your creations are as beautiful as they are functional. Your love for woodwork speaks from every object you make."

Joseph brushed shavings from his hands and smiled as he acknowledged his abba's words. "Yes, Abba, but you have known this since I was a child."

When Abba opened a conversation with praise, Joseph

knew a difficult conversation was soon coming. He took a long, slow breath and settled on a stool near his abba.

"We need more men to farm our land, Joseph. One day you will inherit Matthan's share, as he is eldest. But he is certainly not interested in farming or faith since he is running with rebels and looking for trouble."

Joseph could hear the mix of heartbreak and anger in his father's voice. Matthan's choices continually overshadowed Abba and Ima's thoughts. His risk of getting into trouble with Roman authorities loomed over the family like swirling clouds in a maelstrom over the Sea of Galilee. Even Abba Jacob was helpless to rein Matthan in, and the family suspected he was involved with the notorious Zealots.[3] If such were the case, then his demise was inevitable—it was just a matter of time.

Joseph sighed in frustration. The family farm was no longer adequate to provide for the needs of the family. He didn't want to disappoint Abba, but he loved working with his hands.

Abba Jacob and his father before him had been farmers. Farming in rural Palestine formed the foundation of Jewish social structure. Joseph respected Abba for his commitment to the land. He often scooped up a handful of dirt and held it to the heavens in gratitude to God. Jacob had often told Joseph that his greatest gift to his family would be to leave his farm to his sons. But Joseph believed that dwindling productivity would not sustain future generations in coming years.

Owning land was a mark of stability and prosperity, but property came at a premium. In Herod the Great's day, most Galilean land belonged to a few wealthy landowners: priestly aristocrats and Herodian families who owned slaves or used sharecroppers to do the work.

Abbas had passed down their land to male children in every generation since the Israelites settled in Nazareth after their return from the Babylonian captivity. The law commanded that the land be returned to the original landowners, even if they had sold or leased the property. This law guaranteed that Jewish-owned land stayed among God's chosen people. The eldest son inherited a larger portion, and younger siblings received smaller plots. By the time Abba had inherited it, the family parcel was small, divided, and scattered. To add to the challenge, heavy Herodian taxes imposed on landowners made profitable farming difficult. These taxes forced many Jewish families to sell their land when their plots became too small and taxes too high to sustain a family. With Rome in control, the legally required fifty-year Jubilee that restored land meant nothing and was not enforced.

It was also rumored that Herod Antipas planned to rebuild Sepphoris into a prosperous capital city on a grand scale. This also encouraged Joseph to pursue growing opportunities in carpentry. He could still keep a small plot to meet family responsibilities for offerings at feasts. He hoped to work as an apprentice to a general builder, which would include carpentry and masonry. The Sepphoris project would offer diverse opportunities for a skilled artisan and comfortable provision for his family.

But Joseph also recognized that the thought of him leaving family farming caused Abba Jacob distress, and he didn't want to disappoint his abba. What he wanted most was Abba Jacob's approval of his career in carpentry—a future Joseph had feared to envision for himself. Matthan's departure had left Joseph no choice but to take on his brother's responsibilities. It was what an honorable son would do.

He turned to Abba, who was waiting for a response. Joseph chose his tone, one of deep respect yet edged in strength. He prayed his father would see beyond his words.

"Abba, I honor your love for the land God gave us and that it connects us to our Creator. You have always been grateful, generous, and a good steward. By the work of your hands, our land has flourished like the Garden of Eden, but our family portions become smaller with each birth and marriage. Our families have had many children, and it will not be possible for all of us to survive as farmers unless some men in the family find other trades."

Abba's fingers tapped a quick rhythm on his thigh—the same rhythm they had tapped during his many arguments with Matthan, or during months of drought, or when Ima had become ill with a fever.

Joseph tried to read the look on Abba's face. Weariness and sorrow had etched their story when Matthan left, and that story had never left. Joseph reached out and placed his hand on his father's arm.

Jacob's head dropped toward the stone floor. Silence stretched painfully between them before he spoke.

"I understand your desire, Joseph, and I bless your efforts to become a carpenter. Wood is scarce in this dry land. I'm sure you will also gain greater skill building with stone. I only hope your *mohar*[4] will be large enough to satisfy a bride's father."

Joseph felt a rush of gratitude mixed with sadness. He treasured the cost of his father's words, but Abba Jacob's devotion to God and love for his family had always come before his own desires. Ima and Joseph's brothers and sisters had always trusted Abba's unselfish love and found him more than faithful.

Abba's sacrifice and sorrow will only make it more difficult to leave for an apprenticeship, but I believe Yahweh blesses my choice.

Abba Jacob slapped Joseph playfully on the back. "Promise you will put your whole heart into your work as a carpenter and honor Yahweh!" His father's voice cracked, and Joseph lowered his head in respect.

"Thank you for your blessing, Abba. I will do my best to make you proud and honor Yahweh through my work.

And whenever you have need of extra hands, I will be here to help."

Joseph hesitated, conflict choking his heart. But he knew he must speak what was in his heart for the family.

"Matthan has no interest in the land, but Cleophas would make an excellent farmer. He has soaked up your teaching. Everything he plants grows strong, and he knows how to outwit the tares that choke our crops. But as the youngest, he has been afraid to show his desires."

Abba nodded and smiled. "Yes, Joseph, I can count on you when I need help. And I have seen Cleophas's abilities and will prayerfully consider your suggestion."

Abba Jacob rose and moved toward the door. "I bless your decision, Joseph. I will farm as long as I can, and when I can no longer manage the responsibilities, Cleophas will inherit the land. Follow the desire God has put in your heart."

Joseph nodded, humbled. He prayed that Abba would find comfort in the thought of Cleophas nurturing the family land and that Cleophas would be happy farming the land Abba loved.

Above all, Joseph prayed that his resolve to work as a carpenter had not broken Abba Jacob's heart.

Four

First Love

Joseph willed himself not to run and disgrace his family by exposing his ankles in public. But even his long, steady strides beneath the midmorning sun caused sweat to drip from his beard. The walk to Mary's house was a short distance, but his thoughts tumbled like waves on the Sea of Galilee.

Mary's abba is an international trader, a man of good reputation. Yes, he has blessed me with his approval, but I must show myself worthy. And Mary's ima *grew up in the luxury of Sepphoris. Even though Heli moved the family to Nazareth to protect them from corrupt city life, they may hope me to be more sophisticated than I am.*

Mary's family was honorable and of good reputation, and Joseph had been ecstatic that Heli had approved him as a husband. Although Joseph had not been looking for a wife, he had lost his heart when Mary offered him a cup of water one blazing afternoon when he was working on an addition to Heli's house. Even though he was more than five years older than she, his heart was taken the moment she lowered her beautiful eyes.

Joseph hastened his pace. It would soon be past the time when Mary drew water at Nazareth's well. He smiled when moments later he spotted women scattered around the community water supply. His beloved was working the rope, the morning sunshine glimmering in her dark hair.

A spark hit Joseph's body like embers from an evening fire striking skin. She glanced up at the sound of footfalls. She wore the veil of the betrothed, but he recognized her smile in the quick crinkles around her soft brown eyes that were the color of aged honey. Her silky hair cascaded over her shoulders and to her waist. Her graceful, fluid movements enhanced her beauty as she poured water into a pot at her feet. She smiled as she tilted her head to turn toward Joseph.

"Shalom, Mary."

"Shalom, Joseph." Her tone was soft, almost shy.

The simple greeting sent chills down his spine. His face flushed as his mind emptied. *Have I become a fool?* Joseph stood frozen. *I cannot speak and I feel like a child.*

He was suddenly both frightened and embarrassed.

Her eyes told him she was enjoying that her betrothed was tripping over his words. But she turned her eyes downward and spoke softly.

"My parents are at home, if you came to speak to them." Her voice flowed like silk drifting in the evening breeze. Joseph's throat tightened, and his heart pounded. Speaking to her parents would not be easy. He took a deep breath.

Is this woman my betrothed, Yahweh? She is beautiful and kind, but I want to know her better.

A sense of urgency flooded through him, and Joseph swallowed.

"Yes, I would like to speak to your parents ... but *you* even more."

Talking to her parents was not something he *wanted* to do but was something he must do. Joseph had declared his intentions according to custom, but he and Mary could not be together without a chaperone. He must honor Mary and tradition, but although he and Mary had been betrothed, they had not spoken. He wanted to spend time getting to know her, and he needed permission to visit her during the betrothal period.

I hope she finds me suitable. Although I'm nearly twenty and she is not yet fifteen, her parents could have pledged her to a much older man. They could still change their minds. I can only pray that my chosen occupation, family honor, and devotion will be enough.

The couple made their way up the dusty path through Nazareth toward Mary's home. She walked a half pace behind Joseph. He took the right, a defensive position near the outside of the road.

We are alone and unchaperoned. We must hurry.

The two families—particularly the woman's—were obligated to ensure a betrothal ended with the joining of two consenting persons in *holy* matrimony that reflected on their families.

Joseph's anxiety grew with each step. What if Mary's father became angry to find that Joseph would not inherit his family's land? Would he break the betrothal?

The incline of the road was rocky, narrow. In spite of obstacles and the slope, Mary kept the water jug balanced skillfully on her head. After breaking for a short rest, Joseph spotted Mary's ima Anna in the distance, seated on a rock outside their courtyard. One hand shaded her eyes, and she stood when she caught sight of the young couple.

Joseph swallowed. *Please, God, let her parents believe that I happened upon Mary at the well and that we came directly to their home.*

He hastened his pace when he recognized Mary's father joining her mother at the gate. Moments later, the couple arrived at the courtyard, winded and dusty.

"Shalom." Joseph forced himself to look into Heli's stone-gray eyes. "I passed Mary at the well, and she graciously escorted me back to your home. May we speak?"

Mary nodded, then slipped past her parents, walked through the courtyard, and entered their large stone house. Anna and Heli embraced Joseph, and the tension in his shoulders relaxed. They led him into the gathering room and directed him to a cushioned bench, then settled into carved chairs with leather woven seats. Mary had disappeared.

Joseph wasted neither time nor words. He had come for a purpose.

"Ima Miriam and Abba Jacob send their greetings. They asked me to further discuss Mary's future with you, now that the betrothal is official and the ketubah is signed."

Silence hung in the room as Joseph waited for a response.

Nothing.

He felt beads of sweat forming on his brow, but he continued.

"You and my parents have already agreed to our betrothal. I hope you trust my great affection for Mary and my commitment to her. I would like to use our betrothal period to learn more about her and gain wisdom to become a better husband. I respectfully ask permission to see her as my work with my abba permits me—with appropriate chaperones. Do I have your blessing?"

Heli cleared his throat and leaned forward in his chair.

"Anna and I have spoken with your ima and abba. Your father told me you will receive the land and the farm since Matthan left."

Joseph's heart froze. He had given away his land and house—something no Jewish son would ever do. How could he explain his choice to Mary's parents and not look foolish? His mind raced as he searched for words.

"That *was* true. But I ... I have chosen ... a different path. The land will pass to my brother Cleophas, who has a gift for cultivating and growing crops. I will continue to develop my carpentry skills and build a business that will provide well for your daughter—a better future than the unpredictable realities of farming."

Joseph inhaled, closed his eyes as he held his breath, and waited for an explosion of anger as he counted silently in his head.

One, two, three, four, five, six, seven, eight, nine, ten, eleven ...

He opened his eyes in trepidation. Heli was smiling at him.

"You are a courageous man, Joseph, willing to take a risk to do what you believe is right. I respect that."

Joseph exhaled as Heli continued.

"Yes, Anna and I are quite willing for you to spend time with our precious Mary."

Joseph's heart leaped. "May we walk today in the olive grove—for a short time?" He prayed that his face did not reveal the shaking he felt in his bones.

Heli hesitated for a moment. "I'm certain you didn't come today just to speak to *us* and go home." He nodded and smiled. "With chaperones."

Jacob smiled as he expressed his thanks, then waited for Mary's return.

The morning air was steaming as the couple began their walk toward the community olive grove and garden that lay at the end of a path a short distance below Heli's home. The gnarled, fragrant olive trees provided a secluded setting for shade, private conversation, and secret trysts. The couple ambled as they made their way down the rocky pathway, and he gently steadied Mary's arm on the descent. Ancient olive trees scattered among large boulders shadowed the valley and made it suitable for seating. The couple walked side by side saying nothing, enjoying each other's company.

Not far behind but out of hearing range, Anna and two of her friends trailed the couple. Following Jewish custom, Heli had found chaperones who would protect the couple's reputation and prevent accusations of misconduct during courting.

Joseph's heart raced with the speed of a lion chasing an ibex as they approached the secluded grove. He longed to entwine Mary's fingers in his own, but a woman was approaching on the path. As they stepped to the side to make room for her, their hands brushed. Mary jerked her arm away, then seemed to relax again. Not long after their hands brushed a second time. This time Mary's fingers lingered against his.

Joseph swallowed. Words would not come, but an unfamiliar intoxication enveloped him. Just *perhaps* Mary was as heart-struck as he felt.

Once at the olive grove, Joseph found comfortable seating on a smooth, flat boulder. He brushed away all signs of dirt and gestured for Mary to sit beside him. The chaperones found seats on another rock a short distance away.

Joseph sat to Mary's right, slightly above her. He angled himself so he could look at her veiled face. Her wide brown eyes were modestly downcast, and a cascade of henna-brown hair tumbled past her shoulders

She is so beautiful, but what is she thinking? Is she happy to be with me? Already I sense that her inner spirit is also beautiful.

Joseph sat motionless and silent, fixated on Mary's beauty, his thoughts running in circles as he searched for words.

Will she reject a husband who gave up his meager inheritance? Is she enduring me because the ketubah has been signed?

His heart churned. *She must think me awkward, if not worse.* Boldly, Joseph reached for Mary's hand. She didn't scowl or pull away but smiled as she gazed at a distant rock.

Joseph glanced to the side to see if the chaperones offered any objection to his advance—but they were talking and appeared unconcerned. At that moment, Mary turned, looked into his eyes, and spoke.

"Joseph, tell me about yourself and family, about things that are important to you."

Joseph scanned her face. Her expression was sincere and open.

She's not afraid to be direct, and she's not fearful. She's asking questions to make it easier for me to talk. How kind!

Mary's simple question encouraged and intrigued him. He regained his composure and spoke—incoherently at first, his words tumbling out in no apparent order.

No matter what she said or did, Joseph couldn't take his eyes off of her. Whispers and quiet laughter told him the chaperones were enjoying their job. After several minutes of what he was sure was senseless rambling, Joseph stopped talking, embarrassed that he was making a fool of himself.

His hands shook as he looked into her beautiful carob-colored eyes. Suddenly, the words that had been pounding through his head tumbled from his lips

"I want to marry you. But I must be honest and need to tell you something."

Mary's eyes widened in surprise. Joseph regretted speaking but continued.

"The ketubah has been signed, and you and I are betrothed. But my mohar no longer includes our family land. I would not blame you if you no longer wanted to marry me."

Joseph glanced down at his hands marked by hard calluses from fitting stones for houses and public buildings, as well as by scars from cutting tools for woodworking. He was afraid to look up and see the look of disappointment he was certain would be in Mary's eyes. The few seconds of silence were excruciating. As he steeled himself for her answer, he caught the scent of narcissus in her hair.

"I delight in your honesty, Joseph, but the land is not important. You are direct and open and honest, and I appreciate that. I am fond of you and enjoy your company. I would like to know more about you, but you must tell these things to my abba. Many brides do not see their betrothed until he comes for her for the wedding. I too prefer we use this time to discover Yahweh's purpose for bringing us together, but my abba must give permission."

A breeze rustled through the trees and tousled Mary's hair.

Joseph was taken aback. She spoke with composure, wisdom, and insight beyond her fourteen years.

"Joseph, I like you and am already learning to trust you. We have a year of betrothal for friendship and love to develop, and I look forward to that. Very much."

She smoothed her soft rose-hued tunic, and Joseph smiled.

He understood that while their families had blessed their betrothal, their parents would not insist on the marriage if either one of them refused to wed. If they weren't a suitable match, they could honorably part. But Joseph had no intention of disappointing this woman, and he was certain she could never be a disappointment to him.

Mary's eyes were saying that she was pleased with him.

This is the beginning for Mary and me. At least I pray it is.

Over the next weeks, Joseph made winning Mary's heart his highest priority. After breakfast, chores, and work on the bridal chamber, he headed to Heli's home to spend time with his betrothed in quiet conversation, walking in the olive garden, even helping with household chores for her family.

And amid the long walks, the dust and heat, and the laughter and growing affection, the mysteries of eternity and hope for humankind unfolded in the lives of these simple people.

Five

Two Miracle Pregnancies

"Mary, come out of the sun," Ima called from the doorway.

Mary ground the toe of her sandal into the dirt, then rose and obeyed. Weeks had passed since Joseph had visited, and she was surprised that she missed him so much. Her concern for his safety had deepened to worry. After whispering her morning prayers each day, she felt drawn to the sitting stone near the courtyard gate, where she searched the road for signs of his return.

But another worry soon overshadowed Mary's thought. Word had come that her aunt Elizabeth was soon to give birth, and her delivery was expected to be difficult, perhaps imperiling her life. Her pregnancy had come at an advanced age, and precautions had been put into place to bring the baby to full term.

Traveling had become risky even in Nazareth, and Mary's parents reassured her that Joseph was wise to visit less frequently. Roving bands of rebels, thieves, and outlaws were threatening travelers throughout Judea and Galilee. Robbers had recently raided a caravan headed to Jerusalem and murdered two pilgrims and the wagoner. They stole and destroyed possessions, overturned wagons and carts, and assaulted caravanners, leaving death and destruction in their wake. Travelers had become fearful, and caravans had increased their size and security. The attacks brought the wrath of the Romans, who took reprisals on innocent travelers. Joseph's lone treks had drawn attention. Mary missed him more with each passing day.

When the house stilled and the dark night air pressed in like an airless tomb, Mary closed her eyes in the darkness as she lay in her bed and prayed for peace and safety for the trip to visit Elizabeth in Ein Kerem—and especially peace for Abba and Ima.

"Daughter, a large caravan leaves Nazareth for Jerusalem in two days. It will provide the greatest safety for you. Within that caravan, a group of travelers is headed to Ein Kerem. A widow named Miriam and her son promised to look after you as if you were a member of their family."

Abba stepped toward Mary and gathered her in his arms. "Your ima and I do not give our permission lightly, Daughter. Your veil will identify your vulnerability as a single betrothed woman. We allow you to go, trusting that God will keep you in His care and that He has a great purpose in this visit—as He does in all things."

Abba's embrace tightened.

Yahweh must have moved Abba's heart. There is no other way he would have allowed me to go. But he is also trusting me.

A mix of gratitude, excitement, and fear rushed through Mary.

"Thank you, Abba. This cannot be easy for you or Ima." The weight of her abba's head rested upon her own, then lifted.

Mary knew Ein Kerem had brought danger to its people by embracing the rebel cause. The whole country now feared retribution because of their revolt. No one could escape Rome's anger or the rebels' attempts to provoke local magistrates and infuriate Roman authorities.

* * * * *

Mary's lungs burned, and her face throbbed with the beating of her heart. Opening her eyes made the world spin.

For three days in a row, she had awakened to a churning stomach before Miriam's daughter-in-law had stirred the fire to begin breakfast. The five-day trip to Elizabeth's was proving more difficult than expected, and doubts flickered through her mind about whether she had made the right choice to visit Elizabeth.

Before the caravan left, Miriam's son had placed Mary beside his dwarfish, withered mother atop the mule-drawn cart that carried their belongings. He insisted Mary ride for the entire journey. Miriam had taken Mary's hand and stroked it with bony, crooked fingers.

"We are taking no risks, *yekirati*. You must be careful."

Miriam's searching eyes reminded Mary of her mother's look whenever Mary had taken to bed with fevers.

"Careful?" Mary asked, confused. *Risks? What does she mean?*

"Too much heat robs your strength and can hurt the child. You must rest, yekirati, especially during midday. This is not a good time for you to be on such a hard journey."

Mary's hand flew to her stomach, and she forced the slow scream rising in her throat into silence.

A child ... a baby? How could this stranger have such knowledge? I have never been with a man. Ever. But God's word has come to pass. I have sensed changes in my body these past days. But I am with child of the Holy Spirit.

She had told no one of the angel Gabriel's visit revealing her earthly blessing and heavenly honor. The events had seemed too strange.

And now Miriam was telling her—with just a glance? Could it be true?

Mary trembled as she choked back tears. She could not let Miriam see her cry. Mary gripped one hand with the other to still her shaking.

But Joseph? How will I tell him, and how will he react?

She released her breath, blinking away tears, her chest aching with pressure.

Yes, this will be a difficult journey.

She wrapped her arms around her stomach and let the tears flow.

* * * * *

A tangle of emotions overshadowed the remainder of Mary's trip to Ein Kerem: shock, fear, euphoria, gratitude, confusion, joy, doubt, and feelings she could not name. Yahweh's divine infant Son was living in her body. The thought was too immense to think about before her mind surrendered, acknowledging total insufficiency to comprehend God's wonder. So Mary reached for things she knew. Worship. Awe. Gratitude.

Her emotions swept her into a world so beyond her experience that she seldom engaged in conversation and sat silently in deep conversation with Yahweh while Miriam stroked her hands or brought her food and water.

Miriam's face filled her days as she tended to Mary's needs and coaxed her to lie her head upon the soft lambskin Miriam's son had brought to them for Mary's comfort.

The caravan arrived in Ein Kerem without incident, stopping around midday near a cluster of small houses that opened on a central courtyard. Just beyond the houses, a road branched off to the west. Miriam's son lifted Mary down from the cart and helped her tie her small bundle to her back.

"Follow the road west, and you will soon come to the house of Zechariah, the temple priest."

Mary turned and hugged Miriam's bony, frail body.

"How can I ever thank you?" She stroked the older woman's face.

"I serve at Yahweh's pleasure, my child, the greatest joy a woman could ever know. I provided comfort—it is Yahweh's gift to both you and me."

Mary embraced the old woman, then turned and headed toward Elizabeth and Zechariah's home, praying with every step as tears streamed from her eyes and words tumbled from her heart.

She soon stood before a carved wooden door with heavy metal hinges and paused. God would be with her. He *was* with her. She was Mary, and though it was difficult for her to comprehend, God had chosen her. She drew a deep breath and called through the door.

"Greetings, Dodah Elizabeth, it is Mary, daughter of Anna and Heli." She tried to keep her voice steady.

Mary heard a shout inside, and the door burst open. Elizabeth stared at her, her puffy, full face startled. "Come. Come inside. I must sit back down. The baby just leaped in my womb at the sight of you! This is the first time I have experienced such a reaction from the child." She stroked her bulging stomach as she eased into a large wooden chair overflowing with bright pillows.

"And why should it be granted that the mother of my Lord should come to *me*? Blessed are you among women, and blessed is the child you will bear!" Elizabeth raised her hands toward heaven.

The Spirit of God had obviously directed her aunt's words. A sudden stirring swept through Mary like the bite of cold water slaking a parching thirst or stepping beneath a cleansing waterfall. Then the words came, from breath not her own but borne of the Spirit of God and the child within her. Mary heard herself speak:

Oh, how my soul praises the Lord.
    How my spirit rejoices in God my Savior!
For he took notice of his lowly servant girl,
    and from now on all generations will call me blessed.
For the Mighty One is holy,
    and he has done great things for me.
He shows mercy from generation to generation
    to all who fear him.
His mighty arm has done tremendous things!
    He has scattered the proud and haughty ones.

He has brought down princes from their thrones
    and exalted the humble.
He has filled the hungry with good things
    and sent the rich away with empty hands.
He has helped his servant Israel
    and remembered to be merciful.
For he made this promise to our ancestors,
    to Abraham and his children forever.
Oh, how my soul praises the Lord.
    How my spirit rejoices in God my Savior!
For he took notice of his lowly servant girl,
    and from now on all generations will call me blessed.
For the Mighty One is holy,
    and he has done great things for me.[5]

Exhausted, Mary slipped to the floor at her aunt's feet to rest, and they both bowed to the power of the moment. As the Spirit lifted, Mary settled Elizabeth on comfortable soft-hued blankets stacked at one end of the gathering room near a sleeping pallet and an herb table. Mary could tell that this was a room where her aunt spent much of her time. Mary found the water jug and brought water sweetened with honey and herbs and a handful of almonds for each of them as Elizabeth confided details about her miraculous but difficult pregnancy. Zechariah's and her own advanced age had convinced them that the opportunity to have a child had long passed.

"But our perception of possibilities or impossibilities does not limit Yahweh. He is God. He has a plan. Trust that. And He sometimes carries out His plan in ways far beyond our thought."

Mary settled on the blankets beside her beloved aunt as Elizabeth continued. "From the time of King David, the twenty thousand Jerusalem priests were divided into twenty-four divisions. The honored 'Abijah' priests offered the incense in the temple. Your uncle Zechariah, who you know is an older priest, traveled daily from the first hour of the day to the third to Jerusalem to perform his varied duties.

"One day as Zechariah was offering incense, an angel appeared to him. He was paralyzed with fear, but the angel calmed him and prophesied that I, his wife, would bear him a son who would be called John. This was an earthshaking announcement to Zechariah, since I was barren, and we were both well along in years.

"But the angel whispered, 'Do not be afraid, Zechariah; your prayer has been heard. Your wife, Elizabeth, will bear you a son, and you are to call him John. He will be a joy and delight to you, and many will rejoice because of his birth, for he will be great in the sight of the Lord."

Mary blinked. Had she understood correctly?

Angels visited Elizabeth and Zechariah and spoke to them, just as an angel spoke to me. Could it be true? Are these two unborn babies' destinies linked?

The idea seemed unbelievable, but she had seen God work in strange ways.

"Zechariah, overcome by the absurdity of seeing a messenger from God, doubted the angel's words and questioned the possibility of such an unbelievable deed."

Zechariah questioned what he was seeing, at least at first.

Elizabeth continued, "He asked the angel, 'How can I be sure of this? I am an old man, and my wife is well along in years.'"

Mary swallowed and fingered a wrinkle in the pale pink mantle she had dyed with flower petals.

Yes, and I am a virgin who has never been with a man. Yet here I am with child. But even though this is part of Yahweh's plan, who will believe me? Who will understand the circumstances of my condition?

A thought slammed into her mind, and Mary reached for her throat.

Joseph. Will he believe I have been faithful? that I haven't betrayed him? Will he be angry and send me away?

Elizabeth was still speaking. Mary forced her attention back to her cousin.

Elizabeth shifted to her left side, and Mary slid a soft blanket beneath her head.

"I am growing tired and have not asked about you, Mary. Tell me, child, about your pregnancy."

Mary smoothed away a dark curl that had fallen to Elizabeth's forehead. The connection of their hearts obscured the distance in their ages. God had brought her to this place as a gift to prepare her for the months ahead. She settled at Elizabeth's side and took her hand.

"Joseph and I were happily betrothed. He's a wonderful, godly man, and I soon came to love him. Then one day I was sitting alone weaving cloth, and an angel appeared. I was terrified and wondered what I'd done wrong. But the angel said I'd found favor with God and that I would conceive a child by the Holy Spirit. The angel told me to call the child Yeshua because he will be called the Son of the Most High."

The apples of Elizabeth's round cheeks shone as she smiled. "All glory be to Yahweh, who has reached down to walk among sinners." Tears formed in Elizabeth's eyes.

Not a word of doubt or question.

Stunned, Mary stumbled on.

"Yeshua will take the throne of David, and His kingdom will be everlasting. Although I don't understand everything, I take all the angel said by faith. The angel also told me you, Elizabeth, were pregnant."

Will these two precious lives be connected?

Over the next hours the women poured out their shared experiences, discussing their pregnancies and the anticipations of coming motherhood. When the time for the evening meal had long passed, Zechariah searched out bread, dried fruit, and wine in the kitchen and sought refuge in the sleeping chamber he shared with Elizabeth, where he once again found himself sentenced to silence.

Six

Betrayal in the Court of Public Opinion

Mary could not shed the fear that had overtaken her. How would Joseph respond when he received news that she was pregnant? She feared childbirth and was afraid that she lacked the wisdom needed to mother a child conceived by God. Would her baby be different from other children? Would it be hard to love him?

Elizabeth listened to questions and fears. She gave counsel. She let Mary talk until Mary discovered that God had given her wisdom to be discovered in her frailty. Even though Elizabeth spent little time on her feet, Mary felt as if she were the one being served.

The days flew by as Mary cared for Elizabeth—drawing water, baking bread, milking goats, spinning wool, even weaving baby clothes. Each simple task strengthened her spirit. She was God's chosen vessel and carried His miracle in her body. She understood these days were preparation—but for what she did not know.

John's birth was joyous but challenging. Mary remained to help Elizabeth through her recovery and transition to her new maternal responsibilities.[6] But an urgency grew within Mary to return to Joseph and her family and to face Nazareth's judgment for what appeared to be her scandalous condition.

Elizabeth's parting words were a warning: "Mary, protect your baby. Powerful Romans and corrupt Jewish religious rulers will try to destroy him."

Mary tried to ignore Elizabeth's ominous words. God would certainly not send His Son, the Messiah, only to allow enemies to destroy Him!

* * * * *

Mary's return to Nazareth did not go unnoticed. As she passed through the village toward home, condemning stares and pointing fingers confirmed that word of her pregnancy had traveled home. She pulled back her shoulders and lifted her head.

Let them talk. God knows the truth.

While she didn't excuse the behavior of the women, she understood—her circumstances looked bad. She was betrothed, had left town for several months, and was now returning pregnant.

During the long trip home, she tried to prepare herself for the accusations that would come: being friendly with a Roman soldier, consorting with criminals, succumbing to a lover while she was in Elizabeth's home, or the worst accusation of all—that Joseph was the father.

Please, God, may he not have heard this news. Not yet, not this way.

She'd prayed the prayer for weeks.

Sheer determination and obedience had brought her home and back to the low wooden door of her house. A wave of nausea rolled through her. She would soon speak the most difficult thing, telling Ima, Abba, and Joseph, but she had no choice. She pushed open the door and struggled to stoop through the low stone entry into the house.

Ima, who had been sitting at the loom spinning cloth, froze. Mary saw her eyes widen then narrow again as they swept from her face to her feet, then back to her face again.

Mary straightened to her full height and forced herself to look into Ima Anna's eyes.

"Is it true, what we have heard?"

"I can explain, Ima ..." Mary could see anxiety etched into the lines around Ima's eyes.

She's distraught. How long has she known? What have people been saying to her?

Mary stepped further into the room and set her belongings on the floor near the loom. She pulled a blanket from a pile in the corner of the gathering room and settled herself on the floor near Ima's feet before speaking.

"I have not dishonored my family or Joseph or Yahweh, Ima, no matter what circumstances may look like. I promise you this is true."

She told her mother the story of the angel's appearance and message. Anna asked question after question. Mary had never lied to Ima, but her explanation sounded impossible even to herself. Still, angels *had* appeared to God's people in the past. A Jew could never dismiss a report of a messenger from God.

"Mary, do you truly expect us to believe an angel told you that Yahweh's Spirit ... made ... made you *pregnant*?" Ima's voice rose with the last word.

Ima had never spoken this sharply to anyone. Mary's hands shook.

"Disgracing the holiness of Yahweh brings serious consequences. Repent! You are fourteen! I have explained to you how a girl becomes pregnant—it is *not* through a divine act of God. What you have done is sin. Admit it. Sin!"

Anna stood and paced back and forth across the small gathering room. "There is no shame if someone forced himself on you. The elders of the synagogue will forgive you and encourage the community not to shun you."

Ima stooped, and her arms pulled Mary close, but a deep sadness pressed into the latter's bones. She wondered if Ima could feel the pounding of her heart. She swallowed a rising sob.

"Mary, your abba and I will still love you. Was it Joseph? Did your love for him cause you to give in to your desires?" Ima reached forward, loosened Mary's veil, and let it drop from her face.

Mary pulled away, her heart broken by the accusation.

"No, no! No man has touched me, and Joseph is a man of honor! I am disappointed by your insinuations, although my explanation defies reason. Yet what I have told you is true. I would encourage you to look to scripture and to pray for answers, Ima. If you ask, God will answer."

Mary's voice broke into a quiver, and she turned and fled to the courtyard, where she could weep before Yahweh alone.

* * * * *

Joseph retreated to the solitude of his workroom, away from sympathetic pitying and away from prying eyes. His family had said little, but their silence told him they had learned of the same rumors he had heard in the village marketplace.

Shaking heads. Sneers. Turned backs.

His first response had been confusion. Until he overheard the whispers.

Joseph did not return home that day until nightfall. Instead, he bought a few provisions in the marketplace and walked high into the hills to be alone. He was unaware of the passing of time as he prayed, wept in anger, and begged God for wisdom. He'd been certain Mary was a righteous woman, committed to her vows. Now he was unsure who she was. A deep, rending ache tore at every part of his mind and emotions.

Joseph sat on a wooden stool near the open workroom door whittling a small chunk of wood. He'd propped the door open with a large rock to draw in the morning breeze.

A figure rounded the corner of the house and walked toward his workshop. One glance told Joseph it was Mary.

Pregnant. And she dare come to my home?

A wave of anger rushed through him, and he drew a deep breath.

He'd spent days trying to think through the consequences of what Mary's pregnancy would mean. Rejection, humiliation, and shunning were just the beginning. He had believed God had brought them together. Was he to refuse to marry an impure woman, as any good Jewish bridegroom would do? By law, he could have her stoned or send her away, denying her the opportunity to wed. The evidence of her infidelity and his humiliation was on public display. Even her own father and mother could demand she be stoned.

Why did she do this, God? Was this Your plan?

He had no time to think before she was at the door, beautiful in a mantle the color of desert sand. Her red, swollen eyes told him she had been crying, but in spite of her tears, his heart still flared with anger.

"Joseph, you have heard?" Her voice shook.

"All of Nazareth has heard, Mary." He forced his voice to remain steady, but disappointment oozed from his words. His voice cracked, betraying his rage. A flush rose in his neck as he gestured toward his stool. "You must get out of the sun. Please sit down."

Mary moved to the stool and folded her hands in her lap. In a few sentences she explained her circumstances, her visitation by the angel, and her assurance that the pregnancy was a miracle. No other explanation was possible. She had never been with a man and remained devoted to Joseph. He would have to choose what he would believe. She loved him. She was hoping for his support and, most of all, his demonstration of faith in God.

Joseph stared back at her, incredulous. That was all she had to say? She was explaining her pregnancy as a matter of faith in God?[6] The muscles in his arms, shoulders, and neck tightened.

You betrayed me! No excuse or explanation can exonerate your behavior. No false spirituality can explain your deception.

He must not say more lest he dishonor God. He stormed out of the workroom, muttering in anger.

God, how could You let this happen? I've tried to serve You. I love her. What am I supposed to do?

In the distance Mary called to him, pleading for him to listen, but her words were in vain. The sight of her had fueled his emotions, and he needed to escape. He sprinted to a secluded place in the hills above Nazareth near his home where he could wallow in his misery beneath the sheltering branches of a favorite oak.

Joseph clawed his way up a narrow path marked by rocks and straggling trees, took refuge beneath a familiar lone oak, and settled in the dust to assess his situation. He pulled his waterskin from where it hung at his hip and drew a quenching swallow.

Calm yourself. You must take time to think.

He could ask that Mary be stoned as permitted by Mosaic law, but the thought made him sick. No matter how hurt he might feel, he could never seek her harm. Or he had the option to divorce her privately—a more compassionate choice. Either decision would shatter him. He reached for a nearby rock and flung it with all his strength.

I loved her and was faithful to her. I thought she loved me, and she betrayed me!

He quarreled with himself as he tried to make sense of her betrayal, spending most of the day hunched in desperation beneath the tree, trying to sort out his best choice.

Mary was to be my life partner, my helpmate, my co-counsel, and ima of my children. Her actions make no sense. She loved me, or so it seemed.

Footsteps crunched in the distance, and Joseph looked

up. Mary stood nearby, leaning on a scrawny olive tree and panting, her tunic stained with dirt and one hand resting on her stomach.

Joseph leaped to his feet and rushed toward her, his anger suddenly replaced by concern. "What are you doing here? You shouldn't have climbed into the hills. It's not safe for you!"

Mary extended her hand. "I'm all right. I need you to listen, but I need to sit down first."

The breeze lifted her veil, and Joseph saw that her face was crimson from exertion. An unexpected stab of guilt pierced his heart. She had followed him. He gently lowered her to a seated position on a nearby shaded rock, then drew his waterskin and offered her a drink, watching as she took several long swallows.

"I will listen, but you must admit what you have done, Mary." He forced his voice to remain even.

Tears flowed from her eyes. "Joseph, things are not as they appear." She looked up at him, her eyes pleading. "Although I have not spoken it, I hope you understand how much I love you. I could never betray you and never, ever betray God in such a way. What has happened is a miracle."

"A miracle? This is your explanation?" The anger rose again. But Mary looked back at him, never breaking her gaze.

"I recognize that my explanation sounds unbelievable, but it is the only thing I can tell you, because it is true. Can you understand how hard this is for me? While I am blessed above all women, I am also an unmarried mother without a husband. I am now hated, ridiculed, and rejected by everyone, including my family and my betrothed. My very life and the life of my child is in jeopardy. Do you think I would betray you, my family, and God and *choose this*? Do you?"

Mary's sobs had increased, and an emotion overtook Joseph—a feeling he could not recognize but wanted to be rid of. He put a hand on her shoulder.

"Tell me again how this came to be."

Between sobs Mary told him of the angelic visit and Elizabeth's confirmation. He listened silently. As she spoke, his anger slowly ebbed.

Yahweh, she is confident in You. She believes this story, yet how can it be true—the angel Gabriel speaking to a common girl?

Mary continued, "Gabriel told me Yahweh had found favor with me, and the Holy Spirit would make me with child. He told me to call the baby Yeshua. I'm not guilty of adultery, Joseph. It was hard for me to accept, but I had to face the truth. God sent His messenger to me, and I became with child. He does not lie. The child inside me is from God. And yes, I remain a virgin."

Although they had been sitting in the shade, Joseph felt as though he were having a heatstroke. His head pounded as his thoughts spun, and he could not absorb what he was hearing. He needed time and quiet. The discussion was over—he had listened to Mary and could bear no more. He needed to weigh her words and decide what to do. His heart battled: he wanted to obey God, but was this a deception?

Joseph pulled Mary gently to her feet.

"I will walk you back to my home, where you can eat and rest before I escort you back to your house. You will have my decision after God gives me direction."

Seven
Joseph's Hope Restored

Joseph stared through the vine-laced lattice awning at the stars blanketing the heavens. He'd chosen a far corner on the roof to sleep, away from the area where his brothers would soon lie down for the night.

The air was quiet, the wind still except for occasional screeches of a falcon in the distance. Peace invited much-needed reflection. The consequences of Mary's circumstances required serious thought—and Joseph found himself pondering the most serious questions of his life.

What does God want? Mary deserves punishment—but death? I could never ask for that, no matter what she's done or how angry I may be. Perhaps if I put her away, we can both avoid further disgrace.

Joseph sat motionless as he struggled. His emotions were at war, and he could feel the pulse of blood in his head. As his mind grappled with doubt, anger, fear, protectiveness, confusion, and heartbreak, his body gave way to deep sleep.

He had no awareness of how long he slumbered before a quiet, persistent voice broke through his sleep.

"Joseph, son of David. Joseph. *Joseph.*" He struggled to recognize the calm yet commanding voice.

Fighting to awaken, Joseph knew he was not dreaming. His head was pounding from resting against the stone wall behind him, and his left arm was numb. He shook it to bring it to life, and burning prickles hammered through his muscle. Yes, this was real. He looked around, seeking the source of the mysterious voice, but a brilliant light blinded him.

"Who is calling me?"

A memory flashed as thoughts collided in thunderous impossibilities.

Mary told me of her encounter with a stranger, an angel. I dismissed it as an absurd excuse for her betrayal. This cannot also be an angel!

Joseph hesitated and then spoke.

"Here I am, my lord!"

His mind struggled like a dying fish as he fought to come to grips with the bizarre vision before him.

What does this mean? Is this an angel from God? But why would an angel appear to me?

"Don't be afraid to take Mary as your wife." The voice was not audible, yet he had heard it.

Joseph swallowed. God apparently understood his fears and knew that he was struggling to trust Mary and believe what she had told him.

So God has sent an angel to tell me that what she told me is true. Mary has not betrayed me. God chose her to give birth to the Messiah, my betrothed. And He chose me, Joseph, a carpenter, to be the child's father.

He strained his eyes and tried to look into the light, but the brilliance was blinding.

"She has conceived a child by the Holy Spirit. God has chosen her to be the mother of His Son. You and Mary are God's chosen family. Be of good cheer, Joseph. Mary has not betrayed you."

Joseph blinked, and his legs weakened as he shifted his position.

The voice continued, "It will take time for your child's mind to develop and to mature into a man. Through Him, God will redeem humankind."

Joseph's thoughts swirled like a streamside eddy as he grappled to make sense of what the angel had told him.

Does this mean I will be the child's father and train him as he grows? How could I be worthy of such a responsibility? It is impossible! Mary and I are people of humble birth.

The face of Abba Jacob flashed through Joseph's memory, and then he felt a flood of guilt as he recalled the disappointment his earthly abba had expressed when Joseph announced he wanted to be a carpenter. He'd carried that guilt ever since, and he certainly didn't want to disappoint his heavenly Av in raising His Son.

The light faded to darkness again. Joseph stood and walked to the area where he and his brothers slept. He unrolled his sleeping mat and lay down, still engulfed by darkness. He rubbed his eyes and forced them open again to the familiar sight of the roof—empty. His brothers had still not come to the rooftop to sleep.

If that was a dream, it was unlike any other. Was it a message from God? If so, another angel must come to tell me what to do!

With his mind in turmoil, Joseph pondered what he'd experienced.

Question after question rolled through his mind as he pulled one of Ima's heavy woven sleeping blankets over his body to protect him from the cold night air. He was once again awake, alone with his thoughts beneath a night sky illuminated only by the stars. The knots in his stomach slowly released their grip.

Yahweh sent an angel to speak to me in a dream. He answered my prayer to show me what to do. To give me peace. To show me my part in His plan. Now if He will just show me how to do it.

Joseph's strength drained. If he hadn't been lying down, he'd have collapsed. A profound sense of humility settled over his heart like a shroud. Then, as he grappled with the full significance of what had happened, his heart exploded with joy, and he shouted into the night air.

"Praise God, who fulfills His promises to His people. Through your mercy may You find me worthy, Yahweh.

"And thank You! Deep in my heart I trusted that Mary couldn't betray me! I pray she will forgive me for my anger."

Joseph's thoughts cleared.

Mary and I don't have the wisdom to raise God's Son, but we can and will do whatever God trusts us to do.

With no thought for the hour, he threw back the blanket, leaped from his sleeping mat, and headed toward the rooftop stairs. He couldn't wait until morning; he had to see Mary.

* * * * *

By the time Joseph arrived at Mary's house an hour later, his sense had returned, and he walked, instead, to the olive grove near her house where they had first talked together. He slept under a tree until the sun rose and people appeared in the street. Then he walked with confidence back to Mary's door, announced himself, and was greeted by Mary's mother, who stared at him.

Moments later, Joseph took Mary's hands and spilled out the remarkable story of his visitor. Mary sank onto a goatskin-covered stool as she praised God.

Joseph dropped to the floor at her feet. In spite of the war he'd fought with anger, the law, his emotions, and community scorn, he had made up his mind.

I am ready to take this wonderful gift from God for my wife. God knows the truth. I do not care what people think. But even though what we are doing is God's plan, this will not be easy.

Joseph asked that both sets of parents put marriage plans into motion. The betrothal year and marriage arrangements had been easy—no haggling over Mary's mohar. Joseph offered what he hoped was a generous price for his wife. The law required a mohar to make the marriage legal, and Joseph wanted his bride to see that she was valued and treasured. Both families agreed to the terms. Neither his family nor Mary's was rich in worldly possessions. While they did record the mohar in writing with adequate witnesses, neither party felt it necessary. They only wanted the best for their children and had a hope of many children to follow. They all understood the importance of family in Jewish society.

Now that he believed the truth about Mary's pregnancy, Joseph wanted to talk to his bride privately. For hours they discussed whether they should wait for the arrival of their miracle baby before they married or if they should marry right away. If they wed soon, the baby would not face being accused of being a bastard child. And yet, they could not consummate the marriage until the baby was born—the angel had instructed them. Joseph knew that Mary, like all Jewish women, dreamed of a beautiful marriage ceremony. The chuppah was the ritual that consummated with the wedding vows and a shared bed and would need to be omitted should they wed right away.

Plus, the indignity of a full wedding celebration with the bride's awkward condition on display for the guests—no matter the drapery of the marriage garment—called for prudence. Mary did not want to embarrass family or make guests uncomfortable. She also wanted to prevent more wagging tongues and unwarranted ridicule. Both she and Joseph knew the well-being of God's Son was more important than their sacrifice of a formal wedding ceremony. Mary was satisfied with a private ceremony, celebrated with family and a few family friends.

And in the weeks leading to the wedding, Joseph prayed for wisdom to be an earthly father to the Son of the Most High God.

Eight
A Fateful Roman Census

The memory of the Nazareth raid lingered in Joseph's mind—raging fathers, wailing mothers, and fear-ravaged children. The soldiers did not return to Jacob and Naomi's home on the outskirts of the town, but they left the townspeople terrorized. Joseph wondered what added oppression the hated Romans planned to heap on village residents to remind them of their subjugation.

His prayers for deliverance rose to the heavens night after night as he gazed at the stars from his rooftop bed and laid his hopes and fears before his God.

* * * * *

Joseph slipped his arm around Mary's back and drew her close to protect her from the burgeoning crowd. What appeared to be several hundred people had crowded into the merchant area of Nazareth, where vendors sold everything from vegetables, spices, and bread to goats, lambs, and homemade foods. Mary could smell the wood shavings that clung to Joseph's soft homespun mantle, and her heart warmed. Since their marriage, he had proved tender and kind—so protective of her and the baby—and thoughtful about the smallest things. Even though their wedding had been small and private and they lived simply, she considered herself blessed far beyond most women.

"Thank you, my husband. I did not imagine such a crowd at this early hour of the day." Mary pulled her soft sea-colored garment closer to her legs as people rushed past her toward the town courtyard.

"Such haste!" Mary shaded her eyes as she looked toward the growing crowd. "Caesar has sent a new posting."

The couple paused for a moment and waited for an opportunity to enter the flow of bodies heading toward the synagogue without being knocked down.

Herod's henchmen often posted official documents on the door or inside the local synagogue. Soldiers enjoyed stomping into the Jews' cherished synagogues to anger them. Sure enough, posted on the synagogue door for all to see was a reminder of Caesar Augustus's absolute control of the conquered lands. The notice read, "By order of Caesar Augustus, every family must return to their ancestral home for a nationwide census."

Mary could hear men sputtering under their breath both in front of and behind her. Her chest tightened, and she fought the urge to hush them. Every Jew had been taught not to draw attention from soldiers who had proven themselves far too ready to strike out at the slightest provocation.

An angry man with a waist-length gray beard pointed his hands toward a row of scowling soldiers who stood at attention, their spears dug into the dust. He spoke fearlessly: "Caesar continues to give us reasons to support the rebels. One day we will give you what you deserve!"

A cry of affirmation rose from the crowd.

Near the center of the courtyard, the soldier who had posted the notice sat tall in his saddle and looked at the graybeard with disdain. "Shut up, you old fool!"

Two foot soldiers beside him stepped forward. One of them retorted, "Perhaps he would like a taste of the flagellum?"

The soldier on horseback raised his hand. "No. Whips have had little effect on these Jewish animals. Caesar is making *new* plans."

Mary shuddered. The look on the soldier's face reminded her of a jackal preparing to shred its prey.

Why can't the Romans take the census where we reside, rather than forcing us to travel back to our ancestral homes? Bethlehem is too far for Joseph to go when the political climate is so unsafe.

The soldiers turned and retreated toward their quarters, laughing among themselves contemptuously. As they withdrew, the soldier on horseback muttered, "We ought to burn the village and let them *all* die. Slowly."

Mary's hand flew to her mouth. She glanced around the crowd and saw similar reactions from other people. Many had heard the same words. Men glared at the soldiers through slitted eyes and raised their clenched fists. As the crowd dispersed, a small group of men disappeared down a side street, and others soon followed.

Mary and Joseph turned to walk back to the home they now shared with Joseph's parents. Mary silently observed Joseph kicking up dust clouds. The look of defeat on his face told her all she needed to know: her husband felt was worries about keeping his family from danger. She took his hand.

"What is troubling you, Joseph?"

He dropped his head. "Mary, I have to go to Bethlehem." His voice shook. "The law doesn't require you to accompany me. I can register us and pay the taxes, and I prefer you *not* go with me to Bethlehem. It would present too great a risk—one I will not take."

Mary squeezed his hand. She was sure Joseph wanted to protect her. That was his responsibility, but she'd proven herself to be strong, trustworthy, and tenacious.

"We must discuss this, my love. You are worried. You fear the danger of a trip to Jerusalem and Bethlehem not because of the difficulties of the journey, but because of the danger of armed conflict, am I right?"

Joseph's grip tightened on her hand. "Mary, this boiling

pot of rebellion throughout the country has brought an end to Roman patience. The Romans turned a blind eye to much of the early rebel violence, but now they think they must teach the rebels a lesson. A vicious crackdown on the revolt has begun, but the rebels won't back down. In fact, this might be the time to make an all-out attack on the weakened leadership in Jerusalem."

Mary had known of the danger for Jews because of the revolt. But she'd not been aware that threats had escalated to the point of ultimate conflict.

Joseph continued, "Major fighting will be centered in Jerusalem, but fallout will undoubtedly reach all occupied territories, including Galilee."

Our trip to Bethlehem for the census would be no normal excursion.

Mary realized the full significance of the day's notification—more punishing taxes. Joseph was worried about her safety. Besides, her condition would inhibit his travel to pay taxes in the census—she knew Joseph wanted to take her but ... She weighed her thoughts.

I don't want to be a burden. Joseph is always so protective, but I think the baby and I can travel in full assurance of safety. God will be with us.

"Joseph ..."

He shook his head as he gazed at the mountains. "No. You are more aware than I how many babies die before birth. You are too far along to make a trip this difficult and dangerous. I can't let you take the risk. I will go alone while you stay here with Abba Jacob and Ima Naomi."

"And risk giving birth without you, Joseph?" Mary kept her voice gentle, but she steeled it with immovable resolve. "I will *not* give birth without you at my side. Only you understand what this birth signifies and how it will change the world. After all I have gone through, I *will not* have this baby without you, if I have to walk to Bethlehem and carry our donkey."

Mary shifted her tone. "Yahweh gave us a job, Joseph. We are in no danger from Roman soldiers. I love your protective spirit, and I'm sure it will serve me well on the journey, my love. But Yahweh will provide all we need." She smiled. "I must believe our heavenly Av is with us in everything, or everything depends on us. On our own strength, we are unable to do anything. But knowing our limitations points to only one conclusion.

"Yahweh has been and will be our provider and strength."

* * * * *

Mary had cleared the evening meal, and she and Joseph moved to the bridal chamber that Joseph had built adjoining Abba Jacob's house. They sat side by side on a pile of cushions in a corner, Mary nestled against Joseph's chest as they talked about the upcoming trip. Joseph was silent, and Mary reached up and stroked his soft beard. He smiled.

"Mary, I think perhaps we should take up residence in the Jerusalem area for a time. Carpentry jobs would be plentiful, and it would be a good place to raise our son, away from the gossip and shunning he would receive in Nazareth."

Mary's eyes widened. "I have thought the same, Joseph … of what the future may hold for our child here." She patted her stomach with her free hand. "He is not truly ours, but I feel like every other mother."

"I believe God chose you *because* of your mother's heart, my dove." Joseph's hand caressed Mary's hair.

"God will direct us."

"I agree, but we must prepare for the unexpected before we travel, as well as the possibility of remaining in Jerusalem. Political conditions are volatile."

Mary sighed. "Yes. Prepare. But we must also focus on God's promises. We must protect this baby, raise him for the glory of Yahweh, and be obedient to all He tells us."

The room was silent. Joseph was already listing needed

provisions and envisioning preparations for the trip: safety, supplies, and routes. A move would mean more baggage and a slower journey.

Joseph looked up and smiled. “I’m sorry, I was already planning. Yes, I agree that we must trust God, but I also believe He expects us to be wise. Now tell me about Elizabeth. You must be excited to see her.”

A few days with Zechariah and Elizabeth during the feast would be enjoyable, even if it extended their trip. Mary and Joseph’s goal was to get to Bethlehem for tax registration. They were aware of the identity of their firstborn but had agreed to keep it to themselves. In due time, God would reveal His plan. For now, being faithful to Yahweh was their most important task.

The need for preparation fueled Mary’s excitement. She packed dried foods in tightly woven baskets, collected grain for the offering at the Feast of Tabernacles, gathered extra clothing, and filled the goatskin water bags. Joseph prepared the animals for the journey and packed their provision bags.

* * * * *

Several days later, they left at sunrise for the outskirts of Nazareth to join a small caravan heading for Jerusalem. Mary sat atop a donkey that drew a small cart. A second donkey carried supplies, while Joseph walked in front carrying a backpack fashioned from a blanket.

They left early enough to attend the Feast of Tabernacles so that they could arrive in Bethlehem in plenty of time before the birth of the baby and for Joseph to register for the census. The many pilgrims going to the feast provided additional safety for travel.

The law of Moses required all adult men to attend the autumn grain Feast of Tabernacles in Jerusalem. Participating would extend their time away from home, but it would save an additional trip to Jerusalem later to pay taxes. The stop in Jerusalem would extend the normal six-day journey from Nazareth to Bethlehem by several extra days, maybe even weeks. The early rains began in Jerusalem during month of Tishri—September–October—which would complicate finding indoor lodging. Even though some of their relatives lived in Jerusalem, Mary and Joseph would be challenged to find indoor shelter because of the crowds of travelers. Fortunately, Elizabeth and Zechariah would welcome them to their home in nearby Ein Kerem, which was on the route to Bethlehem, where they would register for the census.[7]

Mary inhaled sharply as a twinge shot through her lower back as she watched Joseph carefully choose each step. This trip would tax her strength to its limits. They could only hope that Elizabeth and Zechariah would have room when they arrived.

Help me do this, God. Give me Your strength to be faithful, no matter how hard this journey may become.

Nine

The Perilous Trip to Bethlehem

The long, jarring first day of caravan travel passed uneventfully. A group originating from Jotapata picked up travelers from Nazareth. Other groups from cities around the Sea of Galilee joined at Magdala. The caravan route would take them from Nazareth south to the Jezreel Valley through the Herod Valley, in view of Mount Gilboa as they traveled east to Scythopolis, then turned south again along the highway that ran beside the Jordan River.

Joseph drank in the magnificent autumn view: craggy mountains glowing in shimmering sunshine and valleys blanketed in colorful textures that resembled intricately woven cloth. He looked forward to passing through the ancient cities of Jericho and holy Jerusalem, and the quaint village of Ein Kerem, before arriving in Bethlehem.

By the end of the first day, Joseph saw alarming signs of Mary's exhaustion. Her color had faded, she was struggling to hold her head up, and she could barely keep herself upright as she sat on the donkey. His rising fears eased when the caravan came to a halt for the night at a quiet, off-the-road site near a nomad camp. They had traveled too far for the couple to turn back, and they could not risk traveling alone. Joseph breathed a sigh of relief as he eased Mary from the donkey. He gave her a skin of water and settled her in the shade of a scraggly gall oak tree on a hand-spun blanket given to them as a wedding gift. Trying to swallow the lump in his throat, he watched Mary curl up on her side for a few brief moments of much needed rest, then turned to tend to their weary donkeys.

Joseph was confident of Mary's determination, but her frail condition worried him. He should have stood firm and not allowed her to come. The trip had already proved too hard. He glanced over his shoulder and saw Mary stroke her belly, and again he prayed for Yahweh's protection.

Dear God, show me how to be a husband to the woman You gave me and a father to the Son You have sent into the world. I'm just a carpenter, and I don't understand how I fit into Your plan, except to love Mary and Your child. How can a pregnant woman sitting in the dirt at the side of the road whose child will arrive embarrassingly too soon fit into the vision of the coming of the Messiah?

The early fall evening breeze carried the sounds of voices from the camp into the air, and Joseph sensed that his voice was being drawn toward heaven with it.

The warm, dry weather meant most caravanners camped under the stars and saved the effort to put up shelters. Local herdsmen had offered to fill waterskins and provide overnight protection from bandits. Joseph tethered the donkeys at a stone water trough near the other animals and returned to Mary. Mary's rest was short but she wanted to be with Joseph. The two joined a crowd gathered around a communal campfire where several women were preparing food. Mary had brought dried meat, figs, and olives wrapped in a cloth.

The evening's lively discussions did not last long. The challenges of heat, dust, uneven terrain, uncooperative animals, crying children, and jolting wagons had taken a toll on everyone. Not long after sunset, the trekkers dispersed to bed down, except for volunteer sentries who would stand guard. Joseph watched the group disband, then stood, trying not to moan at the ache in his lower back. He extended his hand to Mary, who had been sitting on a rock beside him, and gently pulled her to her feet. The flickering flames revealed dark circles around her eyes.

"The travel is too much, my dove." His hand cupped her cheek.

"This is what I want, Joseph. We are together." She slid her arm around his waist, and Joseph felt her sink against his side as they walked. "This child will be born in Bethlehem, you will see." She rubbed her stomach lovingly.

Joseph didn't answer. He simply shook his head in silence.

* * * * *

Joseph laid out two woven bamboo mats in a secluded spot he'd located and marked with a blanket when they'd arrived. Then he layered the mats with the blanket and soft sheepskins. He helped Mary lie down, then covered her with a soft-spun husk-colored blanket, tucking it around her to protect her against the cold night air. He didn't know much about pregnancy, but he was certain an expectant mother shouldn't be chilled. Joseph then lay down on his side close to his bride, his eyes fixated on her already sleeping face, and pulled a second blanket over himself. Mary rested on her side facing him, her knees pulled up toward her stomach, one hand supporting her head and the other resting on her abdomen.

He traced every feature of her face with his eyes. Her beauty captivated him. Every few minutes her petite frame twisted or stretched to accommodate the moving baby, and Joseph felt a surge of protection for both, coupled with a rush of fear-tinged wonder.

Suddenly, a bolt of dizziness shot through him, as if he'd been struck and sent spinning. He blinked, and the spinning slowed. His face burned, and he moved a hand to his face. It was wet. He was crying, but why?

Joseph turned his head and stared into the evening heavens, where the stars glittered. A warm wind engulfed his body, and the deep stillness of the night drew him into a strange void as the wind increased, waking him. An alluring voice whispered from the wind—a voice unlike any other Joseph had ever known. At the sound, he froze.

"Joseph, look upon your bride—how beautiful she is. And she is yours. Take her now and fulfill your marriage vows. It is God's design for a husband to show love to his wife, and you and Mary have wed. No one else will share in your most sacred moments together, as these matters should be. Nothing should hinder the *lawful* and *deserved* fulfillment of your role as husband."

The voice hung in the air—eerie, tantalizing, unlike the solemn holy voice that had spoken to Joseph when the angel told him not to fear marrying Mary.

This voice echoes Yahweh's words and sounds beautiful, but the message contradicts the words Yahweh's messenger spoke. This is a different voice and a different messenger, with a contrary message.

Joseph strained his eyes to see, but he could discern nothing but blackness.

He looked toward Mary. Had the voice woken her? He strained to listen. Was there more? But the darkness only echoed silence. Joseph lay stone-still, struggling to regain his composure and discern if he could safely move.

He laid a hand on Mary's stomach. She flinched. He inched closer and laid his head on her bulging belly as if to listen to the baby's movements. Mary's hand moved to his hair and fingered his curls.

"My Joseph, remember our promise to Yahweh. We will wait until after the baby is born." Even her whispered rebuff made him want to draw closer.

Joseph flinched at the gentle rebuke. "I know, my love. Lying here beside you is all I need for now. I must discipline my longings. I want to do God's will." He inched away from Mary and pulled his blanket back around his shoulders as thoughts about the voice and its seductive message raced through his mind.

This messenger did not come from God. Then where?

The answer sent a chill to his bones.

Are Mary and I now targets of the Evil One himself?

Joseph reached for Mary's hand, and as suddenly as the warm breeze had wafted over him with its mysterious voice, it disappeared, and once again the evening called for the comfort of blankets. Joseph lay perplexed and silent in the night, trying to comprehend what he had experienced and how he could protect his family against the powers of Satan unleashed against his child—God's child.

Had God foreseen this unholy opposition and already provided for it? Had His plan for His Son and humanity been set in place long before Joseph met Mary?

As he pondered these things late in the second watch of the night, Joseph fell into a restless sleep.

Ten

Journey's Long-Awaited End

As the caravan limped into Jericho two days later, patrol riders warned the travelers about danger from a marauding rebel. Simon, a radical Zealot revolutionist, was stirring up trouble in Jericho.[8] His unorthodox methods of spreading his violent message of revolt to the masses had forced Roman authorities to target him as a threat to their military dominance. Hence, Rome arrested dozens of innocent Jewish men and boys in Jericho in a search for Simon and his cohorts. The soldiers' violent activities had been intended to intimidate—but they had, instead, energized rebel support.

A week before Mary and Joseph's trip, a caravan from Galilee had set out and fallen under the wrath of an impatient Roman garrison. Any male who set foot on a Roman road did so at risk of harassment, searches, detainment, or arrest. Crucifixions and slaughter of so-called "suspects" were common. Coldhearted, callous soldiers treated caravanners with disdain—no Jewish traveler was deemed innocent.

So Joseph felt relief when the voice of the lead wagoner cried out that the caravan had reached the outskirts of Jericho. He issued further instructions.

"We must avoid patrolling soldiers, so we need to bypass Jericho. Therefore, we will bivouac at the Samaritans' caravansary up the road. They require payment for rooms, but bedding in the open-air courtyard will be inexpensive."

Joseph noted a man several families ahead of them kick the dirt angrily. "I was counting on a stop in Jericho! I need supplies!"

His wife, who sat on the seat of the rough cart beside him, tugged on the sleeve of his robe and leaned toward him. Joseph couldn't hear her words, but he saw the hurt in her eyes and the quick recoil of her head as her husband raised his hand as he spoke to her. But other loud protests pulled Joseph's attention away from the couple.

"I have relatives in Jericho and planned to stay the night with them!"

"This is our first opportunity for years to shop in Jericho!"

"We need supplies!"

The wagoner, who was walking among the travelers, waved them off and ignored their murmuring. "I am responsible for your safety first—safety for *all* of you. We will proceed beyond Jericho, but *no* further."

The protests quieted. Yes, many in the caravan wanted to shop for fresh figs, dates, and other produce famed in Jericho. The detour meant inconvenience, but most people in the group agreed that they should avoid confrontation with soldiers. In addition to the dangers the soldiers presented, the road was well-known for highwaymen, thieves, and rebels looking for booty and food to help them survive in the harsh desert.

The rocky ascending trail from Jericho to Jerusalem followed the steep and winding Wadi Qelt. Hazards lurked with every step and slowed the trip. Weary travelers had been told that although this was the final leg of the trip, this section presented the greatest challenge.

Soon, the evening sun disappeared below the horizon, and again travelers began grumbling. "How much longer?"

Over and over, the wagoner asked the group to be patient.

But Joseph did not feel patient. Every step endangered

his beloved Mary, who had stopped speaking and sat atop her donkey staring at a spot on the horizon. Her eyes never wavered, despite the blinding glare of the sun, and she had threaded strands of the donkey's sparse mane through her fingers in an unyielding grip. Once again Joseph berated himself for having allowed her to come. How could he have put her at risk? Would God be willing to help them out of the mess he'd created? He feared to even ask.

Dear God, protect her. We must go forward. We can't leave the caravan and go back alone. Please protect Mary, in spite of my mistakes.

* * * * *

Not too much farther up the winding trail, the caravan began the grueling ascent. Every step challenged their endurance, and Joseph found himself overtaken with guilt as he watched his wife cling to the donkey as she fought to lean forward against the upward incline. The tightness around her mouth told him she was fighting enormous discomfort from pressure being placed on the baby. Once again Joseph prayed for Yahweh to protect Mary and the child, but his prayers had become wordless cries of anguish.

Although the remaining distance up the steep incline taxed both Mary and Joseph's resolve, they, along with their exhausted group, straggled into the courtyard of the welcoming caravansary. The popular Wadi Qelt Caravansary had become well-known because of a historic event that immortalized a Samaritan who had taken a wounded traveler there to heal after a Jewish priest and a Levite refused to tend to the injured man's needs. The event was significant in that it hailed a repugnant Samaritan as the moral hero of the tale.

As Joseph and Mary approached the rough-hewn stone building, Mary sighed in relief. "Praise Yahweh for bringing us safely to this desolate place. I can see why somewhere in this area ravens fed the prophet Elijah. Certainly, no living creature could be sustained in this rocky barrenness." She gestured to the surroundings.

"I have never been so grateful to arrive at a destination. The child too." Mary attempted a smile as she slid from the donkey and into Joseph's waiting arms. He brushed dust from her nose, tethered the donkey to one of the many posts in front of the first stone structure, and then guided her to the door as she leaned heavily on his side.

The caravansary was similar to most hostel-like facilities scattered along major trade routes throughout the land. Thick brick walls topped with thorn branches enclosed the compound. Walls constructed of stone and sun-dried brick provided safety from brigands and protection from weather for the animals. Two-story hostel buildings with guest rooms on the upper level marked two sides of the compound. Sentries at the walled entrance provided protection.

Two large gates opened for caravans, but a smaller "needle's eye" door in the gate allowed people to enter without opening the larger gates for camels and carts.[9] Inside the courtyard, travelers could resupply water containers and enjoy dry, warm shelter. Oxen and camel drivers accompanying the caravan stayed in the smelly courtyard, while more affluent pilgrims could stay in the upper deck and, if the weather allowed, seek the cool of the evening on the rooftop.

Gathering at the caravansary provided an opportunity for travelers to talk to people from all over the empire. Politics, rumors, scandal, news from afar, and hopes and dreams were typical subjects at meals. Joseph chose an eating spot under a cypress tree near a young couple from Magdala whom he and Mary had met as they traveled: Obed and Rachel. Joseph was excited about hearing about the political upheaval throughout the land.

The wind swirled through the evening and light pranced over the open fire, sending flames and sparks soaring into the air, muffling conversations. Rachel, who had been speaking of the curfew Herod Antipas had placed on Magdala, raised her voice. She spoke with disgust.

"I am weary of the trouble we have had in Magdala and in neighboring Arbel. One local Zealot was so fed up with the Herodian dynasty that he assassinated our local magistrate. As a result, the Roman officials severely controlled the city and imposed a strict curfew. They searched houses, arrested men, and destroyed homes."

Rachel had obviously been traumatized, and she seemed unable to contain her feelings.

"We were not sure when our house would be ransacked. We feared for our family's safety."

Joseph noted her trembling hands, even though Rachel had clasped her hands tightly. He pulled Mary closer to his side. He had overheard that even some of Herod's soldiers and advisors had become concerned about the severity of the crackdown, fearing it would precipitate further rebellion among locals. In fact, Herod Antipas had built Sepphoris for his capital, rather than rebuild at Arbel or Magdala, both Zealot strongholds.

Joseph noted Rachel peering at Mary's tummy. Everyone who saw Mary recognized her condition.

"Mary, I can see you are uncomfortable. This trip must be very hard for you." Joseph could sense the quiet concern in Rachel's voice, and something inside him relaxed. He was grateful a woman had taken an interest in Mary's welfare.

Although Mary was exhausted, Joseph was certain she would honor Rachel's compassion. As expected, Mary responded with a disarming smile.

"I don't think any of us has been comfortable since we set out. Discomfort is part of any journey, I have found."

Rachel swished her hands in the air to brush flying sparks from the robust fire away from Mary. "I see you are with child."

"Yes, I am to deliver in a few weeks."

Mary's arm laced through Joseph's, and her fingers threaded through his own. He squeezed her hand.

"This is our first. I'm sure it is a girl," Rachel blurted, hope edging her voice.

Her husband, an obese, angry-toned man whom Joseph knew as Obed, turned from where he was unloading a wagon not far behind them and growled, "Yeah, a girl is worth a large mohar, if nothing else."

Mary's eyes grew wide. Joseph saw her measure her deep-seated emotional words before she responded. "Joseph and I are grateful for our baby. You must be too, Rachel." Mary reached out and stroked the woman's arm.

Joseph broke into a smile.

Rachel lowered her head so Obed wouldn't hear. "We want a healthy baby, a girl or boy. What about you?"

Mary replied with enthusiasm, "A son. We want a son. I so look forward to motherhood."

Unable to hold her excitement in check, Rachel gushed, "If it's a girl, my daughter will marry a wealthy man from a good family and have many children. We will name her Mary."

Rachel's words flowed like an untamed river. Joseph squeezed Mary's fingers gently several times, signaling that it was time to slip away to rest, but her eyes remained fixed on Rachel, whose husband had abandoned her once he had finished tending his cart and animals.

And so Joseph stood beside his wife until she finished listening to the dreams of her newfound friend. Then Rachel turned away to find her husband, who had procured their sleeping room.

Because of their limited funds, Joseph had found a quiet corner of the courtyard for their sleeping area. Here he laid out their sleeping mats. Together they said their evening prayers and lay down, Joseph's arm thrown protectively over Mary's thick waist.

Joseph fell asleep quickly in the cool night air. Sometime

later, he was awakened by Mary, jostling his shoulder and calling his name.

"Joseph! Joseph!" The urgency in her voice frightened him.

He rubbed his eyes and strained to measure the light.

What hour is it? The fires have burned down. Only smoldering ashes remain.

The darkness beckoned him to return to sleep, but he couldn't deny the panic in Mary's voice and the pain in his shoulder.

"What is it, my wife? We must not wake the others."

"I feel pain, unlike the sickness earlier today. Could this be a sign I am about to give birth? How am I to know?"

Joseph detected a tone in Mary's voice he had never heard before. Was it panic? Pain? He had never seen her sick. What if he did the wrong thing?

"Do I need to call one of the women?" Mary reached for his hand.

A woman would certainly know what to do.

"No, no, perhaps I spoke too soon. I'm not sure. I don't know what to do. I'm confused!"

Her big brown eyes had grown huge. Joseph pulled her close to him. The nasturtium soap she used to cleanse her hair teased his senses.

"I am here to help you, Mary." He paused as he floundered for what to say next. He only knew he needed to sound confident and was grateful for darkness.

"Is ... is the pain you are having how women have described it?"

Drops of sweat were forming on Joseph's brow, and he prayed that Mary couldn't hear the pulsations of his heart. She could *not* have this baby without a woman present. He refused to even think about it.

He forced himself to ask only one question at a time while he silently counted the weeks since Mary believed she had conceived.

Moments passed, and Joseph forced himself not to speak as he held his bride. Finally, Mary spoke. "You are not panicking and overreacting at all. Who would have thought it would be me? The pain has passed. I think it may have been my stomach reacting to the unfamiliar food our friends shared with us.

"Thank you, Joseph, for your steady spirit. Other than Yahweh Himself, you have been my strength these past months."

A strange warmth coursed through Joseph's body at Mary's words. She drew back and lay down. He tucked her blanket around her shoulders, then kissed her on the forehead. He watched her sleep until after midnight, then lay down beside her, being careful not to wake her.

Expecting arduous travel, the caravan departed before daybreak the following morning. They hoped to reach Jerusalem by nightfall. They crested the Mount of Olives that afternoon along a long mountain ridge marking the eastern border of the city, and the travelers caught their first breathtaking view of the city.

Eleven
Fleeting Joys: Succoth Celebrated

Jerusalem was bustling with visitors, who occupied every niche and cranny around the city. The caravan's mission complete, the small group of travelers dispersed.

But Joseph reminded himself that his family had not yet reached their final destination. Time was crucial, and he had to focus on his pregnant wife and the child who seemed destined to be born at any moment.

Holiday overcrowding in Jerusalem would make staying in the city impossible, so Joseph and Mary continued another wearying 4.5 *milla passuum*[10] to Ein Kerem, where they would find welcome with Zechariah and Elizabeth. Zechariah would be busy with temple duties, and Elizabeth would be doting on their new son, but Elizabeth and Mary insisted on being together whenever they were near each other. With Mary so near the time of her delivery and Elizabeth's birth experience, it relieved Joseph to know that they would find lodging with beloved relatives.

As a priest, Zechariah's life ran on a strict schedule. Temple duties required order. He rose early, took a ritual bath, then proceeded to Jerusalem's Chamber of Hewn Stone on the Temple Mount to draw lots for his daily duties. His obligations included offering sacrifices, cleaning the altar, trimming the lamps, and at dawn, sacrificing a spotless ewe lamb as a burnt offering. Later in the afternoon, priests recited additional prayers and offered more sacrifices. When he finished, Zechariah faced the long walk back to Ein Kerem to be with his family for the evening.

During feasts, requirements intensified, which included formal attire. Even Joseph admitted that Zechariah looked impressive in his long white linen robe secured with a wide girdle and topped with a stately tall white hat. As the wife of a priest, Elizabeth did not share garment restrictions and wore traditional Jewish clothing: a long sleeveless tunic tied beneath her bosom and hitched up at the waist with a band to keep the tunic out of the way while she attended to the new baby and cooking.

Mary had expressed concern that their visit might disrupt the family at one of the busiest times of the year, but they were excited about the visit. It was always fun to catch up on family news, and Joseph was happy that Mary would have time with Elizabeth, Mary's precious mentor. A deep bond had drawn them beyond friendship into a God-given love for each other.

As the sun beat on their heads, Mary and Joseph arrived at Ein Kerem late in the afternoon. The journey had worn them out, and they looked forward to rest, home-cooked meals, and family conversation. Joseph slid his hands around Mary's sides and lowered her from the back of the donkey as Elizabeth hurried down the gravel path, her infant son, John, in her arms, to welcome her kinsfolk.

"You're here!" she called as she stumbled over a small stone in haste.

Mary winced as she attempted her first steps. "Elizabeth, this is a busy time of year. We will ..."

Elizabeth placed her index finger to her lips. "Shh. You are no trouble at all. We are thrilled to see you and show off our John. Is he not beautiful?" She extended the baby at arm's length, then drew him back and kissed his cheek. "May our feast days together be blessed."

With that blessing, Elizabeth ushered Mary and Joseph

up the stone pathway and into her home, accompanied by the sounds of her squealing child.

Joseph found the home of Zechariah to be quite comfortable. The rooms were larger than most, and the house was furnished in a manner suitable for a ranking priest. Frescoes decorated the plaster walls, and mosaics similar to those found in the homes of wealthy families paved the entryway. An exquisite array of stoneware and glassware adorned a finely carved table in the midst of a large common room. The specialty pottery required by sacramental purity laws was appropriately cleansed and stacked on shelves. Beds in a small private room at the back of the house provided a welcome for visitors. The temple required a large number of priests, and the compensation dictated in the Levitical laws made it possible for priests to live better than the average Jewish family.

Mary had described the luxury of their kinsfolk's home to Joseph when she returned home from her first visit with Elizabeth. Joseph was still impressed—the house was far more than a step above their modest home in Nazareth.

With Elizabeth's permission, Mary gave Joseph a brief tour of the house.

"I especially enjoy the picturesque surroundings of the village. Zechariah and Elizabeth are favored to have a home in this location, nestled in this peaceful valley between mountains and rolling hills."

Joseph watched Mary's eyes as she soaked up the serenity of her surroundings.

"I love the beauty of green forests, manicured vineyards, harvested fields, and olive trees. Yahweh gives us such abundance, and He gives it with such beauty."

Joseph nodded in agreement. In spite of the frequent discomforts of their life, Mary had always expressed gratitude for God's provision, even in small things. She often seemed like a child overcome with delight with gifts from her Abba. He found her gratitude and lack of envy endearing.

Elizabeth had made plans for Succoth, the Feast of Tabernacles. The annual feast required attendance of all males over the age of thirteen. Like Passover, the Feast of Tabernacles celebrated both historical and agricultural events, commemorating the forty-year period when the children of Israel had wandered in the desert, living in temporary shelters. *Succoth*, meaning, "booths," referred to the command for the Jews to live in temporary dwellings during this celebration. The Festival of Succoth began five days after Yom Kippur (the Day of Atonement), from the fifteenth to the twenty-first day of the Hebrew month of Tishri. Preceded by the High Holy Days of the New Year and Yom Kippur, they were all a part of the fall holiday season. Succoth was also a harvest festival that lasted seven days. Work was not permitted on the first day of the holiday. Joseph and Mary, as well as Zechariah and Elizabeth, were always careful to follow all requirements.

Elizabeth was decorating for the holiday and placing palm branches on the sukkah roof to prepare for the feast's required temporary living quarters. Conversation turned from family news to the significance of the holiday.

Mary listened as Elizabeth recited the passage from the Pentateuch where the Lord instructed Moses to tell the Israelites the following:

> On the first day gather branches from magnificent trees—palm fronds, boughs from leafy trees, and willows that grow by the streams. Then celebrate with joy before the Lord your God for seven days. You must observe this festival to the Lord for seven days every year. This is a permanent law for you, and it must be observed in the appointed month from generation to generation. For seven days you must live outside in little shelters. All native-born Israelites must live in shelters. This will remind each new generation of Israelites that I

> made their ancestors live in shelters when I rescued them from the land of Egypt. I am the Lord your God.[11]

Elizabeth reached for Zechariah with the free hand that wasn't supporting baby John, who was sleeping peacefully on her shoulder. She paused. "Mary, this feast will find its fulfillment in the baby you carry in your womb. Don't fear."

"The Feast of Tabernacles memorializes our nation's exodus from Egypt and will see its fulfillment in the Messiah's deliverance."

Joseph glanced at his wife. She appeared to be pondering Elizabeth's words.

"That must be what the angel meant when he said, 'You will conceive and give birth to a son, and you will name him Yeshua,'" Mary mused. "He will be very great and will be called the Son of the Most High. The Lord God will give him the throne of his ancestor David."[12] She turned to Joseph, her expressive eyes wide with wonder.

Elizabeth smiled, and Joseph noted her expression of quiet confidence, reflecting the faith of a woman who had just experienced a miraculous birth.

"Mary," she said, "when Zechariah finally acknowledged the miracle God had done for us in giving us John after many fruitless years, God gave an amazing glimpse into the future of your son. God revealed these words to Zechariah in a beautiful song: 'Praise the Lord, the God of Israel, because he has visited and redeemed his people.'"[13]

Elizabeth rose from her cushion, walked across the room, and embraced Mary. "Mary, you are highly favored by God. You and Joseph will make wonderful parents for His Son."

A smile engulfed her plump face and lit up her olive skin.

"Our son, John, will play an important role in preparing the way for your son. We are both blessed by God. We must both live up to the responsibilities God has placed on us, whatever those will prove to be."

Together they gazed lovingly at baby John and then went to the kitchen to prepare the evening meal, share recipes, and exchange birthing secrets.

Joseph remained alone in the adjacent gathering room, while Zechariah went outside to care for their donkey and bring in their packing baskets and supplies. Mary and Elizabeth cooked, laughing as they watched John babble and kick from his cloth sling on his mother's chest. Elizabeth sat Mary on a stool at a table and gave her vegetables to peel. Her belly hung lopsided and low, heavy with child. Time ticked by as the women exchanged pregnancy and birth stories from other mothers who had described their childbearing experiences. The consensus seemed to be that the period of gestation varied among women—for some, eight and a half months, and for others, nine-plus months.

Joseph noticed that Mary listened attentively and asked questions. Was she concerned that her birth might be different because of the unique circumstances of her conception? Why wouldn't she have questions? He did; he just tried not to think about them.

Will she suffer birth pain and delivery discomfort as other women? Will God protect her from those things? Lord God, am I going to be the one to deliver this child? I am Your servant, as is my wife, but I would be most blessed if You desire to send an angel or someone else to accomplish that task.

Just then, Zechariah entered through the front door and disappeared into a side room with several bundles of Mary and Joseph's clothing and blankets. "We can wash these for you before you leave. Elizabeth can help with that," he called out as he strode back into the kitchen. "Does John need time with his abba?"

Elizabeth brushed the baby's head softly and laughed. "He's perfectly content right now. Don't worry, I'll give him to you after he has eaten." She turned toward Mary. "You soon learn that your firstborn becomes your husband's true love." Elizabeth winked at her husband and laughed.

Zechariah reached out and good-naturedly pinched his wife's cheek. "He is my favorite son. And you, my beauty, are my favorite and only wife and love of my heart. No more-blessed man lives." He stroked Elizabeth's hair, and Joseph's eyes shifted to Mary.

I don't care how the child arrives, God, I'll do whatever I need to do to bring Yeshua safely into this world. Please give me wisdom because I am a simple man, but I know that already I long to hold Yeshua in my arms. I promise to do my best to raise Him for You. Please accept the gift of my faith as enough.

With those prayers pounding through his heart into the night, Joseph tended to Mary, restocked their supplies, and prepared for the final leg of their journey to Bethlehem.

Twelve
A Child Is Born

Coiling mountainside roads and steep inclines slowed the pace to Bethlehem, and Mary sensed Joseph's frustration. Had they not diverted to Ein Kerem and traveled into Jerusalem as the crow flies, then the distance would have been much shorter, and they might have entered the city before midday. But rocky, winding trails topped the mountain ridges and descended into treacherous valleys streaked by hillside terraces, making the trip long, hazardous, exhausting, and painful. Days walking and jolting on the back of a donkey was more than enough. Every movement of the beast sent pain shooting through Mary's lower back and hips. She prayed she would be able to walk once they arrived, as she felt like she never would walk again on this earth.

An hour after leaving Ein Kerem, contractions began to tighten in Mary's womb, a gripping ache and crushing pressure unlike anything she had ever experienced. She forced herself to slowly count to fifty over and over while she slowly breathed. This gave her one answer about the birth: she *would experience* pain. She winced as the next contraction swelled.

At the sight of a grove of pomegranate trees, Mary called out. Joseph was walking a few steps in front of her, leading her donkey as it pulled their small cart.

"Joseph, can we stop for a moment to rest?" She tried to force her face to remain in its natural smile, but the contraction won, and her entire body contorted in pain as a low moan rolled from her lips.

In one glance, Joseph erupted into panic. He rushed toward Mary, which startled the donkey, who balked, sending Mary tumbling into Joseph's arms. He deftly shifted his feet, and his grip tightened around her back and under her knees as he caught her like a child.

A new pain seized her, and she writhed. "Joseph, please! Put me down at the side of the road, in the shade if there is any."

Joseph rushed her to the base of a nearby acacia tree and sat Mary in the shade. "Is it time?" He knelt and stroked her face. "Are you all right? Do you think this is the time? What do you need me to do?" The panic in his voice was obvious.

Bethlehem was still some distance away, and Mary was in dire discomfort, but she patted her husband on his upper arm.

"Joseph, I need a short rest. Yes, I'm in pain, but that doesn't mean the baby is coming right now. The pains are far apart and irregular. I think my body is preparing, but I think he will come within the next day or two. If I don't take breaks today, it may be sooner, and I will be less than pleased." She tilted her head and forced a smile.

Minutes later, she was resting comfortably. After a refreshing nap, the couple resumed their journey under darkening clouds. Soon an unseasonal rain began, the temperature dropped, and a squall engulfed them. Covering their heads with woolen blankets to protect themselves from the downpour, the couple surveyed the area for temporary shelter. Joseph pointed to a small olive grove and sheepfold shelter. Mary's eyes darted toward the grove.

A stench-filled sheep's lean-to? Will it offer a spot to rest not befouled by filth? I do not want to seem ungrateful, Yahweh, but there is still some daylight. Perhaps we can find something farther on.

Mary peered through the rain at their surroundings. Shepherds were tending sheep grazing in the fields, feasting on the grain that remained after harvest. In November, farmers planted wheat and barley, followed by peas, lentils, and flax in December. Sheep were often kept in shelters attached to their shepherds' homes during planting season so they wouldn't eat the new grain. But during preplanting season, sheep feasted in the fields.

After gaining permission from the shepherds, Mary and Joseph took refuge in the grove to wait out the cold rain. Mary found a clean corner of the lean-to and used the time to rest. Although she'd experienced contractions throughout the day, she'd hesitated to tell Joseph.

The late afternoon passed drearily, marked only by a visit from lonely shepherds who were delighted for an opportunity to chat. The cold, pounding rain continued.

Joseph knelt beside Mary's nest of clean hay and dry blankets he'd found in a corner of the stable-like shelter. "Please, my love. This is not proper lodging, but it is warm, clean, and safe. Please rest tonight, and we can continue the journey tomorrow."

"This child will be born in Bethlehem. Perhaps even tonight—but in Bethlehem, Joseph," Mary insisted.

One of the visiting shepherds spoke up from near the door. "Bethlehem? You might possibly make it by nightfall."

His words washed over Mary's heart like cool water in the heat of the day.

Not too far.

She turned toward Joseph and mustered her most persuasive smile.

* * * * *

Mary had been adamant: bad weather would not deter her. Yes, she knew there would be no more villages or relatives to provide lodging and protection from the cold rain. Still, she urged Joseph to push on.

In a short time, they ate, warmed themselves, and were back on the road. With every cold drop of rain that stung her face, Mary determined, clinging to the hope that His Son, her baby, would be born *in Bethlehem.*

Joseph had stopped speaking. In the short time they had been married, Mary had observed this signal. He was distraught. Joseph had grown up in a farmer's home, and he could endure rain and cold, but her husband was worried about protecting her and the baby. Mary's heart swelled with love.

You could not have given me a better husband to raise this child and to care for us. Joseph always strives to honor You, Yahweh.

Mary's donkey was lagging, and she did her best to dig her heels into its sides, but her legs had become paralyzed by the force of her weight pressing against the animal. She called out to Joseph, who was leading her donkey by a length of rope.

Straining, she uttered, "Rest for the animal and me, Joseph. If we could sit beneath a sheltering tree for a short time."

Joseph turned and helped her from the donkey, then took her by the arm and directed their steps through the mud toward a tall, scraggly tree. "We should take this last distance in segments that allow you to get off the donkey and take shelter. This weather must be increasing your discomfort, my precious one."

Joseph turned Mary toward him and drew his face close to hers. The rain streaming down his weathered cheeks looked like tears, and Mary felt a sudden urge to bury her face in his shoulder and have her husband gather her close.

This is not the time. Or the place.

She swallowed and stepped back. "I must sit down, Joseph. Perhaps try to lie on my side—my back is aching from trying not to slump or to fall from that rocking beast. When I get off, my body seems to think I am at sea in a tempest. And for reasons I should not speak about, I would prefer that donkeys not have bones in their backs. At least this one." She groaned as Joseph gently lowered her to the ground and smiled.

God, I am trying to have a willing heart, but obedience is not easy. You have performed a miracle in me. I can do this because You called me to do it, but You must give me strength. I cannot go farther on my own.

Hours later as dusk turned to darkness, Mary and Joseph, drenched and shivering, passed the scattered homes and stables that marked the outskirts of the small village of Bethlehem. In the dim light, it was difficult to discern one house from another. Joseph had been praying for guidance to their kinsmen's home the entire journey. Joseph had never been to this house before, so Zechariah had given him directions, but the rain and greasy darkness was making it difficult to spot the landmarks Zechariah had named.

Aching and chilled to the bones, the couple stopped and asked for directions to the home of Joseph's cousin Eliakim. Once. Twice. A third time. Everyone knew Eliakim and his wife Deborah, an experienced midwife who had delivered many of the village's babies. Everyone pointed them farther down the road. And each time Mary winced at the thought of more jostling and pain.

But soon after the third stop for directions, they spotted the two flat stones that marked the path to Eliakim's home. With a quiet moan, Mary slid to the ground and clutched her back. "I will need to lie down as soon as possible, somewhere private. Although we are family and welcome, we are hungry, drenched, and unexpected, and I am about to give birth." Mary slumped against Joseph's shoulder and reached for his cold, dripping hand as they walked the path to the modest stone house. "Who wouldn't want to open the door and welcome us in?" She turned her face upward toward her husband and smiled.

The chatter of voices coming from inside the home told

them that other visitors had sought shelter before them. Mary noted disappointment flicker across Joseph's face as he knocked on the heavy wooden door.

The door flew open. Eliakim—a tall, gray-bearded man with thick, unruly eyebrows—greeted them and pulled them out of the rain and under the grassy awning. Joseph introduced himself and Mary, and the two men embraced. Then Eliakim ushered the couple into his home as a rounded, laughing woman moved through the crowded gathering room to join him.

Like most of the homes in Bethlehem, Eliakim's house was modest and built from exposed stone walls. A small stone oven gave off the scent of bread baking in the kitchen. Wall niches held small oil lamps that lit the rooms. In the large gathering room, clay plates and small bread baskets sat atop a wooden slatted table that was flanked by woven cane stools. The smells of pots simmering in the kitchen swirled through the house, and Mary tried to ignore the hunger pangs rumbling in her stomach. Eating a big meal before delivering her first child would probably not be wise.

Mary noted the well-stocked shelves and the dried fruit hanging on a small rack in the corner, hooks loaded with dried fruits, and baskets bulging with nuts and olives.

The main living area functioned as a gathering room for talking and work. Comfortable chairs, sleeping mats, and wooden stools filled the space. Two small private rooms for bathing and guests completed the house. Off of the guest room, a low arched door opened into a cave cut into the porous hillside for protecting animals from winter's cold or for summer's needed storage. The cave opening permitted animals access to shelter without entering the living area of the house.

"We have had many unexpected guests," Deborah spoke apologetically. "Our extra room is crowded with sleeping mats, even the gathering room." She pointed to the room behind her, filled with nearly a dozen people.

Eliakim chimed in. "We are so sorry. We barely have space for the guests already here."

"But," Joseph blurted, "Mary's time to deliver has come, and she is cold and sick with exhaustion."

Deborah stepped forward and wiped the rain from Mary's face with the sleeve of her rose-colored tunic. "I'm so sorry, my dear. Let me see if other guests might give up ..."

Mary shook her head and broke in before Deborah could finish. "Thank you. I appreciate your kindness. The other guests were here first, and I can't have them sent into the night in this weather. God will direct us, just as He has provided for your other guests."

Deborah turned toward her husband and placed her hand on his arm. Eliakim nodded in agreement, although she never spoke a word. Emotion edged his voice as he spoke.

"There is no room in the guest room, but you are welcome to the stable. I will put down a clean bed of straw next to the cattle manger for you. The stable will be clean and warm, and provide shelter from the rain. The animals are in the fields with the shepherds."

Mary's fear and disappointment melted into gratitude, then confusion. Certainly God had not destined this baby to be born in a stable. But were they to turn back into the cold night? She glanced up at Joseph's rain-streaked face.

"We are grateful." A sigh of relief escaped Joseph's lips so loud that Mary was sure it was heard throughout the noisy room. But she sensed new confidence in her husband. This was where they were to spend the night, he was certain.

"Thank you. It will feel wonderful to be warm, dry, and out of the rain."

Deborah herded the couple through the living area into the cave. Moments later, with the exhausting day behind them, the couple bedded down for the night in dry borrowed clothing in a nest of fresh hay.

Silently, Mary counted the time between the birth pains.

* * * * *

In the fourth watch of the night,[14] Mary nudged Joseph. He moaned and rolled farther from her. She poked him sharply in the ribs.

"It's time, Joseph!"

This time he sat bolt upright. "Tonight? In a stable? I thought perhaps in a few days I could secure better lodging ..."

Mary cut him off. "No, *now*! The baby is coming, and he's not waiting for anyone." Mary tried to hide her fear. The pain was more than she'd expected. "Get Deborah."

Joseph leaped to his feet and headed to the kitchen, where intoxicating aromas had already told Mary that Deborah was preparing the day's menu for the many guests.

God, thank You for leading us to the home of an experienced midwife. As much as I love Joseph, I didn't want him to deliver the baby. I am certain that he has feared the thought. We've honored Your request, God. He's never seen my body or violated modesty. Delivering a baby would have been a startling and perhaps frightening introduction to my body.

Deborah rushed into the darkness of the cave. Mary was now feeling the pain and pressure of cramps every few minutes. Deborah ordered Joseph to stay with his wife and comfort her while she brought lamps and gathered the birthing materials.

Mary squeezed Joseph's hand with the pain of each contraction and struggled not to cry out. She moaned, praying silently that the baby would come.

Deborah settled into place and pointed at Joseph in the wavering light. "You. Out. I will let you know when Mary has delivered and when you can see the baby. Your wife and I have work to do. Now go!"

Mary could not remember ever hearing a woman speak to a man in that tone, but Joseph turned and fled the cave. Deborah turned back to Mary.

"Your job is to push hard when I tell you to." She draped

Mary with a blanket and examined her, then turned and pulled midwife supplies from the basket she had brought into the stable with her. "It appears your body has already done much of the work. Did you have pains on the journey?"

"Ye ... ye ... yes." Mary struggled to speak through a swelling contraction.

"I have good news for you. You are ready to push; your body is ready. The next time a pain comes, push as hard as you can."

Deep, throbbing pain. A teeth-gritting, agonizing push, followed by several more. Then a tiny cry, and Mary forced her tiny son from the safety of her womb into the world. She felt a release of pressure as Deborah pulled him from the birth canal. Wonder overcame her as Deborah gently cleaned him, cut the umbilical cord, gently rubbed salt on the tiny body to prevent infection, then wound linen cloth around his arms and legs, according to custom, to help ensure proper growth. Deborah cradled him briefly in her arms, then placed the infant in Mary's arms. A moment later, Joseph was at her side.

God had chosen the baby's name before the foundations of the world: Yeshua. But before sunset the next day, Mary was calling him Yeshi, her own endearing term for the baby God had entrusted to her care and Joseph's.[15]

Mary asked Joseph to bring a blanket she and Elizabeth had woven by hand months before. She lovingly swaddled Yeshua, making sure the blanket was snug against his body. Then Mary slipped the baby into Joseph's waiting arms as Deborah gathered her supplies and disappeared back into the house.

"They both need rest," Deborah called over her shoulder. "Especially your wife."

But Mary's maternal instincts were not to be quelled.

"Joseph, I'm sorry, I need him back for a few more minutes. I think I should try to get him to nurse ..." Her voice trailed off.

"You just gave birth. You don't need a reason to want to hold your child." Joseph grinned as he handed her the baby. Then he leaned forward and stroked Mary's cheek. "Do you know how brave you are? The trip was hard. I can only imagine the pain you endured. Are you going to be all right?" His tone reflected concern, but Mary's attention focused on the tiny hand wrapped around her little finger. Yeshua had already captured her heart.

"Pain, yes. But Joseph ... there are no words for this feeling. He is beautiful, and he is here. But what does the future hold? The questions in my mind seem too great to even imagine. I am sometimes afraid ... but I do not doubt God."

She snuggled her newborn son to her breast and gently kissed him on his forehead and watched his wee eyes struggling to remain open. She whispered, "Do you know what lies ahead for you? The burden you must carry for all mankind—the Savior of the world?"

A cloud of sorrow suddenly hung over her joy as she grappled with the mysteries of the future for her precious Yeshi. But then, the music of God's hosts of heaven echoed in the stillness a calm resolve and she quietly hummed words that were running through her mind:

> "Oh, how my soul praises you, Lord.
>
> How my spirit rejoices in You, my God and Savior!
>
> For You took notice of this lowly servant girl,
>
> and blessed her beyond measure.
>
> For you will not now abandon your servants.
>
> Your hands will sustain us forever."

Joseph leaned down and kissed her on the forehead. "God does not mind our questions, as long as they do not stand in the way of our obedience. Together we have pledged to raise Yeshua to honor and obey God as best we can."

Mary scooped out a tiny nest of hay beside her and laid the swaddled Yeshua where both Joseph and she could see him. Whatever destiny God had ordained for him, that day was far off.

Today he was a newborn, and she was a new mother.

Thirteen

Yeshi's First Visitors

Voices at the cave entrance awakened Mary from her brief rest. Her eyes adjusted to the blackness, and she made out Joseph's dim form striding toward the gated opening to the cave, where she saw the silhouettes of several men. She pulled Yeshua closer to her and covered him with his blanket.

Joseph spoke. She couldn't understand his words. His statement was followed by men's voices interrupting one another, then Joseph interjecting questions and the men answering.

Then there was silence, followed by the sound of Joseph's voice and footsteps approaching in the darkness.

"Mary, it's all right. There is no reason to be afraid."

No reason to fear? It's the middle of the night, and I have just given birth. Strangers are stopping to visit us in the home of our relatives, where we are sleeping in a stable. Is this a test of my faith in you, Husband?

She drew Yeshua closer and adjusted her clothing. "May I ask who has chosen this time of night to visit and how they found us?"

"Shepherds, but not ordinary shepherds. Mary, this is a miracle, just like your pregnancy, the baby's birth in Bethlehem, and the angels who spoke to us. I will let them explain."

Mary's apprehension faded to curiosity.

Another miracle, just hours after I gave birth?

She smoothed her garments and brushed away a few clusters of straw that clung to her sleeves. Then she gathered Yeshua in her arms, cradled him to her chest, and pulled the blanket away from his face as a small group of shepherds made their way toward her. They were all speaking at once, trying to explain the reason for their visit. A star had beckoned them, and they had followed, engulfed by the most beautiful music imaginable. But something was odd. Mary recognized several of the men as the shepherds who had offered them shelter to rest.

Their story tumbled out as Mary sat stroking the face of her sleeping child and Joseph stood beside her.

"The night began as any other night ..."

"We were looking after our father's flocks ..."

The shepherds interrupted one another until one hushed the rest and continued.

"The cold, damp air had chilled us, and we huddled around a fire in a shelter we built out of rock for protection from storms, heat, and cold—you saw it earlier. Suddenly, a blinding light illuminated the darkness. We were terrified. We fear Yahweh, try to obey the law, and attend synagogue. What had we done? Was God angry with us?

"An angel appeared and spoke out of the darkness, reassuring us. 'Don't be afraid!' he said. 'I bring you good news that will bring great joy to all people. The Savior—yes, the Messiah, the Lord—has been born today in Bethlehem, the city of David!'"[16]

Mary looked at Joseph in astonishment. Had an angel truly appeared to shepherds to announce that the Messiah would be born in Bethlehem? Her eyes welled with tears. All that Yahweh had promised was being fulfilled. God had spoken to these men through an angel, and they had sought Yeshua, her child, the Son of God.

God, You are affirming all You promised. Please give me wisdom and strength to fulfill the task You have entrusted me to serve as mother to Your Son. I am not worthy of Your favor and bow in obedience to Your will.

The shepherd, who appeared to be the oldest, continued. "It startled us when a mighty choir of angels sang God's praises. A brilliant light shone on us as an angel spoke, telling us where the Messiah was to be born. We wanted to depart for Bethlehem immediately, but our father would be angry if we were to leave the flock unprotected. We had also been told about thieves on the road taking advantage of seasonal travelers."

His voice slowed.

"But nothing could keep us from following the angel's directions and searching for the Messiah's birthplace."

Mary listened to the shepherds' story, fascinated. She glanced at Joseph and noted his solemn attention to the young men's words. The wonder in his eyes revealed that he, too, believed God had guided the shepherds to welcome Yeshua to the world. Her mind spun with the wonder of what was happening and the responsibility that lay before them.

For a moment Mary thought she might faint. God had chosen shepherds, a carpenter, and an unremarkable Jewish girl to partner in His plan: simple people, flawed people. The magnitude of all that had happened within the past day overwhelmed her, and she reached for Joseph's hand, only to find that, like the shepherds, he had slipped to his knees in reverence of the child in her arms.

Fourteen
The Marriage Bed

Joseph completed the tax registration before Shabbat began. Rebellion and fighting that had erupted throughout Israel made it too dangerous for the family to travel. They delayed their return to Nazareth. This provided an opportunity for Joseph to investigate housing and job opportunities in Bethlehem—building, repairing plows, or making goads and furniture.

Joseph spent months pondering the best schooling option for Yeshi. Jerusalem would provide unparalleled opportunities for a scripture-based education. The city would also offer other opportunities for spiritual instruction until God provided further direction about the family's return to Nazareth.

After the feast and census, Eliakim and Deborah's guests left, and Mary and Joseph moved from the stable to the guest room, where they remained with Eliakim's family for several days so Mary could rest from the difficult trip and the birth. This freed Joseph to look for a small house in Bethlehem. But knowing suitable homes were few, Eliakim approached Joseph one morning at breakfast with an alternate solution.

"Joseph, why not finish the small addition I began for our family? You are welcome to stay with us as long as you like. That way, you and Mary can have private living quarters without the expense of your own home."

Joseph placed his bowl on the table. How had Eliakim known the few homes Joseph had found in Bethlehem were far more costly than he could afford?

He turned to Mary, who had joined him for breakfast. "God not only answered our prayers but also made a way for you to remain with your dear friend Deborah. He granted your heart's desire. Yahweh blessed you, my wife. Even our unspoken prayers are known and answered."

Mary smiled and lowered her head, and Joseph noted the glisten of tears in her eyes. His wife had endured much and asked for little. Deborah's friendship would be a sweet balm to Mary's soul, but Joseph also knew his wife's deep yearning for a home to call her own.

* * * * *

When Yeshua was eight days old, Joseph took him for the first time to Jerusalem, where Yeshi was circumcised and inducted into the covenant of Moses. Forty days later, Mary and Joseph made another day trip from Bethlehem to Jerusalem. Mary was purified, and they offered a sacrifice to consecrate their firstborn, as required by the law.

In answer to his prayers, Joseph secured several small carpentry jobs and one somewhat lucrative contract that required making mud bricks and fashioning large Jerusalem stones into "Herodian" blocks. Herodian blocks were also called ashlar stones, which were large stone blocks cut flat and even, with narrow margins around the edges and smooth, raised knobs in the center. If work was as plentiful as it appeared it might be, the family would remain in Bethlehem.

Tension had hung between Joseph and Mary since Yeshua's birth—as if every cell in their bodies was asking the question, *When? Tonight?* It was hard for Joseph to admit even to himself that he was nervous. Living in the home of friends seemed to heighten their physical tension. Mary seemed nervous too. Although they had been wed for nearly a year, talking about the timing of their coming together felt awkward, as if they were discussing a household purchase or everyday chore.

Joseph broached the subject in his own unique way: with a gift for his beloved. Eliakim had divided a portion of his stable, and Joseph used it for a workshop. Sharing his workspace with animals posed no problem for Joseph. He spent hours after sundown for several days working on a bed for their new sleeping room. Although Eliakim and Deborah had generously offered space, Mary and Joseph once again made their bed on a sleeping mat, topped by blankets. A bed would be a luxury.

Joseph kept the wood frame hidden behind sheepskins hung on a rope tied across one side of his workspace. He stretched woven strips of camel's leather over the frame and covered the lattice with soft sheep's wool, topped by soft-hued blankets Mary had spun and flower-dyed during their betrothal. Joseph was as eager as a child to see Mary's reaction when he revealed his gift.

Eliakim and Deborah had vowed to keep his secret. They added to the surprise by offering to visit cousins in Jerusalem for three days: the first day, second day, and third day after Shabbat. Joseph arranged for an expectant friend and neighbor to ask Mary to help bake bread the morning of the first day once Eliakim and Deborah left. During Mary's absence, Joseph dragged the new bed into their sleeping room in parts and hastily assembled it, drawing the entry curtain when he finished.

Early that evening, Joseph gulped down Mary's meal of freshly baked bread and fragrant stew. Cooking had kept her busy in the kitchen for the afternoon. He couldn't allow her to wander into their sleeping room and spoil the surprise.

"My dear wife, once again you prepared a wonderful meal, but that was one of your best stews ever."

Joseph dragged the last bit of his bread through the

sauce at the bottom of his bowl, then savored his last bite with his eyes closed.

"But I'm tired tonight. I worked *very* hard while you were visiting this morning, and I think I need extra rest."

From the corner of his eye, Joseph saw Mary staring at him. She tipped her head to the side and smiled, a different smile. A shiver went down his neck.

"Yes, Joseph, it has been a tiring day. *Quite* tiring. I think I will join you. The table and bowls can wait."

Joseph stood. His legs felt like water, but he walked slowly toward Mary. Confused, he knew his goal, but he didn't have an idea in the world how to achieve it. He prayed that the bewildered thoughts racing through his mind didn't show on his face. Smiling, he took Mary by the hand and led her to the curtain outside their sleeping room and lifted the sheepskin.

She caught her breath and lifted her hand to her mouth at the sight of his cherished gift.

Together they lay down, hearts pounding, silently speaking, guided by their love and devotion.[17]

Fifteen
A Star in the East

Yeshua squealed as he playfully tugged a lock of Mary's hair.

"Come inside, my love. The time is long past for Yeshi to be asleep."

"Yeshi doesn't appear to agree with you," Mary called over her shoulder into the house, her eyes fixed on the deep sapphire night sky. "Joseph, come outside and join us. There is a bright star in the sky just beyond Bethlehem."

"I have seen stars, my dear. But I have not seen enough of my bed since the day this child entered the world. Come inside, put him down, and we will try to sleep. Again."

Mary turned away from the pulsating glow in the night sky and turned to enter the house. But in her heart, the glow of the star and an unspoken question flickered.

* * * * *

Joseph awoke to the sound of deep voices in conversation outside in the front courtyard. He pulled a tunic over his head and went to investigate. He opened the heavy wooden door to find three opulently dressed men who introduced themselves as magi from Persia in the East.

Bewildered, he invited them into the gathering room and offered them refreshment. They appeared to be wealthy, learned men, perhaps Gentiles,[18] and had obviously traveled far. The leader, who called himself Melchior, claimed the men had studied the heavens and banded together to follow a heavenly star that had led them to the King of the Jews. He introduced his fellow travelers as Caspar and Balthazar.

"A star in the east beckoned us to follow and led us to Jerusalem and now here to worship the King of the Jews. We have traveled here to honor God's gift to the world."

The men bowed their heads in respect and dropped to their knees. Joseph turned to Mary, who had dressed and come into the kitchen. She was assessing their clothing, jewelry, and servants to determine if they were who they claimed to be. No one could be trusted these days, and Joseph was continually alert to protect his young family. But Mary was also shrewd, and most men underestimated her gentle exterior.

Joseph nodded, and Mary gestured for the men to follow her. Joseph's eyes widened. She had invited three Gentile men into their home in the middle of the night, yet she appeared at perfect peace. Should he stop her? But something in the men's faces told him they were telling the truth. They had come to worship Yeshua. The thought seemed beyond his comprehension.

They passed through the kitchen and crowded into Mary and Joseph's sleeping chamber, where Yeshua lay sleeping in the middle of their large bed, layered in handwoven blankets. The men dropped to their knees and bowed in worship. Then they raised their heads and gazed at Yeshua in adoration as prayers fell from their lips and filled the room like music. Joseph's heart pounded. God had again confirmed His promises. Moved by their sincerity, Joseph invited their visitors to share bread and soup and tell their story in detail. He was pleased when Melchior spoke for the group and agreed.

The men settled in the crowded kitchen on stools Joseph carried in from the workshop. After a few bites of bread and sips of soup, Melchior launched into their story.

"When we arrived in Jerusalem, we went to the Jews, thinking they would be excited to learn the identity of their prophesied King. We sought out Jewish priests. Caspar, our spokesman, bowed to the chief priest and quoted from your sacred scriptures: 'A star will rise from Jacob; a scepter will emerge from Israel.'[19]

"Caspar told the priests that our large caravan, which included attendants and guards, had traveled for forty days[20] from Persia to worship the new King. We pleaded to be taken to him.

"But when they heard this, the chief priests responded with arrogance and mockery. 'Is a king coming?' they sneered. 'Will this king diminish our authority? Who brings such news to us? We serve only the God of Abraham.'"

Melchior stretched his legs, and Caspar, who wore a matching purple turban and robe, took up the conversation.

"The priests' ignorance surprised us. They know about the coming King clearly revealed in their writings but were dismissive. I noted fear in their voices."

The men nodded in agreement.

"We soon learned that religious and political authorities in Jerusalem are corrupt and the thought of a rival terrifies them. A new King would be a threat—not only to King Herod but also to Jewish leaders. So they sent word to Herod, knowing he would take care of their 'false king.'

"One of the chief priests entered Herod the Great's private chamber for an audience. Other priests followed at a safe distance to listen in. Melchior also went. We all wanted to hear Herod's response to the announcement."

Melchior spoke once again. Balthazar appeared content to let his companions do the talking. His head had fallen forward, his raggedy white beard splaying over his deep blue robe.

"The Jewish priests knew Herod was wracked with disease, gout, and possibly diseases from his reported illicit sexual activities. He was also ill-tempered. Everyone feared being in his presence. He had doused his body in sweet perfumed oils to mask putrid body odors. But nothing could shield the stench of a body covered in sores and robes soaked with pus and sweat. Disgusting."

Mary turned her head away and covered her mouth.

"Herod disrespected the priest and me from the moment we entered, demanding to know what he wanted.

"The chief priest seemed fearful of reproach when Herod called them in for interrogation. Reliable sources had told Herod that a king had been born who would seek to rule Israel. A new king was a real danger to his throne.

"The priest watched Herod. It appeared he was assessing his mood, which shifted to rage. Herod shouted at the chief priest: 'Return with your so-called wise men. Tell no one of this rumored king, or you shall receive the full weight of my wrath.'

"Herod left no doubt about the force of his warning. I left as commanded and hurried back to report to my companions, and the chief priest returned to the temple to report to the high priest."

Melchior took a long drink of water, set his cup down, and wiped his mouth.

"I returned, gave the news to Caspar and Balthazar, and communicated Herod's despicable disposition and his threat.

"The three of us hurried to the royal palace. Our conversation with Herod was short. He interrogated us about where this king was to be born. Given that we were under threat of heavy punishment, guards warned us that he would not ask a second time.

"He convinced us he wanted to worship the king. We tried to keep the age of the child secret, but he guessed the baby would be around one to two years old. Convinced he was a worshipper, we told Herod where the child would be born. Assuming the child would jeopardize his power, he became violent, screaming and throwing furniture and artwork. We were fearful of what he might do next.

"We have since learned that Herod lives in constant fear of a Jewish uprising that would attempt to put the Hasmonean kings back on the throne. Fear seems to fuel his self-protective cruelty."

Melchior looked into Joseph's eyes.

"His rage told us he'd betrayed us. We regret revealing the whereabouts of the birth. But our regret does not change facts. We needed to warn you of Herod's hatred for the child. Then, as we hurried toward Bethlehem to pay homage to our newborn King, the star appeared again and led us to you."

Melchior stood.

"But we must leave before Herod finds us. Be warned of danger from this demented king. We have brought you gifts from Persia of gold, frankincense, and myrrh. All of us pray they will help you in your God-appointed task to raise the King of Israel. Now we must go. We have been warned in a dream to return another way. But we warn you: you and the child are not safe."

With those words, the magi left as quickly as they had appeared. Joseph stood in the door, Mary beside him, as the caravan disappeared in a cloud of dust in the distance.

That evening an angel of the Lord appeared to Joseph in a dream warning of Herod's evil plan to kill Yeshua. The angel said with all urgency, "Get up, take the child and his mother, and escape to Egypt until I tell you it is safe."

Moments later, Joseph and Mary huddled at the table, planning the fastest means of escape from their home and the best route to safety. The magi's gifts had come at the exact moment they needed funds to pay for Yeshua's fugitive escape to Egypt. Yet another miracle, Joseph pondered.

And yet another journey into the unknown for Mary, the baby, and me—an unknown to us, but a destiny that was written into eternity before time began. Praise be to Yahweh.

Sixteen

Fleeing Herod's Slaughter

Joseph kicked at a pile of wood carvings at his feet as he tried to push away memories of threats and the near escape he and his family had experienced in Nazareth months before.

God's love of surprises is sending us to Egypt to keep Yeshua safe from Herod after all our people endured to be delivered from Egypt? Joseph's silent words dripped with irony.

Mary and Joseph stood in their small kitchen packing baskets with dried provisions for travel, wrapping them in dried animal skins secured with ligament strings. "Praise Yahweh for the magi alerting us and my heavenly visitor warning us to leave for our safety, or I would not have thought to step foot in Egypt.

I know this is only the beginning. Dear Av, I will do all I can to protect Your Son from the evil one and all enemies seeking to destroy Yeshua. But I need Your help.

Like thieves in the night, Mary and Joseph prepared themselves and Yeshi as they moved stealthily into the streets and out of Bethlehem. Joseph recognized that abandoning their new home in Bethlehem was heartbreaking for Mary, but she understood their grave situation. Taking only belongings they could carry, they might reach the Egyptian highway by the next day.

* * * * *

The terrifying rumble of armed horsemen exploded in the quiet unarmed village of Bethlehem, shattering the late afternoon serenity. A new recruit from Gaul known for his elite military skills rode at the rear, where he hoped the dust would obscure him from attention. The troops received word that residents would be preparing the late evening meal, making it easier for soldiers to carry out their sadistic orders to murder every male child two and under.

Although he had joined a band of hired mercenaries, the recruit had believed it would be a privilege to serve as a soldier of Herod's elite guard stationed in Jerusalem. Dressed in full armor as if confronting the greatest of enemies, his eager men were armed with spears, long, heavy-bladed swords, and sharp, short daggers. Most were hell-bent on killing every male child without conscience or regard for the morality of the deed.

"Kill them all. Every male child under two."

Herod's command had been unequivocal. And unthinkable.

But rumor had spread among the ranks that Herod had become wild with fear about the birth of a Jewish king who would threaten his rule.

No soldier who served under Herod's rule dared disobey a direct order and hoped to live. The Gaulian was no saint. He had seen soldiers carry out their orders with cold impunity, deaf to the screams of mothers clawing the air for infants torn from their arms or children crawling through dirt clotted thick with blood. Other warriors like himself did not believe that male children posed a threat to Herod or the empire. They had joined the Roman forces to fight enemy powers, not to slaughter innocent women and children.

He remembered the face of his sister Diana as she had bid him goodbye before he left, her body swollen in pregnancy.

"If you cannot live as a man of conscience, come home to us, Brother. Even Herod is not worth the price of your soul."

The recruit clung to the image as he searched the town

and took a position behind a fabric vendor's tent that stood among a cluster of carts and wagons. He slid from his horse, knelt behind a wagon, and watched the slaughter until his stomach churned. Then he clenched his eyes shut. The soldiers had timed their arrival in evening, when families were together and unsuspecting. All the easier to massacre—such was Herod's evil mind. The air thick with mingled scents of baked bread, slaughtered lambs and goats, the putrid aroma of human flesh and blood, and acrid urine from the muddied dirt beneath the feet of donkeys and camels tethered around the perimeter of the central marketplace.

Mothers tried to shield their children, who were torn from their arms brutally butchered before their eyes. Other imas clung to their children so tightly that soldiers hacked through them to murder the child. Screams of mercy from mothers and fathers cut through the night air of the village and rose above the chaos of snorting horses and soldiers' blood-infused shrieks at the thrill of killing.

The recruit slid forward in the dirt, dipped his hands in blood streaming fresh from a slaughtered child tossed near him, and wept.

* * * * *

Anxiety and anger surged through Antipas's veins like floodwaters as he sat in the portico and stared at the beauty of the palace garden. News had reached his father, Herod the Great, that the mission in Bethlehem had succeeded.

You would think the fool had conquered Egypt.

He glanced toward his father, who was prancing around the portico like a child in filthy, reeking garments, long gray unkempt hair covering his face like a donkey. His sycophants stood by, watching in fear as over and over his father bellowed, "I have no rival! I am king of all Judea!"

In his peripheral vision, Antipas saw his father lean in his direction, his spittle-stained royal robe dragging the floor. "Let that be a lesson to you!" he roared. "To all of you!"

He turned and pointed at his terrified followers, his voice echoing from the wall of the massive stone porch.

Antipas sat motionless and silent. As likely successor to his father, he feared for his life. Herod's insanity and capability for atrocities terrified everyone.

Let him think the child is dead, but can we ever know? The thought pounded through his mind while his father raged.

* * * * *

The young family's walk to Egypt, a Roman-controlled province out of reach of Herod's rule, would take nearly thirty days. The heavenly messenger's ominous words had warned Joseph that danger lurked in Bethlehem. Mary and Joseph's hearts were heavy with sorrow for their many friends and family left behind to face what would undoubtedly be a bloody onslaught. Mary and Joseph paused, knelt in the dirt and rocks beside the road, and wept as they thanked God for delivering Yeshua from the hands of Herod's murderous henchmen.

With every step down the Egyptian highway, Joseph's growing burden of responsibility to raise God's Son pressed more heavily. Perhaps it was the awareness that his family would live in the land that had held his people captive for hundreds of years.

I have no special ability or wisdom, my Av, to give to Your Son. I am just a simple man.

A sense of profound humility, gratitude, and wonder sank more deeply into Joseph's soul with each passing day.

Awareness of his dependency became a sweet bond. Joseph daily reaffirmed his dedication to keep Yeshua safe, guide his heart, and teach him scripture. Joseph understood that their precious baby Yeshi lay in the hands of their heavenly Av. But he wondered, *What is next? Will we ever settle down and be able to give Yeshi a stable life?*

Joseph did not doubt his Lord's plan, but he was weary

of uprooting his family. They had left everything behind in their simple home. Mary had to be heartbroken, although she had not said a word since they had fled Bethlehem.

They headed for Alexandria, a city with a large Jewish population that had remained after the Babylonian captivity. The community would provide safety and steady work to support the family. Who knew what God planned for them there?

Joseph turned to Mary. She had been carrying the toddler too long. She preferred to walk with Yeshi in the cloth sling that cradled him across her stomach. But the sun had risen to midmorning, and her pace was slowing.

"Let me take our son, my wife. It is time for you to rest."

Mary smiled and nodded agreement as she untied the cloth that bound Yeshi to her chest and handed him to Joseph, who bound the infant to his back.

"I will need to feed him soon. How many more days before we arrive at Alexandria, do you think?" Her eyes looked at him hopefully.

"Three, I would guess." Joseph surveyed the horizon, praying it would reveal buildings in the distance. Mary had been displaced too many times. Perhaps Alexandria would become their home.

Mary smiled and took his hand. "Joseph, I am with child. Our child." Her eyes sparkled with tears.

"Our child? And we have been walking all these days?"

Mary laughed. "Joseph, I am fine."

Joseph had wanted a son of his own flesh for some time. Yeshua's birth had been a divine act without his participation. He loved Yeshi very much, beyond words. But he wanted a larger family. He had wondered if Mary could conceive children, as much as they had been trying.

The announcement was beyond Joseph's wildest expectations. He tipped his face heavenward.

"Thank you, heavenly Av, for this added blessing to our family."

Mary turned to Joseph. "Amen. I love you so, Husband."

Months later, Mary and Joseph's second child and first humanly conceived son came into the world with few complications.[21] It was a special day for Joseph. He loved Yeshua with all his heart, but this child was conceived of his flesh and blood—and born in the land of the prophet Moses's birth, Egypt. Joseph named his son after his own father, Jacob, and called him James [Hebrew, Ya'aqov, Jacob].[22] Yeshua, nearly two years his new brother's senior, laughed with joy as he played with his infant brother. Together, Mary and Joseph smiled in wonder as toddler Yeshua gazed for the first time into the face of baby James, his fully human brother.

Seventeen
The Return to Israel

A small, single oil lamp cast a low glow across the black of night, its light radiating faint shadows on the rock wall near the bed where Joseph lay. Drifting between consciousness and sleep, he prayed for God's direction and protection for his family, when a voice spoke and interrupted his prayers.

"Joseph." The voice spoke with quiet authority. "Get up! Take the child and his mother back to the land of Israel, because those who were trying to kill the child are dead."[23]

The words soaked through the fog of sleep, and Joseph sat up with a jerk. But the voice stilled as quickly as it had come. He lay stunned for a moment as his thoughts swept back to an earlier encounter with an angel who had reassured him of Mary's faithfulness to him.

Quiet joy blanketed him, and Joseph sighed.

Yahweh Himself will help me father this child.

We can go home. God has not left us in this lonely place. Mary will be elated to return to our beloved Israel and, hopefully, to our home in Bethlehem. We will leave as soon as James is able to travel.

* * * * *

An uprising began the day of the Feast of Pentecost but was repulsed by the Romans, which allowed safe travel for Joseph and his family from Egypt back to Israel. King

Herod had died, and while his death did not bring peace, it brought relative calm. With newfound purpose, Joseph led Mary, toddler Yeshua, and baby James on the return trip with a hopeful heart.

But the welcome news of Herod's death brought reminders of his unforgivable cruelty in the last days of his rule. The joy of the journey home was muted with mourning over the news from Bethlehem of the insane savagery of the massacre of the innocents.

Yeshua had been spared, but Mary and Joseph's hearts were ravaged. They could almost hear the screams of mothers weeping for their slaughtered sons.

* * * * *

The journey brought them to Joppa, the crossroads of Bethlehem in Judea and Galilee, where they stayed with a distant relative in the unpopular tanner's section of town.

International travelers entered Israel at Joppa, where taxes were assessed. The city was also a news center for dangerous regime changes caused by Herod the Great's death. Joseph had spent much time in Egypt assessing the dangers of the ever-changing political situation. He visited with countless travelers from Galilee and Jerusalem, trying to better understand his people's predicament. Dire news brought him repeatedly to his knees as he pleaded with God to reveal His will for the future.

Over the past years, Rome had stationed four legions of 6,000 men in Israel: the Third, Sixth, Tenth, and Twelfth. Each legion was divided into cohorts, which were subdivided into six centuries, each with ten maniples. A cavalry of about 120 horses, archers, a camel corps, engineers, and men in charge of siege weapons accompanied each legion. Roman thinking was that keeping the rebellious Jews in line required an overwhelmingly large army.

The Bethlehem experience from which Joseph, Mary,

and Yeshi had fled still lingered in Joseph's mind. While they had lived in Egypt, Joseph had learned many details of the ongoing conflict. Rebel victory had seemed within reach in Jerusalem.[24] To add to Roman troubles, many of the royal troops had joined the rebels. Roman procurator Sabinus developed a well-founded fear of the large group of disciplined, resolute rebels who fought with little regard for their lives.

Fierce conflict raged. Jerusalem's ornate buildings were reduced to rubble. Those fighting on rooftops fell into fires below, and both soldiers and civilians burned alive in the debris. Some Jews put themselves to the sword to prevent capture or a cruel death at the enemy's hands. The temple was breached and looted, and Sabinus stole four hundred talents from the treasury. These deeds enraged the Jews and encouraged sympathetic Romans to join the rebels. The newly formed fighting force laid siege to Herod's palace. Although victory looked certain, the battle signaled the beginning of the end.

Joseph considered himself an Israeli patriot, but the rebellion had lost focus and was doomed to failure. Rebels were accusing law-abiding Jews of complicity and treating them as enemies of the cause.

"I refuse to give credence to men who defy authority and the law without conscience and cause," Joseph had told Mary more than once.

The well-disciplined rebel militia achieved early successes and took advantage of their good fortune in the early stages of fighting. They forced Sabinus to dispatch a letter to Roman general Varus for immediate assistance. In hopes of averting interference from the heavily armed Varus, the rebels offered to allow Sabinus to escape with certain guarantees, but the fearful Sabinus did not believe their promise. He refused, believing Varus would come to his aid. His calculated risk paid off.

Varus's arrival turned the tide of the battle. The Romans set fire to the strongholds of the rebels, and they fled, abandoning their positions. Varus quickly brought the rebellion under control. The plundering of God's treasure from the temple assured the resolute rebels the battle was not over—until all were dead.[25]

Joseph had heard of the leader of the rebels in the Galilee sector: Judas, the son of Ezekias, who played a disturbing role in forming a rebel army to attack Sepphoris. Joseph feared his action would engulf family and friends, who might be forced to join the rebels.

He was right.

Well-meaning rebel groups were hell-bent on bringing independence to Israel and reestablishing a Hasmonean king to the Jewish throne.

Joseph's ancestors had been involved in the rebel cause during the Hasmonean reigns. All Israel longed for the long-past days of independent Hasmonean rule. But they had sterilized and idealized their history. As a result, the nation was in turmoil, with constant infighting among the Jewish factions.

This trouble would not end with Herod's death. Joseph remembered the "good old days" his father Jacob had recounted many times. However, his father had warned him against idealizing the days of old—they were not idyllic.

Joseph worried. Danger lurked everywhere: Jerusalem, Galilee, and in any city in Israel. Traveling with a family forced him to face these dangers, and he accepted his daunting responsibilities with trepidation.

In an early will, Herod named one of his sons, Archelaus, as his successor. Later, in his fifth will, he named Antipas as his sole successor. In his sixth and final will, Herod divided his succession three ways, naming Archelaus to rule Judea, Antipas as tetrarch of Galilee and Perea, and Philip as tetrarch of Gaulanitis, Trachonitis, Auranitis, Batanea, and Paneas. Archelaus called upon Rome to confirm his position, but Rome was conflicted by the various claims to the throne and was unwilling to choose a side. Rebellion broke out in Judea, and the Jews insisted that none of Herod's sons inherit the throne and that Israel be given independence. Rome succumbed to Archelaus's claim, and the emperor Augustus appointed him as ethnarch of Judea, Samaria, and Idumea.

Joseph feared the dangers he faced, especially risks for Yeshua. Even with the death of Herod the Great, the rule of his heirs offered little hope for better times. But Joseph placed his family's future in his God, not in men. Yeshua would face dangers throughout his life, and this was only the beginning.

Lord God, You are with me and will help me protect Your Son and our family. This is not a daunting task to You, and I choose to trust You.

With that reassurance, Joseph prepared to face the future, no matter its outcome.

* * * * *

Joseph was breathless by the time he reached the house. He had walked as fast as he could without running. As a newcomer in the town of Joppa, he did not need criticism about immodesty and exposed ankles. He stumbled through the shoulder-high wooden door of their small stone house. Mary was at work spinning yarn from sheep's wool. Yeshi sat at her feet, jabbering at his brother and making James laugh.

"Mary, I have news. From Jericho."

Mary turned toward Joseph, her eyes wide in surprise and fear.

"Now that he is dead and his power but a shadow, those who were part of Herod's rule have already gathered to plan the future. They have divided Palestine into four districts."

"Oh." Mary went back to her spinning.

The news was far from comforting to Mary, but he continued. Facts had to be faced.

"Archelaus, who you know is an upstart, was made ethnarch of Judea, Samaria, and Idumea. Herod Antipas, whom everyone hates, will rule Galilee and Perea. Philip, the most affable of Herod's sons, received the tetrarch position of the Transjordan, east of the Sea of Galilee."

"This is *not* what we hoped and prayed for, Joseph," Mary interjected. "Archelaus ruling Judea? What does he know of ruling?"

Joseph forced himself to hide his discouragement. Word of Herod's death had brought hope of reprieve from injustice and persecution. But Joseph's hope had shriveled to disappointment.

"God is still in control, my wife. Whatever comes will pass through His hands. Yahweh will look after His Son—we are only His servants."

The night before Joseph and Mary were to continue to Bethlehem, Joseph slept fitfully, slumbering and awaking in an exhausting cycle. As he hovered at the edge of sleep, a familiar voice drifted into his consciousness.

"Joseph."

He opened his eyes. The room glowed with golden light.

Again?

The voice was familiar—the angel who had spoken to him before. Joseph understood now that scriptures told that Yahweh used Gabriel the archangel to communicate messages to humankind. The angel gave further instructions to preserve the safety of Yeshua and his family.

"Go to Nazareth in Galilee," the angel stated.

Gratitude flooded Joseph's heart.

Yahweh has a plan. We must obey and change our destination. God is overseeing our steps.

The family departed early the next morning and proceeded along the caravan route that stretched along the flat Mediterranean Sea coastline toward Nazareth. Mary repeatedly voiced her excitement about going home. She had missed her parents deeply, as well as her extended family.

Life in Nazareth would not be easy. Joseph bore a nagging

fear for his family—especially Yeshua and Mary—that they would be judged, misunderstood, shunned, and shamed.

And what of their own children? How would they respond to their oldest brother? Would they grow to resent a brother unlike themselves?

Act 2

Struggle: Self-Identity (ca. 4 BC – AD 15)

(Hebrew Calendar ca. 3757–3776)

Eighteen
A New Beginning in Nazareth

Life for Joseph and the family settled into a routine after their return to their beloved Nazareth, and the days passed swiftly. Joseph busied himself finding work, and Mary delighted herself in setting up their home.

But even in Nazareth they were not exempt from the tyranny of Herod Antipas, who ruled Galilee. Nazareth was a small, obscure village where Yeshua would draw little attention from authorities. Nearby Capernaum was a larger city of fifteen hundred to eighteen hundred residents. Joseph and Mary both preferred raising their children in a small village near their extended family.

Sepphoris was being rebuilt as a new capital for Herod's son Antipas, and the major city of Tiberias, an unclean forbidden city to Jews, was also under construction, which promised Joseph an abundance of carpentry and building jobs. Large projects in Sepphoris and Tiberias provided a lively economy for farmers, builders, and fishermen. However, a heavy tax burden prevented most urban families from climbing out of poverty.

Herod Antipas's building projects demanded basalt and limestone quarrying, agricultural products, fish, and meat. Capernaum was near enough to profit from the expanding economy. Builders also used tesserae for the mosaics that adorned the floors in affluent private homes and public buildings, as well as limestone for frescoes and plaster.

Local non-Herodian cities lacked such amenities and, therefore, the architectural beauty. Their simple structures were built with walls constructed from a mixture of mud and straw and floors made of packed mud, as opposed to opulent homes and public buildings in Herodian cities. The building profession flourished in larger, wealthier towns. Joseph hoped his business would grow and that he could provide a secure income for his family because of the family's strategic location in Galilee, within walking distance to Sepphoris, Tiberias, and Capernaum.

Joseph and Mary's new home was small but adequate for their young family. The gracious gifts from the magi of gold, frankincense, and myrrh had provided funds for their stay in Egypt. They used the remainder to purchase a small house in a multihome compound. The house needed minor repairs, but Joseph could make them while he looked for work.

Wooden beams covered with small branches and reeds and a thick layer of mud plaster formed the roof. Because their house was slightly larger than normal, two pillars in the middle of the gathering room helped support the roof. The roofs needed continual maintenance, and flat roofs developed leaks and needed annual waterproofing. Joseph and Mary had chosen a home with a flat roof because it would provide additional living area.

Joseph offered to build Mary a thatched awning over half of the roof for protection from the blistering sun.

"Any other repairs or additions you would like, my wife, I will build for you."

Mary, delighted to be back in Nazareth, had expressed her gratitude. "I have my family. That is what is important."

The inner walls of their home were constructed of exposed stone with multiple niches and hooks to store cookware and place oil lamps. Joseph couldn't afford the frescoes and plastered walls often seen in more affluent homes, so they furnished their home with several wooden benches and woven chairs, wood-framed beds, a table, and a clay oven that Joseph crafted. Joseph also built a brick staircase that led to the roof. Mary found the house more than adequate.

Mary arranged cushions on the floor for eating and for guests to sleep on. Straw-filled mats provided beds. Joseph had promised he would put his creative carpentry into practice and build well-crafted tables and beds, a luxury not available to many living in Nazareth. They lived modestly on a small income, growing a few crops in a communal garden.

Family and visitors entered a common courtyard shared by other families in the complex to gain entrance to their respective homes. While Mary and Joseph loved their home, the inside rooms were small and windowless, so they spent as much time as possible on the roof. The roof also offered comfortable sleeping on hot summer nights, space for weaving and spinning cloth, and a covered area for drying fish, raisins, figs, and flax. Open space made living tolerable in their small home.

A courtyard also added space for socializing and activities. Because it served a community of observant Jews, it featured a mikvah for ceremonial cleansig. In addition, a community cistern provided water for all the compound residents. The compound also shared a mud brick oven and a donkey-driven millstone for grinding grain. Livestock was kept near the back of the compound in a corral fenced with thorny branches.

Joseph and Mary took up residence in their new home, settled in, and enjoyed a quiet and peaceful life that had eluded them for the past several years. The Romans had brutally stamped out the rebellion that had caused so much upheaval before they had left Galilee. Larger cities were still marked with the remains of crucifixions of those who had defied and escaped the Romans until the bitter end. The fragile peace was in jeopardy—if not from the rebels, then certainly from the Romans.

Living with a sense of normalcy and safety was a precious

gift. When Joseph learned he could build a small carpenter's shop at the end of the courtyard within their compound, he could hardly contain his excitement. Residents readily agreed with the decision when they heard he would assist them with his carpentry skills.

While he was not yet a master craftsman, Joseph worked at every job and contract he received and learned quickly. He soon developed a reputation as a trustworthy and competent carpenter. His experience working with the local Aleppo tree used in larger construction projects gave him an advantage in procuring more lucrative contracts.

Above all, Joseph enjoyed being with family. Abba Jacob was growing older, and Joseph treasured learning from his experience and advice. His father wouldn't be with them much longer, so every moment with him was valuable. Mary's family was also close, and she visited them frequently. Everyone enjoyed watching Yeshi grow. He was walking and talking in full sentences.

But his first word had brought tears to Joseph's eyes. In the days they were preparing to leave Egypt, Joseph had lifted Yeshi into his arms for an embrace. His son gazed into his eyes with loving trust, and spoke, "Abba."

Nineteen
Illusions of Joy

Joseph burst through the door so abruptly that Mary jerked, the wooden spoon in her hand flinging hot broth and vegetables across the room. The simmering pot of lentil stew teetered on its hook, then swung back over the fire.

"Joseph, where have you been? I have not seen you since morning, and you rush into the house late for the evening meal with your work clothing soiled, yet a smile on your face?"

Joseph cast a mysterious look in her direction. Mary heard a jingle of coins coming from his direction. It was too hot in the kitchen. She did not have time for a game.

She stirred the lentil stew, adding bits of lamb from the neighbor's recent butcher as she waited for Joseph's answer. Her hands were gummy from kneading bread dough. She had secretly prepared a special feast for this day, but her expression didn't reveal the surprise to the husband who was late for his meal.

Breathing heavily, Joseph blurted out his news.

"A project superintendent in Sepphoris contacted me today and asked me to help build a new theater."[26] His voice rose in excitement. "The construction will take several months and maybe even years. Not only did I agree, but also, although I'm only an apprentice carpenter, the superintendent offered me a retainer fee, and I accepted."

Mary smiled, not because they would have more income,

but because carpenters and contractors appreciated Joseph's skills. She was proud of her beloved, and he deserved to be recognized and honored. She was glad she had prepared a special meal.

"Now we can build an additional room," Joseph continued. "I know you have wanted more space for some time."

Mary almost laughed.

Yes, we will need that room.

"More room as Yeshua and James grow and a guest room for family traveling from Galilee southward or from Philippi."

Mary stepped toward her husband and laid his hand on her stomach. "Joseph, I am with child!"

He stared back at her, speechless. Then he scooped her up in his arms, spun her in circles, and shouted with joy.

* * * * *

Jose, named after his father, came into the world a handful of months later. With three children, Joseph's successful contracting business, and the shimmering illusion of peace rising across the blazing desert land, Mary and Joseph rested in the arms of God.

Twenty
School Days

Mary was wiping crumbs from the kitchen table when she felt Yeshi tugging on his favorite corner of her apron. For the fifth time that morning Mary paused as she patiently smiled down at her son's inquisitive faun-brown eyes.

Yahweh, how gracious You are to grant me the privilege of mothering this wonder child.

"Is it time for school yet, Ima? I am ready."

Mary had thought of little else than Yeshua's first day of *beit sefer* for days. She and Joseph were pleased that Rabbi Hakim agreed to have Yeshi begin school. The boy was six, the recommended age, and showed an extraordinary aptitude for learning.

"Yes, Yeshi, it is nearly time, and I know you are ready. You have told me many times."

Mary sighed. Her concerns about Yeshi entering school had tied her stomach in knots for days. He did not understand that he was different from other boys, and children could be cruel. Joseph had been teaching Yeshi about his unique mission in life, but the six-year-old was often more interested in playing with friends, taking Joseph's scrap wood to build miniature toy soldiers, or exploring outside. Yet often he could be found sitting alone, as if pondering and contemplating the mysteries of his life.

Mary's thoughts were interrupted as Yeshi tugged again. She knelt to meet his gaze. "We will leave soon, my son. You must be patient, just as I will have to be patient as I wait each day for beit sefer to be over." She kissed him on the forehead. "Go put away your soldiers now." Mary wiped flour from the side of the stone oven with a rag.

She couldn't help remembering Joseph could always liven him up. Joseph would often wrestle with Yeshi until he was breathless and screaming with delight. When his abba released him, Yeshi begged for more. Yeshi loved for his abba to roughhouse with him.

Mary was never so happy as when she spent time with Yeshi helping him interact with nature and life. She was determined not to let his school interfere with her nurturing him.

She recalled his voice squealing from atop her shoulders, gripping her neck so tightly that she thought she couldn't breathe as they ran through the fields of flowers. Yeshi's love for chasing birds across the road led Mary to explain the flight patterns of birds. She often talked about the habits of wildlife. No wonder in spite of his childishness, Yeshi's comprehension of the world seemed beyond his years.

Unlike most Jewish women, Mary had learned to read as she was growing up. Yeshi loved to have his ima read stories from the Good Book and then act out the characters. Yeshi would scramble to her lap and clap his hands in delight as Ima read dramatically. He especially loved the story of David and Goliath. Ima would lower her voice to imitate the words of Goliath with arms raised in a boyish terrifying manner, bouncing him on her lap, "Am I a dog, that you come to me with a sling?"

Then Yeshi, remembering the story, jumped in with his version of David's response: "You come with a sword in your hand, but I come in Yahweh's name. I will kill you."

Mary remembered her visit with Yeshi to the market. She was pleased with his understanding of the things she explained to him. As they sauntered purposefully through the market, Ima identified various fruits, vegetables, and the freshly butchered raw meats hanging from the rafters of the makeshift lean-to. Yeshi didn't like the flies circling the meat and, as he put it, eating the farmers' kill.

Mary's heart swelled with pride the day she and Yeshi passed a regular beggar sitting near the spice mats. Yeshi asked, "Why is that man sitting there begging for morsels?"

Mary paused, *What an observant question.*

"Yeshi, his name is Ruben. His legs were broken when he was very young, and they healed improperly. Both of his parents were murdered in the uprising, and he has no way of earning a living. Our heavenly Av wants us to show mercy and give him what we are able." Mary reached into her pouch and gave Ruben a small loaf of fresh bread she had planned for their lunch later on and a few shekels.

Yeshi spoke up with his eyes bright as the morning sun: "Ima, I'm glad you helped that man. I am sorry he doesn't have an ima and abba. I am glad I have you and Abba. But won't El Shaddai care for him?"

Mary was surprised that at his young age, Yeshi understood El Shaddai and was learning important life lessons of compassion and empathy from his ima.

Yeshi had picked up some Latin by listening to Roman soldiers. His actions and speech revealed a precocious mind, but he was also quite like other boys: inquisitive, rambunctious, and curious. Yeshi's complex questions frequently puzzled Mary, but she reassured herself that he was fine. Joseph and she were doing their best to parent God's sacred trust and still look after their other children.

As a busy ima, Mary had to cease daydreaming. It was time to get going. She tucked the baby into a sling-like swath of cloth that nestled between her bosom and waist. Then she took the hands of the younger children and set out on the path to Rabbi Hakim's house, pausing along the way so Yeshi could examine creepy crawlers and chase squawking chickens.

Young "scholars" sat on benches outside the priest's

peeling whitewashed stone home where classes were taught, weather permitting. Yeshi spied a buddy, who slid over and made room beside him. With scarcely a goodbye wave to his ima, Yeshi struck up a lively conversation with his friend. A moment later, a tiny withered man, his head obscured by his priestly *migbihat*, appeared in the doorway and clapped his hands. The boys filed in.

The walk home was slow, giving Mary time to muse.

How will Yeshi interact with his classmates? As the oldest child, he's always been in charge. How will older boys respond to his confidence?

Mary shifted the baby to a more comfortable position.

I can no longer protect him, El Shaddai. He is in Your hands.

With her prayer, a realization dawned.

Why am I worrying, Yahweh? Yeshi is Yours, and Your protection far exceeds mine. You sheltered us from Herod's evils in Bethlehem and Egypt. You will care for Your Son.

He will be great one day as You promised, but right now he is my little boy entering his first year of school. Please comfort my heart.

As her fears subsided, Mary returned to the house to share Yeshi's first school day goodbyes with Joseph. She was aware that Joseph also pondered questions about Yeshua's future life with some anxiety. He was the Son of God, but Joseph worried that Yeshua didn't yet seem to understand the enormity of his mission on earth. Joseph shared his concern with Mary.

Mary took Joseph's strong, weather-beaten hand in her own.

"Remember, Joseph, he is only six years old. He may be God's Son, but he is also a child. You are worrying about something God controls. Do not be anxious—you have taught Yeshi well. God knows that." She squeezed his hand.

Joseph had spent many hours teaching Yeshua and the other boys about their history from the sacred scriptures. In all Jewish families, the father was the head of the household and absolute authority in the home. Joseph was a dedicated, patient teacher and mentor to Yeshua, who demonstrated early an astute ability to learn. Not only did he appear to Joseph to have a photographic memory, but also his ability to comprehend complex spiritual and theological issues was uncanny.

Yeshi's school schedule soon became routine, and Mary observed her bright, loving son adjusting to school as friends were absorbed into his life.

Yeshua was sometimes boyishly rowdy and eager to finish his daily lessons, but he never displayed unkindness, lied, took things that didn't belong to him, or cheated in games with friends. His teacher expressed his pleasure with Yeshi's success in school and his ability to get along with his schoolmates. The young boy impressed adults with his memory and compassion and frustrated his siblings and classmates with his obedience.

Mary couldn't help but note that, unlike other children, Yeshi required little, if any, discipline. While his compliant nature was in many ways a blessing, it also stirred feelings of anger, jealousy, and confusion in his siblings and classmates. His goodness separated him from other children his age, who often grew angry at his winsome nature and contentment to be alone.

Yahweh, what kind of world is this that goodness stirs contempt in the hearts of mere children? Is this what You see when You look at us? Is this contempt rooted deep within our souls, and does it separate us from You? Do we all, in our own way, turn away from Your goodness to seek the desires of our own twisted hearts?

* * * * *

While Joseph enjoyed woodworking, he understood that carpentry's greatest profit was found in stonework and brickwork, which were the most demanding skills. Nazareth, like most villages, employed a number of master craftsmen, potters, blacksmiths, cloth dyers, basket weavers, mat makers, leatherworkers, and carpenters. He had gained experience and confidence in the stoneworking side of carpentry by working as a mason's apprentice in Sepphoris and Nazareth. He was grateful for men who had come alongside him and taught him this skill.

Most Jewish fathers trained their sons in the family trade, and Joseph longed for the day when Yeshua would be old enough to learn carpentry.

One afternoon, Yeshi returned home from playing with friends, his face despondent. His father met him in the courtyard, and they walked to Joseph's workshop side by side.

"What is wrong, Yeshi?"

"I … I tried to do a miracle today, Abba, but nothing happened." Joseph could hear the near tears in his son's voice. He laid his hand on Yeshua's shoulder and smiled.

"And why would you try to do a miracle, my son?"

"We were playing soldiers, and I tried to make a soldier out of the dust of the ground—that's what God did in the holy scriptures. You have told me I will do special things someday. I thought that if maybe I did a miracle, my friends would want to play with me."

Joseph was silent for a moment. "Yeshua, miracles are not for play or proving something to friends. They are for pointing people to God and showing His greatness. You will do miracles when God says it is time. Listen first for His voice, then obey. God's answer is often to wait, so you must learn to obey Him, which is the most important lesson of all."

Yeshi nodded.

Joseph took Yeshi by the hand and walked him to a leather-woven bench seat. They sat down, and Joseph looked into Yeshi's solemn mahogany-brown eyes. "Yeshi, you are God's own Son sent to earth, and one day you will change the world. You are a child, but you are also God's own. As you grow older, you will come to comprehend who you are and your mission in life, but your mind and body are a child's mind and body. I am your earthly abba, and Yahweh is your heavenly Av. When the time is right, Yahweh will speak to you and reveal what He wants you to do."

Joseph felt as if his heart would burst as total inadequacy flooded through him. No words existed to explain this child's mission in life. In fact, he wasn't sure what it was. He only trusted that Yahweh would reveal all that when it was needed.

Yeshi tipped his head to the side. "But I want to know now."

Joseph fought the urge to roll his eyes. Yeshi was a human child. "Yes, I know you do, but your time has not yet come."

And with that answer, Yeshi ran off to play.

Joseph recognized that Yeshua's destiny would require a thorough traditional education beginning in beit sefer. Rabbi Hakim held small classes in a room of his home. If Yeshi showed promise in his earlier training, he would also attend secondary school, beit midrash. Before Yeshua was born, Rabbi Shimon ben Shetah decreed that all youths aged sixteen or seventeen were to receive a formal education, but to the disappointment of some Galileans, leaders in Jerusalem appointed teachers. Children as early as six began formal education at their parents' discretion. By the time Yeshua reached adolescence, Yehoshua ben Gamla[27] had formally instituted elementary education for boys from the age of six and personally appointed teachers for specific schools.[28] Education was not mandatory but recommended for one son from every Jewish family.

And so Yeshi began his training in the holy scriptures that were and would become the very outpouring of Himself.

* * * * *

The rabbi looked at the child sitting at his feet, the son of Joseph the carpenter. Yeshua, was that his name? The boy was working hard to look like he was soaking in every word, but he was obviously distracted. With his tablet in one hand and stylus in the other, Yeshua was tracing the twenty-two[29] alphabet letters of the Hebrew language from their textbook, the Torah.

Astounding.

While the lingua franca for Jewish communities was Aramaic, Jewish boys learned Hebrew, the language Yahweh had used to write the scriptures. The rabbi quickly observed that Yeshua found learning exciting and even fun. When the morning lessons were finished and the teacher announced it was time to go home and practice, Yeshua stood to ask a question.

"May we write a few more letters? And can we read?"

The rabbi felt a flash of admiration but withheld it. The child seemed overly confident, and he did not want to encourage pride among the students.

"Tomorrow we will continue, and you will learn more of the Torah letters. We cannot learn everything in a single day, Yeshi. It is time to end our lessons. Class, you may go."

Yeshi collected his tablet and ran to catch up with his classmates, calling back as he raced out the door.

"But I can read the Torah letters."

In the following months, Yeshi demonstrated unprecedented learning. The rabbi soon came to the uncomfortable conclusion that Yeshi was best left to figure things out on his own and to draw him into as little discussion as possible to avoid confusion among the other students.

In the meantime, the rabbi learned that Yeshi's parents welcomed yet another son into the family, Simon, named after the Jewish Maccabean hero. The additional child was a sign of blessing on this Jewish family, the fruitful womb of the mother. With more than slight anxiety, the rabbi wondered if the future children of Mary and Joseph would prove to be students as perplexing as their brother Yeshua.

Twenty-one
God's Child Explores the World

Mary adored her sons. Yahweh had blessed their family with male children, and she daily poured out her thanks to Him. Jewish families held sons in high honor. Boys helped with the family business and inherited the fruit of their father's labor. But Mary longed to give Joseph a daughter to dote upon and to cherish. And she longed for the close bond she had shared with her own ima.

While Yeshi was leaning in school, Mary gave birth once again. Joy washed over Joseph's face when Mary laid his tiny daughter in his arms, bound in a blanket, red-faced, and squalling. They named her Rebecca, after the beautiful wife of Isaac and mother of Jacob, the father of Israel.

Mary had cupped her hands over her mouth as joyful tears spilled down her cheeks. She and Joseph had questioned many times whether or not they would have a daughter, and God had granted their desire. Rebecca would be their first, Mary silently prayed.

* * * * *

Yeshua continued to excel in school. The rabbis were surprised at his progress and enthusiasm for complex studies. His ability in languages baffled his fellow students and astounded the rabbi. Yeshua simultaneously learned Hebrew, Aramaic, and Greek, and spoke Latin to the Roman soldiers, although he had received no formal instruction in the language. Most Galileans spoke Aramaic and Hebrew that they learned in school. A few also picked up some Greek, the trade language. But few—even adults—learned multiple languages at the same time.

Yeshua's somber side impressed Mary most. Every evening he retreated to the garden or the roof with his prayer shawl and the Torah borrowed from the synagogue and meditated. Mary was curious about his deep spiritual devotion. One evening after Yeshua came down, she questioned him.

"Yeshua, you spend much time in prayer. Why is this so important to you?"

Yeshi looked up at her, his eyes wide, as if surprised at the question.

"My heavenly Av talks with me. He speaks to me every day like you do, Ima."

"What does He tell you?"

"That He will teach me all wisdom and truth as I grow and that I will not always understand. I must be patient. He tells me how much He loves me and says I am part of His plan for the world. I must learn obedience, Ima, but that is not hard because I love Him so much, like I love you and Abba."

Like I love you and Abba? Is it possible that Yeshua's love for his earthly parents could be compared to his love for his heavenly Av?

Mary dared not inquire further. Yeshi had given her much to think about. She was certain that her special child would face challenges. She also was convinced that, as despised as Rome was by every Jewish youth, the road before him would be difficult.

Dear Yahweh, give me wisdom. I am a simple woman—give me answers when I should speak and wisdom to know when to be silent. Help me discern when to protect him and when to step back and trust You.

* * * * *

Intimidated by Yeshua's precocious verbal abilities, soldiers loved to verbally spar with him.

"Boy! You are a Jew, yet you dare use our esteemed language and speak like an adult," they slung at him, but Yeshua refused to respond to their insults.

Locals viewed soldiers as vile pagans, but Mary knew many to be kind and, as much as Herod allowed, men who minded their business and were even compassionate toward the Jews. Herod Antipas had warned the soldiers to keep a close watch on all teenage boys, as they were potential recruits for the Zealots. The jealous, insecure ruler was always searching for potential rivals to his throne. His father's massacre of male babies in Bethlehem years before apparently lingered in his mind. It was still rumored that the baby king had escaped in the Bethlehem raid. Although it would seem unlikely that a rival king would risk living near a metropolitan Roman city, Herod Antipas's paranoia drove him to monitor anyone who simply attracted a crowd or spoke a provocative new message.

Local youths often hurled stones at soldiers to harass them. The soldiers typically ignored the boys, but after being hit too many times by stinging stones, guards sometimes gave chase. They rarely caught troublemakers. Locals helped the boys elude their pursuers by allowing them to dive into homes, shops, or piles of merchandise so the hooligans could disappear at any moment.

Mary shrunk in embarrassment the day a soldier came to the door with Yeshi, who was struggling to get free, slung over the soldier's hip. The captain's strong hand kept Yeshua firmly in place.

"Woman," he announced with a stern voice, "your boy was throwing stones at soldiers. I will ignore his insolence this time, but if he continues, I will take measures to punish him."

The rough, sun-darkened soldier compressed a grin

behind his forced scowl. Mary effusively thanked the captain who had brought Yeshi home, rather than taking matters into his own hands. She tried to explain that this behavior was unlike her son, saying that he was well-behaved and obedient.

What in the world possessed him to throw stones at soldiers? She sighed, confused. Nothing like this had ever happened before. *What shall I do? Punish him? Scold him?*

Mary looked at her wide-eyed son, whom the captain had lowered gently to the ground. Yeshi, bewildered, rubbed a red spot on his arm where he had been gripped.

He's not angry or ashamed but confused. Her son shook his head as he stared at the ground.

Mary promised the soldier that when Yeshua's abba returned, he would discuss the matter with the boy. She crossed her arms. Yeshi understood what those words meant. His father was a loving and gentle man, but he was also a disciplinarian. He had seen Abba discipline his brothers, and it wasn't pleasant. But Mary had never known Yeshi to misbehave, and she was shocked that he had done such a mischievous thing. But she did not question Yeshi further. Later that night at the evening meal, Joseph talked to Yeshua about the incident.

"Abba, older boys told us Roman soldiers were evil, saying it was our job to help drive them out of our country."

"One of my friends insisted, 'These soldiers are occupying the land our rabbi told us God gave to the Jews, His children. When I am old enough I will join the Zealots, and we will defeat them and take back what is ours.'"

Yeshi took a bite of bread and continued, "When the boys pelted the soldiers with rocks, the men ran after us. The older boys ran off, but I couldn't keep up with them. I didn't throw the stones, but when my friends yelled, 'Run!' I ran."

Mary searched her son's face. His animated eyes told her he was telling the truth and giving a simple, factual explanation of the incident.

"The soldier caught me, but the other boys slipped away into Benjamin the wagonmaker's yard. I told the soldier I didn't throw the stones, but he wouldn't believe me."

Joseph raised a hand. He had heard enough. Yeshi had never told them a lie. If he said he hadn't thrown stones, then he hadn't. The matter was closed. Joseph thanked Yeshua for his explanation and apologized for the confusion.[30]

"You are obedient, and lying is not a part of your nature, Yeshua. You are growing in wisdom—learning how to live in this world, growing into manhood, learning about the nature of the human heart and mind. You are also learning that friends can hurt you, even when they are trying to be friends. These years are preparing you for your heavenly mission. Your heavenly Av will continue to speak to you and teach you. Listen and obey. People will often tell you to do things they think are right, but the only thing that matters is what Yahweh says—your heavenly Av.

"You told me that your Rabbi Hakim tells the students, 'A child ought to be fattened with the Torah, as an ox is fattened in the stall.'[31] He is right. As you study Yahweh's written Word, you learn how to live the life He designed for you. Your heavenly Av will continue to speak to you personally, but many of His lessons will come as you devour His Words written in the holy scriptures, and your obedience will make you a man who reflects His character."

Mary studied Joseph's face. He was watching Yeshi to see if his words had taken root in his son's heart.

Did Joseph's words reach him, Yahweh? Will he listen to his abba and me, simple people who have been taught so little? Has he already surpassed our influence?

"Abba, I want to grow up to be like you."

Joseph's eyes brightened.

"I will obey you and my heavenly Av in all I do. I am glad you believed me. It is hard when I speak truth and am not believed." Yeshua's voice carried a deep sadness.

Mary watched as Joseph took a moment to absorb his son's words.

"Yeshua, you speak things beyond your years and share the heart and nature of your heavenly Av. You are not like any other child, and you will not grow to be like any other man. Those who believe you will choose to believe by faith.

"When hearts are blinded by pride and self-love, men will reject even the greatest truth the world could ever offer."

With those words, Joseph drew his son tightly into his arms.

Twenty-two
Yeshi's Hunger for Knowledge

Joseph stood at his workbench, patiently sanding the fragrant grain of Lebanese cedar. Yeshua had done an excellent job planing a block of wood into a smooth oar, and Joseph was proud of how quickly he had picked up carpentry skills. He was excited to teach his son the final step of the repair: sealing the wood with pitch. Yeshua was growing, and he and his friend Josiah would soon turn ten.

The boys had both demonstrated keen abilities in academics, and their enthusiasm for learning had prompted their teacher to invite them to advance their education in beit midrash. While their studies continued to focus on Torah, Yeshi's new rabbi, Baruch, recognized the value of liberal studies in addition to Torah, although his teaching methods continued to be focused on memorization and repetition.

Hellenistic influences had exposed Israel to a broader education. As a result, more-liberal Jewish rabbis were encouraging their students to study mathematics, history, music, rhetoric, and philosophy so they could better understand the world and how Judaism fit into God's grand scheme.

Yeshi and Josiah's beit midrash rabbi delighted in introducing these new subjects to his favorite students. Although the boys' teacher was skeptical about philosophy, Yeshi loved it and delved into complex philosophical issues with his teacher and his abba. Rabbi Baruch determined to guide him according to the teachings of Hillel by teaching Yeshua to apply the traditional phrase "taking upon him the yoke of Torah." This phrase helped students recognize God's authority over all aspects of life and learning and assured that even scientific inquiry complied with the Torah.

Although Joseph's family had been forced to escape Alexandria, Egypt, under Herod's death threat, their short stay had brought him into contact with the greatest library in the Western world. His eyes had been opened to a world beyond Judea, and he took every opportunity to learn.[32] He found science, medicine, and astronomy most fascinating and developed a strong desire that one day Yeshua's curiosity would lead him to learn about the mysteries of the universe.

In the workroom, Joseph caught the approaching sound of footsteps and turned as Yeshi ran through the door and approached him with a quizzical look. Standing on his toes at Joseph's worktable, Yeshi stretched his slim body to stroke the smooth grain of the oar Joseph was repairing. A look of satisfaction flashed through his son's eyes. No matter the task, Joseph always pushed for excellence—not out of pride, but out of love for beauty and completion.

"It must be finished," he often said.

Yeshua looked up. A streak of dirt marked one cheek.

"Abba, I have so many questions. What is the origin of the wind and the rain? When it rains, how does the water get to the leaves? And why are stars different colors?"

Joseph frowned. The questions shocked him and took him by surprise.

How does a boy of such tender years have insight to ask such questions?

Yeshua continued as his fingers ran up and down the wood, "Why are eclipses sometimes invisible? What is the size of the earth? Why does the wood of the oak tree look different from the wood of a sycamore? Why don't the stars fall from the sky? What is Arcturus, Orion, and Pleiades that the Holy Book speaks about?"[33]

What am I to say? The depth of these questions is far beyond my knowledge. How can I teach the Son of God about such things? Yahweh, I have no answers for the child You have given me.

Joseph took a deep breath and turned to face his son. "Yeshi, only your heavenly Av knows the answers to these questions. He created the world. I have limited knowledge, but you can ask Him these things. You alone are His Son. He will teach you all you need in the proper time."

Yeshua smiled.

"Yes, Abba, but I want you to teach me too. I need to understand how you see the world. That is also your gift to me."

Joseph stood speechless as he absorbed Yeshua's words, but in a breath Yeshi turned and scampered from the workshop in answer to his ima's call.

Joseph's growing awareness of Yeshua's destiny drove him to the scriptures. As he read the great prophet Isaiah, he saw that Yeshua was the Promised One from Yahweh. But his heart grew heavy as he realized for the first time that God's Anointed One would suffer and die.

Our Yeshua, suffer and die?

The thought was too devastating to think, much less speak. Was death Yahweh's plan for the Messiah?

Am I reading too much into this prophecy? Could this be God's plan for His Son? Death?

Questions pounded through Joseph's head day and night like the blow of a hammer against unyielding iron. He read Isaiah again and again, and each time the prophecy seemed clear.

The Messiah would not bring a glorious earthly overthrow of Roman tyranny. His salvation would not be the salvation the people of Israel envisioned, but rather a life that ended in suffering and death.

This *is Your plan, Yahweh—why Mary and I gave up*

everything to live as fugitives? This is why angels came to us—to announce the birth of a baby who would live in obscurity and die in shame? How can a loving father put his own child to death? Unthinkable.

Joseph did not absorb the truth without anger. His heart froze with sorrow, then raged in anger at what seemed senseless. Questions flooded his mind. As the days unfolded, he barely spoke, worked, slept, or thought of anything else.

What is Av's plan? How could life ever be the same again if Yeshi's destiny has been foretold by the prophet Isaiah? Whom can I talk to?

In his anger and sorrow, Joseph poured out his heart to Yahweh. Sometimes his prayers were met with silence. At other times, words of the Psalms came to him as if whispered by a dear friend. Slowly, the anger faded and was replaced by a quiet peace.

Yahweh would not leave His own or forsake them.

But what of Mary? His heart was shattered thinking she would have to endure even the thought of Yeshua suffering and dying. Should he tell her or try to prepare her for the agony that might face her—that her Yeshi had been born for such a destiny?

Time crept by as Joseph poured his energy into his work. Yeshua was never far from his side, helping with small tasks, carving, and honing his carpentry skills as Joseph guided him.

And in his heart, Joseph stored up the memories of each day like a soldier stockpiling weapons for the war ahead.

* * * * *

The family sat together in the gathering room in the quiet of the evening. Mary busied herself carding wool as Joseph read from the book written by the prophet Isaiah. Joseph noticed Yeshua squirming where he sat on a cushioned mat across the room. Joseph paused to let the silence provide the invitation Yeshua was seeking.

"Abba, I have told you and Ima before that I am often teased at school about my birth. The boys in my class have said shameful things about you and Ima. I always walk away and have never believed them to be true. But Ima has told me that my birth was like no other child's birth."

Yeshi looked at his father, eyes wide with honesty and sincerity.

Joseph drew in a breath as his blood began to boil. Ugly rumors about the circumstances behind Mary's premature pregnancy had circulated throughout the village from the moment they had returned. No man had dared breathe dishonor about Mary for fear of Joseph, who defended the poor and widows and had more than once forced merchants to give back what they had overcharged. Mary had found refuge in several close friends and ignored the tongue-waggers.

But unbridled tongues should never force a young child to defend his mother's honor, Joseph fumed. However, Yeshi seemed more curious than frustrated as he continued his questions.

"Abba, how was my birth different? I understand that a man—a father—must be with a woman for a child to be born, and this is to happen after they are married. Did you participate in my birth? Ima is honorable, and she did not disgrace you. What happened?"

Joseph's face flushed hot. An abba did not discuss such matters with his son, but Yeshi kept pressing him with questions. Joseph was aware of the scripture's teaching on the origin of his divine son. The words of angelic visitors, wise men, and shepherds still resonated in his memory. Yeshi had raised questions that would be difficult for Joseph to answer even if his son were older. Joseph knew of Isaiah's prophecy but hesitated to explain it because of its many implications. But the family was waiting for his answer, and he could feel his ears reddening.

Yeshi had discussed these delicate matters earlier with his ima. Mary had talked to him, and Joseph had inwardly heaved a sigh of relief that he would not have to broach the subject in the future.

But the future had come, and Yeshi was directing questions to him.

Mary had been working that day in the kitchen preparing the evening meal when Yeshi had burst through the door with questions the first time. She had told Joseph about their talk. Yeshi told her that his friends at school had told him that having a baby required a man and woman to touch each other in a special way after they were married. The boys were laughing and making jokes, using language Yeshua didn't like. He had said he didn't understand what they were talking about, but the conversation disturbed him.

Joseph sighed as he tried to form the appropriate response. Yeshua was obviously not going to allow him to postpone the discussion until later, so Joseph dove in.

"Yeshi, before your ima and I got married, God sent His Holy Spirit to her to be your abba. An angel spoke to me and to her and told us this was Yahweh's plan. God chose your ima to be your mother, and it was and is a special honor."

"And he chose your abba Joseph to be your earthly father—also a great honor," Mary quickly added.

Joseph glanced down and tried to envision a way to delay further discussion until after the evening meal, or perhaps save it for another month or year—or more.

But Yeshua wasn't about to wait. He laid out question after question about his birth, as well as the passage in Isaiah.

Joseph prayed for Mary to help him by diverting their son to another topic or activity. He glanced in her direction, and Mary smiled back at him as she often did when she recognized he was in trouble and was leaving him to figure his own way out.

Yahweh, many things are best left to Your instruction. Who am I to teach the deep things of scripture and of the way of a husband with his wife to Your Son? Surely I am not adequate to ...

Mary cleared her throat, and Joseph released his breath.

"Yeshua, you are the fulfillment of Isaiah's prophecy," Mary spoke quietly. "I conceived and gave birth to you, but the Spirit of God participated instead of Abba Joseph. This is a miracle that many cannot and will not ever understand. People are confused by who you are, and that may always be true. It takes faith to believe the truth. Do you understand, Yeshua?"

Yeshua was silent for a moment as he looked at his mother, then back into Joseph's eyes.

"Yes. I think I do. I am His very own, but some will choose not to believe."

The joy of Joseph's call to be father to the Son of God once again swept over him in a whirlwind of awe and worship that nearly took him to his knees.

Mary's brief answer seemed to satisfy Yeshua. Joseph watched as his son moved to the table in the kitchen and quietly traced invisible words in the air as he whispered. Before long, he drew his prayer shawl over his head and disappeared out the back door that led toward the stairs to the rooftop.

Yeshi closed the door behind him, and Joseph did not follow. His son had matters to discuss with his Av.

Twenty-three
Yeshi among Friends

Mary could overhear the boys as she sat in the fragrant kitchen that opened to the larger gathering room of their home, separated by only a woven curtain hung on a narrow hemp cord. The scent of dried myrtle leaves, coriander, coriander leaves, cumin, dill, garlic, and mint filled the room. Her hands worked at the wheel as she spun fibers for a new rich brown mantle for Joseph. She hoped the color would please him. He had observed that the dyeing process was long and tedious, and he would appreciate her work.

The boys' voices rose and fell, and Mary smiled. Yeshi was well-liked by his schoolmates, but some teased him because of his advanced knowledge and academic success. Their hurtful actions tore at Mary's heart. They often ignored Yeshua in group activities. They goaded him and tried to prod him to anger. His refusal to retaliate infuriated them.

All but Josiah.

Unlike the other boys who envied and taunted or ignored Yeshua, Josiah treated Yeshi like an equal and a friend. Josiah, who loved to learn, was a farmer's son. His long curly hair, lean frame, and bright, inquisitive eyes made him stand out among his classmates. He preferred studying to farming or doing the chores his father assigned. Slightly older than Yeshua, Josiah had found a friend who challenged him academically, physically, and mentally.

Yeshua and Josiah sat across from one another on the floor of the gathering room, fashioning puppets out of cloth and sticks similar to those they had seen on occasional trips to Sepphoris. Mary listened to their chatter as they played, enjoying their good-natured banter.

"Ima, do you have any cloth to make clothes for our soldiers?" Yeshi called through the curtain.

Mary stopped her spinning, pulled a few scraps of cloth from a basket beside her, and called Yeshi, who accepted them.

The boys had formed rough terra-cotta puppet figures with pieces of cord that secured the limbs and enabled Yeshua and Josiah to manipulate the arms and legs.[34] Yeshi's crudely carved wooden toy soldiers provided the army that could be attacked by the swinging limbs of the puppets. The boys dressed the puppets in Roman red and Zealot gray to represent the competing fighting forces. They had varnished the hand-carved Roman soldiers with red coloring from the outer clove of a red shallot, and the Zealots with gray shallot.

Mary pulled a corner of the curtain aside and watched the two. Their lips were tightly drawn as they manipulated their puppets and spoke challenging and threatening words to their toy enemies.

"I've got your captain," Yeshi's voice rang out as he banged his puppet into Josiah's soldier, but Josiah fired back.

"Yes, and I attacked your flank and destroyed your catapult."

Mary envisioned Josiah imagining how this fatal blow would make him the victor.

The imaginary battle raged on, with clay arms pounding and stick swords striking as if the fight was to the finish. Before long the boys grew weary of the toys, tossed them aside, and continued the battle in a playful wrestling match as the figurines lay still at their feet. There was no turning back for either of them—victory or death.

A strange discomfort stirred within Mary. She didn't feel comfortable about the boys playing games of battle and death, and she had told Joseph as much. But her objections had fallen on deaf ears as Joseph reminded her, "The boys see soldiers all around them. Their play helps them cope with the reality of the occupation."

Mary wasn't convinced, but she understood Joseph's reasoning and allowed Yeshua and Josiah to express their feelings through play, according to Joseph's preference.

When the boys grew tired of their battles, they went outside to play ball. Joseph had devised a sling that dangled from a neighborhood tree. It served as an anchor for a ball suspended by a goat hide strip for hitting and catching. All of the local boys joined in playing this game of ball. While Yeshua excelled at studies, he was less athletic than some of his classmates and often found himself on the losing end of neighborhood games. But what he lacked in size and athleticism, he made up for in enthusiasm.

On one occasion Yeshua and his friends were caught playing gladiators on the synagogue grounds. They had cut branches from a local pomegranate tree and were pretending to sword fight with one another in Jerusalem's great xystus, also called a stadium, built by Herod the Great for the pleasure of Roman citizens. The Jews bitterly condemned the Roman practices of dueling, gladiators fighting to the death, and abusing wild beasts. Many adults—especially conservative Jews—refused to attend the Roman games.

As a result, many Jewish parents forbade their youngsters from mimicking such activities and glorifying bad behavior. The gladiator games represented the evil practices of the sadistic Romans to cause their enemies' suffering. Allowing children to imitate the barbaric sport of the Colosseum was much debated among parents of the empire.

Most parents did not allow it, but some intentionally permitted it.

"It's just a game" was the most common excuse. However, many parents took disciplinary action when their boys played Roman games.

Mary wasn't sure if Yeshi had been goaded into playing with his classmates, but he received the same discipline from his teacher as the other students. Mary was embarrassed but supported the rabbi's decision and sat dutifully on a stone bench outside his home until Yeshi emerged. He walked quietly beside her, watching the sun sink below the horizon on the return trip home, while she remained silent, caught up in thoughts of what she would say to Joseph. But Mary was certain she heard Yeshi, who was swept away by the beauty of the night, singing softly to himself.

Like most Jewish boys, Yeshi and Josiah argued about whether or not the Torah forbade them from pretending to be gladiators. Mary had heard their playful debate more than once and hoped that staying after school would help firmly establish their commitment *not* to imitate ungodly behavior. However, she concluded that time after school was not an effective punishment for young scholars. At least not for those who broke into songs of praise on the way home.

* * * * *

Josiah gathered his stones in his hands then laid them in a row on the flat rock he and Yeshi had painstakingly etched with the lines of a mills board. They sat in the latticed shade of a sycamore tree in the courtyard outside Yeshi's home as the midmorning heat rose. The words had been burning in Josiah's mind for months, and now they poured from his mouth.

"I have been told you can perform miracles, Yeshi. Some of the other boys have told me this is true. I am your best friend, and if this is true, I am the one who should know. Show me a miracle."[35]

Yeshi's eyebrows rose, and his forehead furrowed. A flash of discomfort flashed through Josiah. Yeshi looked at him for a long time before he spoke, and Josiah regretted his question.

"You and I have been friends for a long time, Josiah. Who told you I can perform miracles? Have I ever made this claim to you? Why is it important to you? Why would you want me to do such a thing?"

Josiah dropped his head as if he had been caught in a lie. He responded sheepishly, stammering as if he were being rebuked. "You have seen the crippled Gentile boy whose father is a mercenary soldier from Camulodunum in Britannia? He told the other boys in town that he saw you create a bird from the sand and send it flying into the air. And sometimes you seem to be listening to voices ... from somewhere. But if you *can* do miracles, why haven't you healed the crippled boy's withered leg?"

Yeshi looked back at Josiah for a long time, then tipped his head to the side as he spoke.

"It is true that the boy asked me to create a bird, and I tried. I also tried to create a toy soldier out of the dust. In both cases I failed, so I asked my abba why. He told me that I am a child and that miracles are not a child's game. If I perform miracles, it will be to glorify God and fulfill His will. Miracles are part of God's mission, not tricks to satisfy curiosity."

Yeshi's face wore an expression Josiah had never before seen, but it reminded him of his abba's face as the family had sat in silence through the night awaiting the birth of his little sister.

Josiah did not want to put his friendship with Yeshi in jeopardy, and he silently vowed not to bring up the subject of miracles again.

Ever.

Twenty-four
The Stolen Lamb Rescued

Elias, Josiah's brother, rolled to his stomach in the fragrant grass and continued his tall tale.

"And the powerful storm arose on the sea, and the men in the boat feared they would drown."

He glanced in Yeshi's direction to assess his friend's response to his tale. But Yeshi appeared to be pondering a wisp of cloud drifting across the sky as he listened to Elias's suspense-filled story. The boys enjoyed spinning tales for one another as they tended sheep, surrounded by serenading birds and the occasional sigh of the wind.

Yeshi's expression changed, and Elias followed the shift in his friend's gaze. A figure was streaking across the field in the distance. The person, who appeared to be a man, reached down and snatched a lamb into his arms, then bolted toward a steep cliff.

Before Elias realized what was happening, Yeshi scrambled to his feet and took off in pursuit of the thief. Elias leaped to his feet and pounded after him.

Apparently, the thief presumed that his choice to approach the dangerous precipice would intimidate the shepherds.

Whoever he is, he doesn't know Yeshi.

Elias wasn't sure what his friend would do, but he was certain of both Yeshi's determination to pursue the crook and his compassion for the sheep. But the thief and Yeshi were drawing close to the edge of the cliff.

Elias yelled at the top of his lungs. "Stop, stop. Let the lamb go!"

The thief circled around an enormous boulder protruding from the ground, apparently hoping the boys would give up their pursuit.

Not a chance.

Instead, Yeshi, who was not a speedy runner, sprinted like a gazelle, vaulted over the boulder, and landed directly on the thief's back with an arresting thump.

But the force of Yeshua's weight was not enough. The thief fought his way free, tossed the lamb over the side of the cliff, and fled at breakneck speed. Yeshi turned back from pursuing the thief to look for the lamb. By this time Elias had caught up with Yeshi and joined him searching for the lamb. Even though the flock Elias had been tending was large and one lost lamb would not be a disaster, Yeshi insisted on searching. Elias's father raised prized spotless sheep for temple sacrifice, and the stolen lamb had been spotless. Its value did not escape Yeshi.

The lamb had landed on a ledge not far below the cliff's edge. Yeshua spotted it first, where it lay shaking and bleating pitifully. Determined to save it, the older, stronger Yeshua lowered Elias by his legs over the jagged rock precipice. Elias extended his arms as far as possible and yelled back to Yeshi, "Let me down a little more."

Elias felt Yeshua's grip on his ankles tighten as he was lowered. Barely touching the animal's back, Elias grasped the lamb by its wool and yelled to Yeshi, "Pull me up. I have him."

Yeshua inched his way backward through the dirt until both Elias and the bleating, trembling "treasure" were once again safe.[36]

As Yeshi and Elias fell on their backs to the ground, exhausted, Elias spoke to his friend with pride and admiration.

"Yeshi, even though you've had little experience shepherding, you are a *good* shepherd, perhaps better than I am. It comes to you naturally. You spotted the thief, and I am so thankful you acted so quickly. Abba will be happy we rescued one of his prized lambs.

"You risked life and limb to save just one lamb. I'm not sure I would have done that." Elias shook his head.

Yeshi lay on the ground for a moment, staring at the sky. Elias wondered what his friend was thinking. He hoped Yeshua knew he admired him, and he was in awe of him for qualities he could not quite name.

When they had caught their breath, Yeshi placed the lamb on his shoulders, and the boys returned it to the flock, rejoicing at the safety of the one stolen lamb.

But for many days a question plagued Elias about his good friend: What drove Yeshua to pursue a lamb at the risk of his life? The lamb did not even belong to him. What had he seen in Yeshi's eyes when he had placed the lamb in his arms?

He was not sure, but Elias understood he had seen something powerful and unlike any expression he had ever seen in the eyes of his father as he interacted with his sheep. It was almost as if Yeshua cared for the lamb as his own.

Elias wasn't sure what he had witnessed, but he knew that it was somehow holy, and he kept what he had observed to himself.

* * * * *

Josiah's brother Elias did not enjoy school. Most young Jewish boys and girls did not attend school—daily housework and labor did not require education, nor did taking on a trade or marrying. Elias felt school was irrelevant and boring and a waste of time. He would rather be in the fields looking after his father's flocks. His limited attendance in the classroom, combined with his disruptive behavior, irritated both the rabbi and his brother Josiah, the latter of whom secretly hoped that his brother's time in school would soon end. Josiah knew that many boys who did not enjoy studies often became successful as farmers, fishermen, carpenters, or potters, or excelled in other needed occupations.

The late afternoon breeze brought relief from the piercing heat of the day. Cool air stimulated Elias to drum up some of his old tricks. Elias, with his slight frame, appeared harmless, but his dogged pursuit of pleasure irritated his classmates and teachers. Woe to anyone not alert to his antics and practical jokes.

One afternoon after classes, Yeshua and Josiah squatted on their heels under a shady sycamore tree, discussing their morning lessons and relaxing. Out of the corner of his eye, Josiah spotted Elias, who had stealthily slipped around a corner of the rabbi's house. Josiah was instantly concerned and called out to his brother.

"Elias, come here! You have been told over and over that going near the rabbi's home is off-limits. Students are to stay in sight in the front courtyard. Don't make me get up and come pull you back here by the ear."

A few moments later, Elias appeared around the corner and sauntered across the courtyard. A bit too casually, Josiah noted.

What is he trying to hide? And how stupid does he think I am?

"What were you doing back there?" His eyes raked his brother up and down for clues.

"Be quiet and I will tell you," Elias hissed. "We don't need everyone looking over here."

He lifted a corner of his brown mantle. A hidden sash secured a small wineskin.

"Abba's finest. I took it this morning when no one was looking, but I'm not greedy. I'm willing to share. Who wants to be first?" He pulled out the wine-stained pouch and extended it.

Josiah ignored the question and pushed his brother's hand away.

Concentrate. Control your anger. The last thing Elias or I need right now is to get into a fight and have the rabbi come running to investigate.

"Are you afraid of getting caught, big brother? Are you afraid Rabbi is hiding under the juniper bushes shpi ... spying on you?" Elias slurred.

He sneered, then glanced over his shoulder. Josiah could see that no one was watching them. The other boys were engrossed in games or had gone back inside. Elias reached for the skin, downed several gulps, then hid the wineskin again beneath his mantle. His dexterity indicated that he had been practicing the move for some time.

"How much have you had to drink?" Josiah's tone was hard.

Elias laughed, then spoke through thick lips, his words barely intelligible, "Yer 'fraid to break rules, ya cow ... cow ... coward."

Elias glared at Yeshua, grabbed the wax tablet from his hands, and threw it to the ground. It landed on a rock and split. Josiah froze in shock. Elias's actions had horrified his brother. But Yeshua stood unmoved, calmly returning Elias's stare. Josiah could read the expression in Yeshi's dark eyes, and he was in no mood to tolerate Elias's foolishness any longer. Retrieving the fragments of his tablet with a jerk, Yeshua tucked the tablet beneath his tunic and spoke. His voice was gentle, yet it possessed the power of a maelstrom.

"You act like a fool, Elias! Consumed by your lust, you stole your abba's wine, dishonoring both him and yourself. Take control of your behavior, consider your selfishness, and have the sense to look at how your actions affect others and influence the kingdom of God!"

Josiah chimed in. "You have been told that we are not allowed to drink Abba's wine until we have completed bar mitzvah—and then only when it is diluted with water and honey. What were you thinking?"

Josiah studied his brother's face. Elias's head had dropped in shame. Yeshua's words had struck Elias's heart. Even though his younger brother liked to prod Yeshua, Elias admired Yeshi.

Later, Elias told Josiah that Yeshua's verbal dart had stunned him—even more than the older boys refusing the wine. It was not the response he had expected from his friend, he admitted sorrowfully, but it was the one he needed.

* * * * *

A warm, dry day welcomed James, Joseph's second son, as he drifted into consciousness on his rooftop mat. The sweet aroma of Ima's baking bread drew him to the kitchen to join the rest of the family who had already crowded into the tiny kitchen.

"James," his abba spoke from across the table as James snatched the last vestiges of bread from a basket, "I need you to come with Yeshua and me today to the small forest outside the village to collect wood needed to repair a cart wheel."

James smiled inwardly. His father did not often ask him to work alongside him. As the eldest, Yeshi worked with Abba most often.

I must do well. Abba is counting on me.

The boys finished their breakfast and morning meditation with Abba, then bolted out of the house and ran full speed toward the forest. Yeshi, whose stride was longer, arrived first. Before long, Abba joined them, showed them which limbs to gather, and left the boys to work on their own until the midday meal. For the next hour the boys gathered fallen limbs and branches, straight and free of knots. Villagers often sought small tree branches and dried wood for cooking or mending fences, so they were difficult to find.

Locating the branches soon became a game, and James and Yeshi kept score to see who could find the most.

Before long, James spotted a long, straight branch, perfect for a wheel spoke. As he reached down to retrieve the stick, he heard a hiss and snatched his hand away, but it was too late. A coiled viper that had been hiding beneath the log struck him near his wrist. He screamed in terror.

"Yeshi, a viper has bitten me! It's poisonous. Please help me!" He tried to keep the panic from rising in his chest, but picture after picture flashed through his mind of children and adults his family had known who had lost limbs or died from snakebites.

Yeshi raced to his side.

"Don't move. Keep calm, James. You must lie as still as possible."

Yeshua understood that moving around would cause the poison to spread—and sucking out poison was dangerous. Instead, Yeshi pressed his fingers into James's flesh just above the bite, attempting to squeeze the poison out of the wound. As he pressed, Yeshi looked into James's face.

"This must hurt, but the pressure can help prevent the spread of the poison and expel it from the wound. Are you feeling much pain?" Yeshua's voice was hopeful.

James knew his grimace betrayed not only his pain but also his fear. Yeshua had not looked to the heavens and prayed for a miracle. The poison was not vanishing from his brother's body.

James would not be instantly healed. The poison was still coursing through his system.

They needed to get home, where someone else could help him. James's head was already pounding, and he wasn't sure if he could walk.

"Yeshi, you must pray for me! Talk to Yahweh—you say He is your heavenly Av. If that is true, He will do a miracle for you!"

Yeshi recoiled, as if he'd been slapped. His eyes grew

distant, and for a moment he stared at his hands, still pressing into James's flesh.

"Ask Him, Yeshua. Is not that the least you can do for your brother? Or is it because you know He will not answer you?" The moment the words fell from his lips, James regretted speaking them. The sorrow that marked Yeshua's face was too much for him to look at, and James glanced away.

Yeshua pulled his hands from James's wound, turned his eyes toward heaven, and cried out.

"Av, show James Your great love. Poison is at work in his body, placing him at grave risk. We ask that You dispel its power, but we ask and do not demand, knowing we can trust You to do what is best for us."

Still, James felt no change, and his heart was racing. His wrist was swelling and had turned an angry red. Yeshua must have noticed the swelling. He tore a piece of his cloak and wrapped the wound.

"We must take the wood now and return home so Ima can look at the bite. We must go. I will carry the wood. Move your arm as little as possible as you walk."

Yeshua tucked James's arm into the sash of his mantle for support, and they set out slowly toward home. James followed, his mind clouding with each step. Each moment of the walk home was a torment for James, as well as for Yeshi, who watched his brother's rage build with every passing minute. Finally, they stumbled through the door of the house together. The family fell silent as Yeshua explained what had happened. James collapsed onto a mat that Ima quickly brought to the gathering room.

Ima Mary was silent as she dressed James's wound and administered herbal antivenin medicines. The world around him was clouded in fog as James lay on the mat as a fever raged, and he struggled to breathe. Swelling and redness that surrounded the bite inched up his arm. He thanked Yahweh when his vomiting subsided, but he still had difficulty thinking, and moaned with the burning pain.

From the moment Ima had brought the mat into the gathering room, Yeshua took a place at his side and did not move from the instant James collapsed to the floor. Yeshi sat with his head bowed, and James could hear whispered fragments of sentences as his brother prayed.

"Abba, why? ... Please ... my time ... Your glory ..."

Even through the fog of pain, James sensed that Yeshi was heartbroken to see him suffering.

I'm still sick. Does this mean that Yeshi is a boy just like me? I have seen that he is different, yet no one has ever seen him do anything miraculous or out of the ordinary. Are Ima and Abba wrong about him? Does he truly have special gifts from God?

The questions drifted through James's mind as he balanced on a precipice of awareness.

Ima Mary had sent someone to find Abba; he was working at a nearby building site. Through the poison-induced haze, James smelled wood shavings, then recognized Abba's voice speaking his name, then sensed a work-roughened hand stroking his forehead.

Abba is here. I will be all right.

Peace settled over him, and he drifted into a deep sleep.

Sometime later, James did not know when, whispered conversation woke him.

"Abba, why did God not answer my prayer? Why could I not heal my brother? We were alone; no one would have known. You and Ima have told me I am God's Son and I have a special gift and will do extraordinary things."

"I am not sure why God does what He does, Yeshi." James listened to Abba's voice but kept his eyes closed. "You are His special gift. He has a plan for your life, and that purpose cannot be thwarted. He *is* healing James, but He has chosen to use the natural laws of His creation that have been set in motion in answer to prayer and the needs of men."

James could hear Yeshi rustling. "But would it not have

proven to James that I am God's gift if I could have healed him? That seemed like a good plan."

James could envision his abba smiling at Yeshi's out-thinking God.

"Yeshi, miracles happen in response to our prayers or natural events when they are part of Yahweh's purpose. Sometimes He has a better plan than ours. Miracles do not take place to satisfy the whims of people or to prove Yahweh can be trusted. We must trust Yahweh to be Yahweh, who loves us and orders all things, not a god who does things we believe are right. Right now you are a child and you are not yet ready to be revealed to the world as His Son. You need more time to grow into manhood and use this time to speak and commune with your heavenly Av."

James opened one eye and watched Yeshi as he drank in Abba's words, his mind absorbing what he had just said. Joseph sighed.

"I only hope, dear Yeshi, that I have explained these things to you in a way that honors Yahweh. I so want to be a good abba and spiritual advisor to you and fulfill the role that Yahweh has entrusted to me."

The evening drew to a close. The girls and Ima had made soup, and the family enjoyed a warm meal. Ima made a bed on a sleeping mat in the gathering room near James so she could continue poultice treatments on his arm throughout the night. The rest of the family retired to their mats and sleeping areas.

When James awoke the following morning, his fever had lifted and the swelling in his arm had gone down. The family gathered in the kitchen to celebrate with a hearty morning meal while James continued his recovery in the gathering room. Abba turned to Yeshi.

"Our heavenly Av *did* hear your prayer, and James is healing. But you must not be discouraged; your time is coming. You must be patient."

A wave of resentment washed over James.

Even when I'm sick, Abba and Ima make it about Yeshua. Everything is about Yeshi and always will be. He's the oldest. He's "special." He's God's gift to the world, but somehow no one else can figure out why. Especially me.

James slipped from his mat, crept toward the door, and left the house. He would find somewhere else to nurse his wounds.

Twenty-five
Lessons from Saba

The month of Kislev had arrived, and the pace of life shifted with the weather. Frequent rains softened the soil, which opened the door for a brief time to ready the fields for planting. Abundant crops depended on timely planting, and the Jewish community abandoned other business and tasks when Kislev arrived. Every able-bodied man headed to the fields to work.

Joseph had risen even before Abba Jacob called out to him. Jacob was responsible for farming the land of the family inheritance and often needed extra help in the fields. Joseph had promised that he would help in the fields when he could, even if it meant leaving his carpentry work, and he was determined to show Abba that he would fulfill his promise with his heart.

Joseph had dressed and been first to the kitchen for the morning meal.

"You can count on me, Abba," Joseph said as he tied the sash of his work garment.

"I will help too, Saba," Yeshua piped up from the table where he sat beside his brothers.

Not to be left out, James chimed in, "I want to go too."

Joseph was well aware that James was too young to be of much help, but his enthusiasm was infectious, and Joseph was also wise enough to know James didn't want to be left out. He smiled and nodded in James's direction, and the two boys raced out the door. Joseph followed at a dignified pace, searching for his father as he walked through the growing crowd of men gathering in the courtyard of the compound. He spotted Saba Jacob, who was striding toward the younger boys, a broad grin on his face.

Joseph was grateful for Yeshua's *saba*, who was rich in knowledge of scripture, farming, relationships, and integrity. Saba Jacob gave his precocious grandsons valuable wisdom, practical skills, and life-changing mentoring. Joseph smiled. Yeshua, who was still a preteen, regardless of his potential, still had much to gain in wisdom and knowledge of human nature.

Saba can make a great difference in teaching the boys character and integrity, things that cannot be taught in a classroom.

Yeshua often spent time after school in the fields with his grandfather, soaking in his warm presence and knowledge of scripture. Jacob also delighted in sharing his love of farming with his grandson. Farming provided a unique opportunity to teach a boy thirsting for knowledge. Object lessons abounded everywhere. And although Yeshua did not desire to become a farmer, he enjoyed time with his saba.

Saba, Abba, and grandsons hurried toward the fields, hoping to get there before the intensity of the early morning sun could overheat the newly planted seeds and place them in jeopardy. Yeshua raced ahead to get the first view of the fields. But when the adults and smaller children arrived, Joseph noticed a sag in Yeshua's shoulders as he surveyed the family plot. His face wore a look of disappointment.

"Why are we going to plant in fields covered in rocks and sprouting weeds?"

Joseph delighted in seeing his son taking an interest in his saba's work.

"Ask your saba. He is the expert on farming. I am a carpenter."

Joseph was glad to deflect the question—especially

when he was curious about the answer himself. He watched Yeshua scurry along the path to catch up with Saba.

"Saba, can this field bring forth a crop with so many rocks?"

Joseph watched the interaction of saba and child, and a swell of warmth grew in his chest. Jacob's face was weather-beaten from exposure to the sun, and his thin hair was white as wool. He stood half a head taller than most Jewish men, which gave him an air of dignity in spite of his humble clothes. His friends praised his gentle spirit, passion for work, and father's heart. Joseph was proud of his abba and loved the time he spent with him or watching him interact with Yeshua. Saba took time to explain matters in a way a young boy could always understand, and he always gave Yeshua his undivided attention, not to mention his limitless affection.

Joseph overheard Abba Jacob's words as the men and boys walked out onto the field.

"Yeshi, I own other fields that we can cultivate by oxen and plow—you have seen them—but today we will plant this field. All of our land must work for us to make a living from it. Don't let the appearance of this field fool you. I have already prepared the soil. I removed the smaller stones and pulled most of the weeds to make the field as productive as possible."

"But, Saba," Yeshua interrupted as he pointed to several large rocks in the field, "look at those huge boulders. Won't they keep the crops from growing?"

Jacob placed his hand on Yeshi's shoulder.

"I prepared the soil and removed all the impediments I could. The rocks and weeds that remain will have to coexist with the crops. Remember, Yeshi, our heavenly Av gives the increase and brings forth the crop. He sends the rain to soften the dirt. He sends the sun to help the seeds grow. We remove the rocks and weeds as our part, but we cannot do it all. We must trust God to work where we cannot.

"Yes, the rocks are a deterrent, but there are always hindrances in our work and in life, rocks in our path and weeds that choke out life. Learn how to face the rocks and weeds in ways that will glorify your heavenly Av, Yeshua. He will not always remove them for you, but sometimes He will leave them to help you grow as you respond to them."

Joseph, who was bent over a bag of seed, caught every word and thanked God for the gift of time his abba was investing in Yeshi's life. Young James, however, had wandered to the edge of the field and seemed more concerned about earthworms sunning on the rocks than the urgency of planting the fields.

With Jacob's final words, he and Yeshi began the day's planting. Yeshi walked beside his grandfather and watched as saba sowed seeds gleaned from the former year's harvest.[37] Lesser-quality fields with rough terrain, thorns, thistles, and an abundance of large rocks had prohibited plowing. Some of the plots were so covered with stones and thistles that they were planted with the mere hope that a partial crop could survive, despite nature's challenges.

Such was the case for this field. Many of the largest rocks and boulders had been removed, but many embedded stones remained. A well-beaten path separated Jacob's field from a wealthy priest's land that bordered his plot. Jacob dared not cross into the neighboring field as he worked, lest he incur the wrath of the temperamental priest, which had happened more than once.

Yeshi tucked the skirt of his tunic into his sash and called out to Saba as he headed into the field to sow.

"Saba, why are you dressed so strangely today?"

Joseph saw his son wrinkle his nose. Jacob wore work clothes and had slung a sack over his shoulder and secured it with a wide leather strap.

Jacob grinned and bent down to fill his sack.

He continued to walk the field, the sack riding on his hip as he scattered fistfuls of seeds in a sweeping motion that evenly covered the area. It was impossible to direct the seed to fertile soil while avoiding the rocks, thorns, and well-trodden pathways.

Joseph again smiled as he mused.

Yeshua watches Abba's every move with such attentiveness. He is storing pictures in his mind of what his saba is doing.

Joseph watched as Yeshua studied his saba's method of spreading the seeds, noting where every seed fell and absorbing minute details of the planting. As he followed his saba, he swept seed from rocks and paths and other infertile areas.

Joseph, who was following a short distance from his father, saw that his abba was turning the day into lesson time. "Look, Yeshi." Saba Jacob pointed his finger to a few seeds that had fallen in the hard boundary path. "The birds are even now swooping down to eat those seeds. Look out! That bird might get you," Jacob joked to Yeshi.

"As hard as I try to control spreading the seeds, some will fall on infertile soil."

As Jacob reached the end of the row, Yeshua responded, "I see, Saba. Look, some seed has fallen on the rocks. They won't grow there, will they?"

Jacob slowed, reaching to pull out more seed. He hesitated and then answered, "Some seed will fall on the rocky soil that was too hard to become fertile. The hot sun and dry wind will burn up the seed, or the birds will find it, as we have already seen."

Yeshi took great joy in learning. Jacob loved farming, but Joseph remembered a stoic-faced, silent father who went to the fields. Yeshi connected with the soil and Saba Jacob in a way that Joseph had never experienced as a child.

I'm sorry, Abba, that you never experienced that connection with me, your eldest son.

Joseph's head dropped for a moment as a wave of emotion overtook him. Guilt? For failing his father? Shame?

That his father had never desired to share his passion with him? Voices drifted toward him and lifted his head.

His father was once again instructing Yeshi.

"Look over there, Yeshua, where seed fell among the thistles. Those will not survive either."

Yeshi piped up, "Yes, Saba, the 'stickers' will choke them to death, won't they?"

Jacob smiled. "Don't fret, Yeshi. Most of our seed has fallen on good soil and will give us a good crop. Some areas will produce crops one hundred times, sixty times, and thirty times what we planted. We will have a good crop despite rocks, thorns, and bad weather. God blesses faithful service, and farming to God's glory is faithful service. Once the seed is sown, everything depends on the weather and nature. Only God controls that."

* * * * *

Loud, angry voices burst from a cluster of olive trees in the neighbor's vineyard.

"Abba, look over there. What are the men yelling about?" Yeshi shielded his eyes with one hand and pointed with the other.

"The landowner is arguing with the tenants who work his land," Joseph answered.

A growing number of sowers turned their attention to the argument as it became more intense. The conversation could not be heard, but angry voices reverberated with the acoustics of an amphitheater down the valley.

Joseph called to Jacob, "What's going on?"

Joseph walked across the field to where Abba Jacob and Yeshi were watching the heated argument. The volatile situation between the men was near a physical confrontation as they stood nose to nose, arms flailing, debating the owner's alleged unfair compensation for labor.

"What is going on, Saba? The men are angry."

"Yeshua, some landowners make huge profits from the

work of the tenants who labor long hours to produce crops and receive little payment for their work. That landowner has built larger and larger barns to store the grain his farmers produced. He has become greedy and has not treated his workers fairly."

Jacob continued, "I know this landowner. He bought his land from neighbors who were taxed so heavily that they could not afford to keep their farms. That is one reason your abba decided not to be a farmer. Our land has been exploited, and many of us have little property left for our heirs."

Joseph nodded.

Thank You, God, that he doesn't resent me for my decision to be a carpenter.

Yeshua listened as Jacob continued to describe the predicament of many farmers.

"The powerful landowner you see influenced tax collectors so they would levy punishing taxes on neighboring landowners, forcing them to sell their property at bargain prices. After humiliating them by taking their land, he hired the owners to serve as his tenants of the fields they had owned—the ultimate degradation."

Joseph saw from the scowl on Yeshi's face that he recognized the realities of evil, injustice, and often-unseen disparities between the wealthy and the poor.

Joseph jumped into the conversation.

"God has promised that men who spend their lives building financial kingdoms will die and their wealth will be no good to them. They will appear before the judgment seat of our great God, naked and empty-handed. It will be too late to say, 'I wish I had been less interested in profits and more concerned about my fellow man's needs.' Yeshua, their words will all be for naught."

During the conversation, Jacob had inched toward a large rock. As he sat down, Joseph noticed his father's jagged gasps as he leaned forward to catch his breath.

"Yeshua!" Joseph cried out as he stooped over Abba Jacob.

Jacob slumped over and slid to the ground, his face ashen.

Joseph placed his hand under his abba's nose to check for breathing.

No air.

Please, no, Av, a few more years, please.

The silent prayer poured from Joseph's heart. Even as the words came, guilt flooded his heart for not taking responsibility for the family property as eldest son. Had his decision to be a carpenter hastened his father's death?

Both Yeshi and James had raced to Joseph's side. He confirmed for them what they all feared. "I'm so sorry, sons. Your saba is with our heavenly Av."

James burst into tears. Sobbing, he screamed, "He can't be dead." He reached out to embrace his saba. "Wake up, Saba, wake up!"

Joseph watched in agony as James stroked his saba's face in desperation. But Jacob was gone.

In desperation James turned to Yeshua. "Yeshi, make him wake up."

Joseph saw the silent tears streaming down Yeshua's dusty face and slipping from his closed eyes. He sat motionless. The event had stunned him too.

Joseph waited.

The Holy Book says the Messiah will heal the brokenhearted and will bring the dead to life. Has Yeshi's time come?

"James, I can't. It is not my time." Tears were streaming down Yeshi's face.

Disappointment flooded over Joseph. He didn't understand, but he trusted Yeshua. Joseph glanced at James, whose face had contorted in anger. James could not possibly understand the complexities of his brother's position or the reasons for his seeming inaction. And Joseph could not provide his younger son with an explanation he could understand. He didn't understand himself.

The law required that Abba Jacob be buried before sundown the same day of his death. The next few days were difficult for Joseph as he mourned his father's death. Joseph's grief took its toll on his sons, especially Yeshi and James. Yeshi had spent many days with his saba in the fields, learning lessons from nature. Yeshi loved Saba dearly and would miss him terribly.

James was shaking with rage. Yeshua had refused to do anything to help his own saba. Joseph placed a hand on his youngest son's shoulder and opened his mouth to speak.

"I do not mean to dishonor you, Abba, but I cannot listen to one more word of defense for Yeshi. Either he has gifts to help others, or he does not. If he will not or cannot help his own saba, then he is worthless to everyone. Especially me."

James turned his back and walked toward the road, disappearing on the horizon.

* * * * *

Because Matthan had shown no interest in farming, and because Joseph had become a carpenter, Jacob's next-oldest son, Cleophas, inherited the lion's share of his father's land. Joseph continued to spend valuable time in the fields teaching Cleophas valuable skills and lessons, but Joseph recognized that everything changed when Abba Jacob died, especially the relationship between Yeshi and his brother James.

Twenty-six
Joseph's Burden

Joseph's heart pounded. He rarely felt such excitement and relied upon calm reserve that provided a solid foundation for sound judgment.

"Hurry, Yeshi," he called. "The trip to Jerusalem is long, and we must prepare for the journey before day's end."

Tomorrow they would depart for Yeshi's long-anticipated first trip to Jerusalem. Yeshi had begged to see the Holy City from the time he had first been told of its wonders. All Jewish boys longed to see Jerusalem, but Yeshua had begged year after year.

But Jewish custom dictated that boys remain at home with their imas until they reached twelve years old while the men of the community attended the feasts in Jerusalem. From early childhood, Jewish boys were taught about the magnificence of the Holy City until their expectations nearly burst.

Joseph had often wondered whose anticipation about Yeshi's first visit to Jerusalem was greatest—Yeshi's or his own. His son's insight into scripture was far beyond his years.

Will Yeshua's perception of God's Holy City be different from that of other boys? Will he understand the city's significance in Israel's history or the significance of the temple beyond its pageantry and spectacle?

Joseph had often observed Yeshua wander off over the

past months to sit among the olive trees in silent meditation with his heavenly Av. He pondered what Yahweh said to him during those long hours of prayer?

He seems so young to already bear the weight of his mission in life. Sometimes he acts like other boys his age preparing for bar mitzvah, and at other times he seems crushed by the weight of the world. Am I to speak to him of these things, Yahweh, or wait for him to speak? I do not know, and I cannot ask other abbas. I didn't even ask my own.

Joseph often felt alone in his impossible position. Yahweh had given him the responsibility of raising His Son and teaching him how to become a godly man—and *God's Son!* But Yeshi was rapidly outdistancing Joseph's knowledge of Yahweh and life. Yahweh had chosen him to be Yeshi's earthly abba, but *how* was he to carry out his part? And how was he to fulfill his responsibilities as abba to Yeshua while still loving, teaching, and caring for his other children?

At times guilt overwhelmed him. Was he failing Yeshua and failing Yahweh?

How does an abba who is a simple carpenter teach a gifted child, train his other children, and love them all without feeding sibling rivalries and resentment? Help me, Yahweh, for Your son stands apart among the others. Help me teach them how to trust him and not use his gifts against him.

Joseph sometimes wondered if he had been tasked with an unfair demand. His unique responsibility and chosen role continually lay heavy upon his heart and mind.

But in spite of his concerns, Joseph was confident that Yeshi's first trip to Jerusalem would be special. He would have time to show him places he had learned about from their people's history and visualize the stories he had learned from the Holy Book in situ.

Josiah and his parents would accompany them to the Holy City for the Feast of Passover, the first day of the seven-day Feast of Unleavened Bread. All males over the age of thirteen were required to attend three feasts annually:

Passover, Pentecost, and Tabernacles. Some nonobservant Jews ignored attendance at the feasts, while others found the exhausting travel or the financial burden prohibitive. Pious Jews with financial ability made every effort to attend all the feasts. But most Jews, regardless of the burden of distance or finances, attended the Feast of Passover. From the year Abba Jacob had first taken Joseph, he had never missed a Passover, which was special to Joseph both as a man and a devoted Jew.

Although Mary was not required to attend Passover, she often accompanied Joseph. Opportunities to shop in Magdala and Capernaum were limited and lacked Jerusalem's excitement. Besides, city dwellers appreciated purchasing villagers' homegrown fruits and vegetables and their homemade garments. A trip to Jerusalem was also an opportunity to make money at its many markets.

Joseph bolted down a bowl of warm kasha Mary had boiled from barley grain, then stood and took a step toward the door before stopping to look down at Yeshua. "We must hurry, Yeshi. Our first duty is to secure a proper sacrificial lamb to offer at the temple. I need someone to help me select the perfect lamb. Can you help me do that?"

Yeshua looked back at his abba with solemn eyes as he munched the last bite of his morning kasha.

"Yes, Abba. I am ready. I will help you choose the lamb that will be slain for our family."

As he spoke, Yeshua's eyes reflected a sadness Joseph had never seen, something so unsettling that without thinking, he turned his face away from his son.

Heavenly Av, what did I see? It was as though the sadness of the world looked back at me through Yeshua's eyes. What could bring such grief to a child's heart? Did I imagine it?

He forced his gaze to remain on the door they would pass through to leave the house, the door they would exit to find the sacrificial lamb.

No answer came. No voice, audible or internal. The haunting memory of the look clung to Joseph's memory.

"Come, Son." Joseph moved toward the door.

Together father and son set out to the pasture with Josiah and Elias's father to select two young lambs without blemish. The law demanded a pure sacrifice. The temple priests strictly judged the quality of sacrificial lambs. Elias's abba's sheep were always in great demand for sacrifices. Yeshua looked over the flocks, hoping to find the one Elias and he had rescued—but the animals looked too much alike. Joseph also searched, and his keen eye spotted a well-proportioned white lamb.

"What about this one, Yeshua?"

"He is perfect." Yeshi ran his hands over the animal. Then he lifted it into his arms and nuzzled his face into the lamb's fleece. "No flaws."

Joseph helped Yeshua sling the lamb over his small shoulders to carry it home. The tiny animal bleated in protest until Yeshi freed it and carried it home in his arms.

* * * * *

"Abba, why can't I go? It is obvious Yeshi is your favorite and you love him more than you love me—or the rest of us."

Joseph absorbed James's anger. Few Jewish fathers would tolerate such disrespect, but he understood his younger son's frustration. Yeshi *was different* from other boys his age, and Joseph and Mary did not understand how to ignore that reality. They also struggled to prevent their children from resenting a brother who did not lie, steal, seek vengeance, or demonstrate pride or selfishness. James was not an unruly son, but he had a bent toward mischief and anger, and he held grudges. He struggled with resentment toward Yeshua.

Joseph turned away from the half-loaded donkey and toward James. Packing provisions would have to wait. He took his son by the shoulders.

"James, I cannot compare the way I love one child to another. I do not love Yeshi the way I love you because you are James. An abba's love for his children cannot be measured. Love is unique to each child. I would give my life for you and want the best for you. I want those same things for all my children, including Yeshi. My love looks different for each one of you because each of you is different.

"Yeshi is oldest. He will do many things first. He is twelve, so it is time for him to visit the temple.

"But you will stay with Savta Naomi, and she will spoil you. And you will have a wonderful time if you allow yourself to."

Please, heavenly Av, help him understand.

Joseph could read disappointment and anger in James's face.

"Is it because I was born in Egypt and not your beloved Israel?" James's voice dripped with sarcasm, and Joseph recoiled.

How could James believe that? Is he this jealous?

"James, Moses, our great lawgiver, was born in Egypt. Your birthplace is unique to you. Each of our children is a special gift from God."

Joseph needed to handle this matter delicately. Yeshi *was* special—*God's Son* entrusted to his care—but James was no less loved.

Joseph moved toward the mule[38] and ran his hand over the animal's nose. There was so much he could not say, so much James did not comprehend.

"The way you and Ima speak of Yeshi, he sounds like God Himself."

James's resentment surfaced often when the boys squared off in verbal banter and Yeshi refused to offer an angry retort. James was also prone to disruption and often had to take responsibility for his words and actions.

Joseph turned his eyes upward and prayed.

Yahweh, help James. Give me wisdom to help him. Help him see that his resentment will destroy him.

The sound of voices, creaking cart wheels, and bleating animals broke through his prayer, and Joseph opened his eyes. The caravan was approaching, and the mule still had to be loaded. He would have to let the subject go for now, but Joseph determined to continue the discussion.

"I'm sorry, James, but you can't go, because you're not old enough yet."

Joseph would not tolerate complaining. James would have to resign himself to the decision and wait until he was old enough, just as Yeshi had waited.

As he reached down to lift provisions onto the back of the mule, Joseph prayed that his decision would not further deepen James's resentment of Yeshua. It would be simpler to give James what he wanted in the short run, but the decision would not serve him well in life. He would have to learn contentment or pay the consequences.

And Joseph feared the consequences would be painful.

Twenty-seven
Abba Joseph, the Hero

The caravan proceeded south from Nazareth, crossing the Nazareth ridge and heading down into the fertile plain of the Jezreel Valley. There the travelers came to the international trade route that ran through the city of Megiddo to Hazor, which Joshua had once conquered. They picked up additional pilgrims along the way who were heading for Jerusalem.

Joseph used every opportunity along the way to teach the boys the history of God's people. The caravan did not slow down for Joseph's lessons, but that didn't discourage him. Sometimes he and his "students" lagged and had to race to catch the group, Joseph winning just often enough not to discourage the boys.

The next few days of travel went by without incident. Yeshua spent as much time as he could reading from the books of Melakhim. Joseph was concerned that Mary worried about Yeshi spending too much time studying, meditating, and questioning complicated philosophical concepts. She loved watching him at play with his siblings and friends.

"Why can he not just be a boy sometimes?" she would say, sighing, when she saw Yeshi studying or in prayer.

His responsibility to teach his son the things of God burdened Joseph, as well as what it meant to be a young man of honor. The trip to the Holy City was an important part of that plan.

But a deep foreboding in Joseph's heart told him his time to teach his son how to grow into a man of honor might be running out.

* * * * *

The outline of Jericho appeared on the horizon like stubble sprouting from the smooth cheek of a youth, at first imperceptible, but growing proudly prominent.

As the caravan passed the ruins of the ancient site of Jericho, Joseph turned to the boys and commented, "See those heaps of broken and crumbling red clay? That is Jericho. It was destroyed many years ago. After our ancestors returned to our homeland, some tried to restore the city, but eventually they abandoned it. This is a fertile valley, so Herod built a new city as his capital with his winter palace in its place. Look over there."

The boys' eyes swept the landscape to visualize Joseph's description.

"Jericho and Jerusalem are only 13.78 milla passuum apart with a difference of 2,437 pedes[39] in elevation. Elevation was a factor. Land features are always important to war … and to building."

"Why is that important?" Josiah asked.

"Jericho winters are more balmy and desirable, while Jerusalem winters are colder and damper. Herod chose this resort-like climate to build one of his most beautiful estates. He used the Roman concrete style of masonry with plastered floors and walls and frescoes."

The boys had overheard these terms used in Joseph's shop but had never asked him to explain.

As the caravan continued at a steady speed, Joseph retold the story of Yehoshua (Joshua) and the fall of Jericho, reminding them, "It is one of the most important events in the long and intricate history of God's chosen people—and Yeshua, your namesake. The story was the foundation for Joshua's conquest of the land of Israel.

"Remember, God fights for us. We need not fear." Joseph looked into Yeshi's eyes.

"Yes, Abba, we do not need to fear."

Arriving in new Jericho would mean the trip was nearing its end. The travelers would be free to visit the city's shops and purchase unique merchandise, foods, and much-needed medicines.

But Jericho was also known for rebel and bandit activity. Although this was true, Joseph felt no threat of danger. The city was one of Herod's pet projects and was built on a grand scale. The stark contrast between the Jericho oasis and the desolate wilderness of Judea beyond its walls made it a favorite stopping place for travelers. Shops along the streets and in open-air markets were stocked with date palms, assorted fruits, and imported goods, and lined with balsam trees that helped to make Jericho a paradise.

Travelers, healers, midwives, and common folk came for medicinal oils that were produced from local balsam sap and were known for their disinfecting properties. The sap carried a fresh scent often used in perfumes. The oils were used to treat burns, colds, coughs, cuts, muscle aches and pains, and more serious wounds. Most travelers spent what little money they had in this marvelous shopping city, then headed for the comfort of the caravansary.

The long day drew to a close, and the caravan stopped for the night. The accommodations were modest, but the tiring trip had exhausted everyone. No one had strength to complain. The travelers took shelter inside a large fortified compound. High walls built from spiked logs protected them from wildlife and brigands.

A single small gate allowed access to the open-air courtyard. A few men were on duty to protect travelers and warn them of impending dangers.

Everyone had settled into their bedrolls when men began shouting in the courtyard.

"Everyone take cover!"

Was it an attack? He wasn't sure, but he directed the boys to hide beneath the wagon.

Most of the travelers froze as they searched for the source of the noise. But Joseph dashed toward the disturbance, Yeshua running just steps behind him. In the growing dark of night, they spotted a small band of thieves attacking a member of the caravan, the abba of a family Joseph had befriended. As the thieves bolted toward the entrance gate, other men from the caravan joined Joseph in pursuit. When the gate didn't open to let the thieves escape, a brawl ensued. Joseph and several other men wrestled the would-be robbers to the ground in a pile of flailing arms and kicking feet as twelve-year-old Yeshua watched in amazement.

But Mary soon arrived and tugged at his arm, pulling him away from the action.

The thieves were rendered helpless and restrained with wrist and ankle shackles. Officials searching the bandits' pouches discovered Galilean coins several pilgrims had been taking to Jerusalem to pay taxes and purchase much-needed goods from area shops. Theft of these coins would have been a terrible loss to the travelers, and their trip would no doubt have been abandoned.

The incident ended. Soldiers stationed at Jericho to protect the aristocracy showed up in time to arrest the brigands—or so everyone thought. Because the fray disrupted the soldiers' evening meal, they beat the bandits and left them on the ground to wallow in their own blood.

After darkness fell, Joseph crept to the side of the delinquents and bound their wounds with the refined balsam oil he had just purchased. Then he gave them shekels he had taken from the garments of the sleeping soldiers—who had kept much of the money when they "arrested" the culprits.

When Joseph returned to the caravan camp that night, Yeshua seemed to be looking back at him through deeper, softer eyes.

Joseph dropped his gaze. The power and love in Yeshi's

eyes was too great for him to bear. In that moment, his son had somehow looked into his soul, and Joseph felt undone. Seen. Exposed. And loved more than he ever believed possible.

Twenty-eight
"Arise, Jerusalem!"

The next day the caravan progressed painstakingly up the steep, treacherous Wadi Qelt. The path was overcrowded with loaded burros and oxcarts, sacrificial animals, and men shouldering clusters of grapes and other foods for the festival. Searing temperature, endless rocky incline, shadeless path, and choking dust made ascending an endurance test, but Joseph observed little complaining. Although everyone was in pain, they anticipated their arrival and sang psalms as they crept toward Jerusalem.

"I was glad when they said to me, 'Let us go to the house of the Lord.' And now here we are, standing inside your gates, O Jerusalem." [40]

Joseph and Yeshua walked side by side up the steep path as Joseph related the history of God's Holy City. Joseph was proud of his Jewish heritage, despite its bespeckled past.

"The city and temple had its origins with King David, who planned to build the temple, but it was his son Solomon to whom God granted the privilege. Babylonian king Nebuchadnezzar destroyed the original temple. In the Melakim, our scripture describes its beauty. The temple was magnificent."

Yeshua nodded. "Yes, Abba, we learned much about the temple and its beauty. I am so excited to see it and to watch the priests perform their duties in their ritual attire."

This first visit to the Holy City would be the highlight of

Yeshi's childhood. And no other earthly father would ever see Jerusalem as Joseph would as he walked the streets beside his son, God's Son. He could hardly contain his joy at sharing this trip with Yeshua, and he wanted to make the most of every moment.

"Yeshi, you have learned that Ezra led our people out of captivity in Babylon when Persia's King Cyrus granted amnesty, and the Jews constructed a second temple. The Babylonians destroyed the ark of the covenant. Worship at the temple continued without the ark, but the office of high priest became the authority in Judaism and competed with the king for political power. The priesthood became an elite class of wealthy men, with the Levites subordinate to the priestly aristocracy."

"The Roman general Pompey came to Jerusalem to intervene in the civil war between our rival kings, Hyrcanus II and Aristobulus II.[41] He besieged Jerusalem and took control of the temple. Rather than destroying the temple, he restored Hyrcanus as high priest, with the real power residing with Antipater the Idumaean. It was another step in dishonoring the holy temple. After Herod's successful conquest of Jerusalem years later,[42] in the eighteenth year of his reign,[43] he rebuilt the temple on a more magnificent scale, not to bring glory to God, but as a monument to his own ego. Your saba Jacob told me as a young boy many times that he remembered when the people respected the temple, even with all its faults. Now what stands before us, as glorious as it is, is the testimony to the glory of Herod. Many have not embraced the temple structure even though they worship in it."

Joseph hesitated, then leaned toward Yeshi. "I tell you these things, Yeshua, because the priesthood you will observe is charged with corruption, power-mongering, and greed. Many people believe the priests are only interested in lining their pockets with money stolen from poll taxes, land taxes, and sacred offerings. I do not want you to reject our heavenly Av because of the behavior of corrupt priests. Keep in mind that Zechariah, Cousin John's father, is a priest and an honorable man."

"I have been aware of the ungodliness of the priestly class for some time, Abba. My teachers defend the way they conduct themselves, and that troubles me." Yeshua bent and picked up a rock.

I must choose my words carefully. I do not want to poison Yeshua's attitude with negative words.

Joseph continued in silent prayer as they walked up the rough path of the Wadi Qelt. But Yeshua was not content to walk in silence.

"Tell us more, Abba."

Joseph paused and shook a rock from his sandal before proceeding.

"Herod the Great secured his power base as ruler of Israel and began a rigorous building campaign. His plan was so grandiose that, although he was a troubled, cruel man, his buildings are marvels of accomplishment."

Joseph wiped his brow to brush away perspiration as he picked his way along the path, maneuvering to avoid stones and cracks in the parched road.

"His legacy stands in his monumental work of building the temple, a work he began in the eighteenth year of his reign. Construction of the temple precincts remains unfinished. Shops stand along the sides of the Temple Mount, and a large bridge routes traffic from the upper city to the mount. The giant stairway protrudes westward from the southern section and gives access to the mount. To the south of the Temple Mount, large steps with multiple gates lead worshippers into the temple area. Our hope is that the temple will last until the Messiah establishes the kingdom."

Joseph smiled, wondering what Yeshua's role would be in the coming kingdom. Yeshua had absorbed the scene without comment or question, pondering what he had been told and locking it away in his memory.

"Abba, when will I take up my role in the coming kingdom? Must I wait until I complete bar mitzvah?"[44]

Joseph saw excitement etched deep in Yeshua's young face and could hear the urgency in his voice. He laid his hand on Yeshi's arm.

"Yeshua, God has not told me these things. I do not know, but He provides every day what we need for that day. You are not yet twelve, and every day you learn more about what it means to live as a boy and a young man in this world—to know disappointment, anger, hurt, and sorrow, and to learn obedience. Yahweh will reveal exactly what you need at the right time. His plan is perfect, and He cannot fail. You need to trust."

Yeshi sighed deeply. "Abba, it is hard."

Joseph lifted his son's chin. "Hard, my son?"

"Yes. It is hard to wait, hard to learn painful things, hard to suffer pain, to live in a dirty world where those who should teach us the things of God know nothing of His heart. It is hard to be a boy, Abba. Sometimes when I am with my heavenly Av, I rest on His shoulder and cry."

Joseph swallowed. Words could not describe the sorrow that gripped his heart and crushed the lifeblood from it.

He excused himself and walked to the rear of the wagon where he could be alone. Stories and lessons could wait.

* * * * *

The caravan ended at the outskirts of Jerusalem near Bethphage and Bethany, and the travelers headed off on their own. Each family would have to find lodging—which would not be easy. Every pilgrim coming to Jerusalem for Passover was seeking housing. Homemade camps and crudely constructed tents dotted the hillsides like knots on a weaver's rug. Pushing, shoving, and shouting often incited physical confrontations as families fought for spots to homestead for the week.

As was the custom at the annual feasts, young boys

from Bethany and Bethpage wandered among the weary travelers, offering places to stay in local homes that provided warm and dry accommodations—some for a fee and some as a ministry. However, the urchins often stole from unsuspecting travelers or swindled them out of their shekels.

About midmorning, a rumpled boy of about ten with a crooked grin approached Joseph.

"My family can offer a place for two adults, one child, and limited animals. Our home is in Bethany, but we have smaller quarters in the city within easy walking distance of the temple. You are also welcome there."

Joseph swallowed. They certainly could not afford this.

"What is the price?"

Joseph readied himself to squabble, but to his surprise the boy raised his hand in protest, his dark curls dancing.

"My family serves Yahweh. We share what God has given us."

Joseph was skeptical. Such generosity was not common, especially near the city.

"We are grateful for your kindness. May Yahweh bless your family for their service to Him."

Mary, Joseph, and Yeshua followed the lad to his family's comfortable home in Bethany, where the boy's abba introduced himself warmly.

"I am Eleazar, and this is my wife, Miriam. Shalom, and welcome."

Mary and Joseph detected that this was a God-fearing family who sought to live out their faith through acts of kindness and generosity.

Joseph noted Eleazar eying Yeshua. "I have daughters about your age … and a son." He smiled. "Martha and Mary, come and meet our new guests for the feasts."

He turned to Mary and Joseph. "You have already met our son, Lazarus, named after me," he added, his voice edged with pride.

Joseph, in equally proud response, introduced Yeshua

to the Eleazar family. Oddly, Joseph sensed a close bond in spirit with the family. By the time his family left, he and Eleazar had become fast friends, and Yeshua had found a home away from home.

Thank You, Yahweh, for this gift to my family. Bless this home and family that feels like our own. You alone know Yeshua's future, but should he have need of a welcoming home in Jerusalem someday, thank You for providing Eleazar's family to assist him.[45]

Twenty-nine

Yeshi's First Passover

Joseph smiled as Yeshua ran down the road that crested the Mount of Olives, his thin legs wobbling, his feet stumbling. With a sudden jerk and tumble, Yeshua sprawled in the dirt. Unshaken, he jumped to his feet and called over his shoulder, "Hurry, we're almost there!"

Racing ahead, Yeshua crested the Mount of Olives, where he would gain his first view of the city. The Holy City had not been visible from Bethany, which nestled on the east side of the mount.

Joseph's heart skipped a beat as he caught up to Yeshi. Morning sunlight was reflecting off the temple's white stone with blinding brilliance. The view was breathtaking, precisely what he'd hoped Yeshua's first view of the sprawling, glorious city to be.

"Abba ... it is magnificent!" Yeshi stood frozen in wonder, drinking in the view as his homespun tunic fluttered in the breeze. "For as long as I can remember, I have wanted to be here and learn more of my heavenly Av." A tear slid down his cheek.

Joseph swallowed. He had not seen Yeshua cry since Saba Jacob had died.

What is it about the city that moves him? He is just a child.

Joseph pulled Yeshi close. "Stay near me. It will be easy to get lost in the crowds."

But Yeshua remained absorbed by the view. "I can see the temple." He pointed into the distance. "Perhaps someday I can come to the temple and study from the Torah. My teachers have told me the temple priests are the greatest scholars in the world."

High stone walls obstructed a view of the temple precincts, but Joseph and Yeshua could still identify the tops of the booths of the money changers and of the vendors who sold sacrificial animals. Joseph was sure the scene looked exciting to a young Galilean boy, but he had concerns about the city.

Have Yeshua's rabbis told him that the temple high priests are "the greatest teachers in the world," when they are proud and corrupt? And is the temple where Yeshua should train for his ministry, even though my knowledge is limited?

Thoughts stirred about Yeshua's future. Should he be closer to Jerusalem? Joseph watched his son drink in the beauty of the temple like a desert-parched soul.

The family began a slow descent down the Mount of Olives, across the Kidron Valley past the revered tombs of Zechariah and of Hezir's priestly family. As they made their way toward the sacred precincts, Joseph watched Yeshi's confusion shift to delight as he detected the diverse languages that surrounded them.

"Will I learn and speak these tongues, Abba?"

Joseph smiled. "Concentrate on your Greek and Latin first so you can communicate with those whom your heavenly Av has placed in your community. He will take care of the rest."

Wealthy men dressed in splendid clothing, master craftsmen about their business while fighting the mobs, artisans looking for employment, and thousands of dazed, lost pilgrims clogged the streets. The chaos captivated Yeshua, but Joseph was saddened by the belligerent hawkers, aggressive beggars, and rude and road-weary pilgrims.

The family entered the eastern gate of the walled portion

of the city, where they could experience the heart of God's Holy City. Tiny shops lined the walls below the massive Temple Mount. Shoppers flooded the streets, all pushing and shoving amid a cacophony of banging hammers, scraping chisels, and screaming merchants.

Cart wheels rattled against rough stone pavers that bore the weight of Jerusalem's throngs: limestones, sacrificial sheep, construction supplies, and farm goods. Travelers fought for space in the narrow streets, where merchandise spilled underfoot from vendors' tables. The air was filled with an acrid mix of odors: burning sacrificial animals, offal, open sewers, sweat, and kosher cooking.

The Jerusalem market was known for its vast variety of wares: clay pots, water jugs, firewood, dung patties, fruits, vegetables, prayer shawls, tunics, leather girdles, robes, mantles, outer garments and bed clothing, money pouches, sword sheaths, and rare imported items. Mary bought the boys slingshots made from leather and designed to be tucked into the sashes beneath their cloaks.

Their first day in Jerusalem had only begun. But every glance at his oldest son told Joseph that Yeshua had fallen in love with the city, and life would never be the same.

* * * * *

Passover arrived. Celebration began on the fifteenth of Nisan and lasted for seven days. The feast commemorated Israel's deliverance from Egyptian slavery under Pharaoh, who had been afflicted with ten plagues, culminating in the final plague that announced death to all firstborn children. God's instructions to Israel had been clear: "Mark the doorposts of your homes with blood, and the death angel will pass over your household." The blood released the firstborn child from the death penalty.

As they walked through the crowded streets of the lower city, Joseph reminded Yeshua why the celebration was significant.

"When Pharaoh gave the Israelites permission to leave Egypt, they left so quickly that their usually leavened bread did not have time to rise. This is why we eat unleavened bread during the Passover celebration and why it is called the Feast of Unleavened Bread. Passover is also a celebration when we remember God's deliverance. Like our forebears, we are to gird our loins, wear our shoes, and consume the meal in a hurry."[46]

As he spoke, a rising clatter caught Joseph's attention. He glanced up as the crowd in front of them parted. In a split second, he reached out and jerked Yeshi out of the path of a donkey-drawn cart filled with baskets of fresh figs. Joseph realized his legs were trembling. He placed a hand on Yeshi's shoulder as his son looked back at him, wide-eyed.

"It's easy to become overwhelmed by the people, my son. You must always be alert to what is both before you and behind you. Danger lurks everywhere in the city."

"Yes, Abba. I will not forget. Ever." Yeshua's face was somber.

Joseph glanced up and down the street jammed with people, animals, wagons, and mounted soldiers. He waited for a gap in the flow and drew Yeshua beside him and into the throng, sheltering him within the curve of his arm.

"Sabbath celebrations at the Nazareth synagogue are beautiful, but nothing I have experienced has been like this, Abba."

Yeshua drank in the city scenes as they walked, his head turning from side to side in constant motion.

Bleating lambs awaiting slaughter.

Lost pilgrims searching for relatives or lodging.

Thousands of bustling priests, brows furrowed as they focused on their tasks.

Occasional stray animals that had found their way into the streets.

The sweet scent of burning incense and the sacred, haunting call of the shofar.

Joseph watched as Yeshua, who had known only a rustic life and education, tried to absorb the flood of sight, sound, smell, and emotion. At times he seemed on the edge of tears.

Among the thousands of priests, administrators, policing forces, Levites, and others crowding the streets were minor functioning priests. These priests came from various provinces throughout Israel for the honor of participating in annual feasts and rituals. Even Joseph enjoyed the splendor of ritual sacrifices conducted by these priests, who wore stunning white linen gowns and tall white hats that added beauty, ceremony, and authority to their work. Yeshua couldn't help but notice them as they passed.

"Abba, the priests' garments are different. Is there a purpose behind the details?"

Joseph realized that his son was thinking far beyond his twelve years. He himself had seldom thought about the meaning behind the detail of priestly garments.

Yeshua continued questioning as they walked, eventually turning his attention to the ubiquitous Temple Guard, policing the streets in full force. Uniformed in polished breastplates and holstered knives, the guards kept watch for thieves and disruptors, but they also protected price-gouging temple vendors from disgruntled pilgrims. The Sadducees had permitted the merchants and money changers to invade the temple precincts instead of the normal markets at street level. For the privilege, the Temple Guard often took bribes in exchange for protection.

The day proceeded with Yeshi asking question after question and changing direction in topics like a hare eluding a fox. By midday, Joseph felt as though his store of knowledge had run dry. Yeshua's questions were often so profound that he had difficulty understanding what was being asked.

As the day progressed, the familiar shroud of inadequacy settled over his thoughts.

What am I to do? I do not have answers for all of his questions, Yahweh. He has an insatiable desire to understand deep things unknown to me. Prepare him for Your work, for I cannot. Yet You chose me for a purpose.

As he walked the teeming streets of Jerusalem beside Yeshua, Joseph understood that with each passing day, he and Mary must completely trust Yahweh for what they could not see or understand.

Thirty

At the Hall of Hewn Stone

The boys sat in the shade of a small canopy that protected the goods of a *shuk* that sold foods, beverages, and trinkets to pilgrims thronging into the Temple Mount area. The High Holy Days and Yom Teruah had passed.[47] Yeshua and Josiah had learned to navigate the city alongside Joseph, but Josiah had decided the time had come for the boys to explore on their own.

"Come on, Yeshi. We'll be careful." Josiah saw his friend's hesitation, so he pressed further.

"We could bring your ima a pomegranate from the *šūqā'* nearby and be back before anyone knows we're gone. You know she's been wanting pomegranate." Josiah used the Aramaic word for *shop*. The boys spoke Aramaic, although they preferred to speak the Hebrew they'd learned at school. Most soldiers couldn't understand Hebrew.

"Abba hasn't given us permission to go out in the city alone." Yeshua's voice was firm.

"Yes, but he hasn't said we *cannot* since the first day. We know our way now," Josiah persisted. "We could visit the Royal Stoa and listen to the rabbis. Perhaps you'd learn something about the Torah, the commandments, or the temple ceremonies." Josiah hoped that mentioning the temple would draw Yeshi in.

The Royal Stoa overlooked Jerusalem's residential and

commercial quarters and was where a priest blew a ram's horn to announce the start of holy days.

"I've been told that the many temple merchants and money changers use God's house to defraud unsuspecting pilgrims who travel from distant countries. I want to see for myself if this is true, but you should not disobey your abba, Yeshi. You should stay."

Josiah suddenly stood, bolting into the crowd and toward the temple. These corrupt merchants refused foreign currencies and offered unfair exchange rates. Their inspections of ritual animals violated the law, and they pronounced many unspotted lambs and doves flawed, forcing pilgrims to pay exorbitant prices for replacements. Yeshua had often expressed his offense at the corruption to Josiah.

Josiah wove through the crowd and headed toward the Hall of Hewn Stone, where the Sanhedrin met.

The discussions there will captivate Yeshua if he follows me.

Josiah ran through the early morning crowd, just fast enough for Yeshua to keep him in sight. He ignored the frowns of disapproval as he sprinted, arriving at the hall just steps ahead of Yeshi. Panting, the two boys slipped through the hall door.

The hall was the highest court of religious law and spiritual instruction. One elderly stately man stood as the other priests remained seated. Discussions among the sages subsided as he spoke, and Yeshua focused on his words. A boy just slightly older than Yeshua sat near the rear of the room and waved at Josiah. He gave Yeshua a gentle nudge.

"Go. Listen and learn."

Yeshua moved near the boy, who made room beside him on the floor. Yeshua sat, then whispered, "Who is this rabbi?"

"That is my saba Hillel," the boy responded with pride. "Over there," he continued, pointing to a man sitting on the other side of the room, "is Simeon ben Hillel, my abba. I am Gamaliel."[48]

Yeshua knew who the sages were. In fact, Yeshua's great-uncle Joseph of Arimathea was counted among them.[49] And everyone had heard about Nicodemus, a respected member of the Sanhedrin. Their rabbi in Nazareth had often spoken of these teachers. Hillel the Elder founded the House of Hillel, a school of interpretation for scholars, and was a preeminent scholar. Gamaliel's father was president of the Sanhedrin.

"They must be masters of scripture, but they seem to misunderstand what I have been learning in the scriptures." Yeshua spoke in reserved awe.

Later, when they returned to their guest house, Josiah overheard Yeshua tell his abba about his disappointment with the interactions between the rabbis but his desire to return. The rabbis' discussions went far deeper than anything he had been taught, but they also troubled him. Surprisingly, Abba agreed that Yeshi could go back.

Each day Josiah tagged along, but when the boys came to the Hulda gate, Yeshua turned toward the Hall of Hewn Stone, while Josiah remained outside, watching the banter and bargaining between merchants and buyers.

So, with Abba's permission, Yeshua sat daily among the sages, who invited him into theological debates.

Josiah wandered in and out, always signaling to Yeshi when he returned. As the days passed, Yeshua moved toward the front of the room, where Rabbi Simeon ben Hillel directed the discussions. One day Hillel asked, "Which commandment is the greatest?"

A white-bearded Pharisee spoke up, his distinctive headdress wound around his head, the ends hanging down his back to signal his piety.

"Honor thy father and mother," he responded.

Another Pharisee jumped up and retorted, "No, the most important is 'Thou shalt not murder.'"

Several voices joined in, and for a few moments the room rumbled in debate. Josiah watched in shock as little Yeshua rose to his feet. All eyes turned toward him; the room went silent. His appearance was uncommon for a twelve-year-old lad. He stood straight and tall. His hair cascaded in thick, shiny black curls. His tender spirit was evident in his fervent eyes. Although his movements were bold and self-assured, he possessed humility.

"May I respond?"

Rabbi Hillel smiled at the impertinence and nodded, but Josiah could see a veiled expression beneath the smile. What was it? Fear? Anger? He couldn't tell.

"You may speak."

"The greatest commandment is 'Love the Lord your God with all your heart and with all your soul and with all your mind and your neighbor as yourself.' Messiah will demonstrate this when he comes."

The rabbis looked at each other in astonishment.

Rabbi Hillel swallowed, attempted to speak, and then stopped.

"What is your name, child?"

"Yeshua, son of Joseph the carpenter."

"Yeshua, who is the Messiah? How will we know Him?" The rabbi asked looking pompously around the room thinking the impossible question would silence the youth.

How will he answer? He is just a boy like me and could not possibly know.

"The scriptures say, 'Look, your king is coming to you. He is righteous and victorious, yet he is humble, riding on a donkey—riding on a donkey's colt,'"[50] Yeshua answered.

Rabbi Hillel reared back and laughed. "You have not been taught my interpretation of scripture, child. This passage is to be understood figuratively."

Many rabbis nodded in agreement at Yeshua's answer. Not everyone agreed with Hillel, and he appeared frustrated, Josiah noted.

"And when will your Messiah come and this age end, Yeshua? Do you also have special knowledge on these things?" Hillel sneered.

Yeshua remained unintimidated. "Do you not know the scriptures?" His voice was confident. "A period of seventy sets of seven are decreed for our people and our holy city to finish transgression, to put an end to sin, to atone for wickedness, to bring in everlasting righteousness, to seal up vision and prophecy, and to anoint the Most Holy Place."

Yeshua continued, his voice growing stronger, his words intense.

> "Now listen and understand!
>
> "After this period of sixty-two sets of seven, the Anointed One will be killed, appearing to have accomplished nothing, and a ruler will arise whose armies will destroy the city and the temple. The end will come with a flood, and war and its miseries will be decreed from that time to the very end. The ruler will make a treaty with the people for a period of one set of seven, but after half this time, he will put an end to the sacrifices and offerings. And as a climax to all his terrible deeds, he will set up a sacrilegious object that causes desecration, until the fate decreed for this defiler is finally poured out on him."[51]

Yeshua had the room's full attention. He continued with a lecture on hypocrisy and corruption.

How do you justify priests living in extravagance and eating the meat of sacrifices while the worshippers who raise and offer the sacrifices rarely eat meat?"

Hillel jumped to his feet. "Are you challenging the law of

Moses that states the first fruits go to God? They are to be given joyfully."

Yeshua remained calm. "First fruits are not to be devoured by the priests but to be returned to the people in the form of charity and grace. How can the people rejoice when the priests sell the sacrificial animals at a great profit and give poor exchange for foreign money? It is bad enough for the people to pay the backbreaking taxes the Romans levy on them, but then you burden them with unnecessary charges to fill your personal coffers."

Hillel sat down, speechless, as whispers rolled through the room. Josiah overheard the comments of several men sitting near him.

"This young man has a remarkable knowledge of the scriptures and speaks with wisdom far beyond his years."

"I am impressed by this boy's arguments, but he is impertinent." However, many scholars agreed with Yeshua—but didn't want to change.

"Hillel will never tolerate such arrogance from an upstart ..."

Joseph of Arimathea listened intently. He was anxious to get to his grandnephew and speak privately with him. He sensed danger in Yeshua's words.

Josiah had seen changes in Yeshi since he had come to Jerusalem. His time at the temple had increased his confidence, wisdom, and maturity as he gained deeper insights into the Torah, worship, the priestly order, and his own history. He did not fear criticism. He believed what he was doing and saying. Sitting in the Royal Stoa day after day had helped Yeshua see the world differently and his role in it.

Every day Josiah grew more excited about Yeshua's future, but it puzzled him, and that caused great concern for this young friend.

Yahweh, I do not trust these teachers who are supposedly authorities on Your scriptures. They seem to twist Your Words to conform to their opinions and theologies. I am worried that their pride will cause them to despise Yeshua and seek his harm.

Please protect my friend, Yahweh, and help me be the friend he needs and become the man who can one day help him carry out his mission.

Thirty-one

Yeshua and the Rabbis—Decision Time

Mary drew in her breath with the first pangs of fear as the caravan heading home crept slowly down the wadi toward Jericho. Forcing herself not to panic, she sucked in slow, deep breaths as she broke her pace and turned back into the flow of people and animals toward the rear of the procession. She walked slowly, her eyes searching, until her legs burned and she could no longer breathe the searing air. When the caravan arrived at Jericho, groups would break off to head toward the Dead Sea and others toward southern Judea and to Galilee to the north. She dared not think about what would happen if she did not find Yeshua before then lest she collapse in fear.

Weaving between goats, children, carts and wagons, mules and donkeys, and occasional stray dogs, Mary found her way back to Joseph, who was leading their donkey-drawn cart. She struggled to force the panic from her face as she approached him.

"Joseph, have you seen Yeshua? I thought he was with Josiah and his parents—that's the only place he ever goes when he leaves our sight—but I cannot find him."

Even as she spoke, Mary scanned the crowd surrounding them. No sign of a pale blue mantle, no sign of her child.

Joseph laid a hand upon her arm.

"We will find him, Mary. Wherever he is, he is safe. People in the caravan know him. He is likely in deep discussion with someone or studying the birds or insects alongside the road."

Joseph sounded calm, but Mary saw furrows of concern on his face. It wasn't like Yeshua not to tell them where he was, and they had thought him to be with Josiah's family. Mary's mind raced.

I should have checked on him. I should never have assumed he was with Josiah's parents. Where is he, El Roi?[52] *Please help us find him.*

"Mary, you lead the donkey, and I will look for Yeshi and ask friends to help. We can search faster as a group."

Mary took the lead rope from Joseph, but she could not look into his eyes.

"Do not waste time blaming yourself. I assumed he was with Josiah, as he usually is. It's not your fault, Mary. We are both his parents."

With those words, Joseph turned and disappeared into the crowd to find Yeshua.

* * * * *

The return trip to the Holy City was excruciating. Every step, every creak of the cart, was a heart-piercing reminder to Mary that her son was a lost, homeless child somewhere in the streets of Jerusalem. She spent every available moment in prayer, trying not to think about what could happen to a child alone in the huge city.

Josiah's parents had offered to accompany Mary and Joseph on the return trip. With deep gratitude, Mary and Joseph accepted. Help in searching would be more precious than gold. Josiah's father Kenan's keen eye in sorting sheep was welcomed in the search.

With every breath, Mary prayed to see Jerusalem's beloved silhouette etched on the horizon, but when they reached the gates, they found a crowd gathered around a city judge to be entertained by a legal dispute. The accusers and defenders had become so angry that they were pushing and shoving, and a fight seemed imminent. Mary's heart cringed.

Heavenly Av, keep Yeshua safe from the violence and corruption of this city. He's just a child.

They searched first in the area where they had stayed, but no one had seen Yeshua. Yeshua could have been within a stone's throw of them and they never would have seen him amid the crush of residents, merchants, pilgrims, sacrificial animals, priests, and beggars. By nightfall the first day, he was still missing.

Mary did her best to calm her heart. She stayed close by Joseph's side and, when modesty permitted, reached for the comfort of his hand.

Have soldiers taken him? Has he been sold?

Questions were asked when any Jewish boy disappeared after the despotic Roman occupation. The cruel Archelaus, Judea's ethnarch, had recently been deposed and banished to Gaul. Even Herod Antipas hated Archelaus's treatment of the Jews. Judea had come under Rome's jurisdiction. The new political situation had caused Mary and Joseph to believe Jerusalem was safe for a child living under the new regime.

Were we wrong to bring Yeshua to Jerusalem? Did we make the wrong decision?

The question plagued Mary as she walked the streets of the city. Joseph had planned for the family's safety, and a trip to the Holy City was part of almost every Jewish boy's education.

They continued the search the second day. Still no Yeshua. At least Joseph and Mary found lodging in the city with Eleazar, praise be to Yahweh. Their new friends could pray with them.

The morning of the third day, Josiah suggested they search the temple area. Yeshua had spent most of his time at the Hall of Hewn Stone listening to the elder rabbis teach. In his anxiety, Joseph had forgotten Yeshi spent time with the rabbis.

In that instant, Mary's heart calmed. They would find Yeshua at the temple.

The group hurried toward the Temple Mount. Joseph took the lead, with Mary a few steps behind. A female could not enter the hall, which was dedicated for the use of religious leaders and aspiring rabbis. She stood in the doorway beyond the Chamber for Women and prayed that she could see into the Chamber of Hewn Stone.

Joseph slipped through the doorway and took a seat. Mary hovered in the doorway behind him, praying the religious leaders would not see her and ask her to leave. Almost instantly she glimpsed Yeshua sitting near the front of the large tiered auditorium, near the two desks where the sages sat to teach. He was talking with a rabbi standing at the front of the room. Although she only made out a few words, it was clear that Yeshi was controlling the conversation. Relief flooded her heart like sunshine pouring through an open door. She turned to whisper to Joseph, but he was already on his feet, waiting for a break in the dialogue. When it came, he spoke, his voice firm.

"Yeshua."

All heads turned.

"Your mother and I have been searching for you for three days. Why did you not tell us you would be here?"

Joseph of Arimathea rose at the front of the room and stepped forward. "Mary and Joseph, I am so sorry, but Yeshua has been with me. His cousin John and I have enjoyed him staying with us for several nights. We weren't aware you were looking for him."[53]

Mary was speechless. John's parents had passed away, making him an extra special cousin to Yeshua and his brothers.[54] Even at a young age, John had known of Yeshua's special birth and felt a unique connection to his cousin. But

John had developed a deep resentment toward the priestly class, including his father's temple ministry. Still, Joseph of Arimathea should have known better.

The learned priest spoke up. "I am Hillel. Your son has shown remarkable understanding of the scriptures, especially the Torah. Even the most learned among us have been confounded by his ability to interpret the law. While he has much to learn about the law, I see great potential if our Jerusalem scholars can take charge of his education."

Joseph thanked Hillel, but Mary wondered why such learned men and particularly Joseph of Arimathea had not made certain that a child's parents had known his whereabouts. She silently rebuked the rabbis as she and Joseph led Yeshua from the room and into the women's chamber. Mary stopped and turned to Yeshi.

"Yeshua of Nazareth, were you aware of how much you frightened us? The city is filled with dangers."

Her stinging words came with a mixture of anger and relief.

"Your father and I have been searching for you for three days. Did you plan to stay behind?"

Yeshua's answer came without an apology or appearance of remorse. "Didn't you know I had to be in my Father's house?"

His answer was an honest and direct statement of his priorities. The response caught Mary off guard. She and Joseph were his parents, but ... he was becoming less dependent. Mary covered her mouth with her hand.

Is his time at hand? He is so young, and yet he is the Son of God—but now?

Mary's mind raced. How would she and Joseph handle his questions if even the high priests at the temple could not? Was Yeshua outgrowing his need for an abba and an ima? Were they no longer needed?

Mary wasn't sure of those answers, but she was certain that Yeshua's time in Jerusalem had ignited a fire deep within him that would move him further toward manhood and Yahweh's mission—wherever that might take him.

* * * * *

For several days after the family returned from Jerusalem, Mary could think of nothing but the scene at the Hall of Hewn Stone and Yeshua teaching the temple rabbis. Conversation with Joseph soon turned to the choice before them regarding Yeshua's next level of education: Would they continue to teach him in Nazareth or find a way for Yeshua to receive his education in Jerusalem?

Was it right to confine Yeshua's brilliant mind to Nazareth's educational limitations, especially when most young men aspiring to be rabbis or priests were educated at the Jerusalem temple? Mary insisted that Yeshi could not live apart from his parents in the city, despite its advantages. They had responsibilities to their seven other children. They discussed the advantages and disadvantages of Jerusalem over Nazareth for days. One morning after prolonged prayer in his workshop, Joseph sat down alone with Mary at the table in the kitchen and took her hand in his.

"Although Jerusalem may seem the best choice and even offer business opportunities for me, I believe we should stay in Nazareth."

Mary sighed in relief, but her spirit troubled her. "Why hasn't our heavenly Av spoken to us? He spoke to the Abraham, Isaac, and Jacob and later to Moses and the prophets. Why has He not spoken to us about this important decision?"

Joseph did not answer Mary but continued.

"Elizabeth warned me that Zechariah was being pressured by other priests to compromise his ethics. Desires for power, money, and authority have overtaken many religious leaders. And Cousin John refused to follow his father's path into the priesthood after his bar mitzvah. Zechariah was disappointed, but he is also disillusioned about the worldly direction of the priests in Jerusalem."

Joseph fell silent for a moment and closed his eyes. His mind swirled as he too wondered why Av didn't warn them of the dangers and give direction to their decision. He'd warned them of the perils of Herod while they were in Bethlehem and told them to return from Egypt. Moments later Joseph raised his head and spoke as if a brilliant idea flashed across his face like a strike of lightning.

"Mary, we don't have to teach Yeshua everything ourselves. We only need to provide a sound environment for his development in mind, body, and spirit in order for him to express the divine knowledge that has always been in him because he is the *God-man.*"

The God-man. As Mary let the phrase sink in, her apprehension faded. They could trust God to provide what Yeshua needed—and what they needed. She could lay down her burden and rest.

"Mary, when I realized this, my fear of being a good abba lifted. I can trust Yahweh to walk beside me day by day and teach me how to be Yeshi's abba."

That night Mary rested at peace in Joseph's decision—it was the Lord's decision. The family would remain together in Nazareth. Hours later in the depths of sleep, her mind summoned words from the prophet Isaiah that she would remember for weeks to come: "From Jesse's roots, a netzer [branch] will bear fruit."[55]

Thirty-two

Bar Mitzvah's Revelation

Joseph wasn't sure how Yeshua would feel about remaining in Nazareth for his education. The boy had fallen in love with Jerusalem, but he would respect their decision. A clan of David had returned from the Babylonian captivity about a hundred years earlier and settled in Nazareth. The name of the town came from the Davidic clan known as Netzer, meaning "shoot" or "branch."[56] Mary and Joseph's families, both descendants of King David, settled in Nazareth after the Babylonian captivity.

The prophecy "He will be called a Nazarene" was a refinement of Isaiah's prophecy[57] "And a shoot will come up from the stump of Jesse, from his roots a Branch [Netzer] will bear fruit." Joseph was acquainted with several priestly families who settled in Galilee during the return from captivity. Some settled in Nazareth.[58] It was a natural place for clan members to homestead.

Living in rural villages was vastly different from city life. That factor played a large part in Joseph's decision for Yeshua to remain in Nazareth for his advanced schooling. City dwellers depended on shopkeepers for their food, whereas a rural diet consisted of local fish, barley, lentil porridge, nuts, olives, fruits, and occasional meat. However, wealthy Sadducees, priests, traders, landowners, and government officials feasted on extravagant catered meals with the finest wines. The wealthy aristocracy viewed mealtime as a social event and an opportunity to display their fine clothing. Joseph feared that these ungodly practices might influence Yeshua. As abba, he was responsible for protecting his family from the corruption of city life.

Residents of Nazareth, like residents of other hamlets, were basket weavers, tanners, shepherds, carpenters, potters, farmers, fishermen, and stonemasons. Sons learned their father's occupation and took over his business after completing an apprenticeship under his supervision. Nazareth was known for its conservative Jewish practices, and the people of the surrounding region considered the town inconsequential because it was located in the often-disparaged region of Galilee.

After Yeshi's birth, Joseph often pondered on God's reasons for bringing his family to Nazareth and not Jerusalem, the Holy City. Shouldn't God's Son be raised in the temple and amid learned rabbis? But the more he pondered, the more Joseph recognized that God, who knew the beginning and the end, had placed Yeshua in the perfect place where his humanity and divinity could unfold according to His plan from before time's beginning.

* * * * *

Joseph rolled over in bed and drew Mary's homespun blanket around his shoulders. Yeshua was now thirteen. Joseph could barely absorb the thought. The years had passed too quickly, and the time had come for Yeshua to accept religious duties at his bar mitzvah. The ceremony also represented the dedication of Joseph's family. "The son of commandment" ritual would include feasting, the taking of oaths, and celebration.

I will no longer be responsible for Yeshi's actions. He will bear responsibility for keeping Jewish laws, traditions, and rituals and will become a member of the community as my equal.

Joseph stared into the darkness. This was Yeshua's first

step into adulthood on a journey that would culminate when he was twenty and reach full manhood, at which time he would be recognized as being at the age of majority[59] and would be eligible for service in war and responsible for paying government taxes.

Yeshi's bar mitzvah was scheduled to begin on the first Shabbat after his thirteenth birthday, today.

Joseph had pushed the ceremony out of his mind as long as he could, but today he had to face reality. Mary would make sure of it.

And he was right. Before the cock crowed, Mary enlisted him to pack a cart with food to take to the building the Jews of Nazareth used as a gathering space and synagogue. She had placed tables at the end of the open space farthest from the door and added arrangements of local flowers.

With the help of friends, Mary had also prepared the finest food the family could afford for the feast. She had chosen food to remind guests of God's provision for His people. Bread, wine, and olive oil represented the three main crops of the Jewish agricultural calendar—wheat, grapes, and olives. Long wooden tables were laden with goat's milk, assorted fruits and vegetables, fish, eggs, and generous amounts of goat meat and mutton.

The ceremony would take place after the guests had eaten.

Yeshua had spent time preparing for his bar mitzvah, studying, memorizing, and preparing a scripture lesson he would present to his guests—the central event.

The morning of the celebration, guests crowded into the room, expressing their respect for Yeshi, Joseph, and his family. Many commented on Yeshua's character, spiritual insight, and kindness. Joseph's gratitude grew as people shared observations about Yeshi.

I can take no credit for Yeshua's wisdom, insight, and compassion, Yahweh. He is Yours.

When the crowd gathered, the lead rabbi introduced

Joseph. As the candidate's father, he was given the privilege of offering the prayer for his son.

Joseph glanced at Yeshua. His eyes were downcast. Joseph's heart swelled with love and pride as he reverently raised his hands.

"Yahweh, we thank and praise You for entrusting us with the privilege of raising Your son Yeshua, of bringing him to bar mitzvah, and of educating him in the ways of Torah and Your commandments."

Joseph continued, blessing and thanking family and friends for celebrating this milestone in Yeshua's life with them. The enormity of the moment overwhelmed him, and words would not come. He glanced up and saw Mary, her face buried in her shawl, her shoulders heaving. He squeezed his eyes closed and swallowed, concluding the prayer with a blessing on the meal.

"Blessed is he who brings forth bread from the earth."

The feast began. Yeshua was seated as the guest of honor with his family surrounding him. The sound of voices and laughter rose and fell, filling the room. The sound died down as the feast drew to a conclusion.

Joseph drew in a deep breath and stood. The moment had arrived. He invited Yeshua as his son and the honoree to present the brief sermon the latter had prepared. Candidates focused on a commandment that highlighted their commitment to be faithful to the law.

Yeshua's words flowed like spring mountain rivers, smooth and refreshing. He had chosen the commandment taught by Hillel in Jerusalem. Joseph watched as Yeshua's teaching mesmerized his guests, his words incisive, powerful, unlike any teaching on the commandment they had heard before.

"The school of Hillel teaches, 'That which is hateful to you, do not do to your fellow. That is the whole Torah; the rest is the explanation; go and learn.' This Rabbi Hillel calls the golden rule."

Yeshua thumped the lectern as he drove home his interpretation of the Torah.

A dissenting interpretation, Joseph observed with raised eyebrows.

Some audience members chuckled, some smiled, and others looked at one another in disapproval as Yeshua continued.

"The true golden rule is, 'Love the Lord your God with all your heart and with all your soul and with all your mind and your neighbor as yourself.' This is the first and greatest mitzvah."

The guests sat spellbound. Moments later Yeshua concluded his sermon and walked away from the podium. Joseph held his breath as the room went as silent as a sepulcher. Finally, a rabbi from the synagogue rose and clapped in affirmation. The room erupted in applause to approve the message—a controversial but scripturally illuminating sermon. Yeshua had challenged the ideas of a respected sage and demonstrated insight, wisdom, and clarity in his understanding of the commandments.

Dancing soon broke out in a corner of the room, as was the custom at bar mitzvah, followed by singing in another corner. Waves of awe and gratitude swept over Joseph, and he reached for Mary's hand.

Did their friends and neighbors understand that thirteen-year-old Yeshi's teaching exceeded the wisdom of the most mature scholars of the temple?

The celebration flew by in a haze of singing, dancing, celebration, greeting, and gift giving. Yeshua received religious items, writing tablets, and small amounts of money, as all boys did at bar mitzvah. The singing and dancing lasted longer than expected. Nobody seemed to want to leave.

In the midst of the celebration, Yeshua's rabbi, Baruch, approached Joseph.

"Joseph, I am mystified by your son. He is like no student

I have ever taught. A prodigy, but something more than that."

He searched Joseph's face for an answer.

Joseph looked into the rabbi's eyes and chose the simplest, most truthful answer: "Yes, Yeshua is a prodigy. He is a gift from God, and I'm certain something special lies ahead for him."

Then he turned to take his son, now a young man, home.

Thirty-three

Joseph's Talk about Birds and Bees

Joseph stood on the rooftop and looked at the mess he'd refused to face for too long. He was frustrated. His procrastination had caused more damage.

As a busy professional carpenter, he had too long neglected maintenance on his own house. If he were to wait any longer, his home would become a hazard.

He surveyed the roof. The red clay outer surface that doubled as the floor had sprouted weeds and leaked—again. If that were not enough, plaster on the inside of the water cistern was peeling, and precious water was leaking out. Repairs were needed immediately. He had wakened Yeshua to help him.

Like all the roofs in their housing compound, theirs had been built to accommodate sleeping, mild weather leisure, crafting, and drying grain. A large area was covered with a reed-woven awning for protection from the searing sun and elements.

Joseph knelt and assessed the roof's three layers: sycamore beams provided the foundation, followed by brushwood, then a final layer of stone-rolled clay. All roofs eventually sprung leaks. Major repairs needed to be completed before the winter rains.

The family spent a great deal of time on the rooftop, often gathering there in the cool of the evening to talk. Mary and the girls used it to do chores such as drying seeds and fruits, and the boys slept there at night. Most of their friends considered the roof to be the most important "room" in the house.

Joseph sent Yeshua to gather tools from his workshop while he cut the sycamore he had already carried to the rooftop. Yeshua soon returned and helped him pull up rotted portions of the old roof and remove rooted sycamore beams. By midday they were laying brushwood and stirring mud and straw for caulking gaps.

Joseph supervised every step with care. Yeshua needed to learn to honor Yahweh in all things. There was no excuse for laziness or half measures. But Yeshi was showing interest in all the details of the roofing process. Even though he was missing his much-loved classes, he sang to himself from the Psalms as he worked and occasionally asked Joseph questions.

"Abba, I like to work with you. The Torah cannot teach me to build." Yeshi sat back on his haunches for a brief rest.

Joseph stood, removed his outer mantle, and hung it from a branch of the awning as he observed scratches on Yeshua's hands.

The Son of God toiling in mud with dirt on his face and bloodied hands. Is this how the Messiah is to come, Yahweh?

He watched as Yeshi leaned forward again and struggled to spread the mud smooth over the brushwood, a skill that requires years of practice. Joseph knelt and laid a hand over Yeshua's to direct the trowel.

Yeshi turned toward his father.

"Abba, I must ask you a question. Why do the boys in my class continue to say I am not your son—your real son?" His eyes reflected a deep sadness.

Joseph's knees went weak. Yeshi had asked a similar question when he was younger, and Joseph thought he'd given adequate answers. But boys seemed to need new answers as they grew. Mary had faced gossip in her own dignified way, and the whispers had died down. But classmates had tormented Yeshi long before his bar mitzvah. He was becoming a man, and it was time they explained the whole truth. Joseph stepped beneath the shade of the awning, sat on a stool, and pulled Yeshua near him.

"The accusations are cruel and untrue, Yeshi. Your earthly father is not a Roman mercenary from Gaul, as some delight in saying, nor are you my illegitimate son. Your mother and I did not come together as man and woman until after your birth, as God instructed us, because you were divinely conceived of the Holy Spirit."

Yeshua smiled.

"I have known for a long time who I am, Abba, and that God has a special plan for me. Rumors and accusation do not trouble me, but my brothers and sisters are ashamed of me. They have been hurt by the gossip and do not know what to think or say."

Joseph's head snapped back. "Yes, I know your brothers and sisters were being tormented by gossipers? Many have told me!"

Yahweh, they are children. Help them understand truth that is beyond them and forgive those who accuse in ignorance and pride. Help them comprehend that Yeshi is not like other children. We cannot be responsible for how they respond but can only tell them what we think is necessary under the circumstances. They must choose what they will believe.

Joseph's thoughts were interrupted by bounding steps pounding up the staircase. Simon was home from school. He flew across the rooftop toward Joseph.

"Abba, can I help?"

Joseph smiled. His rambunctious son wouldn't be much help, but time with him was more valuable than the sum of Rome's wealth. He nodded.

"Simon, your job will be to make new rope to tie reeds to the beams."

Joseph often weaved rope from flax, reeds, or rushes, but

he preferred rope made from strips of camel skin for roofing. Simon only knew how to make cord from reeds, but it was important that he be included. Joseph could teach him to make camel skin rope another time.

Yeshua continued the conversation as Simon drifted away to gather reeds.

"I am sad for Ima—and you. She's endured endless mistreatment from the townspeople, yet she does not defend herself."

"Yeshi, your ima does not care what people think. God chose her, He is her defender, and she knows the truth. She finds no purpose in stinging responses or persuasive answers. She is compassionate and merciful toward her accusers. Someday they will remember their words."

Yeshua nodded and moved further down the roof to continue his work.

"Yes, I understand, Abba."

Joseph bent to stir the bucket of mud and straw.

"Your brothers and sisters sometimes listen to your critics and seem unkind, but they do love you, Yeshua. You mystify them."

Yeshi nodded. "They are angry. My little sisters seem the most accepting."

Simon had clattered downstairs to work in the kitchen, closer to Ima's cooking.

"Your brothers and sisters have been confused by the rumors," Joseph continued. "They want to defend you but don't know what to say. We have been reluctant to tell them the truth that you were conceived by the Holy Spirit. They are not old enough to understand.

"So much is at risk. Herod attempted to kill all of the infants in Bethlehem because he was told a king had been born. He feared that child would threaten his reign. An angel warned us, and we escaped to Egypt. If we had not fled, Herod would have killed you too.

"Herod presumed his butchery killed the rival infant king. But Yeshua, you were that baby."

Yeshi looked at Joseph with solemn eyes.

"Yes, Abba."

Joseph stood and stooped over the final coat of mud plaster to inspect their work as he chose his words.

"We told your brothers and sisters that your birth was special and that God chose you for a unique mission. But they have seen nothing special about you except your unique intelligence. We felt it was unsafe to say more than that. Children are children. We could not place your safety in their hands."

Joseph hoped Yeshi understood. He and Mary had done what they thought best, still fearing Yeshi's siblings might struggle with resentment and embarrassment.

Joseph wiped the sweat from his forehead.

"We chose to live in Nazareth knowing Herod Antipas believes the child lived and would search for him to kill him. He believes the Messiah king will be the leader of the Sicarii or the Zealots and will attempt to overthrow his kingdom. He sees this boy as a threat."

Yeshua nodded.

"If Herod Antipas suspects who you are or where you are, he will attempt to kill you. Do you understand why we could not tell your brothers and sisters? They are too young to keep their tongues or to be fearful. We never wanted secrets, but neither could we fully reveal the truth."

Yeshua had become somber and plucked at straws that clung to his sandy-hued tunic.

"I wish they understood. Perhaps they would not resent me so much. But someday they will see me for who I truly am, won't they, Abba?" Yeshua looked into Joseph's eyes.

"Yes they will. Many things come later, Yeshua. For instance, you asked God to use you to heal the crippled boy you saw in town the other day, but it did not happen because it is not yet your time. Everything happens for a purpose known only to God."

Yeshi's eyes filled with tears.

"I wanted to heal him, Abba, but I discerned it was not my time. My heart has been so heavy. My heavenly Av's heart breaks because the boy cannot walk, but the child's destiny is tied to eternal things. Only Abba knows the right moment."

The conversation had run its course.

Joseph and Yeshua began the final section of the top surface of the roof. This required sifting of a mixture of earth, ash, and chalk, followed by a four-inch application of a strong lime solution for waterproofing.[60]

A short time later, the task was finished.

Joseph, Yeshua, and Simon washed up and, at Ima's bidding, sat down for a much-anticipated evening meal with the family. Mary served cooked legumes with beets and aromatic spices, and dried and fresh fruit with fresh bread and honey. Mary presented Joseph and Yeshua with small bowls of cucumbers and almonds to acknowledge their work.

After the prayer of thanks, the family ate, but Yeshua asked for permission to rest. Joseph's eyes followed his son in concern as he slipped across the room, out the front door, and into the early evening twilight to sit in the presence of his heavenly Av.

Thirty-four
James Seeks Independence

Joseph bent over the oar, stroking the pumice stone with the grain. The transition of new wood to old was indiscernible. He hoped the fishermen on the Sea of Galilee would be pleased.

Joseph was proud of his work. Abba Jacob had taught him to do all to the glory of God, and Joseph strived to honor Yahweh in his vocation. Word had spread among the fishermen of his talent for working on boats and fishing equipment. He had tried to enlist James to learn his craft, along with Yeshua, but had received James's unexpected and rebellious refusal.

Joseph sighed as he brushed dust from the oar. A cloud rose and fell to the floor. His firstborn after Yeshua battled anyone in authority and resented family expectations. He disdained the family as too traditional and scorned rituals of worship. James finished beit sefer school and did well but was prone to truancy, wouldn't do homework, and often claimed illness to stay home. He longed for adventures at sea and was susceptible to bouts of moodiness, anger, and rage.

As soon as he completed elementary school, James announced, "I quit." He didn't want to be a carpenter or a farmer and didn't hesitate to disappoint or anger his abba.

James's disrespect angered Joseph, but he was also

saddened by his son's ingratitude and determination to pursue a faithless path.

Joseph had put off the dreaded conversation for months, but an opportunity came as James stuck his head through the workshop door.

"Ima said to tell you that midday meal will be a little late. She is accompanying Rebecca to the well for more water."

"James, come in. I'd like to talk to you."

Disdain flickered over James's face, but he entered and settled on one of the extra stools near his father, refusing to meet his gaze.

"James, what are you planning to do since you do not want to continue your education?"

James stared at the ground and muttered, "I am looking for adventure. I find excitement fishing on the Sea of Galilee, not in books, not in lectures from hypocritical rabbis, and not in stone and carpentry. I can read and write. I will seek my future as a fisherman."

Joseph had stopped his work to listen. "Go on."

"I seek the thrill of the raging sea during storms, navigating boats from shore to shore, and fishing the depths of the waters for living creatures. This is the life I want." His tone and bearing presented his choice as rebellion and a badge of honor.

A deep ache settled upon Joseph's chest. For a moment no words would come. His son's choice was rooted in anger and could not bear good fruit.

"James, I can support you choosing to become a fisherman, which is an honorable profession. I only wish you would wait until you reach majority age before you strike out on your own. You will be older—responsible for paying taxes and other adult duties—and mature enough to make the best choice for your life.

"A fisherman's life is hard and dangerous. But you will have to learn that on your own. Fishermen live hard lives—are you ready for that?"

Joseph warened, "Violent storms quickly transform the Sea of Galilee. Winds funnel through the Galilee hill country and stir up the waters. Violent winds come off the hills of the Batanea [Bashan] to the east. The winds become deadly for fishermen trapped on the sea, which nests in the basin."

James's face remained fixed and confident with teenage arrogance. "I understand what life at sea is all about."

Joseph almost laughed. James refused to listen.

The conversation came to a halt as James stood and walked out the door. Joseph did not follow but instead bowed his head.

I leave him in Your care, Yahweh. Please pursue him with Your love where I cannot go.

* * * * *

"A fisherman's life is hard and dangerous—are you ready?"

Abba's question had pounded through James's head since he had crept out of the house before the rest of the family had awakened. But despite his best efforts to be quiet during his secret departure, James failed. He spotted Yeshua standing at the corner of the house watching him as he disappeared down the road.

I have worked alongside Abba, and I can be tough and work hard. I will prove to him that I'm a man and can make my way in the world.

James headed for Tiberias on the Sea of Galilee to seek employment in the predawn darkness. The walk would take an entire day, and it was important that he leave early if he hoped to find fishermen along the shore before dusk fell. He made good time in the early morning hours, but by midday his calves were aching and his feet throbbing. He pressed on, driven by anger and pride.

The salty sea air called to him as he reached the outskirts of one of four of Judaism's four holy cities. But religion, faith, and God had become an annoyance. Adventure called, and despite aches and pains, he headed toward the seafaring boats that dotted the pier and the men tending their nets on the shore.

An elderly man walking the shore and chewing on a reed responded to James's question about employment and pointed toward a fisherman.

"His name is Simon, but people call him 'the big fisherman.' He hires extra help when the fish are running." The old man paused and sucked on his reed. "Be careful, he's always in a bad mood."

James was unsure about the warning. Should he be afraid? He decided not to think about it and headed in Simon's direction. The man was barking orders to other fishermen as he inspected several boats pulled on shore.

Spotting James, Simon approached, his brown mantle wet to the knees and clinging to his legs. His rounded nose and almond-hued squinting eyes set him apart from other Jewish fishermen.

"You looking for work, young man?"

James was hopeful.

"I am James ben Joseph, and yes, I am looking for work."

The man eyed him hard from head to foot.

"Do you have fishing experience?"

James paused as his mind raced.

"I am a willing learner and strong. The life of a fisherman is difficult, but I am willing to work and to learn."

Simon smiled.

Perhaps my enthusiasm convinced him I'm worth the risk.

"You have your abba's permission?" Simon narrowed his eyes.

"Yes, my father, Joseph the carpenter of Nazareth, has given permission."

Simon raised an eyebrow.

"Joseph the carpenter? We fishermen of Tiberias are pleased with his skills in boat repair. And you are his son? Then you have been taught how to work, and I am shorthanded. It appears we are a match."

James breathed a sigh of relief. Independence. Freedom. He had escaped. His new life was about to begin.

* * * * *

James was grateful for Simon's kindness. The fisherman was rough, humorless, and erratic, but his fellow workers respected him for his strong leadership and trusted loyalty. Simon began teaching him the secrets shared by fishermen. He seemed pleased with James's work ethic, and James quickly gained acceptance and respect among the fishermen.

Under Simon's tutelage James soon developed a reputation for exceptional skill and aptitude as a fisherman. The other men soon joined Simon in caring for James but did not hesitate to confront his rebellion. Fishing required cooperation and trust, and rebellion was regarded as both destructive and dangerous.

On one occasion, Simon confronted James about his disregard for instruction and his quick anger. James had responded with a roll of the eyes and a comment that he would do his job but that his personal life was his own business.

When Simon cut off the conversation, James assumed his boss had recognized his irritation. But for months after, James felt Simon's eyes watching him like an abba. His only choice was to ignore the scrutiny and do what he chose.

James quickly learned how to identify fish, find their favorite spots, and learn their spawning habits. His eagerness impressed the other fishermen, and they enjoyed teaching him.

James was growing into a young man, and women were drawn to his rugged features, sun-darkened skin, and amber-flecked eyes. The rigors of fishing had muscled his tall, lean body, and he soon learned that the power of his appearance on women, combined with his lonely, male-dominated life as a fisherman, magnified his fleshly desires. Temptation haunted him, and he never missed an opportunity to win young women's attention. He was acutely aware that Abba and Ima feared this very thing—that his fishing "adventure" was really about abandoning God and his family so he could pursue selfish pleasure.

And they were right.

But his parents were not aware that a question had pounded through James's mind relentlessly after he had left—a question that haunted him: Why did pleasure feel so pointless? And did life offer a greater purpose?

* * * * *

James worked hard not to complain as his body acclimated to punishing conditions, for instance, being drenched in cold seawater for hours at a time. The profitable tilapia and sardine fishing seasons took place in the dead of winter. But by the end of the first winter season, James was known for his courage for plunging into the freezing waters of the Sea of Galilee to free trammel nets stuck on the rocks or to retrieve fish.

He also learned not to complain when the men ran their nets during the night, emptied their catch on shore in the early hours of morning, then washed, mended, and hung their nets to dry at sunrise to prevent mildew or rot. The calluses on his hands grew thick, and he learned to subsist on brief naps snatched between endless tasks.

James thrived on challenges. The harder the work, the more he excelled: rowing, pulling in heavy nets, hauling in large catches, cast net diving under the cold water to untangle or retrieve nets. He became known for his knowledge of various species of catfish and sardines and the *musht* known for their long dorsal fin that looks like a comb.

James also learned to mend the varied kinds of nets. The seine, a type of dragnet with openings of various sizes that allowed certain sizes of fish to be trapped or escape, was the most difficult to mend. The large, heavy eight- to ten-man net measured 222 *pedes* long and 254 pedes wide.[61]

But James preferred mending smaller one-man circular cast nets. They were easy to mend unless the bars of lead attached to the edges needed redistribution or replacement.

With the seasons, the months passed. James seldom spoke of family to his friends. His occasional visits home felt awkward and painful, and he stopped going. The village of Tabgha, a fishing paradise, became his occasional refuge.

His bond with Simon grew stronger. James's reputation continued to grow in the fishing community around the Sea of Galilee, and beautiful women continued to find him attractive.

But no matter where he found himself, James no longer had a place he called home.

Thirty-five

Fish's Treasure

James's success as a fisherman came with complications. After several years at sea, he still did not own his boat and often had more work than he could manage. Overwhelmed, he reluctantly asked Abba Joseph and Yeshua to repair his oars and boat. He promised in return for their help to recommend their work to the fishing community. He retained a portion of the fee as a subcontractor, and they were pleased to gain additional steady work. Besides, the contact gave him an excuse to see Ima, whom he missed more than he would ever admit. He was painfully aware that she longed to see the family reunited, but James wasn't ready. However, working near Abba and Yeshua gave James the opportunity to show his maturity and success at his chosen vocation.

He was making his way in the world, but he showed no sign of willingness to follow his family's faith or legalistic restrictions as demanded by the law of Moses. He longed for a measure of grace, as well as justice.

On one occasion, he returned to Nazareth with a large barbel fish. Thinking it was a catfish, Ima swept it off her table and sent it skittering across the floor.

James reassured her that he would never bring an unclean catfish into their home. The fish was a barbel, he explained.

"Barbels are a species of the carp family. Carp species

are the largest fish in the sea, and of course you are aware that they are popular for Shabbat and festivals."

James glanced sideways to see if Yeshua was listening.

You've always been so smart and think you know everything. Well, it's my turn. You're not a fisherman, and you don't know everything about the sea. I have mastered the sea, Yeshua.

But Yeshua's steady gaze met James's glance. He stood near James—too close for comfort—and looked steadily into his eyes, a smile tugging at his lips.

What was that look? What was he thinking?

Angry, James forced his attention back to the fish and continued, "Barbels are one of the three species of the carp family and have barbs at the corners of their mouths. Fishermen must memorize hundreds of details about the fish in the sea to be successful."

Again, James glanced in Yeshua's direction, this time receiving an affirming nod and smile of approval that only irritated him more. But he'd saved the best for last. James asked family members to circle the table, where he'd placed the fish on a platter.

"I brought *this* fish because it's special. Yesterday I was hook fishing from a boat moored at Magdala, where I hooked this fish. Yeshua, open its mouth and look inside."

The family waited in anticipation as Yeshua pulled open the mouth of the barbel, reached inside, and pulled out a small, shiny object.

"It's a denarius!" Rebecca exclaimed. "A fish with money in its belly. How strange, and how exciting."

James stood tall, eager to make the most of the moment.

"These fish scavenge in the mud for food and often swallow foreign objects as they search the sea bottom. Evidently a swamped boat lost cargo that included coins, and the fish swallowed a coin. I caught this barbel while I was waiting for Simon and the other fishermen to return to shore with their catch."

The family expressed their delight and admiration. Yeshua turned to James and laid his hand on his arm. His eyes held the power of an arrow released from a Scythian composite bow. Immediately, James's stomach began to swirl at the sight of his brother's quiet confidence.

"You are a skilled fisherman, James. Thank you for sharing your love of the sea with us. What other things have you come to love since beginning your adventure?"

James felt as if he had been kicked in the stomach. The question was innocent on the surface, but did it carry an underlying message? He tried to maintain his smile and keep his eyes from narrowing, but he refused to answer.

Yeshua continued. "Thank you again for bringing the barbel and showing us the coin. Don't you also find that people often have something hidden inside? I'm sure this is as true with fishermen as it is with all humankind. Would you agree? The barbel was not created to live with a coin in its belly, which is deadly waste for a barbel. God created the coin for a different purpose."

James was overcome by a sudden urge to escape. He excused himself from the conversation, turned his back to Yeshua, kissed Ima, and fled out the back door.

Thirty-six
Kindred Spirits

Joseph slammed down his knife in frustration. Despite his efforts, the blade barely scored a mark in the finely polished wood he was trying to carve. The tool had barely survived its last sharpening, and the wooden handles were slipping on their metal axis. He had grown weary of inadequate equipment that made it difficult to produce acceptable-quality merchandise.

His tools were as important as the wood and stone he worked: knives and chisels for chipping and carving, adzes, saws to shave and carve furniture, and a bow lathe and plane to repair boats and nautical equipment. His carpentry skills were in ever-increasing demand. Sepphoris and Capernaum offered tool suppliers, but Jerusalem boasted the best specialty blacksmiths.

A trip to Jerusalem would kill two birds with one stone, Joseph mulled as he sorted through his tools to find a drawing knife still in good repair. The Torah required every male to attend Yom Kippur, soon to be celebrated in Jerusalem. He could see a blacksmith while he was there. Along with Yeshua who was familiar with the city, it was an excellent opportunity to fulfill his desire to introduce Jose and Simon to splendors of the Holy City.

The boys were delighted to learn that they would be staying with in Bethany with Miriam and Eleazar, whose son, Lazarus, would help entertain them. They had no interest in Miriam and Eleazar's daughters, Mary and Martha, who in turn had no interest in boyish games and preferred attending to household duties.

The trip to Jerusalem was uneventful, and soon after arrival Joseph found himself at a table in the kitchen, immersed in conversation with Miriam and Eleazar.

"Joseph, how is James? We have been told by friends he is no longer at home."

Miriam's brow knit in concern as she cut vegetables. Joseph told himself that his son's choices were his own, but guilt flooded his heart.

I didn't do enough. I wasn't firm enough. How can God trust me with Yeshua when I failed with James?

"James is fishing these days and is doing well in business, but we are concerned for his future. We would ask that you pray for him."

Joseph wanted to be positive yet truthful, and most of all, he wished to ask his friends for prayer for his son.

Eleazar spoke up. "We are honored to pray for James. It's a burden to a parent's heart when a child's feet takes them in directions we would not choose." Eleazar reached across the table and placed his hand on Joseph's arm.

Joseph continued with a report on his girls, and Miriam updated him on Mary and Martha.

"Martha has the spirit of serving and is a great help. Mary is compassionate in all her dealings with people. Both girls have great faith in God and want to serve Him."

Joseph smiled. "Miriam, I am pleased to hear this about your daughters. You are wonderful parents."

Eleazar redirected the conversation.

"Jerusalem continues to have outbursts of activity among the rebels. Soldiers here are preoccupied with fear of a Jewish king who will bring open rebellion."

Joseph sighed. He didn't want to talk about the rebellion in front of the boys, but he did answer his friend, who was concerned about growing tensions.

"Galilee is still a hotbed for the Zealots, but we have not observed many violent Sicarii, whose influences are much more alarming. Fortunately they are concentrated in Sepphoris, Magdala, and Capernaum. We aren't concerned for our children, but family can always become drawn in, and that worries us."

Joseph did not want to bring up Matthan's involvement, so he redirected the conversation. Everyone soon dined on porridge, fruits, and nuts at the table before preparing for bed. Eleazar had prepared a comfortable sleeping area for Joseph and the boys in the gathering room.

When time came to end the day and say *laila tov*, Eleazar turned to Joseph. Apparently, he had been holding back a question all evening.

"May I speak with you privately before you return to Nazareth?"

Joseph recognized the serious expression on Eleazar's face. The two had been close for many years, and his friend did not become easily concerned. Possibilities flashed through Joseph's mind.

"Ask anything. I will do whatever I can for you."

"You must be exhausted from the trip, but we'll speak soon."

Joseph agreed. Then he succumbed to his weariness and retired to his bed mat. Sleep had already overcome the children, but he tossed and turned, pondering Eleazar's request to talk with him privately and his serious tone.

He appears worried. Is there something he has not told me, perhaps news of Matthan?

Much later, Joseph fell into a restless sleep with Yom Kippur swirling in his head.

Thirty-seven
Yom Kippur Revelation

Joseph stood near the door in the gathering room, prodding the boys to hurry.

"The high priest will soon be at the east gate inspecting the cows, rams, and sheep. We do not want to miss Yom Kippur, my sons. Many pilgrims from throughout Israel have already trekked to the Holy City to offer their annual sin offering at the temple, and they will block our view if we do not hurry."

He continued with dramatic emphasis, "The high priest stayed awake all night to ensure he did not become defiled and disqualified from performing his tasks. Priests-in-waiting stood ready nearby to snap their fingers if the high priest appeared to be nodding off to sleep. How would you boys like that job!"

The boys shoved the last of Miriam's fresh barley bread into their mouths as they laughed. Abba often expressed humor.

"I want to see the priest's spectacular garments as he performs his duties," Jose piped up.

"I'm sorry to disappoint you, Jose. No one is allowed to observe the incense burning or the offering of the blood for atonement.[62] But we will see great pageantry and ceremony unlike anything you have seen in Nazareth."

Jose seemed satisfied with the answer and joined his brothers as they headed out the door for the journey to

Jerusalem over the Mount of Olives and down the Kidron Valley.

* * * * *

Joseph and his sons entered the city near the Siloam Pool in the southern section of walled Jerusalem. They passed through the lower city, where dwellings spread out before them in a tangle of narrow, crowded streets and ancient buildings.

The eerie quietness of the Holy City shocked him. Yom Kippur was unlike any other day of the year. No merchants hawked their goods, no farmers sold fruits and vegetables, no business was done. Only the sounds of shuffling of feet on the stone pavement and the occasional bleating of sheep or squawks of camels interrupted the stillness.

They paused at the steps leading to the plaza on the Temple Mount. Should they climb the huge stairs at the southwest corner of the mount or enter through the double gate? Joseph was thinking about how much he wouldn't enjoy the challenging climb when he spotted Mary's *dod* Joseph of Arimathea in his priestly garb. Beside him stood a pudgy young man, a neophyte priest. Joseph of Arimathea greeted Joseph.

"Joseph ben Jacob, this is my nephew Joseph ben Nebo, who is here to observe Yom Kippur to learn how to participate in the ceremony himself one day. He is from the priestly line of Levi and related to the royal family of Aristobulus. I must attend to duties. May he accompany you and your boys?"

Joseph knew Joseph of Arimathea had many duties. Anxiety lined his furrowed eyebrows. Joseph gladly absorbed the "young" Joseph into their group, and they continued on to the top of the daunting stairs.

The upper and lower city, the Hasmonean Palace, the council house, and the xystus—a covered portico of the gymnasium—presented a stunning view below. As they entered through the double-gate tunnel, they were awed by floral decorated walls and ceilings.

When they emerged, the magnificent Royal Stoa greeted them with rows of columns stretching the distance of the mount, supporting a long hallway. The site glittered in the golden rays of the dust-flecked morning sunlight.

"My classmates in Cyprus would never believe this," Joseph ben Nebo whispered.

As they walked, the young student peppered Joseph with questions. As an aspiring priest, he expressed concern about the Messiah's influence on God's plan for him as a priest.

"When the Messiah comes, will He offer sacrifices?"

"Will He address the corrupt temple priests?"

"How will the coming Messiah fit into the old covenant?"

"Will the Messiah not come if our people are disobedient?"

Joseph answered to the best of his ability. The young aspiring priest's questions showed he was well versed in the Holy Book.

Yahweh has a remnant who is seeking to be obedient to His Word and will accept the Messiah when He reveals Himself.

The group drew close to the *soreg*, a fenced area that prevented Gentiles and unclean Jews from entering the temple area. Limited space on the Temple Mount restricted many among the Jerusalem crowds from gaining a close-up view of Yom Kippur events. Everyone in the temple area wanted the extraordinary view, so pushing and shoving was the norm. The boys gripped one another's mantles tightly and pushed through the crowd to get close enough to see the ceremony and the high priest. Simon, who was leading, wiggled under arms and around hips without irritating the crowd. Before long, he let out a cry.

"There he is!"

Hands all over the crowd pointed to a figure in white.

The high priest was moving through the throng clad in

his morning attire. He had both morning and evening garments—a linen coat and linen breeches girded with a linen girdle and topped with a linen miter. All were made from white flax, designated as "white garments," and woven with six-ply thread.[63]

Yeshua was ecstatic to see the high priest's ephod, an apron-like vestment that was white in the back and fastened in front by a long belt. The front of his garment was set in a gold frame with an onyx stone at the top of each corner of the garment with the twelve tribes engraved on them.[64] Under the two onyx stones, gold chains fastened the breastplate to the garment. The Urim and the Thummin were placed within the framework of the breastplate, by which heavenly answers came to enable the high priest to make correct critical decisions.[65] Joseph was certain his earthly sons would never again see garments with such significance and splendor.

The crowd stood in silence as the high priest moved toward the sanctuary and the sacrificial animal. He placed his hands on the bullock's head between its horns, then made his confession.

"I beseech You, O Lord; I have sinned, rebelled, and transgressed against You, I and my household. I beseech You, O Lord, grant atonement for sins and for the iniquities and transgressions which I have committed against You ..."

Joseph leaned toward young Joseph's ear, but Yeshua spoke first. "The Messiah will be sinless and will not need to confess His sins. He is from a better priesthood than Aaron—after the order of Melchizedek.[66] His priesthood will last forever."

Joseph drew in a quick breath. *He already knows.*

Jose pointed his index finger toward a group of worshippers and whispered, "They seem to be confessing with the high priest's prayer of confession. Are they repenting too?"

"Yes, Jose. This is a spiritual ritual on behalf of all our people."

The high priest, accompanied by two men, moved to the eastern section of the court.

"One man is the high priest's stand-in, and the other is the head of the family clan responsible to serve at the temple this day. They are awaiting the lottery, God's method of deciding the part each will play in the ceremony.[67] One goat will be sacrificed, and the other, the scapegoat, will be sent into the wilderness."

Yeshua watched the wooden box holding the two lots. One was marked "For the Lord" and the other "For Azazel."

Joseph explained before one of the boys could ask: "'For Azazel' is named for the rocky precipice in the Judean wilderness where the goat will be sent."

A collective sigh of relief swept through the crowd when the high priest drew the lot. The goat had been chosen to pay the price for their sins for another year. As the high priest placed the designated lot on the head of each animal, with a united voice the people spoke: "Blessed be the name of His glorious kingdom, forever and ever."

The priest tied pieces of dyed crimson wool between the horns, then left the animals to attend to the rest of the ceremony. He returned later to the goats, continuing to offer the bullock as a confession for the priests. He slaughtered the bullock himself, collecting the blood in a *mizrak* vessel. Then he handed the vessel to another priest, who swirled it to prevent the blood from coagulating. The high priest then returned to the court.

He ascended to the top of the altar, carrying a long-handled golden incense spoon. Gathering burning coals from the fire, he scooped up incense with the golden spoon and disappeared behind the sanctuary curtain. The audience was forbidden to see the remaining part of the ritual.

"What is he doing now?" Simon was standing on his tiptoes, straining to see.

Yeshua bent down near his ear. "He is offering incense on the foundation stone in the holy of holies. The original ark of the covenant disappeared after the Babylonian conquest of Jerusalem, leaving the current holy of holies empty.[68] The ark rested on the foundation stone. The priest will set the coals and incense on the stone in the position where the poles of the original ark[69] would have been, and that will provide a smoke covering to protect the high priest while he offers the blood sacrifice. When the chamber completely fills with smoke, he will return to complete his duty."

As Yeshua finished his explanation, the high priest emerged from the holy place and walked toward the priest holding the blood of the bullock. He collected the vessel and returned to the holy of holies to place the blood on the foundation stone for the sacrifice for himself and the priests.

A priest brought the goat designated by lottery as "for the Lord" to the high priest, who slaughtered it and collected its blood in another mizrak vessel. Again, a third time, the high priest disappeared behind the temple curtain and offered the blood for the sins of the people. Following this portion of the ceremony, the two mizraks were mixed together and sprinkled on the horns of the altar[70] and on the western side of the outer altar's foundation.[71]

The boys were engrossed in the ceremony. Young Joseph from Cyprus stood transfixed, soaking in every detail. He fixed his eyes on the high priest heading for the eastern gate, where the scapegoat waited. There the priest placed his hands between the goat's horns and confessed the sins of the nation.

Abba Joseph, Yeshua, his brothers, and Joseph of Cyprus joined the congregation as they spoke in unison, "Blessed be the name of His glorious kingdom, forever and ever."

Joseph observed the boys' fascination as the goat was handed over to the designated person who would take the animal into the wilderness.

"At one time a series of booths were built along the way to provide food and drink in case the scapegoat's warden got tired or couldn't make the journey to the goat's predetermined location in the wilderness," he explained. "A man from each booth will accompany the priest to the next station and so on until a warden reaches his final destination with the scapegoat."

The younger Joseph sighed. "Maybe, perhaps someday, I will be the scapegoat's warden."

"Perhaps you will, Joseph ben Nebo." Joseph smiled.

The boy looked up into Joseph's face. "My good friends don't call me Joseph but by the second of my names given to me to honor a family friend. Call me Barnabas."

For the first time that he could remember, Joseph welcomed a new friend who already felt like one of the family.

Thirty-eight
Nuptials for Yeshua?

Returning to Eleazar and Miriam's house that night, Joseph directed the exhausted boys to bed. They lay down and were asleep almost before Joseph exited the door of the spare room. He was focused on Eleazar's request to talk.

Is he in some kind of trouble? Does he know of concerning political matters? Could Miriam be sick?

He entered the gathering room, where Eleazar and Miriam sat side by side on goatskin chairs talking in low tones. Joseph chose a trunk across the room and sat.

"I have to admit, I'm nervous. You sounded serious when you asked to talk, Eleazar." Joseph ran his hand up and down his arm self-consciously.

Eleazar laughed. "Something serious but good. I wanted to suggest a betrothal between our Martha and your Yeshua."[72]

Although Eleazar's opening statement stunned Joseph, he released his breath. A betrothal discussion was not life-or-death.

Eleazar went on, "They have much in common and enjoy each other's company. Martha is a hard worker, is strong, and can give us many grandchildren." He breathed a deep sigh and waited for Joseph's response.

Joseph read the apprehension on his friend's face. Marriage proposals had strict protocols. Joseph and Eleazar both were aware of Jewish marriage customs. Shiddukhin arrangements would be made preliminary to the legal betrothal. As a bride, Martha would have little voice in decisions. As was custom among Jewish parents, the father of the groom selects the bride for his son. Next would come the written agreement, or the ketubah, which would include the provisions of the marriage proposal. Yeshua would agree to support Martha with a dowry of money and property (mohar), and Mary would stipulate the mohar. The groom would pay the bridal price to the bride's family. The bride would then be released from her family's household and become her husband's responsibility.

Joseph froze.

The silence was uncomfortable, almost palpable. Both men bowed their heads over their clasped hands. Miriam stared at the embroidered curtain that separated the gathering room from the guest chamber. Eleazar broke the silence.

"Joseph," he said, his tone respectful, "I hope my broaching the subject has not offended you. We have always been friends."

Joseph tried to mask his shock at Eleazar's request, not at its impropriety but at its unexpected nature.

He took a deep breath. "Dear brother, you are free to speak honestly with me. We have been friends for years, and I respect your family and have the greatest admiration for you. I think Martha would make a wonderful wife and ima. But Yeshua is a special child of God, and obedience must take precedence over personal needs."

Joseph struggled to find gracious words. The groom's father chose the bride, and Joseph did not want Eleazar to think Martha was not an acceptable match. But he and Mary had never thought about Yeshua marrying, nor had they ever asked him if he desired to wed.

Before Joseph could speak, Eleazar spoke a second time.

"Joseph, I understand. It was only a question. There is no pressure. Yeshua is a special child. Mary has told Miriam the details of Yeshua's divine conception. Let's say no more.

We will be good family friends all the days of our lives. Mary, Martha, and Lazarus admire Yeshua and his brothers and sisters. We don't want to change that. Think no more of it with our blessing."

Joseph felt a wave of relief. Eleazar appeared to understand. Yeshua was focused on becoming a rabbi/teacher. Training meant many years of intense study. Local rabbis taught young students of the law in Hebrew schools for their early training, followed by advanced studies in Jerusalem, where the finest teachers taught. Their life required long periods away from home during and after their education. Men of the sacred shawl married much later than the usual eighteen to twenty years of age—often late into their twenties or thirties.

It would be unfair for young, beautiful Martha to wait that long—even if Yeshua wanted to marry. I don't think marriage is in the plans for Yeshua—at least he has never discussed it with us.

The conversation ended with the lateness of the evening.

The next morning Joseph and the boys purchased the needed carpentry tools and had Abba's saws and axes sharpened. That afternoon they set out for Nazareth. But Joseph carried more than a profound sense of worship and new tools. A question burned in his heart.

Is Yahweh best served if Yeshua marries or remains single? Please, heavenly Av, give us wisdom, and show us Your will above our own.

Thirty-nine
Yeshua Speaks on Marriage

Eleazar's question set Joseph's mind reeling and preoccupied his thoughts. He'd never thought about whether or not Yeshua would take a bride. Yeshua's confluence of humanity and divinity confounded him, and he had chosen to defer the question. Joseph had never spoken about marriage to Yeshi, but the time had seemingly come.

The evening meal was over on their third night home, and the younger children were playing a game around the kitchen table. Yeshua had settled in the gathering room to meditate, the fringe from his tallit brushing the tops of his feet as he sat with his head bowed in a leather lattice-woven chair. Ima Mary sat adjacent to him at the spinning wheel.[73]

Yeshua was reading scripture, part of a morning and evening routine he had begun several years before. Joseph watched him in silence from the kitchen.

He won't be ours much longer. The time has passed too quickly.

A pang struck his heart. Was Yahweh pleased with what the young man Yeshua had become? What lay ahead for him? Joseph forced himself to focus on the moment and trust God for the future. He headed for the gathering room and chose a seat facing Yeshua.

"Forgive me for interrupting your prayers, Son, but I need to speak to you."

Yeshua looked up. "Yes, Abba?"

Joseph's heart warmed at the word *Abba*. He often sensed distance between himself and Yeshua—not because of lack of affection or communication, but because of Yeshua's unidentifiable sense of "otherness." He was growing more introspective with each passing day.

Joseph took a breath and plunged in.

"Yeshua, Eleazar asked me to offer betrothal between his daughter Martha and you. Ima Mary and I have never talked to you about marriage. I told Eleazar that your mission took precedence over marriage, but you must speak for yourself. Martha would be a wonderful wife, *if* you are seeking a bride."

Yeshua hesitated, and a wave of insufficiency swept over Joseph. What advice had he to offer God's Son on marriage? Yet Yeshua always treated his words with great respect and seemed to value his opinions.

"Abba, thank you for considering my opinion. Make no mistake, I enjoy being with girls. I appreciate and admire their beauty, wisdom, creativity, and strength and take joy in them as marvels of God's creation. I enjoy conversation with several female friends. But getting married and having a family is a different question altogether."

Jewish law warned young men about lust. The sin of adultery and sex outside of marriage was so repulsive to God that Joseph had feared talking to Yeshua about it.

Yeshua paused, as if collecting his thoughts.

"Jewish men are expected to marry and have families—and God blesses marriage. But the central issue for me is this: would my ministry be more or less effective if I had a wife and family?"

The question had never crossed Joseph's mind, but he replied with a Jewish proverb: "It is good for a man *not to have sexual relations with a woman*. But since sexual immorality occurs, each man should have sexual relations with his wife, and each woman with her husband."

Joseph's response stirred a thought. *If Yeshua doesn't*

marry, will he be sexually tempted as other men? Is he saying he should marry or should not marry?

Yeshua smiled confidently and replied, "The problem is the same with all humans. Those who marry do not commit sin when they express love to their spouses, but God forbids sex outside of marriage for many reasons. I must consider what Jewish men and women would think an acceptable choice for a rabbi, but more importantly, I must consider what would further my mission."

Yeshua had spoken with wisdom. Joseph was relieved that his son had pondered the issue.

"To the unmarried and the widows, God would say it is well for them to remain single. Younger women should remarry to raise a family. But if they can't control themselves, they should go ahead and marry, for it's better to marry than to burn with lust."[74]

Yeshua continued, "If a man remains single, he is free to serve God. A married man must care for his wife, thus dividing his attention and priorities."[75]

Yeshi laid his hand on Joseph's arm. "I have no intention of marrying, but I want to consider your concerns. Grandchildren are a sign of blessing for a Jewish abba, but grandchildren will come from your other children—not from my loins."

Joseph understood. Yeshua's ministry must come first.

"And what kind of children would I have if I married? I was not conceived by a human male but from Ima and the Holy Spirit. Would my children be god-men or god-women or normal human beings? Would they be like the Nephilim, offspring of the 'sons of god' and the 'daughters of men' before the deluge as recorded in Hebrew scriptures? No, Abba, I will not marry—but I also will not sin. Although I am tempted like all men, sin is not in my nature."

Joseph forced himself to speak, although he was stunned. "Thank you, Son, for your wisdom. I will not seek a wife for you."

Joseph felt relief that the discussion was over, but Yeshi's words had brought clarity to his unique nature as both human and divine, the God-man.

Again, Joseph's mind flooded with questions.

The God-man. Surely Roman authorities would want to kill a Jew who claimed God's authority and power.

Fresh fear gripped Joseph's heart. How could he keep Yeshua safe from the power of Rome? Was it even his job to try? He stared as Yeshi, like in appearance to other men, pulling his tallit back into place as he returned to his prayers.

But Joseph's eyes fixed on one obscure detail—the tassels of Yeshua's tallit brushing the surface of the floor, the white threads gathering traces of dirt and specks of debris, the sacred now soiled. Memories of the Passover flashed before Joseph's eyes and the sight of a blood-drenched lamb upon the altar, and he left the room for the solitude of his workshop.

Forty

Carpenter Yeshua Practices His Craft

Zebedee shaded his eyes from the rising sun as he peered into the distance, his green mantle flapping in the cool sea breeze. Zebedee gained his reputation as an expert in use of the trammel net, a three-“wall” compound net with three layers held together by a single corked head rope and a single-headed foot rope. The three layers with varying meshes enable the fisherman to catch different sizes of fish. James and John, Zebedee’s sons, often mended nets while in the boats. An unseaworthy boat meant delays in fishing and men out of work.

Still no sign of Joseph.

The carpenter had always done exceptional work and delivered on time, and Zebedee hoped this wouldn’t be his first disappointment. But the thought had barely crossed his mind when a familiar figure appeared striding down the beach, a shorter figure at his side.

Perhaps he has brought the enigmatic son so popular among gossips.

Zebedee had little patience for gossips and idle talk, among his crew or with anyone. He ran through his list of questions once again. This job was important, and he did not have the funds to pay for it twice or even to pay a boatwright to do it the first time. The carpenter would have to do, and do it well.

A moment later Joseph and what appeared to be his eldest son called out to him as they neared. Zebedee's lips tightened.

"Shalom, Joseph. I see you are not alone. Is this Yeshua, your son?"

Joseph smiled through his slightly graying beard. Joseph was Zebedee's brother-in-law, but this visit was strictly business.

"Shalom. Yes, I have brought my eldest son Yeshua, a skilled carpenter and well trained ..."

With a fling of his hand, Zebedee cut Joseph off.

"Yes, I'm sure he's well trained, but this is a job for a boatwright. This ship carries men with families and maintains their livelihood. Repairs must be meticulous and of the highest quality. I cannot have your son learning on the job—too much is at risk."

Joseph tried to speak, but Zebedee shook his head in protest.

"Joseph, you have done much work on our boats here in Magdala, and I trust your work, even though most of your work has been building in Sepphoris. You are skilled and you have proven yourself, but I know nothing of your son, my nephew." Zebedee crossed his arms with finality.

Joseph paused, then smiled.

"I promised that you would receive the best work at the best price, Zebedee. I am a man of my word. This is why I am leaving you in the capable hands of Yeshua and will return later tonight. Trust me and allow him to repair the hull of your boat. His skill has bypassed my own."

Zebedee scrutinized Yeshua from head to toe as the young man stood silently at his father's side, his eyes drinking in the sight of fishermen off-loading a catch on shore. He appeared unaware of Zebedee's concerns.

Joseph has always delivered what he has promised, and his son is rumored to be gifted.

Zebedee addressed Yeshua, his voice stern. "Your father's reputation for excellence at a fair price is known among the fishermen, including my sons, John and James. Your abba has also done work for Simon, the big fisherman, who speaks highly of him. Do you think you can do this job, Yeshua?"

Yeshua smiled politely. "Fishermen live hard lives. They pay punishing taxes, are separated from family, and withstand violent storms and grueling weather. I do my work to the glory of Yahweh—with all my heart, soul, and mind. Yes, I am ready. My abba has trained me well."

Joseph gripped Yeshua's hand, then turned and strode toward the streets of Magdala.

Zebedee nodded. "I guess you should get to work, then. Let me show you the boat."

Yeshua followed him across the beach until Zebedee approached his battered boat drawn on shore near a pier that extended a few *graduum* into the sea. The pier was shared by local fishermen who worked together to maintain it. Several other boats in varying states of disrepair were tied to the pier. Zebedee stepped into his boat.

"Let me show you what needs to be done."

Yeshua got in behind him and dropped to his knees. He crawled from bow to stern, examining every board, running his hands over the grain, and probing for rot. Zebedee had not expected such a meticulous inspection.

"We have made many repairs ourselves, but they never last long and make the problem worse. The boat took on so much water last week during a storm that we nearly swamped. We would have lost everything."

Yeshua stood and met Zebedee's gaze. There was something arresting about the young man. His features were not remarkable, but his eyes conveyed a serenity, peace, and kindness that overwhelmed Zebedee's spirit. He found himself hoping the young man would take the job, no matter the cost.

"I can complete the work," Yeshua assured him. "The boat needs major repairs that will require special materials. I am not a boatwright, but I can make it seaworthy for you and finish the job today if I can secure the right materials."

Zebedee did not want to doubt Yeshua's word. The boat must be made seaworthy quickly. Every day they did not fish, he and his men lost income. Fishing from shore was not profitable enough.

Zebedee discerned that the young man was calculating needed materials and planning his strategy. He was also aware that wood was scarce because of Herod Antipas's building projects in Sepphoris and Tiberias. Imported cedarwood would be out of the question, but perhaps a local wood could serve as a substitute.

Yeshua glanced toward Zebedee. "Do you have scrap wood I could use? I can save you money if I can use leftover materials and just purchase a few planks."

A craftsman who's looking out for me? He could have used a lack of materials as an excuse to raise the price.

"Yes, I think we do." Zebedee turned to John, who was waiting for instructions from his father. "Go to the pier storage shed and bring any quality scraps you can find."

Moments later, John returned, his arms filled with pieces of scrap wood, some taken from other boats, some that had washed ashore, some salvaged from the city. Wood was a treasured commodity among fishermen.

The boat had been Zebedee's for more than ten years. The original construction consisted of Lebanese cedar in the hull with oak framing. Many of the iron nails had rusted and were failing to hold the boards in place. Faded red splotched the hull, originally applied to prevent rot. Many of the replacement timbers had been made from soft wood from local trees and had badly decayed.

After an extended assessment, Yeshua spoke. "I can do this." His voice was confident.

Zebedee was reassured, although he wasn't certain why. *Certainty* did not guarantee skill. But this young man looked at the boat and its scars and imperfections as if he had designed it and understood how to make it whole again.

Zebedee sighed in relief. "Maybe your abba was right about you."

Yeshua smiled.

"It will help if you can send someone to Capernaum to fetch a few Aleppo pine planks and some local cypress wood. The softer pine won't be as good as imported Lebanese cedar used in the boat's original construction, but it will get the job done. The cedars have all been designated for Herod's building projects."

"Yes, Sepphoris gets the best of everything, but I think we can get a good price on pine at the Capernaum Works Exchange."

"My abba visits that shop often. The owner has a thriving business and a reputation for fairness and honesty."

Zebedee appreciated Yeshua's interest in doing business with shop owners of integrity. Shop owners often tried to take advantage of fishermen, thinking the latter uneducated and ill-reputable. Yeshua apparently held no such prejudices, even though his brother had turned to fishing as a rejection of his family and faith.

Zebedee dispatched John to purchase the needed wood, and Yeshua set to work organizing tools and preparing the boat: identifying areas of needed repair, scraping and digging away rotted wood, preparing resins, sharpening planes and adzes, and scraping and shaving the wood smooth. By early afternoon, John had returned with the needed wood.

Yeshua worked late into the afternoon and finished up as light was fading. Zebedee had watched from a distance but had waited to assess the final repairs once Yeshua had finished. The moment had come. Yeshua called him from his net mending, and he trudged through the sand to inspect the boat.

Yeshua had saved the older cypress planks for their strength but had cut away all rot and reinforced the cypress with new wood, using wooden plugs to join them. The quality of the work was evident, and Zebedee was impressed.

The young carpenter had repaired each flaw, weakness, and breach whether it had been visible or invisible to the eye. He used every piece of scrap wood available to him.

No wonder fishermen had been passing by to watch Yeshua work.

Zebedee observed that Yeshua had used jujube wood from a sidder tree on the aft part of the keel.

How did he know that sidder grows to such great sizes that it is uniquely suitable for construction of a keel? Where would he have gained such knowledge?

He had also shaped dozens of small, precisely shaped mortise fitting pegs that slid into matching holes to form strong joints. Finally, he had surfaced the entire boat with pine resin to ensure both a watertight exterior and interior.

Twilight was breaking as Yeshua applied the last brushes of resin at the base of the boom and double-checked the mast as Zebedee waited, amazed at the end of the pier. How could such an excellent job have been completed so quickly? He barely recognized his boat—it looked brand new.

Yeshua approached him, a smile on his face as he rubbed resin from his fingers.

"It is finished."

No pride, nothing to prove, as if he were unaware of the amazing thing he had done, Zebedee observed.

"Yeshua, you realize you have done an outstanding job, an unbelievable job. Your abba must be proud of you! I'm not sure I can pay you for the quality of the work you have done and the skills you possess. What do I owe you?"

Yeshua smiled. "I'm glad you are pleased. My work honors my abba. I owe my skills and training to him."

Zebedee pressed for an answer to his question.

"But what do I owe you and your father, Yeshua?" Zebedee recognized that his livelihood had been restored—the greatest gift he could imagine. As a man of character, he must pay, at least whatever he was able.

Yeshua smiled a captivating smile. "Zebedee, I cannot and will not put a price on my work. My abba trusted this work to my hands, and it is my gift to you. I only ask that you tell others about what you have seen and what you know of the work I do for my father as his representative. It will bring him great honor and bring me great joy."

Zebedee was mystified. He could not fathom such a gift given so freely. *Who is this nephew of mine, this Yeshua? What are his motives? And how could such seeming greatness reside in the son of a mere carpenter?*

Act 3

Emergence: Self-Awareness (ca. AD 15–25)

(Hebrew Calendar ca. 3776–3786)

Forty-one

Dangers in the Fox's Den

Joseph hadn't slept in days. Telling Mary his concerns would only make her fearful in spite of her faith. He wouldn't place his worries upon her, but the time had come to take Yeshua into his confidence and speak with him as an adult son.

Joseph chose a rainy afternoon when work in the shop was slow. He turned to Yeshua and asked him to put down the yoke he was mending so they could talk. They faced one another, sitting on tool crates as the pounding rain thudded on the roof and the scent of wood shavings rose from the damp floor.

Yeshua was growing into manhood. He stood nearly as tall as Joseph, and his body was muscled from physical labor. But his eyes often made Joseph want to weep—an uncomfortable sentiment Joseph had long since tried to understand.

"Times are challenging, Yeshua. We must talk about the future and how we will continue to provide for the family. You will soon leave your work as a carpenter to become a teacher."

Yeshua nodded, his brow knitted in concern. "Abba, I will do all I can to help care for the family and you and Ima. Always."

Joseph swallowed. He was no longer in the prime of life,

and more than once he had decided not to tell Mary about the pain that sometimes left him breathless.

"I've given thought to doing more work in Sepphoris. As it is Herod's capital city, designed to be rebuilt in stone by Herod Antipas, we could easily find work. With our special stone-carving skills, we would earn a good, steady income for the family."

"Yes," Yeshua interjected, "but Sepphoris also comes with all the entrapments of a major city—crowding, crime, corruption, high taxes, and religious and political infighting, not to mention the constant presence of Herod Antipas's soldiers."

Joseph was grateful for Yeshua's insight and delighted that his son had no interest in the lure of the large merchandise center near Nazareth.

How does he discern so much about city life when he has not experienced it? He speaks as if he has lived there.

"Your excellent work for Zebedee has made us popular among the fishermen of Magdala. And we may eat tilapia for a long time if Zebedee keeps bringing us fish."

Yeshua laughed. "The fish have been a welcome gift to the family."

Jacob lowered his head and scooped up a pile of wood shavings. "Making a living for a large family in Nazareth is difficult. Profitable trades are not in abundance here, but neither are the prying eyes of Herod's guards and informants as they search for the rival king Herod believes threatens his rule. The man is paranoid. He never believed the child died in the Bethlehem massacre ordered by his father."

Joseph looked into Yeshua's eyes. "We have always tried to protect you, Yeshua. Soon we will no longer be able to. You will step out of our home and into your ministry here on earth. We will still be your family, but it will not be the same."

Yeshua looked out the door at the rain, as if watching for someone to come.

"You are right, Abba. There are no words to thank you for what you and Ima have done for me, but one day you will understand. Yahweh Himself will tell you. Whatever happens, trust Yahweh to be fulfilling His plan through me. And trust me to speak for Him."

Joseph's heart skipped a beat.

I am looking this moment into the eyes of Yahweh, who was made flesh and came to earth as a man. Dare I think that I am fit to speak with Deity? But isn't that what Mary and I have done since the moment Yeshi breathed his first breath? Yes, but hearing Yeshua speak on behalf of Yahweh is a jolting reality that all is being fulfilled.

The air went out of Joseph's chest, and an overpowering awe pressed him to his knees.

Yeshua's breath brushed his face as he leaned forward. "Abba, do not be afraid. My time has not yet come. I will always be Yeshi, your son. Nazareth provided a great home for me. You and Ima wisely brought me here to protect me. You have given me a valuable trade, taught me the honor of toiling to serve others, and protected me from restless rebels who draw the attention of authorities. Abba, you have loved me well."

The gentle pressure of Yeshua's hand fell upon Joseph's shoulder, and he lifted his head. "Most of all, Abba, you taught me to do all to glorify my heavenly Av as my one true joy. That is your legacy as I move into my mission."

A quiet peace settled in Joseph's spirit. His every decision in raising Yeshua had been to honor, obey, and please Yahweh. If he succeeded in this, he had done well. For now, the family would work in Nazareth, Magdala, and Capernaum. Herod's royal cities of Tiberias and Sepphoris presented too much danger and could wait.

Yeshua had attained the age of majority and was legally an adult with all the legal rights of religious participation, property ownership, and tax responsibilities. His mind and personality had nearly reached its pinnacle.

And he was subject to Herod's laws, Herod's tyrannical obsession, and prosecution under the law.

Forty-two
Yeshua's Career Change

Joseph leaned back and let the evening sounds of the compound wash over him. A cool breeze riffled through his hair as he sat beneath the awning on the roof of their home. He had just returned home after completing a job at Magdala, and his services had been requested on another site there. Simon and Jose had quickly learned stonecutting skills under his tutelage, and their services were in increasing demand. And Yeshua's quality work in the carpentry shop was beyond successful. As a father, Joseph couldn't be prouder or happier.

Footfalls padded softly behind him and turned to see Yeshua coming up the stairs. He directed him to a fabric-strapped chair beside him.

Yeshua sat, placed his elbows on his knees, and looked Joseph in the eye.

"Abba, yesterday two men came to speak with me. They were elders from the city and local synagogue in Nazareth and surrounding villages, Levi the Galilean and Nahum ben Hophni. They were most gracious."

Joseph silently groaned.

Oh no. Are they unhappy with work Yeshua or I have done for them? Did one of the children get in trouble while I was gone?

Yeshua continued. "They told me that my knowledge of scripture is known in the region and asked me to teach beit sefer for boys living in Nazareth and Lower Galilee. They would combine students from the villages and hold classes in the synagogue and at various sites around the area. I would teach, which I love, and be close to family, yet still far from the eyes of Herod Antipas. Your thoughts, Abba?"

Joseph fingered his beard. Yeshua's question was unexpected although anticipated. He and Mary understood that Yeshua could not remain living with them forever. This situation would allow him to teach and receive lodging as an itinerant rabbi, and he could still help in the business and be with family as time permitted. It seemed an ideal situation.

After a long pause, Joseph spoke. "Yeshua, what is in your heart?" He searched his son's face, knowing Yeshua's desires would mirror his heavenly Av's heart.

"I would like to teach children about their heavenly Av's great love for them. They will one day lead our people, and they will lead in righteousness if they know and love Av."

A breeze stirred the branches in the awning.

"Of course I give my consent, Yeshua. Your ima and I have seen your passion for teaching. Perhaps this is the time to give more responsibilities to Simon and Jose. They have already learned much on our projects in Sepphoris."

Yeshua nodded. "Simon has spent a great deal of time with me in the workshop, and he has grown skilled at woodworking for his age. He knows the fishermen who come to us and how to calculate fair pricing. I have done my best to teach Simon, and I will still have time to train him."

Joseph sighed. "Yes, I am pleased with all the boys have been learning, and I, too, have known this day was coming. Your ima and I want what is best for you, Yeshua. The family business cannot come first."

They sat together in silence, the sounds of life in the apartment compound below drifting on the wind.

Together, Joseph and Yeshua came to an agreement. Simon and Jose would take on greater responsibilities in the business, and Yeshua would begin teaching beit sefer. With one mind, they returned to the house, where Mary had prepared fresh bread and sweet wine.

But fear still lingered in Joseph's mind. Traveling to the hamlets scattered around Lower Galilee and becoming known outside of Nazareth would put Yeshua at even greater risk for being discovered by Herod's soldiers.

* * * * *

Days later, Joseph sent Yeshua to Tabgha, a fishing village known for its hot springs and winter musht, to carve replacement boards for a fisherman's boat. Yeshua's skills had become known among Magdala fishermen, and sending him to Tabgha—a fishing haven—would draw in new business.

At the same time, Joseph traveled to Sepphoris to begin construction of a gymnasium designed after Jerusalem's gymnasium. Jose accompanied him to hone his skills in stonework, and Simon remained home to oversee the carpentry workshop. Plentiful work meant increased income for the family.

Joseph was proud of his family, content with life, and grateful for Yahweh's goodness. He considered their most recent child, Judas, named after the famous Jewish hero, as Yahweh's special gift. Releasing Yeshua into the adult world was proving more difficult than Joseph thought. The delight of young Jude running around the house would help keep his mind off his concerns for Yeshua. But the reality remained that Herod Antipas was still searching for the rumored child-king who had grown into adulthood.

But once Yeshua begins teaching, word will spread about his profound wisdom and unconventional teaching, and it will only be a matter of time before rumors reach Roman authorities.

Forty-three

Rabbi Yeshua in the Flower of Galilee

The pace of life had changed. The children of Galilee were receiving exceptional instruction under Yeshua, and Joseph relished Yeshi's visits and stories about his hungry learners. Yeshua's itinerant teaching position brought added income to the family and still allowed him to develop skills as a mason and carpenter.

As time passed, and in spite of danger, Yeshua became involved in carpentry jobs Joseph had contracted to rebuild Sepphoris. When Yeshua was in the city, he often visited the newly constructed theater, which was in full operation. Joseph often observed him drinking in the movements, actions, and oratorical skills of actors. The men projected their voices at great distances, in spite of noisy crowds. Yeshua also studied the structure of their dialogues—the cadence, poetic expressions, and melodic phrases.[76]

Yeshua lived in two different worlds, that of a carpenter and that of a teacher, enjoying and excelling in both roles. His carpentry and masonry were flawless, and his students were enthralled with his exciting, challenging lessons. Discipline problems were nonexistent in his classes. Like all rabbis, Yeshua was closely scrutinized, but parents could find little to criticize.

On several occasions Yeshua's old acquaintance Simeon

ben Hillel traveled to Nazareth as an itinerant lecturer. Yeshua invited him to teach so his students could hear a well-respected scholarly rabbi interpret the Torah. However, the rabbi's teachings always disappointed Yeshua, he told Abba Joseph. Rabbi Hillel's teachings focused on interpreting the Torah and neglected the Writings and Prophets.

The rabbis interpreted the laws in the Torah so literally and applied them so strictly that they often compromised integrity and defied common sense. To aid their interpretation of the law, Jewish sages added oral tradition. To guarantee the law was not violated, they placed a "fence around the Torah." The "fence" included added laws to hedge against violation of the written laws. These rigid, oppressive laws extended far beyond the intent of the written law. Adherence to these nonscriptural, legalistic laws were often used to measure an individual's spirituality. Competition developed about the degree to which observant Jews followed oral traditions to the letter. Yeshua's teaching drew a sharp distinction between prideful Jewish legalism about minutiae and observing God's intent for the commands with a pure heart.

Yeshua and Simeon's son Gamaliel had become friends—at least respectful of each other. But Yeshua feared that Gamaliel's interpretation of the law, learned from his father, Simeon, distorted the law's intended meaning.

In contrast, Yeshua used unique teaching methods, incorporated illustrative stories, and used only biblical sources.

In the spring, Joseph took a day off from his duties at Sepphoris to visit one of Yeshua's unique classes. He followed students and Yeshua out of their small classroom to a hill outside Nazareth. When they reached the top, Joseph sat down among the students on a knoll arrayed with wildflowers—lilies of the field, poppies, and daisies, along with spring grass, on the site locally known as Flower Mound, overlooking the sprawling valley below. The majesty of Mount Tabor rose above the hills behind them, and the Sea of Galilee glistened before them on the distant horizon.

No wonder Nazareth is called "the flower of Galilee." The beauty here is breathtaking.

Joseph's heart resounded with praise.

Yeshua, who was standing a short distance away, lifted his head and hands to heaven.

"How the flowers of the field grow. They do not labor or spin. Yet not even Solomon in all his splendor was dressed like these. As my heavenly Av clothes the grass of the field, which is here today and tomorrow is thrown into the fire, will he not much more clothe the people of Galilee? They must have faith."[77]

A small group of student fathers had followed to listen. A father stood and interrupted Yeshua.

"Master teacher," he said, "we appreciate your instruction of our children."

Joseph sensed there was more to the man's comment as Yeshua politely acknowledged the abba's statement.

"Thank you. I hope the Word of God penetrates their hearts."

Yeshua, this abba is like a man with a knife to a lamb's throat! Beware!

Yeshua smiled.

The man cleared his voice and continued. "We have followed Yahweh all our lives and observe the law. Nevertheless, our children tell us that you teach a different interpretation of the Ten Commandments. That contradicts the rabbis' teaching." He paused, waiting for a response. Yeshua remained silent and composed.

The Ten Commandments are sacrosanct to faithful Jews, and contradicting a rabbi borders on heresy. He is baiting Yeshua! Be careful how you answer, my son.

The man continued, and other fathers chimed in with support.

"The second commandment, 'You shall not murder,' is

interpreted by Rabbi Simeon ben Hillel to refer strictly to one who commits premeditated murder. My son said you have expanded on the interpretation of the commandment. Explain to us what you meant."

Emboldened, the group nodded in agreement.

Joseph held his breath as Yeshua responded. "It is good that you are devoted to obeying God's commands. I assure you that your children possess a keen desire to learn scripture. My commitment is to teach them the truth of God's Word, no more and no less.

"I know the rabbis and Hillel say, 'Do not murder, for the offender will be subject to judgment.' But the commandment goes beyond forbidding murder to speaking to the *intent* of the law. Anyone so angry with his brother that he *desires* to commit murder will be subject to that judgment."

Joseph watched the fathers' responses. Their expressions told him they had misread Yeshua's calm demeanor and had expected timidity. His passionate conviction inflamed them, as well as his refusal to respond with bluster and arrogance, like most rabbis who spewed arguments like camel's vomit. They had hoped to provoke him and had failed.

A second parent fired a follow-up question. His tone displayed his insincerity. "Then what *shall* we do to inherit eternal life?" he sneered.

Despite the public show of disrespect, Yeshua replied sincerely, "Keeping the commandments does not bring eternal life." He looked the inquirer in the eye. "Love the Lord your God with all your heart and with all your soul and with all your strength and with all your mind, and love your neighbor as yourself."

Heads turned and some men gasped, but they were obviously mystified by Yeshua's response. Joseph didn't know whether to laugh or grieve.

"Who is our neighbor?" someone called out.

They believe following laws is the same as loving God.

Loving God by loving and serving others is unfathomable to them.

"What does that have to do with anything?" another man muttered.

Yeshua responded with a story Joseph had told him on a trip to Jerusalem when he was twelve about a kind Samaritan. Joseph smiled, recalling the memory of the day.

"Who acted as the 'neighbor' in that story?" Yeshua asked.

"Obviously, the Samaritan who showed mercy was the neighbor in the story," a father in the front of the crowd answered. "I think I now understand."

The protesting abbas turned to one another, whispered, nodded in agreement, and then dispersed. The men trailed off into the distance, and Yeshua returned to instructing the boys, who sat in rapt attention at his feet. Joseph listened to his son with the heart of a student, eager to learn.

A short time later the two men walked side by side down the Flower Mound, the boys trailing behind them like ants. When the children were dismissed to return home, Joseph and Yeshua began the walk home at a rapid pace, hoping to arrive before sunset.

But soon Yeshua lagged. Joseph slowed his steps, but Yeshi struggled for breath.

"My head hurts, Abba, as if a hammer is pounding inside."

Joseph was instantly concerned. Yeshua had seldom been sick as a child, and he had never expressed extreme pain. Had he stood too long in the sun while he was teaching, while students and parents had sat in the shade of a tree? Had the walk in the extreme heat made him ill? Even the strongest of men succumbed to the Galilean sun.

Yeshua moaned, staggered, and reached for Joseph's arm. Joseph removed his girdle, moistened it with water from the skin that hung from his waist, and wrapped it around Yeshua's head.

He is a man, Yahweh, and I no longer have the strength to carry him. If he cannot walk, I cannot get him home. Please, send help. I don't know what to do.

At that moment, Yeshua's strength gave way, and Joseph reached out to catch his son as Yeshua's body crumbled beneath the weight of human frailty.

Forty-four
Yeshua Afflicted

Mary had worried about Yeshua's health for months.

The moment she heard Joseph crying out at the door for help, she knew her instincts had been right. Months of intense preparation and teaching, walking long distances to teaching sites, and work in Sepphoris had exhausted Yeshi's body. Even worse, disease-carrying mosquitoes harassed anyone who ventured into the summer heat. Yeshua also struggled with sleeplessness. He constantly meditated, prayed, or reflected on private thoughts.

Joseph carried Yeshua's limp body over the threshold and laid him on his sleeping mat. Joseph helped him into bed clothes and gave him water while Mary prepared cooling cloths to place around his body.

Mary knew that sickness was far too common in Judea and Galilee: paralysis, epilepsy, insanity, ophthalmia, skin diseases, parasites, and malaria. Dysentery from infected goat's milk was common. In addition, many people lived with defects from accidents, from birth, or because of other infirmities. Rabbis and religious leaders attributed illness and defects to insanity, demons, or sin, and the ill were often blamed for their suffering. Mary, like most imas, had become skilled in preparing natural remedies, and her family had endured the same illnesses as others in Nazareth.

But Yeshua? Serious illness? How can sickness coexist with deity?

Mary struggled with the question through the long night hours as she changed moist cloths on Yeshua's forehead to help bring down his fever.

Near daybreak, Yeshi's moaning interrupted her listless dozing. She replenished the oil in the lamp and stumbled as she hurried to his bedside. Sweat was beading on his face and body as he tossed and turned, and his legs were drawn to his chest in pain.

Mary placed her hand on Yeshua's forehead. He was burning with fever. He opened his eyes and smiled.

"I have been sick all night, Ima, with stomach pain and vomiting many times. I believe I have dysentery, perhaps from something I ate when I last traveled to teach. Perhaps I ate impure food or drank bad goat's milk. It is challenging to learn to give thanks in *all* things in a vulnerable body." He smiled again.

Mary recognized the symptoms of dysentery and prayed Yeshi did not also have deadly malaria.[78]

Mary hurried back to the kitchen to prepare the mixture of herbs to relieve Yeshua's vomiting and cramps. She prepared a small amount of opium from local poppy seeds. A gentle measure of the drug would provide pain relief and promote restful sleep. Next, she mixed oils from balsam tree sap they often purchased from a shop in Jericho. She had learned that when the oils and herbs were combined, they helped reduce fever and ease cramps, muscle aches, and even vomiting.

Yeshua's symptoms soon eased, and he slept through the morning, but Mary remained worried. She sat in a favorite chair near her loom and pondered Yeshi's sudden illness. Before long Rebecca joined her, sitting silently for a time, picking at the threads of her country woven mantle.

"Ima, is Yeshua sick?"

Mary paused. She had to be careful. The rabbis taught that illness was often caused by sin, and people were quick to condemn and judge those were ill or maimed.

"You're worried about him, aren't you?" Mary searched her daughter's face, knowing she adored her oldest brother.

Rebecca pulled harder on her dress. "I don't want people to think he's sinned and done something bad, Ima, or think ugly things about him that aren't true." Rebecca's olive-green eyes blazed with anger.

Mary leaned forward. "Rebecca, we cannot control what others think. They are responsible to God for their judgments, as we are for ours. We know who Yeshua is, and Yahweh knows who he is. Yes, he is sick, but I don't think it is because he has sinned. He is sick because illness is part of life."

Yeshua is God's Son, the Messiah, so he cannot sin. The rabbis are wrong. I trust in God's revelation spoken by the angel, and I will continue to trust it, no matter the circumstances.

Mary took Rebecca's hand. "I can promise you that Yeshua will recover. God has a plan for Yeshua's life, and that plan will not be cut short by illness. I respect our religious leaders, but they are men, and they are not always right."

The worry on Rebecca's face eased. "I will make Yeshua broth, Ima. Thank you for helping me understand. I will do all that I can to serve him." Rebecca rose and disappeared into the kitchen.

Mary sighed and returned to Yeshua's room. He was awake and resting. She sat beside him and stroked his forehead with the back of her hand.

"Much better," she pronounced as she caressed his face. Yeshua looked into her eyes, searching her soul.

"Ima, this illness does not surprise me. I am a man and am subject to the same frailties of the body as other men. I fight anger, sadness, grief, and other human emotions.

"I am God's Son, and I cannot sin, but I am tempted as other humans. Because I am the Anointed One does not exempt me from human frailties."

Mary was confused. Yeshua was speaking about himself as *the Messiah.*

"Ima, sickness is not caused by a person's sin. Sickness came as part of the curse because Adam and Eve sinned. They disobeyed God's direct command, which brought both physical and spiritual sickness and death. That sinful nature is passed down to all generations through the blood. Our people's history—every generation—bears testimony to the wickedness of the human heart."

Mary shifted and looked down at her hands. It was uncommon for young men to talk to their mothers about spiritual matters. Religious instruction passed from father to son, and she and Yeshua often spoke about practical matters, although she had instructed him in prayer, devotion, and obedience to Yahweh. It was Joseph who instructed him in deeper spiritual matters. But Yeshua had initiated this conversation, as if he were preparing to tell her something.

"Our spiritual leaders teach that illness indicates the sick person has sinned, but they are wrong. I was conceived when the Holy Spirit came upon you—a union of the Divine and humanity. Ima, I am the God-man, Son of God, Son of man. Do you understand?"

Mary stared at Yeshua as the world faded to black then back to light. She had thought she understood, but perhaps faith had carried her. She was now looking into the eyes of Yahweh Himself in human form, born as a baby, birthed from her womb. Her hands flew to her eyes.

How dare I look upon Him, the Most High God?

"Ima, I am your son, but I am also God's Son, and as such I must explain what is to come. Sin passes from generation to generation through the blood of the father. My father is heavenly, not earthly, and I do not possess a sinful nature. I am the only human born into the world who could ever bear the sins of the world and pay an eternal price. A lamb or heifer or dove—those served as symbols. My body is human, but my essence and soul are divine. I am God's

Lamb. This is the reason the Messiah must die and shed His blood to pay the price for the remission of sin."

Mary had stopped breathing. She had nursed Yeshua through the night and prayed for him to return to health, only to have him tell her he was going to die! Anger flared in her heart. The Messiah was coming to die, not to establish a political kingdom for His people? She forced the shock from her face.

Yeshua placed his hands on his abdomen. "My body cries out in pain, I bleed when I'm cut, and my head hurts when I'm in the sun too long or I don't duck when I come through the door of the house." He smiled and continued.

"The prophet Isaiah tells us this," he said, and then he quoted the following:

> See, my servant will prosper;
> he will be highly exalted.
> But many were amazed when they saw him.
> His face was so disfigured he seemed hardly human,
> and from his appearance, one would scarcely know he was a man.
> And he will startle many nations.
> Kings will stand speechless in his presence.
> For they will see what they had not been told;
> they will understand what they had not heard about.
> Who has believed our message?
> To whom has the Lord revealed his powerful arm?
> My servant grew up in the Lord's presence like a tender green shoot,
> like a root in dry ground.
> There was nothing beautiful or majestic about his appearance,
> nothing to attract us to him.
> He was despised and rejected—
> a man of sorrows, acquainted with deepest grief.
> We turned our backs on him and looked the other way.
> He was despised, and we did not care.

Yet it was our weaknesses he carried;
it was our sorrows that weighed him down.
And we thought his troubles were a punishment from God,
a punishment for his own sins!
But he was pierced for our rebellion,
crushed for our sins.
He was beaten so we could be whole.
He was whipped so we could be healed.
All of us, like sheep, have strayed away.
We have left God's paths to follow our own.
Yet the Lord laid on him
the sins of us all.
He was oppressed and treated harshly,
yet he never said a word.
He was led like a lamb to the slaughter.
And as a sheep is silent before the shearers,
he did not open his mouth.
Unjustly condemned,
he was led away.
No one cared that he died without descendants,
that his life was cut short in midstream.
But he was struck down
for the rebellion of my people.
He had done no wrong
and had never deceived anyone.
But he was buried like a criminal;
he was put in a rich man's grave.
But it was the Lord's good plan to crush him
and cause him grief.
Yet when his life is made an offering for sin,
he will have many descendants.
He will enjoy a long life,
and the Lord's good plan will prosper in his hands.
When he sees all that is accomplished by his anguish,
he will be satisfied.

And because of his experience,
my righteous servant will make it possible
for many to be counted righteous,
for he will bear all their sins.
I will give him the honors of a victorious soldier,
because he exposed himself to death.
He was counted among the rebels.
He bore the sins of many and interceded for rebels.[79]

"You see, Ima," Yeshua spoke, "I am a high priest who understands men's weaknesses, for I faced all of the same tests men do, yet I am without sin.[80] As the Messiah I know what people feel because I have also felt those things."

Yeshua's words were not entirely new revelation to Mary. God had told her she would bear the Messiah, but a Savior who would die for the sins of the world? How could she move through the days ahead knowing Yeshua was walking toward death?

Yet how could she not trust, knowing that the life and salvation of the world rested on Yeshi's shoulders?

Forty-five

Rebel Overreach

Simon Cananeus sat cross-legged atop a large rock, his eyes fixed on the worn path that led to his house, as he listened for the sounds of children. The hillside behind his large home blazed with red anemones.

They will be here soon, and I will see for myself the truth about the rebel rabbi from Nazareth.

He shaded his eyes as he looked again down the road that led from Nazareth to Cana. It was Cana's turn to host beit sefer school for children in the lower region of Galilee. Simon Cananeus had been waiting for this opportunity to assess the rabbi on behalf of the rebels. Was this rabbi one of them? Word was that his teachings were contrary to tradition and defied religious authorities.

Just what I like—controversy and fear. Simon the Zealot's name will be known and remembered!

Simon was curious about Yeshua since John had first talked about him. John had watched Yeshua repair a boat for his father at Magdala near the Sea of Galilee. He had also often accompanied his abba, Zebedee, to Cana to purchase wine for the family. Simon's abba, Laban, owned the finest vineyard and winery in all of Galilee, but a cohort of Roman soldiers had plundered it, stolen the finest bottles, and smashed the storage jars, destroying his entire inventory.

Simon was outraged. His anger seeped deep into his

spirit, like rot eating through the hull of a ship. John didn't share his rage. The two friends had grown apart and then separated. Simon's anger led him to the Zealot movement, where he found justification and an outlet for his rage. He was not alone in his hatred toward Rome. Many youthful Galileans had banded together to harass Roman authorities as Zealots.

Simon's suspicion of Jews who could be collaborating with the Romans grew. His involvement in Zealot opposition transitioned from covert, to occasional nighttime forays, to public ambushes that further incited the Romans and angered the Jews. As a result, many locals who were fond of Laban distrusted Simon.

Still, he boasted of his exploits, proud to be feared as Simon the Zealot.

He slid off the rock as he continued to observe the road.

Today I will hear the teachings of Bo John's cousin Yeshua and see for myself if he is a friend of Rome and danger to our movement.

A cluster of boys appeared down the Cana road, each carrying a wax tablet and stylus. Simon judged that they were five to ten years old.

It is time.

Simon hurried across the road and entered his ima's house. He tried to hide by sitting in a back corner of the large gathering room behind a pile of blankets. The room had been built to accommodate weddings and bar mitzvahs. Benches had been placed along the walls, where the scholars would sit. The rabbi would stand in the center to instruct.

Simon himself positioned near a hand-hewn support beam that further obscured him from view as the boys filed in and took their seats. Yeshua arrived with the first students and called each one by name as they entered. The children greeted him enthusiastically.

Simon was curious. Yeshua's students seems to respect him yet not fear him.

Yeshua moved to a space in the center of the benches. "Young men, today we will begin with an object lesson that will help you understand that Yahweh is Creator of all and that all creation declares His glory. Today we will study in the field behind the house. The ground is covered with anemones, just one small display of God's creativity, beauty, and design."

Students stared back at their rabbi, gape-faced. Beit sefer students did not study outdoors or sit among flowers. They sat on wooden benches and listened to lectures. Simon had been told that this Yeshua was unlike other rabbis, that he defied tradition, and the man had proven the rumors were true without teaching a word.

Simon seethed. Who did he think he was, changing tradition? Even his bearing was inconsequential. This Yeshua was not a man of comely appearance or of the appearance of wealth, yet he carried himself with quiet authority. His eyes and manner drew the children to his side, and he did not turn them away. He bent down and answered each question at eye level—something Simon had never seen a rabbi do.

This Yeshua rebels against even the smallest traditions. He cannot be trusted.

Simon trailed behind as Yeshua led the class to the anemone-painted field, the boys clutching their wax tablets as they whispered to one another. Simon resigned himself to being seen because Yeshua had brought the class outside.

The boys settled on the ground in a cloud of flowers in hues of pink, blue, and red as Yeshua began a lesson interpreting a passage in Deuteronomy

"No Ammonite or Moabite or any of their descendants for ten generations may be admitted to the assembly of the Lord. These nations did not welcome you with food and water when you came out of Egypt. Instead, they hired

Balaam son of Beor from Pethor in distant Aram-Naharaim to curse you."

Simon watched as the students listened to the rabbi read the text as if the story were his own.

"But the Lord your God refused to listen to Balaam. He turned the intended curse into a blessing because the Lord your God loves you. As long as you live, you must never promote the welfare and prosperity of the Ammonites or Moabites. Do not detest the Edomites or the Egyptians, because the Edomites are your relatives and you lived as foreigners among the Egyptians."[81]

Yeshua smiled and stroked his beard. "Many Sadducees misunderstand this passage."

Simon's eyes widened, and he saw students glance at one another, confused. No one *ever* said the Sadducees were wrong.

Yeshua continued. "They say God's hatred of evil is often affirmed in the Psalms and in this passage in Deuteronomy. Therefore, those who embody evil are God's enemies, and God's people should hate them. They teach to 'love your neighbor but *hate* your enemy.'"

Yeshua paused and leveled his eyes at Simon.

"But I tell you, *love your enemies* and pray for those who persecute you, that you may be children of your Father in heaven. He causes His sun to rise on the evil and the good, and sends rain on the righteous and the unrighteous. If you love those who love you, what reward will you get? Are not even the tax collectors doing that? And if you greet only your own people, what are you doing more than others? Do not even pagans do that? But you are to be perfect, even as your Father in heaven is perfect."[82]

He looks at me when he speaks those words, yet he does not know me. He is not a Zealot, so he must be a collaborator. Why else would he say we must love Roman infidels who persecute us?

Yeshua sipped water from a skin he carried beneath his

robe. His confident voice caught the attention of several men resting on the hillside. They moved closer to listen to the rabbi wearing his teaching tallit.[83] Soon other Jews from the village saw the group on the hillside and investigated.

Before long, Simon stood among a throng focused on the rabbi's teaching. Many whispered to one another, their words drifting on the wind: "Wonderful interpretation ... hear more ... wisdom above the Sadducees ..."

Yeshua teaches contrary to the scholars of Jerusalem, and he does so in the garb of a priest!

"Why are you here, Simon? Are you not a friend of Dod Matthan?" Yeshua's voice rang out as if he were standing beside Simon, yet he stood beyond the seated students.

Simon felt uncomfortable. He tried not to blink.

"I came to hear your message from God." He hoped his words would deflect the rabbi's interest in him.

"So you are seeking religious instruction?"

Simon flushed.

The teacher looks through me, but he cannot possibly know I think he teaches heresy. Does he know I am Simon the Zealot and will report his seditious teaching to my commander? And that my report could bring an order for his execution?

But Yeshua's gaze did not waver, and Simon's heart suddenly trembled with a chilling fear.

Who is this man who seems to read my thoughts and show no fear? And what is his sudden interest in me?

Forty-six

Intruders: Surprise!

The gathering room hummed with the sounds of family as Mary sat working her much-used circular millstone. The smell of oil lamps burning in the gathering room niches cast a swaying glow across the small space. Joseph had not yet returned from a long day of work. Yeshua sat near the door talking with Anna and watching the younger boys, who were grappling on the floor. With each rotation of her hand on the mill, Mary added to her storehouse of gratitude: a good husband, steady income, healthy and happy children, food and provision, and a faithful Yahweh who answered their cries for wisdom to raise His Son.

I am blessed above all women. Thank You, heavenly Av.

She glanced over her shoulder and saw Hanna kneading mixing flour, water, salt, and starter with the previous day's dough. From the time she could toddle, Hanna had required little supervision. She loved to work and loved to please her ima and abba. She was still struggling to learn that in bread making and in life, doing the right thing did not guarantee the desired result, and as one grew older, the right choice was not always clear.

Mary sighed.

Dangers of bad choices could even reach my family. Guard our family, Yahweh.

Hanna worked the dough in smooth strokes. When she sensed the precise texture, she would shape it into round loaves. Then it would rise and be ready to bake in the courtyard ovens, to help keep heat from rising in the house.

A sudden *thud* shook the front door, and Mary turned. "Joseph? Is that you? Are you all right?"

Silence.

Her heart dropped. Several men in the compound had been beaten and robbed while traveling, and danger had increased in recent months with new attacks from malcontents and thieves. Mary's hand flew to her throat.

"Yeshua, open the door! Abba may be hurt." She strained to keep her voice composed, but the boys on the floor stopped their wrestling as Yeshua stood and slid a broad board from its bracing position.

A shadowy figure wrapped in a dark cloak crashed through into the room.

Then another, and another, and another as Anna screamed and recoiled, as if trying to climb the stone wall behind her.

Yeshua was shoved aside by the tumble of bodies but quickly moved into position in front of his sister as the boys stumbled to Mary's side.

Mary forced herself to focus. The men carried Roman-style swords but wore the garb of Jews. The small gathering room echoed with angry commands and threats, and she straightened her back, the heavy mill pinning her where she sat. She prayed for Yahweh to help her break free of the smaller top stone.

The smallest of the three men stepped forward. "We mean no harm to you." He gestured toward Mary and the children. "We are here for the one called Yeshua." He pointed. "Are you the rabbi, the one teaching our youth?"

Yeshi quipped, "You have entered our home without consent or welcome."

The man's face reddened. "We come as agents of Yahweh. We are His Zealots. You dare to teach our children to love their enemies? Rome is our enemy. They occupy our land

and disrespect our God. We will not love them or tolerate those who teach our children to do so!"

"Yet you approach me as a trespasser in my home. Are not all men trespassers and in need of blood sacrifice? And do you not yourself ask for Yahweh's forgiveness, which He has provided? Does Yahweh not love His enemies, and should you not love Him with all your heart, soul, and mind by forgiving your enemies as He forgives?"

The man glared at Yeshua, obviously searching for words as his companions mutely shifted their weight.

"We exhort you—no, *command* you—to stop teaching this heresy in Galilee. If you continue, we will stop you. You have been warned, and we will not be held responsible for the outcome. We represent many men whose zeal must sometimes be expressed in violence."

The man paused, waiting for a response. Anna had retreated to a corner and slid to the floor. The sound of her soft sobs filled the room as the intruder waited. Mary fought the urge to speak up for her son; she remained quiet and held her breath and her tongue.

He is a man and must speak for himself. My voice would only escalate the anger.

Jose opened his mouth to speak, and Mary motioned him to be still. She was sure the boys were debating whether to engage physically or verbally. How could they not? Jude was wide-eyed, probably wondering whether he would see battle right here in his house. Mary turned her head to the boys and raised a finger to her lips with a frown, and they nodded in understanding: remain silent and still.

Mary fixed her eyes on Yeshi and prayed that Joseph would not come home before the men left. His presence would escalate the tension. Yeshua stepped forward, and Mary sighed inwardly. He was not frightened. He was in control, but his accusers and critics were unaware of his power. They believed they could tell the Son of God what to do.

They had no idea whom they were talking to.

Yeshua's response was short.

"Go. Stop harassing your own people. God controls Rome, as He does all things. Messiah will bring you freedom and salvation. Trust in Him, and you will know peace. He who lives by the sword will die by the sword."

He spoke softly, but a sudden stirring of fear filled the room as his powerful spirit penetrated the men's minds.

A taller intruder reluctantly sheathed his sword and muttered under his breath, "You are spreading nonsense throughout Galilee! We have been told that Messiah is called the Teacher of Righteousness and is with the Essenes in the Judean wilderness. But this so-called Messiah has done us no good in Galilee." His words dripped with contempt.

Joseph had once told Mary about a sect of religious Zealots along the Dead Sea at Qumran who were skeptical of a Messiah who would overthrow Rome and establish a Jewish kingdom. Many Zealots supported the Qumran sect, who broke with traditional Judaism because of corrupt temple priests. However, the Zealots became disillusioned when they learned the Qumran Messiah was a spiritual leader and not a warrior and political leader. Other rebel movements throughout the country were making revolutionary statements to Rome: the Sicarii, the followers of John of Giscala, and the soldiers of Simeon bar Giora. All were anxious to overthrow Roman tyranny.

Another *thud* sounded at the door, and Mary's heart pounded.

Not now, Joseph! Please, Yahweh, protect us and protect my husband.

The smaller soldier turned and opened the door. A man exploded through the door, tall and muscular with long flowing hair, unlike Joseph's curls. His unruly beard bore streaks of gray. He wore a basalt-hued tunic, and a short sheathed knife hung from his girdle. A look of terror flashed across the faces of the three other intruders at his entrance.

"Who gave you permission to enter this house?" he

bellowed. "Under whose authority have you disturbed the peace of this family, Simon?" The long-haired man shook his fist in the face of the intruder he addressed as Simon, then grabbed the shortest of the three by the throat and pulled his face forward until they were nose to nose.

"Get your men out of this house *now*, Cananeus! We have spoken of this before, yet you dare to defy me? I would advise you not to cross my path again."

Mary watched as the man released Cananeus, who crumpled against the wall and then rose, turned, and slithered out the door with his friends. The intruder who remained turned suddenly and faced the wall.

How strange that he turns away. This man wields great power, but why has he used it so forcefully for our protection?

Mary tipped her head.

The voice is familiar. A merchant or distant neighbor, perhaps. Or … no, it couldn't be possible.

A rush of heat flashed through her body from the top of her head to the pit of her stomach. She reached for Jose's hand as she watched Yeshua step forward and lay his hand on the intruder's shoulder. The man flinched but remained staring at the wall.

Mary drew a breath, struggling for words.

"Matthan … is it you, Joseph's brother?" Her hand flew to her mouth to stop the rising sobs. Even speaking the words pained her—she had locked them away for so long.

He turned, but he faced the stone floor. Yeshua moved his hand to Matthan's arm.

"We have waited long for this moment. Come talk to us, Dod. But not before Ima looks into your face and holds you in her arms."

The next minutes were a commotion of embraces, brief comments on the changes brought by age, and good-humored arguments about where Matthan would sit, what he would eat, and who would sit beside him.

His apology came at the first lull in conversation after

everyone was seated again. His eyes told Mary the sincerity behind his words. He had meant to stay in touch. He had not known the intensity of the Zealot cause when he joined.

"These men are radically committed to protecting Jews from Roman oppression, despite their claims to be guardians of God. Their zeal is often misguided, and they punish Jews who are not as 'zealous' in their attitudes and actions against Rome. I rose to leadership, but I also became entangled in a group whose actions I often question."

Matthan had accepted a glass of wine. He quickly swallowed a drink, stood, and stepped toward the door.

"I put myself in danger of my life coming here. You must not speak a word of seeing me to anyone. Anyone, do you understand? Even Joseph. Especially Joseph. Any knowledge of me could endanger you, and he should be able to honestly report he has not seen me. I promise you, I will take care of the three idiots whom I threw out of here tonight."

Matthan fingered his dagger, and a chill crept up Mary's spine.

Should she tell Joseph anyway? How could she not? They had never kept secrets, and this was too important to keep from him. Besides, he would read the secret in her eyes.

But what would she say—that Matthan was a hero who had saved them from Zealot threats? Or that he was a violent criminal, even more rebellious and in greater danger than the day he left?

For the first time in her marriage, Mary felt alone. She feared for her family and did not know what to do. But her greatest heartbreak was that she could not turn to Joseph for help.

Forty-seven
Rabbi Showdown at the Mound

The midmorning sun streaked through the sycamore branches in tremoring fingers of light as Rebecca watched pilgrims trail like ants to honey up the south side of the Flower Mound outside Nazareth.

"So many, Yeshua. I cannot believe so many are coming."

She clasped her hands together in excitement, bubbling with gratitude that her brother had chosen her to be part of the day. In spite of her siblings' endless debates about Yeshua's enigmatic nature, Rebecca had always suspected that God had chosen him for a unique role in Israel's history. She refused to be drawn into resentful conversations about his flawless behavior or introspective nature. Yes, he was often annoyingly good, but he was always kind, and most of the time he seemed just like anyone else. Rebecca had to admit Yeshi confused her too, but her heart told her to trust the love she saw in her brother's eyes.

Rebecca always chose a seat beside Yeshua during his evening meditations in the gathering room. When they talked, he answered her every question with patience and understanding and fed her thirst for knowledge about theology, politics, current affairs, science, and other subjects often restricted to women. In Yeshua's eyes she was not just a woman; she was Rebecca, honored and respected for who she was, with God-given abilities and interests.

During a recent talk, Yeshua had told her about the

death of Hillel the Elder and the severe blow his passing had struck to Judaism. Even Abba was sobered for days. Just months before Hillel the Elder's death, his son Simeon ben Hillel had resigned as president of the Sanhedrin in Jerusalem, the religious sect responsible for training rabbis.

Schools in local synagogues depended on rabbis who received advanced education in Jerusalem to pass their education on to students in smaller villages outside Jerusalem. Religious leaders considered Hillel one of the most brilliant and influential rabbis of his generation. Simeon had lived beneath his father's shadow for many years and was now free from control and expectations. Rabbi Simeon wanted to chart a different path and shape the lives of young Jewish leaders. He believed that teaching hungry young minds would fulfill his vision, rather than navigating the corrupt politics of the Sanhedrin. He moved back to Gamla, the city of his ancestors, which was located on the east side of the Sea of Galilee. There he took up an itinerant ministry teaching and preaching. His brilliant son Gamaliel accompanied him.

Simeon ben Hillel traveled throughout Galilee preaching a fabricated narrative of the scriptures and gaining support for his view of Judaism. Yeshua had often expressed his concerns about Simeon's teaching to Rebecca. Students in his school were being led astray by his teaching. All of Galilee was talking about Simeon's interpretations, and Yeshua had to respond.

Rebecca pledged to do all she could to help him and spread word to nearby villages that Yeshua would be at the Flower Mound outside Nazareth to discuss Simeon's teachings of Rabbi Hillel.

But she had not expected such an overwhelming response.

Yeshua's reputation as a rabbi had grown, and he had been drawing attention from locals and surrounding villages for some time. This had given him the opportunity to teach parents and community members that true worship engaged the spirit and followed truth. He corrected misunderstood teachings regarding the intent of the law of Moses, as well as teachings on the neglected books of the prophets.

Open-air sermons were unusual. Menacing Roman soldiers were often in earshot of outdoor gatherings. Rome feared dissenting factions poisoning the minds of youth and inciting rebellion. Soldiers were quick to break up crowds, and they attempted to silence anyone they deemed to be a threat. Increased activity among rebel groups fanned the flames of fear.

Rebecca had shared her concerns with Yeshua before they left the house: "Be careful to avoid using words authorities could construe as treasonous or inciting."

Her brother had smiled. "When men do not know God, they always find His Words inciting."

Synagogues hosted most religious instruction, and this new outdoor venue would appeal to many hungry, hurt, and confused hearts. Jews were expected to practice the law, but in reality, many were Jewish by nationality, not by faith. The spiritually hungry willingly risked Roman interference to receive instruction from this radical rabbi. Legalistic and restrictive Judaism did not appeal to the masses. They wanted teaching that would save their souls and give them freedom from their oppressors. Rebecca's heart also longed for freedom, and Yeshua somehow provided it.

Rebecca watched as Yeshua took his place at the top of the mound, where his voice would be carried down the slopes where people were gathering. He had prepared a message short enough not to irritate the soldiers yet to allow for questions and interaction with the crowd.

Anxiety stirred in Rebecca's heart as the crowd sat down and quieted, anticipating Yeshua's opening words. But his face wore the same warm sincerity she had always seen in their talks together. He raised his hands to indicate he was beginning.

"I have followed Rabbi Simeon ben Hillel's teaching with great interest. I thank God for men dedicated to preaching holy scripture."

Yeshua's voice rang clear and strong, and Rebecca's clenched fingers relaxed.

He is wise. He does not mention his many reservations about Hillel's teachings and practices.

"However," Yeshua said, his voice becoming firmer, "Rabbi Hillel sometimes undermines the *intent* of the law, which does not represent biblical Judaism."

Rebecca watched a wave of shock roll through the crowd like a living thing, stirring people into agitation.

His words have caught them off guard. He has expressed strong conviction against a respected authority in a confrontational manner on an emotionally charged subject.

Her fingers clenched again, this time with her neck and jaw muscles, as Yeshua continued.

"You have heard the commandment that says, 'You must not commit adultery.' But I say, anyone who even looks at a woman with lust has already committed adultery with her in his heart. So, if your eye—even your good eye—causes you to lust, gouge it out and throw it away. It is better for you to lose one part of your body than for your whole body to be thrown into hell. And if your hand—even your stronger hand—causes you to sin, cut it off and throw it away. It is better for you to lose one part of your body than for your whole body to be thrown into hell."[84]

Oh no, not that.

The crowd reacted. Voices began to rise.

A well-dressed man near Rebecca spoke to his obviously wealthy companion, whose clothes were fashioned from silk in shades of blue. Both had arrived on donkeys. The blue-robed man sneered a comment to his friend.

"What does he mean, we should gouge out our right eye? We know the expression an 'eye for an eye,' and a 'tooth for a tooth,' but what is the purpose of gouging out an eye?"

Rebecca, too, wondered about the meaning but dismissed the men for their disdainful attitude.

Yeshua continued. "I speak in hyperbole. The right eye is your most important eye. I use hyperbole to emphasize that even the most important part of your body—the vital part you need to survive—is not as important as God."

The listeners murmured, realizing that Yeshua was not speaking of the need to literally cut off a hand or poke out an eye, but was saying that one's eternal destiny is more important than physical things. A sigh reverberated through the crowd.

Rebecca scanned the faces near her. Her instincts told her that the people were fascinated with Yeshua's unconventional methods of delivery more than they were grasping the spiritual message he was proclaiming.

Yeshua struck at the heart of personal sin—lust. This was not what anyone wanted to hear. It was now obvious that Yeshua's message was being presented not to tickle the ear but to proclaim God's message and to establish his authority as the one to whom Yahweh gave that message.

Most people in the crowd favored Simeon's teachings and less restrictive demands of the law. They believed the law of Moses required restrained behavior. To hear that it also placed demands on the motives and intentions of their hearts would trouble them. Yeshua's teaching was radically different from anything they had ever heard.

Rebecca's heart raced. She glanced over the crowd to gauge their reactions. Were they angry? Were Pharisees in the crowd? She twisted the hem of her mantle, fears and questions racing through her mind.

Please, Yeshi, don't say things that will get you into trouble! Abba and Ima have often spoken of Herod's fear of Jewish militants.

A man in rabbi's garments spoke to the people sitting near him. "He does not question the grave transgression of physical adultery. But how can this man teach that scripture compels us to go deeper than the words of the commandments?"

Yeshua responded as if he had heard the man's question.

"Adultery not only violates another person but also breaks the marriage contract. It tears apart a relationship that represents God's love for His people. By law, the offender could be severely punished."

A murmur swept through the crowd as listeners voiced their doubt and some their anger as a man a stone's throw down the hill stood and crossed his arms.

"Rabbi Yeshua has extended the offense of adultery to include the intent of our thoughts. How can this be? This is a hard saying. How can we do this?"

At his words, Roman centurions who had taken position beneath a tree began to banter sardonically, pushing one another in jest.

"A Roman soldier certainly never *thinks* bad thoughts for fear of divine retribution."

"Never!" came a response, accompanied by howls of laughter.

"We have pure thoughts and noble motives."

Rebecca winced at the laughter, but Yeshua's face remained fixed on the crowd as he continued from the Torah.

"Again, you have heard that it was said to the people long ago, 'Do not break your oath, but fulfill to the Lord the vows you have made.'"

He continued, his vibrant voice carried by the wind to everyone who had come to truly listen.

"You have also heard that our ancestors were told, 'You must not break your vows; you must carry out the vows you make to the Lord.' But I say, do not make any vows! Do not say, 'By heaven!,' because heaven is God's throne. And do not say, 'By the earth!,' because the earth is His footstool. And do not say, 'By Jerusalem!,' for Jerusalem is the city of the great King. Do not even say, 'By my head!,' for you can't turn one hair white or black. Just say a simple 'Yes, I will' or 'No, I won't.' Anything beyond this is from the evil one."[85]

Rebecca held her breath again. The crowd understood that an agreement could be voided unless it were sworn to. Yeshua was saying that a person's integrity is not reflected in words but in the intent of their heart.

The murmurs had escalated. People didn't like what they were hearing: Don't swear at all; one's integrity should stand on its own without need of an oath.

The crowd had been listening, and some had become enraged at Yeshua's words. They stood and trailed away down the mound, muttering in disgust as they walked. Yeshua took a drink from his waterskin, pushed back his hair, and continued as a faint breeze rustled the tall grass and flowers.

"Giving of alms is an act of gratitude expected of all Yahweh's faithful subjects."

Galileans acknowledged that alms were demanded by the law, but the people in Nazareth's small, depressed villages were overtaxed by Rome—and Yeshua was fully aware of this.

Be careful! Don't give the soldiers an excuse to disperse the group or arrest you for condemning Roman taxes.

She rustled her hands in her lap and tried to draw Yeshua's attention, but he remained fixed on the crowd. He continued, expressing concern that priests often sought public recognition for their good deeds. In fact, they often gave to the poor just for public praise. Pharisees often hypocritically did the right things for the wrong reasons, putting on masks to play various roles, as Yeshua had observed from attending the theater in Sepphoris.

Rebecca sighed.

What are you doing, Yeshi? You are offending Romans, Jews, Pharisees, everyone! How can this be your message—that everyone has been deceived?

Yeshua continued to address pharisaical practices.

"Watch out! Don't do your good deeds publicly, to be admired by others, for you will lose the reward from your Father in heaven. When you give to someone in need, don't do as the hypocrites do—blowing trumpets in the synagogues and streets to call attention to their acts of charity! I tell you the truth, they have received all the reward they will ever get. But when you give to someone in need, don't let your left hand know what your right hand is doing. Give your gifts in private, and your Father, who sees everything, will reward you."[86]

With these words, Yeshua concluded his sermon on the Flower Mound, and the crowd dispersed as Rebecca tried to summarize what she had just heard. Yahweh is concerned with our attitudes more than our actions. Good deeds are for the purpose of honoring God and people, not for earning reward or praise. Give in secret, not for reward. Do not seek the praise of human beings.

His message will certainly offend the Sanhedrin and Pharisees, who live to be seen and praised, as well as rabbis who long to follow in their footsteps. Ima and Abba will ask about today. What should I tell them? I can't let them how Yeshua has set all of Rome and Galilee against him in one day.

And yet her brother seemed as serene as ever. He had retired to the shade of the sycamore tree and seemed unconcerned by the sputtering crowd streaming away.

A gray-bearded man leaning on a walking stick approached Yeshua. "I wasted two day's journey to listen to your blasphemy. I have been taught by many rabbis in my years, and none have ever spoken like you. You do not speak the teachings of my rabbi."

"I would have nothing to offer if my message were the same as that of other men." Yeshua held the man's gaze, yet his look was gentle. "My purpose is not to teach vain repetition, but the Word of God as He directs."

The old man's eyes grew wide. "You say you speak at God's direction?"

Yeshua continued to look squarely into the old man's eyes but remained silent as Rebecca watched, icy tentacles of fear gripping her heart.

Why am I so afraid? What changed in that one sentence in the old man's eyes?

With an angry thump of his cane, the man turned and walked away, and Yeshua pulled Rebecca closer to his side.

"I knew my message would not be popular and would stir anger. Thank you for being here and supporting me, Sister. This was not easy for you. It may appear to you that I do not struggle, but I do. I am tempted to lash out and seek my own way and indulge in pleasure like anyone, but my love for Yahweh, my heavenly Av, compels my life. More than ever, that love must compel me in the time ahead."

Rebecca reached for her brother's hand. Had Yeshua meant to comfort her or warn her with his words? She wasn't sure. But she did know he needed to be careful what he taught and where he taught in the future.

She knew Yeshua was concerned about carrying out Yahweh's plan. But he was not concerned about offending anyone. Being careful was Yahweh's last concern.

Forty-eight
The Ultimate Seductress

Dusk slowly shrouded daylight, and deep shadows fell over the narrow paths that led home. Yeshua and Rebecca made their way down the Flower Mound and across a large meadow past a popular water well.[87] Rebecca pondered Yeshua's message as they walked in comfortable silence, each buried in thought and surrounded by familiar night sounds.

Before long they drew near to Nazareth's community well. The well had always held special sentiment for the family. Ima had often told the story of Abba meeting her at the well and walking her home so he could see her.

But as Rebecca neared the well, a sudden chill fell over her. Her heart pounded, and she struggled to breathe. The air grew thick and sticky, as if she were about to choke. Something told her to stop, but Yeshua continued his pace toward a lone figure drawing water.

Rebecca tried to call out a warning, but she could not speak. She leaned on a nearby tree to steady herself.

An attractive woman was drawing water unaccompanied. Yeshua watched as the woman lowered her bucket into the dark hole. The night sounds went silent, and a seductive voice spoke in a soft whisper, yet Rebecca's head seemed to be splitting apart with the sound.

"Look at her, Yeshua—a lovely, beautiful woman created by your Av. You desire her—skin as soft as dove's feathers and bountiful breasts cradling the sachet of myrrh. Her dark hair is like strands of silk between your fingers, and her lips taste like fine wine. Every sway of her hips releases the fragrance of her perfume."

Rebecca's hand flew to her mouth, and her face burned. She had never heard such words, and to witness them spoken to Yeshua was beyond disgraceful! She pressed her hands over her ears, but the voice persisted, as loud as before.

"Beneath her tunic, her legs are as soft as a sheep's belly, and her womb is as lush as a verdant hillside. She will pleasure your every desire. Imagine your bodies entwined, her lips pressed to yours ..."

Please stop. Please stop. Please stop. Yahweh, help us. Satan himself has devised this plan to destroy Yeshua. Please help him![88]

"Take her, Yeshua. Experience what it feels like to lie beside the warm body of a woman. She awaits you. Go now. No one will ever discover your secret."[89]

Rebecca watched as Yeshua turned away from the figure at the well and spoke into the darkness. She drew her hands from her ears so she could hear him and trembled in the chill air.

"Depart from me, temptress. I know who you are. So you come to test the teacher on his own lesson? It has been said, 'Do not commit adultery.' But I say to you that anyone who looks at a woman lustfully as you have described has already committed adultery with her in his heart.[90] Women are God's crown jewel of creation, made in Yahweh's own image, and are not objects to be used. The experience you describe might be pleasurable, but it would not be beautiful or good."

Yeshua's tone intensified, and Rebecca inched toward him, not wanting to distract him as he spoke.

"Lying with a woman does not make a man a man, and pleasures taken outside their purpose destroy and kill. Men and women never find peace and joy until they know and love the one true God and find their pleasure in Him."

Rebecca was dumbfounded. Was her brother debating with the devil or one of his demons? Was this even possible? The voice continued.

"You misunderstand." The insincere voice, feigning confusion, tried again. "Pleasure must not be forbidden. You can take her to your marriage bed. You have suffered at the hands of God. He has withheld life's greatest joys from you—close friends, love, marriage, children. You have endured ridicule since your childhood from your community and family, and you have endured serious illness. The time has come for you to experience the joys of love so you can speak about it with authority."

Rebecca had drawn close enough to Yeshua to see his expression. His eyes were turned upward, his lips moving. After a brief pause, he opened his eyes and spoke.

"But Yahweh says, 'The single man is concerned about the Lord's affairs—how he can serve the Lord. But a married man is concerned about daily living—how he can please his wife. While it is good for men and women to get married, that is not my mission on earth. I am here to do the will of my Father and complete my mission for Him."[91]

The chill lifted, and the sound of insects and birds returned. Rebecca walked toward her brother, questions tumbling through her mind like rocks down a hillside.

"Yeshi ...?" Rebecca could not find courage for the question, as the truth her heart told her to be true was too great for her to comprehend. "Are you ..."

Yeshua looked into her eyes and pulled her close. "Listen for the voice of God, Rebecca, in all things." He sighed. "The Prince of Darkness has launched a full attack upon me. I am sorry you had to witness it. More is to come, I am sure, but I do not want you to worry. And I do not want Abba and Ima or the rest of the family to worry. I will tell them privately tomorrow. Our brothers and Anna need not be told.

But Abba and Ima must trust me and God's plan, no matter what comes."

He lifted Rebecca's chin and cupped her face in his hands. "No matter what comes, know I am in Yahweh's hands. What I do, I do willingly—always remember that."

The deep sorrow in Yeshua's eyes and the touch of his hands on her face seared Rebecca's heart as tears flooded from her eyes. She nodded.

But fear pounded in her heart as they walked silently home.

Forty-nine

Rabbi Yeshua Rejected

Rebecca had taken her morning work to the roof. She sat beneath the awning in the open-air, carding wool needed to make family clothing. Coaxing the wool through her treasured carding combs, she gazed into the distance, squinting against the early morning sun. She needed time alone to think about what she could do to help Yeshua.

The day after Yeshi had spoken at the Flower Mound, religious leaders in Nazareth had come to the house and asked him to remain home until they addressed concerns that had arisen among parents about his teaching. Some had sat under his teaching at the Flower Mound, and others had heard reports about his message, but many were purportedly alarmed, believing his teachings were contrary to traditional interpretations of the law.

Yeshua had graciously complied with the request, and for three days he had worked at Abba's side in the carpentry shop as if nothing had happened.

Rebecca tugged at a clump of wool that had become stuck in a comb.

Yeshua did nothing wrong, yet he didn't speak a word to defend himself against their accusations! I don't understand.

A familiar knot tightened in her neck. She slapped the carding combs together, pinching her finger between the two flat surfaces. "Ai!"

Her head snapped back with the pain, and her eyes

glimpsed the road that led from their house to the business center of Nazareth. In the distance, a group of men, some dressed in the garb of Pharisees, were stopping to pray in the street, drawing their feet together and bending near the ground as they entreated God for all to witness.

Rebecca's hands shook, and the carding combs fell to her lap. They were headed to the house to confront Yeshua!

I must warn Yeshua! If he hurries, he will have time to hide or flee.

Rebecca threw her work into a basket beside her and hurried down the stairs and to the carpentry shop that stood a short distance behind the house. She threw open the door, but one glance told her Yeshua wasn't there. Abba sat alone repairing a damaged hand plow. She closed the door and raced back to the house and into the courtyard.

But she was too late. A contingent of Pharisees and Galilean rabbis stood in the courtyard facing a serene Yeshua, who did not appear surprised or concerned. Rebecca smiled inwardly. Behind her, she heard footsteps and turned her head to see Abba close behind her.

The men made no attempt at pleasantries or introductions. A Pharisee spoke first, on behalf of the local rabbis who were unable to vocalize their opinions.

"Yeshua, we have tolerated your unorthodox teaching for some time, but ..."

Rebecca sensed caution in the man's words—perhaps because he knew Yeshua was one of the most effective teachers ever to instruct in the region.

"Our superiors have instructed us to dismiss you from your post at the Hebrew school. Your services are no longer required."

This is unjust! Their pride and lust for power is behind this action. Parents and students are pleased with Yeshua's teaching of the Torah and tell him so often. This is an attack by legalistic rumormongers and power -grabbers.

Rebecca's heart fell. No matter how Yeshua responded,

this news was disastrous for his students. With their beloved teacher gone, they would be taught by a priest who would not put their best interests first but would promote his personal agenda to gain status. Rebecca knew that priests hid behind masks of false piety while they sought power and prestige. They and other religious leaders feared Yeshua's teachings, which threatened their absolute authority.

Yeshua appeared composed, his hands clasped before him in humility, but his gaze was level as his eyes swept over the faces of the men standing before him.

"Your limited understanding of God's commands has led to self-centered interpretations of the law and tainted thinking that has brought about this decision. God knows the intentions of your hearts. I withdraw for the sake of peace, but the price of your action today will be paid for generations to come in the spiritual peril of the children of this community and their children."

Yeshua's eyes never flinched as he spoke evenly, his words cutting through the air like a lash.

For a moment the men froze, as if they were struggling to understand his words. Then a squat man with the tassels of a Pharisee and a warty nose burst out. "Insolence and blasphemy! Pharisees and temple priests have been Yahweh's spokesmen to His people for generations. We protect Yahweh's truth."

A half dozen voices broken out in protest with him, accompanied by shaking fists.

"I honor the synagogue as God's divine institution for worship." Although he spoke quietly, Yeshua's voice overpowered the clamor of the men, and they quieted.

Stunned, Rebecca replayed what had just happened. Had her eyes and ears tricked her, or had Yeshua quelled these angry men in one sentence and without raising his voice?

"Yes. I will give up my teaching in the school for the sake of peace and to honor Yahweh. The people of Galilee and the spiritual leaders of its community have rejected me. They have heard God's message and chosen."

"Your reasons are of no concern to us as long as you comply," snapped a priest.

Yeshua smiled. "I do not comply. I offer peace beyond your understanding, but your pride blinds you."

"I know my mission and have known you would come. Your decision is part of something much greater, a plan that is not your own."

With Yeshua's words, the men turned on their heels and retreated, stirring a dusty cloud behind them as they departed.

Fifty
Yeshua's Pre-Messianic Message

Joseph sat under the rooftop awning in the cool evening air. Yeshi sat across from him, meditating as Joseph carved cooking spoons for Mary in the fading light. He and Yeshi had talked for a time until the latter had closed his eyes, signaling he was communing with his heavenly Av or meditating on scripture.

Joseph had grown comfortable with his son's frequent lapses into meditation and prayer. Yeshua appeared to have developed a deep relationship with Yahweh since he'd reached majority at the age of twenty. He'd taught several more times since his teaching at the Flower Mound, and each time Rebecca had accompanied him, curious about how his preaching and teaching style were developing and how people were responding. She'd come home and eagerly talked to the family about every detail.

Galilee showed no signs of shifting their thinking on traditional rabbinic Judaism, which was based on strict legalistic interpretations of the law. Meeting God's standards required keeping rules and rituals, no matter the attitude of one's heart.

Joseph had been hearing rumors that sincere seekers wondered if the Messiah would come as two Messiahs with two different missions, as some Pharisees and the Essene community at Qumran claimed. Yeshua's divine commission had weighed heavily on Joseph. How could he possibly help a divine son? He'd searched his heart for years. But he'd also searched the scriptures, seeking out passages speaking of the Messiah or prophesying of His coming.

Yeshua had spoken to him about a forerunner who would make a way for his ministry. The people would need to deny the grip of the power-hungry religious aristocracy, and they would be asked to choose: God's Son or corrupt Judaism.

The hope of the coming Messiah was in the heart of every pious Jew. Yet pharisaical Judaism preached the minutiae of the Torah while denying its intent and neglected God's overarching plan. The people longed for relief from Roman oppression, but religious leaders taught nothing about the Messiah whose throne was promised through King David. Many false prophets were claiming to be the Messiah. The Jews didn't even have the knowledge or understanding to recognize the true Messiah.

Joseph laid his carving in his lap and looked at his son. Yeshua had draped his tallit over his head as he bowed his head in prayer. Of course Yeshua wanted to teach from scripture the purpose of the Messiah's coming. He planned to begin an itinerant ministry to Galilean synagogues, in open-air markets, and in private gatherings to lay the foundation for the fulfillment of true Messianic Judaism.

But the past days had made it clear that Yeshua would face opposition. The Sadducees, Pharisees, and rabbis would continue their confrontations. This would elevate their fury and draw attention. Yet when would the time be right for Yeshua to reveal his role in God's messianic mission?

Joseph's heart quickened as the breeze moved the tallit and he glimpsed Yeshua's moving lips. Joseph had no idea when the time would be right. But he was certain that when the day came, Yeshua would come under the wrath of the paranoid fox Herod Antipas.

Fifty-one
James Hears the Rabboni

James pelted the choppy waters of the Sea of Galilee with stone after stone. The sun warmed his back, and a gusty breeze flung his long hair into his face as he sat on a stump that had washed ashore. In the distance, a voice rang out over the sound of waves slapping the rocky shoreline.

"James! James!"

The call grew louder as a figure drew nearer. A young man was struggling to keep his footing as he walked atop the uneven rocks that had washed along the shoreline of Bethsaida.

James squinted and tried to identify the man. It appeared to be his cousin John, son of Zebedee, flailing his arms to keep his balance as he made his way upon the rocks.

James's cousin Yeshua had given the name Boanerges, meaning "sons of thunder," to his uncle Zebedee's two sons, James and John. They were both known for hot tempers and impetuous spirits that often incited physical confrontations. To distinguish the name John from so many others by that name, his friends had dubbed him Bo John, shortening the name Boanerges.

"Yes, Bo John, it is I," James called.

Bo John stumbled over the final rocks. "James, I come from Gamla, where I heard Yeshua preach in the synagogue," he spurted out.

Bo John was enamored with the rebel cause centered in Galilee, but Gamla in Batanea was known to be a safe haven for insurrectionists and Zealots. Like many young men, Bo John sought adventure, and the lure of Zealot activity had misdirected his enthusiasm. He and other naive young men had been led unwittingly into a tangled web of rebel groups.

Bo John's regular visits to Gamla heightened his desire to join the Zealot efforts—against his father's wishes. But Bo John found the group's exploits exciting and fodder for bragging among friends who hung on his every word as he recounted rebel adventures. His storytelling about the Zealot cause eventually brought him respect and a following among admirers—but it was all talk. It was also met with upraised eyebrows from his family, including outright disapproval from his abba.

James read the excitement on his cousin's face as he approached. What story would Bo John have this time? James tried to brush away his irritation.

"I had an encounter with your brother Yeshua on the way to Gamla. It changed my mind about many things, James. I saw him use the special gifts you and others had told me about ... and I came away with a new regard for him."

Bo John's eyes were wide as he spoke. James swallowed and gazed at his cousin with renewed interest. Their families had raised them side by side, and they'd grown up like brothers. He knew too well John's propensity to exaggerate and tell tall tales. His cousin's winsome personality had won Bo John great favor with James's parents—more favor than James had liked in his younger years. Although he told himself he'd grown out of the jealousy, the truth was that he had tried to forget it and couldn't.

Bo John continued, "I was traveling to Gamla when I spotted Yeshua sitting on the side of the road resting. His work as a carpenter has made him strong and muscled, and his carob-colored hair makes him stand out. He'd draped his prayer shawl over part of his head. I saw that a slingshot secured his linen tunic, and I later learned he had hidden a leather money belt beneath his black and white striped woolen tallit. On his arm he had bound a tefillin[92] as a reminder to be obedient to the law of Moses, not for show, as some pious rabbis do.

"I recognized Yeshua immediately.

"I was headed to Gamla to check on rebel activity. Yeshua agreed to my company, and he and I departed from just outside Bethsaida on foot.

"He secured his bedroll over his shoulder and girded up his robe with the slingshot he carried for protection from animals, and we set off. He told me he was on his way to fulfill a task given him by Yahweh. I was curious because Gamla is the home base of the young rabbi Gamaliel, son of Simon Hillel, whose teaching Yeshua opposes. I wondered why he would head into Hillel's territory. Certainly, Yeshua wouldn't confront Gamaliel by teaching in Gamla—at least that's what I thought."

Where is this story going? Why am I wasting my time listening to another of Bo John's ramblings? James thought.

But his cousin continued.

"The trail in the mountainous area of Gamla is rocky and hazardous. As we turned a bend in the path, Yeshua stumbled. His sandal strap broke, and he injured his ankle. He limped the remaining distance to our destination—the local synagogue grounds—with a broken shoe. Yeshua was given a room on the synagogue grounds, and I was directed a short distance to a home where I was offered a room and hospitality."

James sighed. Bo John was a *talker.* His stories often became lost in the details. James forced himself to hold his tongue and not stop his irrepressible friend.

"The following day after he finished his morning prayers, Yeshua found me."

James cleared his throat. "Bo John, I'm glad you got to

spend time with Yeshua." He willed the sarcasm from his tone. "But is there a point to your story? If so, it is eluding me. I'm just going squirm on this hard surface and wait for an end, for it appears we are going to be here a long time."

A gust of wind caught Bo John's long curls and tossed them in his face. He swatted them away as he carefully settled on a rock, tucking his robes beneath him and crossing his arms.

"Yes, I have a point! You are always so impatient. After a bit of bread and honey, we walked around Gamla and found a shop that could repair Yeshua's sandal. Yeshua offered his carpentry services in barter, and the cobbler agreed, so Yeshua set to work repairing a broken brace on the leg of a workbench."

James's concerns had been growing as Bo John spoke. He could hold his tongue no longer and broke in.

"Were you spotted by rebels and followed? Yeshua has become known, and Gamla is full of Zealots and Roman soldiers posted to keep an eye on the city's many visitors and to spot residents with rebel connections. Did you go undetected?"

"Yeshua prayed for Yahweh's protection before we approached the city, and we were careful. But Yeshua seemed to intuitively know where soldiers might be and what areas to avoid. We stayed away from gatherings and kept to back streets."

James nodded and pulled his mantle closer. The sea winds were growing colder. Gamla was strategically located in Herod Philip's territory at the southern part of the Batanea,[93] overlooking the Sea of Galilee to the south and Syria to the northeast. Gamla's position had made it the perfect location for a military stronghold, which forced the Romans to place soldiers within the walls for defense and security.

"James, as we left the cobbler's shop, two soldiers threatened and questioned us.

"'Who are you, and what have you been doing? Where are you from, and why are you here?' they demanded of us. I was terrified."

James was skeptical. He'd long ago grown tired of his cousin's exaggerated tales and found it difficult to trust Bo John's reports. He'd found it much wiser to wait and see whether a kernel somewhere within the story proved to be true. But he continued to listen.

"The soldiers recognized us as visitors and as Jews and were trying to intimidate us. The taller of the two soldiers slapped Yeshua sharply on face and yelled, 'Who are you, and why are you here?'"

James recoiled inwardly at Bo John's words. The thought of someone striking Yeshua was revolting. He hurled a rock into the sea, the water rippling out in rings and dissipating into the waves. He didn't want to hear more of Bo John's story.

"Yeshua staggered backward, then stepped forward, his eyes never moving from his attacker's eyes. His voice was steady and fearless as he spoke: 'Why do you lash out at someone unknown to you? Have I given a reason for you to be cruel? Do you believe assault to be a sign of strength? I am Yeshua, son of Joseph from Galilee.'

"But as soon as Yeshua identified himself, the soldier challenged him again. 'Are you *Jesus* Barabbas, the insurrectionist and murderer who stalks Gamla?'"

Hairs prickled at the back of James's neck. Bo John's story had to be true. The terror in his voice told him that John was reliving the moment, fearing for his life and Yeshua's. James leaned forward and placed a hand on John's shoulder.

"You stood with him, Bo John. You did not leave his side. It was a brave thing. I am not sure that if I had been at his side in that moment, I would not have run."

Bo John hung his head. "My enthusiasm for joining the rebels certainly faded in that moment. We were facing real danger, but Yeshua responded calmly. He simply answered, 'It is not I. You seek another.'

"And in that moment, peace descended. His spirit caught the men off guard. I saw them flinch. They were bewildered and didn't know what to do. He waited while they stared, and their belligerence turned to awe. Eventually one man spoke.

"'Who are you then, Lord?'

"This time the attacker was quiet and respectful. He addressed him as *Lord* and even bowed as if conceding Yeshua's authority over them. I'm not sure what I witnessed, but those moments were powerful."

Bo John's face shone.

"And Yeshua, what did he do?" James asked, trying to paint a picture of the moment, to glimpse the power himself. What Bo John described felt somehow familiar …

"Yeshua smiled, as if … as if one of his students had just grasped a new teaching."

Can this be true? Could Yeshua have silenced his adversaries with just a few words? Why did their hearts change? And why had they called him "Lord"? Was it out of respect or something deeper? How can this be?

"The men trembled as they waited for Yeshua to do something. Then he spoke to a soldier who had stood aside and not participated.

"'You are a mercenary from Camulodunum in Britannia. You are also the abba of a beautiful crippled son. What would your son say about what these men have done today?'

"The soldier appeared shocked that Yeshua knew his identity and about his son's illness. But Yeshua addressed him kindly: 'Go and live in peace. I have not come to bring contention, but kindness and hope.' The men dispersed, and the mercenary soldier separated from the others."

Bo John took a deep breath and gathered his windblown mantle around him. James was aware his cousin was waiting for affirmation that he had played a central role in a grand event. But had the meeting been monumental, as Bo John described, or had Yeshua simply spoken his mind and the soldiers left? Or had battle-hardened soldiers seen something in Yeshua that had caused them to bow to his authority as if he were a king? What authority would they have seen in the son of Joseph, a simple carpenter from Nazareth?

"Yeshua did not back down, James. My curiosity was raging, so when we left the soldiers, I followed him to the synagogue in Gamla. Religious leaders had flocked to listen to him and were infuriated that an unknown from Nazareth had come to teach learned rabbis.

"Yeshua's teaching stirred up leaders of Gamla's religious community. They twisted like branches in the wind as they listened to his unorthodox teaching. Rabbi Gamaliel could barely contain himself as Yeshua spoke about a new covenant. This is what he said," Bo John told James, and then he quoted as follows:

"The day is coming," says the Lord, "when I will make a new covenant with the people of Israel and Judah. But this is the new covenant I will make with the people of Israel after those days," says the Lord. "I will put my instructions deep within them, and I will write them on their hearts. I will be their God, and they will be my people. And they will not need to teach their neighbors, nor will they need to teach their relatives, saying, 'You should know the Lord.' For everyone, from the least to the greatest, will know me already," says the Lord. "And I will forgive their wickedness, and I will never again remember their sins."[94]

Bo John continued, "Then Yeshua shifted his focus and described those whom God blesses: the poor in spirit, those who mourn, the meek who will inherit the earth, those who hunger and thirst for righteousness, and the merciful, for they will be shown mercy.

"James, I see Yeshua now as someone far more than my cousin. I'm not even sure what that means. I cannot explain;

you need to experience it for yourself. But I am certain of that desire to be near him, sit at his feet, and have him teach me."

James stared at the restless sea. In one encounter with Yeshua, Bo John had profoundly changed. What had happened? Was he a fool, or was Yeshua truly a gift from God, unlike no other man?

James scooped up a fistful of stones from the rocky soil between the boulders and flung them aimlessly, wistfully into the waters of Bethsaida.

Fifty-two

James Finds Love

The familiar odors of Magdala's shore greeted James with the acrid smell of seaweed, the stench of gutted fish, and a bracing sea breeze. Magdala presented a sharp contrast to the pleasant scents of Sepphoris' and Nazareth's wood-burning fires, sweet wildflowers, and whispering wheat fields. Fishing boats crammed the harbor as men scrambled to get their vessels out to sea, claim favored fishing spots, and outrun afternoon squalls. The goal was the same for every captain: bring in a haul before the opportunity slipped away.

Magdala's mystique and reputation had always attracted James. The city offered safe haven for rebellious Zealots as well as spirited fishermen, although the city's reputation suffered. The city was also known for its colorful history. During a Jewish revolt, Romans and Jews fought a great sea battle at Magdala. The Jews lost, and the Romans put twelve thousand inhabitants of Magdala to death in the theater in Tiberias. Another six thousand were forced to build Nero's canal in Corinth, and an additional thirty thousand were sold into slavery. For generations, Jews viewed Magdala as a dangerous village populated by rebels.

The city also provided harbor for those traveling the Sea of Galilee. Magdala was strategically located at the convergence of conflicting weather systems. Winds funneling through the hill country frequently transformed the placid sea into raging mountains of clashing waves. Winds pounding down from Batanea's eastern hill threatened fishermen's lives and livelihood. Waves reaching a height of two men crashed down on villages and harbors with explosive destruction. Sailors and fishermen tried to avoid the tempests—but James had learned by experience that bringing in a catch came first.

Many boats had already pulled away from the docks. He would need to hurry if he hoped to bring home a catch by day's end.

James hastened his pace, hesitantly praying to the God he had long ago rejected that the day would bring a lucrative catch instead of troubled waters.

* * * * *

Compelled by his rebellious spirit, James had come to Magdala for fishing *and* adventure. His parents were blindly devoted to Yeshua as their "special" child, which James found harder to stomach with each passing year.

What was so special about a brother who shrouded himself in a prayer shawl and claimed Yahweh spoke to him? Yeshua got sick like everyone else, and when the family faced trouble, time after time he seemed unable or unwilling to intervene. James had tired of Abba and Ima's obsession with Yeshi. Magdala had been as good a place as any to forget about his family, along with their irrational faith.

James's only regret was hurting Ima. His departure and indulgent life had broken her heart. Yes, he'd determined to find his own answers in his own way, but he'd never wanted to hurt his parents. Even in his unbelief and anger, James's godly upbringing lingered in his heart and would not let him go, tapping him on the shoulder every day and calling him back to righteousness. He was awkwardly aware of Yahweh's presence in the world and with him. And although James seldom saw his parents and family, he sensed Yahweh's quiet presence pursuing him.

The more he sensed Yeshua's love and concern, the harder James ran. And Magdala seemed the right place to drown his anger and bitterness in the putrid latrine he called pleasure.

Magdala and Tiberias served as administrative centers in the region. Both were important fishing centers that catered to the lusts of men who often lived apart from their families. Intent on thrill seeking and snubbing his faith and family, James joined other fishermen who sought the pleasures offered by the city.

A memorable encounter occurred one night as he was celebrating a large catch of fish. He sat beside his boat, enjoying a loaf of rye bread, roasted sardines, and the warmth of a fire before heading into the city for the evening. As he was licking his fingers, a white-haired, stoop-shouldered man approached him.

"Shalom, young man. You appear to be alone here on the beach. My name is Silas, and this is my daughter. Are you looking for companionship tonight?"

James took another bite of fish. It wasn't uncommon for businessmen to approach fishermen returning to shore to sell goods or offer services. Silas appeared to be wealthy enough, and James recognized the reason why in the young woman's eyes.

He is offering his daughter as a prostitute—if she is his daughter. She looks like a child.

The girl was staring at the ground, her long, straight black hair dancing as it curtained her face and then slapped her neck and cheeks in the gusty air. The steady wind bound her deep pink garment about her petite frame, and she clung to her father's arm as if the next slap of wind would drag her away.

A memory flickered through James's mind—his sister Rebecca as a child, standing near a precipice, her long dark hair tossed by gusty winds, and James running to her rescue before she was blown off balance and plummeted to the rocks below. The girl standing before him was also in danger. Rebecca's face flickered through his mind again. He would kill any man who dared to violate his sister, but had he not violated women over and over again? They were all somebody's daughter. His anger suddenly flamed toward the man standing before him.

For the first time in many years, James's conscience stirred to life. He faced a choice—indulge his desires as he always had or be a different man. He looked at the young woman standing before him again.

"I was going into the city tonight anyway. Lead on."

James rose and brushed the remains of his dinner from his tunic.

"What is your daughter's name, Silas?"

The man leered through ragged teeth. "Mary. Mary Magdalene."[95]

* * * * *

Silas led James to his home and took him to a room at the rear of his large, comfortable house, then pointed to an embroidered curtain hung across a doorway to a small anteroom. James slipped inside and took a moment to let his eyes adjust to the dim light. Apparently, Mary had prepared before he was permitted to enter her room.

"Wait until she tells you to enter," Silas growled, "but pay up."

James had already drawn a few coins from a small purse skin hidden beneath his tunic. He handed them to Silas, who skittered away.

A few moments later a woman's voice called out. James entered and found the girl lying on a straw-stuffed mat laid atop a wooden-framed bed. A multihued robe strategically exposed Mary's breasts, and her hair seductively splayed over her shoulders.

James was familiar with many women whose circumstances had forced them into prostitution, but he had never seen a woman whose eyes were so void of life. Her eyes were expressionless, as if she were unaware he was in the room. When he had entered, she asked him to sit on the bed. Her voice was a haunting monotone.

He approached the bed. "Mary, my name is James. I'm not going to hurt you."

She laughed soundlessly, her eyes fixed on a candle flickering in a niche on the wall opposite her bed.

"Get it over with."

"I'm not going to hurt you," James repeated. "I want to talk to you."

"Talk?" she spit out as she jerked to life. "You want to talk, so Silas can beat me for not doing my job? Because you feel sorry for me? Do you think you can make my life better? That you're not like all the rest who come night after night to take what they want? What do you want, really? What are you trying to prove, because you're not fooling me!"

Mary's words came like a punch to the stomach. Having lowered himself to a cushioned trunk that sat beside the bed, he rested his head in his hands.

What am I doing? Why am I here? I don't have any idea what to say to this girl.

Revulsion for his life had swept over him, and he thought he might be sick. His abba would have given his life to prevent his daughters from being abused by a man.

James raised his head. "How old were you when it began?" he whispered.

The silence in the room was broken only by the sound of James's breathing. He was afraid to stir for fear he would frighten her. As he opened his mouth to repeat the question, Mary sat up and pulled her robe closed.

"Silas is *not* my father. He is my husband." She paused and turned her face toward the wall. "Everyone told me I was beautiful when I was young," she whispered. "I didn't understand that beauty came with a curse. When I was thirteen, Abba Obed and Ima Rachel betrothed me to Silas, who was a wealthy Magdala fisherman. He claimed his wife had passed away. Silas owned two large and very profitable fish markets. His success had come by paying bribes to Roman centurions who forced fishermen to sell their fish to him. Silas was notorious for underpricing and undercounting the fish when he paid the fishermen. He is despised for his greed.

"My parents wanted me to bring a good price, and Silas was financially successful. They believed I would be in good hands and that they would be rewarded with a generous mohar. They did not care that he was old, and they refused to see his evil nature.

"However, before the betrothal was signed, Silas forced himself on me. I fought to free myself from his putrid breath, rotting teeth, and foul-smelling body. But the attacks became routine. My ima and abba told me not to complain—we would be married soon."

Mary lowered her head. "If I fought, ran, or tried to hide, he would beat me. If I recoiled at his advances, he whipped my legs and bare back with a leather strap. By this time he was my husband, I was powerless. My parents refused to listen—Silas was a wealthy businessman. Maybe they knew the truth. Maybe they didn't want to repay him the dowry. It doesn't matter. I lost hope a long time ago, years ago."

"I do not understand your pain or what it feels like to lose hope," James whispered. "But I have felt alone, rejected, and lifeless—this is what often brings men to women who are not their wives."

Mary nodded. "Perhaps."

Another silence hung in the air.

"Continue your story, Mary. I want to listen." James locked his hands on the back of his neck and leaned against them.

"My mind became unstable. I would lie in bed for days, unable to do anything. I was in a continual state of despair. What could I do but submit to my torment? I learned to let my mind take me to other places, but Silas grew angry when I drifted away. So as punishment he offered me to fishermen."

James didn't want to hear any more. But this was the truth of Mary's life. Who knew what the truth had been for the women he had used? He had never thought about it before. They had all been somebody's daughter, hopefully loved ... until.

Until.

Mary continued. A stillborn child. A second child sold to slave traders in Sepphoris. Periods of mental torment—for how long she couldn't be sure. But she had not recovered with full restoration of her mind. Nightly voices and nightmares replayed the physical and emotional torment of her life, accusing her, shaming her. Simon accused her of being possessed by demons, and she didn't doubt his word. She knew she lost control of her body and her mind. Some days she became violent, attacking everyone who crossed her path. Other days she sat for hours speaking nonsense to herself.

"I am certain of one truth. I am a hopeless, damaged harlot, worth every abuse I have received."

Fear flashed through James, and his blood went cold. Demons? Could it be true? He had heard reports about demons but never witnessed someone believed to be possessed. And as adventurous and inquisitive as he was, he had a healthy fear of demons.

Everything inside him told him to flee from this woman. *Only trouble, danger, and heartache lie here. Get out!*

But James could not take his eyes off the shuddering woman sitting on the bed. Everyone had abandoned her. Logic told him he had no duty to her. She was a stranger. Yet something in him told him he should not leave. He was a man at sea, adrift in a tempest. An image of his mother's face drifted through his mind. Strangely, he did not feel ashamed here in the room of an unwilling harlot.

"James, I have talked to you longer than I have talked to any man. Perhaps now you would like ..."

James cut her off. "Mary, I am not going to touch you."

She turned to face him. "You find me repulsive?"

James fought the urge to reach out to her, as he had many times when his sisters were troubled.

"You are beautiful. But my abba and ima taught me to respect women—my sisters, my ima, all women. I have not always acted honorably. I selfishly used women. You have helped me see that the problems in my life are about someone else. I have myself to blame for many things." James hung his head.

"Guilt is a terrible thing, James. It torments you."

"Yes. But there must be a way to be freed from our guilt. People did evil things to you. Yahweh did not create you for this horror."

"Well! He didn't stop it, did He?" Mary challenged. "Maybe He helps others, but not me. I'm not worth it."

"I don't believe that. I believe Yahweh loves us because He knows we are not worthy."

James couldn't believe what he was saying. He was speaking about a good Yahweh, a Yahweh who cared about people. Did he even believe what he was saying to this woman? He wasn't sure, but the words somehow rang true.

"You're not responsible for the terrible things people have done to you, Mary. You don't deserve to be treated this way."

A single tear slid down Mary's cheek, and she slapped it away. "I don't understand why I'm even speaking to you. I don't know you. Why should I trust you?" Yet she continued to tell the repugnant details of her life. After a time, she paused.

"You must *never* tell Silas I have told you anything about my life. He will beat me—or worse. He controls everything about me."

James wanted to reach out to comfort her, but he was afraid his actions would be misinterpreted or they would trigger the emptiness he had seen in Mary when he'd first entered the room. Or perhaps he was afraid for himself. He was strangely attracted to her, but he wanted to protect her and see her restored.

She frightened him. Her behavior was erratic, driven by survival. She had somehow retained a fragment of sanity. James was humbled and amazed that she had told him so much of her story. The more she had spoken, the heavier his heart had become to honor her. He wanted to help her—but he didn't know how, or even if he should.

How can it be wrong to help someone who is being abused? I don't want to hurt her further. What would Ima or my sisters do for her? How would they help her?

Most of James's friends had no interest in honoring or helping the women who frequented the wharf and sold their bodies for pleasure. More than once James had willingly joined in their pursuits of pleasure. But when James looked at Mary, he saw a broken woman, cornered like a stray dog waiting to be kicked.

"I will demand that Silas release you."

Mary grabbed James's arm, her eyes wide with terror. "You must not do that! He is powerful and dangerous. He will not give me up and will find ways to harm you. Silas is relentless and controlling to the point of madness."

She was shaking like a child in the cold. James pulled a blanket around her shoulders.

"I can take care of myself, Mary. Fishermen are loyal to one another. Silas would be unwise to come after me, because he would incur the wrath of all of us." He patted her arm reassuringly.

"He is my husband. He tells me a wife must do anything her husband demands."

James winced. He had glimpsed the lash scars on her shoulders.

"My abba honors and protects my ima. He taught my brothers and me to protect our sisters and treat them with respect. I never saw my abba raise a hand to my ima or sisters, and he held Ima's opinion in high regard. If anything, the girls in our house were treated with extra care."

"Perhaps as a son you were treated with extra care," Mary whispered, "but you were too angry to see it. Most fishermen run from something because they are angry. Did anger bring you to Magdala and the sea, James?"

Her question caught him off guard. He had never spoken to anyone about his feelings toward his family and the anger that had drawn him to Magdala. Somehow Mary had seen the rage he struggled so hard to hide. He did not want to talk about it—now or ever. James stood and walked toward the curtained door.

"Yes, I *am* angry, and I will demand that Silas release you. Trust me, I can persuade him, and you will not be punished. Stay here and gather your things. If there is anything of value in this room, take it. And take this." James pulled his money belt from beneath the sash that bound his cloak and threw it onto the bed.

Then he turned and stormed out, leaving a speechless Mary behind.

Within just a few steps, he stood facing Silas, who was sitting in the kitchen gnawing on what looked like a chunk of roasted meat. At the sight of James, he dropped it into a bowl and wiped his hands on a grease-stained cloth on the table. He flashed a leer.

"Did you find everything to your liking?"

James grabbed Silas by his graying hair and pulled him to his feet, then leaned into his face.

"Everything was *not* to my liking, but *you* are going to make everything right. First, I will tell you how things are going to change. Among my thirty or forty friends who are fishermen, I am the smallest, not nearly the strongest, and one with the mildest temper. They consider me family and my friends family. Remember that, Silas."

James cocked back his right arm and landed a blow to

Silas's nose, then another, and another. Silas fell to the floor, blood oozing from his face and screaming.

"What are you doing? What do you want? Was she not to your liking?"

"Not to my liking, you animal?" James kicked him in the ribs. "Consider yourself fortunate if you are alive when I leave. I will be back, perhaps later tonight, perhaps tomorrow morning or tomorrow night. And when I come, I will bring my friends, fishermen who would all love to pummel a coward who sells his wife to men to be raped.

"You will not go near Mary tonight or ever. If I learn you have spoken a word of threat or condemnation or taken any action against her, you will suffer severe consequences. Do not go near her room! You are to release her in the morning, give her one hundred denarii,[96] and allow her to return to her parents."

The muscles in Silas's neck drew taut and his teeth clenched as he lay in the growing puddle of blood.

"You think you can talk to me this way in my home? You have no power over me or my wife." Silas spit the words out.

"Yes, but I *do* have control over many things. My friends, first of all, and their preferences in where they sell their fish." James cocked his arms in a defensive stance. "It would be a terrible thing to see a decline in business, wouldn't it, Silas, if suddenly all the fishermen in Magdala were to take their fish to your competitor? It would be unfortunate if the businessmen of Magdala began to question why the entire fishing community turned on you."

"I am a man of power," Silas screamed. "I own the authorities on the waterfront. Roman legionaries are some of my best customers. One word from me, and they will throw you in chains."

Silas struggled to stand. James stretched out his leg and shoved him back to the floor with his foot.

"You don't intimidate me. You're a coward and a cheat. Your biggest problem is that I don't care about consequences, and you do. I care about helping your wife—not to use her, but to set her free."

"You're digging your grave." Silas wiped blood from his face with the back of his hand.

James stepped on his throat.

"Promise you will allow her return to her family—without threat or coming anywhere near her. And you will give her one hundred denarii as token compensation for all she has lost. Now! Don't force me to crush your throat."

Silas writhed in pain. "Yes ... yes, you have my word, I will let her go. No harm will come to her, and I will leave her in peace tonight and forever. Now get off of me!"

James sensed Mary's eyes watching, and he glanced over his shoulder. She stood just out of view, hidden by the curtain to her room, her hands covering her mouth, her eyes wide in fear. James gave her a reassuring smile.

He turned back to Silas and lifted his foot. Silas grabbed his throat and moaned, then slowly raised himself to his knees and groped for the greasy rag on the table and held it to his bleeding nose.

James turned toward Mary's room.

"You are free to return to your parents' home in the morning. Silas will not approach you or speak to you. He will leave one hundred denarii on the table in the kitchen before morning and will be gone before you arise. I will send someone to accompany you home. If Silas speaks to you or threatens you, tell the man who will meet you in the morning. You are free."

As he made his way back to the wharf later that night, James wondered if his threats were enough. Would Silas see through his show of bravado? Would he let Mary go? And would she be safe until morning and have the courage to leave?

He suddenly found himself praying, pleading, aware that he knew he was not enough to help this woman, that the evil in the world needed a solution greater than he could provide.

For the first time in many years he considered that perhaps faith was not senseless and that a senseless world needed answers beyond human understanding.

Fifty-three
Revenge: James Visits the Rophe

Mary retreated to her sparse, filthy quarters in Magdala, trembling and in despair.

She was in deep trouble. She had told her deepest secrets. Voices screamed that she had ruined everything and her life would never change. Silas would bring her back and kill her. How dare she hope? And why should she trust a man to keep his word?

The evil voices screamed relentlessly—accusation, condemnation—taunting her with commands to take her life.

She curled into a tight ball in the center of her bed, rocking back and forth like a child, crying out from somewhere deep within her for help to survive the night.

* * * * *

Silas's hold on Mary was diabolical. James had tried to console her before leaving, but eventually he walked out the door, followed by Silas's threats and curses.

He wasn't naive about Silas's power and influence. The tyrant wouldn't give up his prized moneymaker without a fight. His promises under duress had been lies he had no intention of keeping.

James's thoughts, along with his stomach, churned as he made his way toward the docks. He had done the only thing he knew how to do, and he thought his abba and ima would have approved. The fishermen at the wharf would also be impressed to learn he had dealt Silas a few blows. Silas was well-known as a cheat, and it would not take much to enlist the help of fishermen.

Menacing rain clouds darkened the sky as James made his way through the center of Magdala, deep in thought. The look of desperation on Mary's face as he'd left lingered in his mind. He clenched and unclenched his fists to drive the pain from his knuckles and his heart.

Three strong burly men rushed out of the darkness as James was reliving his conversation with Mary. He had turned down a dark, narrow alley leading to the business district when the club-toting men jumped him. Within minutes, Silas's henchmen exacted revenge and left James in a heap at the side of the road, bleeding and writhing in pain. The attackers had given James no opportunity to defend himself. Blow after blow found their target until James could no longer raise his arms to protect his head.

He wasn't sure how long he lay unconscious and bleeding. When he awoke, he struggled to stand, but the pain was crushing, and once again he blacked out and slumped back to the ground.

Hours passed before a man from the village discovered James lying in the gutter as he passed down the narrow street on the way to Magdala's market. He helped James stand and half dragged him to the synagogue *rophe*, who treated his many wounds and found someone to help James back to his boat.

Recovery took several painful days, but James did not forget his promise to help Mary gain freedom and safety, goals that involved innumerable challenges. Something about her had taken hold of his heart. He charged Bo John, Zebedee, and several other fishermen with returning to Silas's house and escorting Mary to her parents'. Reluctantly, and somewhat surprisingly, Silas let the men escort Mary to her home. Bo John and Zebedee convinced

James that Mary would be safe in her parents' home. Silas dared not mistreat her after James's threats.

But James could not trust their word. When he was well, he made frequent visits to check on Mary's well-being. Eventually, Mary's parents invited James in, and before long he was given permission to talk with Mary to help bring her back to health and correct her distorted thinking.

Mary sometimes recognized him when he came, and other times she sat as if in a trance or babbled black thoughts.

James had experienced far more than physical blows from Silas's lackeys and Mary from Silas's hand. Mary had captivated his heart, but her mind was troubled, and she needed a friend. At times discouragement overwhelmed him when he acknowledged how slowly her mind was healing.

Whenever James's visits dwindled because the fish were running, Mary's condition worsened, as did his fears for her recovery.

Mary's ima confided that James seemed Mary's only tether to reality. On one occasion when Mary was lucid, she whispered that she was being tormented by seven demons. During some visits she was lucid, but at other times she appeared to be in another world—singing, dancing, and whirling around the room unaware of her surroundings.

Although not religious, Silas appeared terrified of the spirit world and was happy to remain at a distance after hearing reports of Mary's behavior. Rumors circulated that Mary had received minimal attention from Silas because of his fear of demons.

Exhausted after months of effort to help Mary, James's discouragement overwhelmed him. He had done all he could do, and it was not enough. His anger with Yahweh fired anew in his heart.

Why have You inflicted this beautiful young woman with such a terrible affliction? Are You punishing her? Will You not act to free her from her torment?

But even as he asked, a gentle voice resonated in James's soul.

"You say you do not believe in Me, that you hate Me, that you owe Me nothing, yet you come to Me in prayer, angry that I have not done things your way?"

In a burst of illumination, James realized he was conversing with Yahweh.

He was looking at the world through eyes of love. What did this mean—for him and for Mary? If life was not about pursuing selfish desires and pleasure, what purpose was behind living, suffering, working, drawing the next breath? His mind overflowed with unresolved questions.

Can Mary ever be well, Yahweh?

He was unprepared for the quiet voice that echoed the answer in his heart.

Yes, James, she can and will be healed.

He fell to the ground, overcome, and remained on his face before Yahweh until the darkness in his soul lifted.

Fifty-four
Fishermen Face the "Bird of Prey"

Early afternoon heat slithered across the Sea of Galilee as James surveyed the surf. Fishing would be slow, and James felt a pressing need to return to Magdala. His time with Mary had disturbed him. He needed time at sea to think, and the trip would help. Simon, Andrew, Zebedee, and Bo John had agreed to accompany him, as well as Yeshua, who had been teaching nearby and was returning to visit his family. With the afternoon heat rising, The men lifted anchor and set sail from Bethsaida for Magdala.

Yeshua had chosen a seat at the rear of the boat, and James sat next to him. The ride was always smoother in the rear, and James longed for quiet, away from the raucous voices of his friends. Without the weight of a fish-filled hull, Simon's large boat skimmed the surface of the placid sea. The ride was eerily quiet. Only the gentle lapping of waves against the wooden hull broke the silence as the boat cut through the water. Perhaps he could talk to Yeshua about his experience in Magdala, if he could find the courage.

James lifted his face to the breeze and hung his fingers in the water splashing off the hull. Simon steadied the rudder as he barked orders to Andrew, who was unmercifully pestering Simon. Andrew simply didn't understand limits, especially when it came to irritating Simon. Simon sometimes overstretched his authority and reveled in bossing the others. Andrew had hard, fast fists and was skilled in using them, frequently taunting his brother into scuffles. While as brothers they often faced off, strangers and troublemakers always met their unified wrath.

James watched the men tussle good-naturedly. He always enjoyed their company and the camaraderie among the fishermen. Occasionally one or another would find himself tossed overboard, but he would always be hauled back into the boat sopping wet, met by jesting and laughter.

The men had lowered the nets into the boat for the sail back to Magdala. Winds were light, but the breeze was refreshing. James never wearied of the warmth of the sun on his face and the brush of the sea breeze in his hair. Each haul of their net came up empty—there would be no nets to clean tonight, only an evening of wine, good food, and stories and laughter among friends.

The men were well-known in coastal villages in the region to relish their leisure and eke all they could from their hard-earned, limited denarii. Most of James's friends avoided brothels, but on occasion some followed the call of temptation and found themselves in conflict with the Roman soldiers and Gentiles who frequented local brothels. Political tensions among Jews, Gentiles, and the fishermen ran high, and even going near a brothel was often considered an invitation for a fight.

As the men docked and tied off the boat upon their arrival in Magdala, James spied the local tax collector on shore. He was making another unannounced visit.

"I see the leech has washed up on shore," Andrew muttered.

"Looks to me like a bird of prey," Simon responded. "A vulture."

James hushed the men, fearing their voices might carry on the sea breeze. But they weren't alone in their frustration. Almost all Galileans despised Levi, the local tax collector, and relished calling him spiteful names.

Levi was required to pay the Roman government in

advance, and then he collected from citizens in his territory to recoup his expenses and bring in a profit. He notoriously levied unfair taxes. Most people regarded him as a Roman sympathizer and a money-grubbing opportunist. He made his profits off the backs of common hardworking fishermen and farmers who earned meager incomes, but from the rich and powerful he accepted bribes to keep their taxes lower.

The locals disdained this unfair system and hated the man who administered it. Levi was the embodiment of the tyranny of their Roman occupiers. Sadly, he was one of their own—a Jew—profiting from injustice. He was beyond disgraceful.

Levi, himself a Galilean, often collected duties along busy highways, demanding taxes on imported goods that farmers, merchants, and caravans brought in. He enjoyed catching merchants and vendors when they least expected it and were transporting their largest catches and inventories.

James watched from a distance as Levi stopped and set up a makeshift table beneath the shade of a cluster of tamarisk trees. He paid two swarthy men to act as guards. His presence made locals' blood boil, and it wasn't uncommon for men to take a swing at him or rob him out of anger. Anyone who landed a blow or stole from him, most area Jews saw him as a hero. Even Romans taunted and despised tax collectors.

But James wasn't looking for trouble. He needed to stay out of the eye of the Roman guard.

All the fishermen knew that Levi came unannounced to the docks to evaluate the day's catch and levy appropriate taxes—normally 12.5 percent of the catch. He was permitted to charge as much as 25 percent for port fees. These taxes were added to property taxes, income taxes, and land taxes forced upon the Galileans. If a fisherman had a low volume, extra taxes were levied, creating a punishing burden for payment, and these came with the threats of Antipas's enforcers to exact payment.

Peter, Andrew, and James had experienced frequent clashes with Levi. They had never hidden their dislike for the man and discovered that beneath his demanding bravado, he was a coward. In confrontations where James and John had participated, Levi had learned to approach the "sons of thunder" with caution.

One by one, the men approached the table and declared "No catch" with a smile, knowing their lack of fish deprived Levi of payment and that he would be reluctant to levy a punitive tax.

Levi chose his response carefully. When fishermen reported no catch, he often searched the hull of the boat, accompanied by local soldiers he bribed and who, therefore, shared his incentive for a full catch.

One soldier called out, "Tax them anyway. If they have come back without fish, it is only to defraud Rome or because they are lazy Jews."

James recoiled in anger, clenching his fists. Hands gently gripped his shoulders to restrain him, and he turned. It was Yeshua.

He could hear other soldiers laughing. Tormenting Jews was their sport. His anger surged, but Yeshua smiled, then released James and approached Levi at the table.

Levi leaned back in his goat-hair chair and crossed his arms. "Pay up. You are not a fisherman and will be charged for all of them." He crossed his arms and waited for a response.

James watched the stand-off in suspense. Moments crept by.

Yeshua leaned over the table and whispered into Levi's ear. When he finished, he leaned back and looked Levi in the eye.

The color drained from Levi's face as his look of bravado was replaced with one of fear. As the fishermen passed by him one by one, he spoke the same words: "No tax. Move on. No tax. Move on."

James watched in wonder. What had Yeshua said? And why had Levi suddenly seemed afraid? How had his words and the look in his eyes drained the anger from his heart?

James had no idea. But he trusted Yeshua, believed his message, and wanted to know him more.

Still, something deep in his soul told him that a decision to follow Yeshua would come at a high cost—perhaps all that he had and even more. Who was Yeshua?

Fifty-five

Unveiling of Mystery Zealot

The day's work had been more exhausting than usual. Joseph had not anticipated that Benjamin would expect the hull repairs to be completed in one day. With Yeshua traveling and preaching, both the skilled and heavy labor now fell to Joseph. Yeshua had not been with him on the job to haul materials or do heavy lifting. The repair was not completed until just after sunset, and Joseph's body ached with weariness with each step home from Tiberias.

With the moon illuminating his path, Joseph's steps brought him to the courtyard of their compound. From a distance, he could see that the lamp in the niche near the door glowed with unusual brightness. Joseph's heart quickened. Something must be wrong. Mary only brightened the lamp to warn of danger or misfortune.

His legs had no strength left to run. His energies were better exerted in prayer. Joseph lengthened his stride as he lifted his heart.

Av, I have no knowledge of what news awaits, but someone needs comfort and Your presence right now. Be with them. Comfort Mary and give me wisdom for what lies ahead.

He staggered the final steps to the door, pushed it open, and bent to enter. Mary rushed to him with open arms, nearly knocking him backward through the open door. She embraced him and clung to him with the desperation of a child who had lost its mother. Joseph waited for her ragged breathing to calm.

"It's ... it's Matthan, Joseph. Your brother has been arrested and taken to the prison in Tiberias."

Mary looked up at Joseph, tears streaming from her face. Joseph had seen her ridiculed and threatened, but she had always stood strong, saving her tears for moments with her Father Av or in Joseph's arms. His heart fluttered with fear.

"They have accused him of insurrection, Joseph. Insurrection. Have they made a mistake, or is he guilty? What can we do?"

Soldiers often wrongly accused Jews of crimes. They would punish Matthan even if he was not guilty and feel no shame. They often unjustly incarcerated and beat innocent men. Roman soldiers believed all Jews were guilty of something.

"They do unthinkable things to prisoners accused of being Zealots. I cannot believe that Matthan—your brother—can be guilty of such charges." Mary's thoughts returned to Matthan's visit months before. Was he really a Zealot?

Mary crumpled into her favorite chair in the gathering room and put her head in her hands. Joseph sat on the floor beside her and took her hand. How much should he tell her? They had never kept secrets from one another, but what could it profit her to worry about what she could not control ... for what he could not control? He drew her face to his chest so she would not read his eyes.

Joseph had learned more than he wanted to about the Zealots. They did not present a serious threat to Rome's dominance, but they were a continual annoyance and drain of resources. They stirred up trouble, sometimes in violent outbursts and sometimes in petty harassment, throwing rocks or pillaging Roman outposts. So it was to be expected that soldiers took their revenge. When they caught rebels, soldiers treated them cruelly, either crucifying them or sending them to maximum security prisons to endure inhumane conditions. Prison provided soldiers the opportunity to punish rebels with impunity, and they were encouraged to be merciless and answered to no one.

Joseph had heard a rumor that Barabbas, commander of a large Zealot militia, had joined forces with Sicarii—a splinter group of the Zealots—led by Judas Iscariot.[97] The combined forces had launched a surprise attack on Herod's lightly guarded fortress at Masada. The Romans believed the natural defenses at Masada would withstand any attacks. Therefore, only a small force was sent to protect Herod's grand palace.

The Romans repelled the initial attack, but Zealot determination sent fear through the Roman forces. Just hours away, a cohort of Roman soldiers from the Sixth Legion stationed at Antonia Fortress, with a cavalry regiment and heavy armor, marched toward Masada. The Jerusalem force had swollen to hundreds of soldiers preparing for an anticipated Zealot and Sicarii assault on weaker Roman outposts. Restless soldiers at Jerusalem were living in cramped barracks and passed the days glutting themselves and playing board games. A poor loser started a brawl. The soldiers had lost ethical and moral restraints and become dangerous, and tempers ran high when they confronted the Jews.

Located strategically atop an isolated rock plateau, Masada's fortress boasted impregnable walls, and Roman forces repelled every attempt to overthrow the stronghold. The Zealots attacked over and over. However, this time the ruthless leader Barabbas tried to breach the walls of Masada.

Boasting a panoramic view of the outlying area for security, the private palace of the king stood on the northern edge of the steep cliff at Masada. A fortress wall separated the secure residence from the rest of the compound. The elaborate administration center was located along the center of the western wall near the main gate. The building housed storerooms, workshops, and apartments—and possibly the king's throne room. If the rebels could take it, the administration center would be a strategic prize.

Over several hours, the rebels inflicted substantial losses upon the Romans, but they were no match for the approaching reinforcements. As the enemy approached and penned them in, the rebels fled and took heavy losses as they scattered in all directions. With the Zealots successfully routed, the Roman army withdrew and headed back to Jerusalem. A contingency of Roman forces remained behind while the majority of the soldiers headed north to seek the escaping rebels, whose names had been extracted from a captive.

Joseph shook his head. Matthan's name would surely have been on the list, but he dared not tell Mary for fear of frightening her further.

In spite of defeat, the surviving Sicarii set their sights on destroying their Roman oppressors. Even Jews feared their ruthlessness as terrorists and assassins.

Joseph had learned that Matthan was accused of taking part in the attack and was on Rome's list of wanted criminals. Matthan was a known associate of Barabbas, and word had circulated that Barabbas had been a leader in the revolt. The Romans were searching for participants in the raid whom they could subject to their infamous torture and execution.

Joseph calmed Mary as he asked her for details. She couldn't remember everything—it all had happened so quickly. Instead, she peppered Joseph with questions about prison conditions and torture.

Joseph answered each question patiently but with as few details as possible. She was obviously distraught. Her voice shook as she recounted the evening's events.

"Matthan appeared this morning right after sunup. He asked if he could stay a few days because soldiers were searching for him. Even though he's been involved with the Zealots, he's your brother. How could I turn him away?"

Joseph tried to hide his anger. Mary had done nothing wrong, but Matthan, having not told her that authorities were on his trail, had placed Joseph's family in danger. Matthan had chosen a life of risk when he joined the Zealots. His capture would likely put Joseph's family in grave peril if soldiers learned that they had harbored Matthan.

His brother had avoided involving family members for many years, so it was probable that he had come to their home because he was in imminent danger. Joseph pushed away the anger he felt about Matthan drawing attention to his family so he could focus on Mary, who had begun to cry. Joseph stroked her head as she spoke.

"Don't be angry, Joseph. Matthan's friends found us—coming against his direct orders. He was furious and had just ordered his men out of the house when soldiers crashed through the door."

Joseph drew Mary into his arms. "There is nothing you could have or should have done differently. If you had interfered, they could have arrested you as an accomplice. You are safe, and that's all that matters."

"I had no idea they were going to arrest Matthan, that he was in danger of arrest."

Joseph continued to soothe Mary. He could not speak to her about his fears.

"They accused me of harboring a criminal and said we could be charged with treason.

"Joseph, could you go to prison?" The look of fear on Mary's upturned face tore Joseph's heart. Why had he not been here? If only he had been home to protect his family!

Matthan, how dare you have brought this fear upon my household, upon my wife, who looks for the good in everyone—even Roman soldiers who persecute us. She has done nothing wrong. Yahweh, please protect us and vindicate us of wrong.

Joseph had known for a long time that Matthan was not just involved with the rebels but was also a chief commander.

He had joined Judas of Gamla, the Zealot founder, before Yeshua was born and had taken a major role in uprisings just before Yeshua's bar mitzvah. In fact, Yeshua's teaching experience in Gamla had been peaceful in part because Dod Matthan was considered a Zealot hero in Gamla.

Joseph cradled his wife in his arms. He could not give her false assurances, but he needed to be truthful about Matthan's situation.

"Mary, Matthan has been a Zealot for many years. The last time I spoke to him, I warned him to leave the group because of his advancing age, and he refused. He believed only a violent uprising could liberate his people. Matthan would not listen to reason. It is true that those who live by the sword die by the sword. This is the tragic path he chose."

Mary listened. Joseph would rely on her respect and trust for his opinion and his word. She was not guilty of any wrongdoing. Yahweh would protect them, but he knew his next words would frighten her.

"Mary, I must go to Tiberias to seek my brother's release."

The possibility of release was impossible, but he must try, even if all he could offer Matthan was comfort, food, and fresh clothing.

"He is my brother. No matter what the consequences, I must go to Tiberias, find a way into the prison, and do all for him I can do."

Joseph refused to utter the final words of the sentence: *before he is executed.*

Fifty-six
Joseph Faces Prison Fears

Joseph forced himself to admit he would face danger in Tiberias. Yes, he had struggled with a strained relationship with Matthan when his brother joined the rebel group, but Matthan would always be his brother. Joseph would be incapable of protecting himself, but his unwavering belief that Yahweh would take care of him strengthened his resolve to search for Matthan in the reprehensible prison in Tiberias. God only knew what help he would be able to offer when he got there.

Yeshua spoke from across the room where he sat near Rebecca. "Abba, I would be less likely to be suspected of conspiracy. I can travel discreetly."

Joseph was adamant. "It is far too dangerous for you, Yeshi. Tiberias is Antipas's city, and if he learned who you were, it would be his highest priority is to find you and question you about your intentions in Galilee. And as Matthan's brother, I should go. Tiberias is also an unclean city by Jewish law. This is not your mission; it is mine."

The other boys chimed in, offering to go in Joseph's place, but Mary hushed them.

"Yes, you must go, Joseph. Matthan is your brother. We will respect your decision. Our task will be to pray for your safety, for Matthan to be spared, and for Yahweh's will to be done in this."

Mary had turned her face toward the wall. The tightness

in her voice told Joseph she was resolved but fighting back tears.

Joseph pulled her close, and the two talked of his travel plans. Not only was it dangerous for relatives to visit a prisoner, but also devout Jews did not enter Tiberias, because it was considered unclean. Joseph's mind was made up—he would never forgive himself if he did not go—but he listened to Mary's concerns, assured her he would be wise, and made the safest provisions possible. In the end, they both would have to trust Yahweh as they had before when faced with the impossible.

"I must go, my precious one. I put my life in Yahweh's hands. We have learned that impossible circumstances do not exist for Him."

Joseph didn't want to show his concerns about going to Tiberias or about leaving after the family had been threatened. Traveling to Tiberias, Herod's capital, meant Joseph would be away from his home for an extended time and would be walking into Herod Antipas's home territory.

He was certain that Yeshua's reputation as a teacher had reached Herod, but hopefully Herod's larger concern was for unruly Zealots. However, anyone who drew a crowd was considered a threat, so Yeshua had avoided preaching in Antipas's region. Even the Romans considered Herod to be a paranoid governor, using all means to capture and eradicate Zealots who plagued him.

Despite his resolve to trust Yahweh, Joseph's concern overrode his thoughts—for Matthan, for Yeshua, and for the rest of the family. He was taking on a grave responsibility that could end in his death.

Yahweh, I ask for Your wisdom and discernment for this task.

Mary laid her hand on Joseph's arm. "We will pray for deliverance for Matthan, but we must be prepared for bad news. Apart from a miracle from Yahweh, he will not be released. We must pray for Yahweh's great love to move him, especially now. Perhaps prison is the place that will force him to pull his hands from his ears and listen."

Yeshua spoke from across the gathering room, where he had taken a seat near the door near Rebecca. "Abba, you must prepare for the dangers of this trip."

"Yeshi, you understand more than anyone that we are safest when we walk where Yahweh calls us. And I will be wise in all I do."

"Yes, Abba."

Roman prisons were typically holding tanks for prisoners waiting for trials that seldom occurred. Months passed before a Roman judge arrived to listen to charges. Most men who entered the fetid jails awaited inevitable execution, crucifixion, or torture and dismemberment.

"I am not unaware of the dangers in Tiberias. Guards expect bribes, and family members are often turned away. But let my actions assure you that if any of you are ever in trouble, I will come for you, whatever the risk."

Joseph hoped his words would comfort the family, especially Mary and Yeshua, the latter of whom so often was set aside because of his true identity. Yet perhaps this crisis might be Yahweh's plan and the time when Yeshi's divine nature might be revealed through a miracle.

Is it even right for me to desire such a thing—that Yahweh's divine nature could be accomplished through a man who has chosen a life of defiance, rebellion, and violence?

James spent little time with his parents but had dropped by to visit them. His visits were usually short and unexpected but always welcome. He settled in a corner, listening. Joseph could see the anger building in his eyes. Obviously, James expected Yeshua to step forward, show his power, aid the family, and prevent Abba's perilous trip to Tiberias. Over the past few months James's hard attitude toward Yeshi seemed to have softened. Now a new test emerged.

Joseph forced himself to remain silent. Would James

ever understand? Or would his resentment fester until his faith in Yahweh flickered and died?

The following day, Joseph prepared for his trip to Tiberias. Mary lingered over packing his food and clothes, knowing he would be gone many days. She packed additional food and clothing for Matthan.

Joseph set out early the following day. The thirty-five-milla-passuum[98] trip from Nazareth to Tiberias proved to be uneventful. The winding rocky road from Nazareth took Joseph along the Nazareth Ridge joining the International Highway, called "Way of the Sea" at the junction of the road that passed through the Turan Valley. Avoiding the Arbel pass toward Magdala, Joseph took the northeast road to Tiberias.

Herod had selected Tiberias as his new capital because of its location on the shores of the Sea of Galilee, which provided commerce and access to major trade routes. In spite of strong objections from Jewish Galileans about building over burial sites, Antipas determined to build the city—be damned with Jewish laws and opposition.[99]

Joseph prayerfully sought temporary living quarters when he arrived in Tiberias. Because the city was considered unclean by conservative Jews, few lived there, and a Jewish synagogue had not been established where he could inquire about lodging. Not acquainted with anyone who lived in the city, he settled for a hostel that accommodated unsavory travelers and undesirables. Joseph had always felt comfortable among the downtrodden and poor, and he thanked Yahweh that he had found warm, dry housing.

While securing his room, Joseph asked the proprietor about the location of the Tiberias prison. The hostelry was a short distance away, and the innkeeper knew it well.

"Everyone in this city is all too familiar with the stinking hole the Romans call a prison. We smell its stench. We see those who enter and never see the light of day again. And many in Tiberias know where and when to stand outside the prison walls so they can hear the screams of the tortured and crucified."

Joseph shook his head and ignored the comment, then hurried to his room, gathered needed provisions, and set out walking toward the prison's main administrative building overlooking the city square.

An ancient Jewish burial cave had been located below the building. Herod had ordered the bones be relocated so the space could be used as holding cells for prisoners waiting to be summoned for trial. Each low-ceilinged cell was just large enough for one or two men to lie down in. Some common cells would hold multiple inmates. The thickness of the outer walls of stone measured more than half the height of a man and included narrow openings for ventilation and food portals. Friends or relatives also used the openings to pass food into prisoners confined in the cells. A narrow stone bench was built into one cell wall, but these were diabolically undersized, making sitting or sleeping nearly impossible.

Prisoners did not come to Tiberias or other Roman prisons to be sentenced and confined as punishment. They *were* often confined for long periods of time, but every inmate faced starvation, illness, torture, disfigurement, slavery, or crucifixion. The almost inevitable death penalty offered Rome many advantages: minimal costs, eradication of suspected enemies, and entertainment for the city's sadists.

Prisoners were manacled in stocks and chains and guarded by soldiers who dealt out cruelty for sport. Chains were often shortened or altered to limit a prisoner's mobility, forcing them to stand for torturous periods of time.

Visitors left the facility with horror stories of putrid, filthy cells and staggering overcrowding. Most prisoners' shredded garments were stiff with filth that hung from their emaciated bodies. Any food was provided by relatives or concerned benefactors. Even when family and friends brought food and clothing, their kindness was thwarted by guards who stole gifts brought to the condemned.

Prison visitors were viewed with suspicion as likely saboteurs and coconspirators. Risk was greater for visitors if the imprisoned was charged with insurrection or treason. Visitors were also interrogated, which often led to confiscation of property, their imprisonment, and torture.

No matter the risk of visiting a prisoner charged with sedition, Joseph knew he must attempt to contact Matthan and show his support, however unlikely it was that his brother would ever be released. But most important, he had to do this because Matthan's execution could be imminent.

As the prison came into view, Joseph paused beside a blind beggar to pray for wisdom and protection. Then he pressed a few coins into the man's hand and strode toward the gate and passed two Roman soldiers, who were arguing.

Once inside the administration building, Joseph was pushed into a line of other hopeful visitors, many bearing baskets and packages. When it was his turn, Joseph approached the stern young Roman guard standing behind a table.

"I am looking for a prisoner here by the name of Matthan ben Jacob," he spoke boldly in Latin.

The guard looked up, his face registering surprise. "You speak Latin?"

"Yes," Joseph responded. Romans did not like to speak in Greek, much less Aramaic, and certainly not Hebrew to a lowly Jew. The man was obviously surprised that Joseph was fluent in his native language. Joseph's extensive work in Sepphoris forced him to learn Latin.

"I am a relative of Matthan ben Jacob."

Joseph feared to tell the soldier he was Matthan's brother, which would place him under suspicion of conspiracy. Perhaps the guard would assume Joseph was an uncle.

"You must wait with the others." The soldier pointed at

the crowd of visitors milling about the room. "The magistrate must grant permission."

Joseph took a quiet, deep breath and forced a look of confidence.

Thank You, Yahweh, for calm. Please, give me wisdom. May I honor You, even here in the presence of my enemies.

He looked steadily into the soldier's eyes, and the man glanced away, rattled.

I have not been turned away or thrown in shackles. Thank You.

Many of the visitors were leaning wearily against the stone walls of the room. Joseph squeezed into a spot in the corner and joined them. He waited until his feet cried out for relief before the guard called him back to the table. Joseph prayed that he would be granted favor as he waited for the soldier to finish a conversation with the man in front of him.

But the soldier never spoke a word and waved Joseph toward a tall, stately man wearing a white robe who sat at a large desk at the back of the room. His aquiline nose tilted upward, making him appear pompous and autocratic.

The magistrate delivered his pronouncement in a monotone, his voice trailing off at the end. "You will have to come back tomorrow. I do not have time to find the cell of this Matthan you seek."

His voice was cold as he continued. "We have had an influx of insurrectionists this week and have not yet recorded where they all have been placed."

The magistrate had given a reasonable answer and not the excuse or questions Joseph had expected. Joseph was dumbfounded. The official dismissed him without further comment.

Joseph left quietly, overwhelmed that he had not been harassed and grateful that the food and clothing he had brought for Matthan had not been confiscated. He could deal with the Roman bureaucracy again tomorrow. Today he would be grateful than he was not in chains beside his brother.

And perhaps tomorrow a well-greased palm might bring him even closer to Matthan's side.

Fifty-seven
Hopeless and Doomed

Joseph was waiting outside the gate the next morning before the administrative offices opened. The same men sat at the tables, and this time Joseph was immediately waved through to the magistrate. Again, Joseph asked in Latin for permission to see Matthan.

The magistrate tapped his yellowed dirty fingernails on the desk in front of him, then sneered. "What do you have for me?"

Joseph bent his head. If seeing Matthan meant groveling, he would grovel. He was not above playing a fool's game.

"I am a poor carpenter from a tiny village in Galilee and have little to add to your coffers."

Joseph omitted reference to Nazareth. The fewer people who heard about a carpenter from Nazareth, the less the risk someone would identify Yeshua as the rabbi and king whom Herod Antipas sought—a carpenter from Nazareth who was the son of a carpenter.

Joseph continued. "Most of the people I serve pay me in trade—fish, meat, wood, wine. But I have brought you something of value."

He reached into his bundle of provisions for Matthan, pulled out a delicately rendered wood carving of a lamb, and set it on the filthy table between them.

"This would make a good gift for someone you care

about. It is valuable, I assure you. I worked on it for many months to create the most realistic detail ..."

Joseph paused. The prison steward was staring at the face of the lamb. He had picked up the carving, and his fingers brushed the creature's ear. Then with a jerk of his arm, he slipped the object beneath his cloak as he turned to a clerk working at the table in front of him.

"Send word to the head prison steward that the man seeking Matthan from Sepphoris is here again."

The clerk rolled his eyes. It was easy to see he hated being sent into the pit to fetch prisoners, deliver messages, or escort visitors into the vile depths of the prison. Who could blame him?

Hours passed as Joseph waited for information about Matthan's whereabouts. But he was wise enough not to show his inner turmoil and impatience. A brusque, clean-shaven interrogator politely invited Joseph into his office.

His office? Why the feigned helpful demeanor? Does this man think I'm a fool? He holds Matthan's fate and mine in his hand. He is hoping to manipulate me for his purposes.

The inquisitor studied a sheet of papyrus, then shook his head back and forth. He glanced up at Joseph with a look of accusation.

"Matthan has been charged with rebellion and high treason, which are serious charges." He matter-of-factly continued, "He will be sentenced to death by crucifixion unless he reveals the locations of his coconspirators and their identities." The inquisitor leaned toward Joseph with an intimidating glare. "What do you know about his activities?"

Joseph had prepared for intimidation and accusation. He straightened in his chair and held his gaze. The accusations had now shifted from Matthan to Joseph's involvement with Matthan—exactly what his family had feared.

Joseph did not respond, and the room fell silent. He would not be intimidated. He was playing a dangerous game but would not back down. He honestly knew nothing of Matthan's involvement.

"I am not an insurrectionist, nor have I supported insurrectionists in their activities. I have been estranged from my brother for my adult life. I have come here to provide a relative with food and clothing for his comfort—nothing more."

Joseph held his inquisitor's gaze, even as he questioned whether his bravado was valor or idiocy. Jews who dealt with Roman authorities often feigned deference to secure compassion. Confidence was seen as rebellion and a threat. Yet Joseph believed his confidence had been bestowed and was not his own—confidence from Yahweh.

"So, you are a relative?" the guard retorted.

"Yes, he is my brother." Joseph had determined before leaving home that he would not use deceit as a ploy.

The interrogator blinked at Joseph's unwavering stare. He swallowed, then abruptly stood and turned toward the door and asked Joseph to follow.

Joseph tried to hold back a gasp and drew in a slow, deep breath as they headed down a long, arched-stone hallway secured by guards to the steps leading down into the prison. The eyes of every prison guard drilled into the back of his neck as he walked the long hall. From the expression on people's faces, he concluded that few who appealed for visits were granted their request.

He had been given favor by Yahweh Himself. And Yeshi, in his wisdom, had prompted Joseph to bring the carved lamb that had captured the heart of a hardened prison steward. Mary would be overwhelmed to learn of Yahweh's unfathomable protection.

As the door leading to the cellblock opened, the stench of human waste, sweat, rotting food, and moldy walls struck Joseph with the force of a blow, and his stomach wretched. He forced his face to remain unmoved. A dead body lay in a corner of a cell, and rats scrambled everywhere, chewing on anything dead or living.

Joseph was shoved toward a cell at the rear of the block of barred chambers. As his eyes adjusted to the oppressive darkness, he made out Matthan's bloodied form lying lifeless on the floor near the narrow rock bench built to accommodate discarded bodies. A second, younger prisoner in Matthan's cell was shackled to a metal ring in the floor.

"Matthan, wake up. It is Joseph your brother. I have come to see you and brought food for you."

Even in the darkness, Joseph could see purple, green, and yellow bruises on his brother's neck, arms, and legs. Clotted blood had matted his hair and crusted his face. Wounds on the bottoms of his dirty feet oozed with pus. Matthan was no longer a young man, and he could not survive long under these conditions.

"You should not have come. Your efforts are a waste," Matthan rasped. He winced as he slowly lifted his head, and Joseph could see that Matthan's eyes were bloody and swollen shut from the inquisitors' beatings.

"I am here, Matthan. Do not make my efforts and Mary's a waste by refusing the food she prepared."

Matthan raised his head. "I will eat, but I will never give them the answers they want. Both you and I know they plan to execute me after beating me. I have a clear picture what lies ahead, Joseph."

Joseph took a step closer. "I'm not sure you do, Matthan, but as long as you are alive I will do my best to care for you. What lies after the grave is up to you."

Matthan grimaced. "Still relentless in your faith, I see. I would think you would admire a brother with tenacity."

He moaned as he lowered himself gently to the floor and inched his way toward Joseph by pulling his broken body with his arm. His chains scraped as he slithered through excrement, urine, and blood, stopping when the chain stretched taut a short distance from the door.

Joseph pushed the food across the vile floor with his staff, nudging the wooden bowl he had borrowed from Mary's kitchen. Stretching his arm until the manacle bit into his flesh, Matthan hooked the bowl with his fingers. He pulled it to his face and scooped up the figs, olive oil, and bread that Joseph had prepared into a soft mash that morning. He had assumed it would be difficult for Matthan to chew or swallow since prisoners were given almost nothing to drink. Joseph tossed a skin of water between the bars, and Matthan pounced on it like a rabid animal. As his brother lifted his chin to drink, Joseph recognized the mangled lines of a broken jaw and a swollen mouth.

"Just sips, Matthan, or you will become sick."

Yahweh, how can men do this to one another? No wonder that only blood will atone for our sins.

They attempted brief conversation as Matthan ate, but he was too weak. Swallowing the simple food Joseph had brought was exhausting his strength. Matthan had already made it obvious that although he was hell-bent on remaining faithful to the Zealot cause, he remained a faithful Jew. He believed his people should frustrate every effort of Roman government in an effort to overthrow Rome's occupation.

Joseph quickly tried to explain that Matthan's only option might not be death. He might not be released, but he might be able to remain in prison with a reasonable level of comfort.

"Matthan, your prospects for deliverance are slim, and I'm sure you are aware of this."

Matthan swallowed painfully. "I have done many things for my people, and I would not change a thing. When I chose to be a Zealot, I chose what my life's end would be. I am ready."

Joseph's mind flashed back to childhood days. Matthan had always been a thinker, the one who pondered his actions and how they would influence the world. Joseph was proud of him, of his commitment to his people, even though he didn't agree with the choices that came with Matthan's commitment.

Joseph leaned toward the bars. "After searching for some time, I found a Jewish family living in Tiberias and hired their daughter Susanna to bring you food every day and keep your garments clean. She will shop daily for fresh bread, nuts, olives, and other foods. Her brother may accompany her into the prison for protection.

"I have fresh garments here for you. Change before you eat, and give Susanna your clothes. She will clean them and return them the next day. Eat all the food so it does not become contaminated. Share with your cellmate to buy his silence."

Joseph knew that the guards routinely stole food and clothing that was not personally delivered, and he must be as discreet as possible. He whispered for several minutes as Matthan listened, his eyes at first half closed, then opening as he took in Joseph's words about Yeshua's message about preparing for the coming kingdom.

"Perhaps I have been following the wrong rebel leader. Is that what you are suggesting?"

Joseph remained silent.

"Are you saying that Yeshua ... that he is the Messiah? My nephew, a child I have known from his birth, your own son and Mary's? Certainly you cannot believe this is true?" Matthan's eyes flashed with a fear Joseph had not seen since his arrival. But why? Would not the arrival of Messiah be good news? Had Matthan been trusting in his actions to secure God's approval with his commitment to the Zealot agenda?

Joseph whispered through the bars, "Yes, Matthan. I believe Yeshua is the Messiah. All that He is and does demonstrates that He is God's Son. His mission has not yet begun, but He is the One."

Matthan grasped the bowl and slid it toward his cellmate, who had listened to their every word.

"Finish it. You need nourishment. And there is water."

Mustering his strength, Matthan tossed the waterskin

the short distance to his manacled cellmate, then turned back to Joseph.

"Little Yeshi is the Messiah who will overthrow Rome but is not an insurrectionist? I will have to ponder this, but then, time is all I have."

"You have Yahweh, Matthan. He has not abandoned you. And your family has not abandoned you. I must go, but I will return to see you again before long. You will be stronger and healthier. I am praying that even in this place you will find peace."

Later, walking the long return to Nazareth, Joseph wondered if offering Matthan physical comfort would be enough. His brother was awaiting death, and only Yahweh could free him from his anger and bitterness.

* * * * *

News came to Joseph and the family less than a month later. Every prisoner held at Tiberias had died. No survivors.

Joseph assumed Matthan had expired during aggressive interrogation. He had sworn that he would never give information about Zealot activities or names of those involved in the movement. Prisoners charged with sedition were led out of the prison and crucified. Those who were too weak to be crucified or who died before execution were dumped in open graves. Joseph and the family hoped that Matthan had not suffered the horrific cruelties of crucifixion.

The Jewish community mourned Matthan's death as one of the nation's great patriots. Regardless of views on rebel tactics, all Jews supported those who fought the despised Roman occupation, and Matthan was a national hero. Joseph thought Matthan's zeal had been misguided, but he admired his brother for his bravery and dedication. Jude was especially grieved. He had always revered Dod Matthan and had chosen to be him when he and his friends engaged in play battle against Roman soldiers.

Joseph and Mary talked long into the night about why

Yahweh had not answered their prayers for Matthan's deliverance, both physically and spiritually. Yahweh possessed the power to intervene for Matthan. Why had He not done so? Had their prayers fallen on deaf ears?

Joseph had no easy answers. His brother was dead, and Mary's compassion and optimism had taken a blow. Trusting Yahweh when they had no answers would have to be enough—Yahweh alone.

Act 4

Crisis: Faith Challenged (ca. 25–28)

(Hebrew Calendar ca. 3786–3789)

Fifty-eight
Catastrophe Strikes

Guilt became Joseph's companion.

He had guilt that he hadn't been able to save Matthan from execution, guilt that he couldn't ease the fear that had overshadowed Mary after the soldiers' raid, guilt about his absence from his construction sites in Sepphoris, due to worry and a lingering painful stomach illness, and guilt about leaving his sons in a wicked and immoral city without his oversight.

Because of Joseph's chronic illness, Simon and Jose were given responsibility for their father's masonry contracts in spite of their inexperience. They still had not mastered the finer points of laying stones or gained proper respect for the dangers of the job. Each rock required precision crafting. Some types of stonework depended upon skills that were learned over time—working with rocks of varying textures that required different angles of splitting. The work was challenging and tedious. One wrong blow of the chisel could ruin a stone, resulting in extra work and expense.

Joseph hurried his pace toward Sepphoris. He finally had gained enough strength to visit the jobsite. Both Simon and Jose had been working there for weeks, splitting their time between the rock quarry and the construction site. Quarrying the stones required that a series of holes be chiseled deep into solid stone. Then wooden wedges were driven into the holes and saturated with water. The wedges expanded, splitting a slice of rock from the stone face. These stones were then shaped and "dressed" to form desired dimensions and shapes, which required unique skill to assure proper alignment.

Jose and Simon had been eager to learn the trade but impatient about the time required to master needed skills. They had come a long way since Joseph had begun their training, but his declining health and advancing age had limited the time he could spend helping them hone their skills.

I cannot fault them for youth, Yahweh, or for what I have not had time or strength to teach them. Give us a good day together as abba and sons.

By the time Joseph reached Sepphoris at midmorning, he was drenched in perspiration. Road dust parched his lips, and his leg muscles trembled as he hurried toward the building site to find Jose and Simon.

He soon spotted the tent used for planning and managing the project. Once inside, Joseph found his sons head-to-head over a table, arguing over the details of a drawing. Simon, having spotted Joseph first, embraced him and then poured out an animated progress report.

"Abba, we have great news. The city magistrate asked us to construct a two-story addition to the city administration building. We signed the contract in your absence. It allowed us to hire extra day laborers and will give us steady work for months, perhaps even a year. Construction is already well under way."

Joseph flushed with pride. Jose and Simon had always been fun-seeking young men, and it had often been difficult to direct their energy. But they had obviously grown during his time away and were shouldering their new responsibilities with excellence. The income from the new project would provide important profits for the family business and security for the future. For a number of months, Joseph had been praying about how he could provide security for Mary and the children. His body was growing weaker with each passing year.

Jose and Simon led Joseph to the site, talking over one another with excitement. Joseph carefully inspected the ongoing work. The craftsmanship was equal to Yeshua's. Pride flooded through him.

"Your work is impeccable. I'm proud of you, both as sons and craftsmen. Roman leadership here in Sepphoris has obviously taken note of your work and will offer us more opportunities in the future. You have done well in my absence, my sons."

A day worker sauntered past, and Joseph noted his side glance at Jose and Simon, who returned knowing smiles. Yes, Joseph was proud and loved his sons, but he also knew the bent of their hearts toward the world. They wanted to please him, but they also enjoyed satisfying their physical desires and obviously had not demonstrated a godly example to the workers.

Joseph was not ignorant of Simon and Jose's activities, indulging in the sinful pleasures Sepphoris offered. The day laborers treated them like other pleasure-seeking men, not pious Jews. Simon often shed his Jewish upbringing and engaged in cursing and coarse sexual talk with the construction workers. Joseph confronted his sons' behavior when he saw it, but he understood that the boys would have to wrestle through their faith with Yahweh Himself.

Working for the Roman government was not as profitable as people assumed. Contracts were generally verbal, and contractors were often fined and their contracts cancelled if Roman administrators could find even a slight imperfection in the work. But even a small income helped provide Joseph's family with the essential food and clothing.

The administration building provided new challenges. The tall stone walls required reconstruction of the roof. Large, heavy beams needed to be lifted high into the air—a task that required great skill. The support beams needed to be long enough to span the entire distance between the walls. Lifting them in place was dangerous and required strong young men who could scale the slippery walls and guide the thick ropes. Despite Joseph's concerns for their safety, Simon and Jose had been unwilling to leave such an important task to untrained day laborers or to lose profits by hiring skilled tradesmen.

Joseph stood in the shadow of the newly constructed walls. A lattice of scaffolding partially obscured the view above him, but high at the top of the wall he spotted Simon and Jose straddling two beams and signaling for the next to be hoisted. Their voices drifted in the breeze, above the sound of pounding and chiseling.

Joseph strained to understand what the boys were saying but only caught occasional phrases.

"Dod Matthan ... Tiberias hellhole ... family safe ... Nazareth."

Joseph shook his head. His sons were blind to God's protection. They were acquainted with men engaged in rebel activity who were in hiding. Zealots had approached Simon and Jose often to enlist them to join the movement. Their refusal had brought escalating harassment and threats. Jose envisioned the Zealot life as exciting, even though he had refused to join out of respect to Abba's strong warnings and Jose's deep desire not to hurt his ima. But while his sons wore the outward garments of belief, they were disillusioned doubters and skeptics.

The boys' conversation continued, their voices dripping with sarcasm. "Special gift from God ... glad he's gone ..."

Every muscle in Joseph's body went limp, like a runner crumpling at the end of a race.

Yahweh, why did You choose me to be an abba to Your precious Son when I have failed to teach my earthly sons? Have mercy on them in their ignorance.

Yeshi's goodness had provoked jealousy in his brothers and sisters—jealousy that had grown with the years. His refusal to retaliate had infuriated his brothers. Yeshua always seemed to do the right thing, and as much as Joseph and Mary had tried to treat him like the other children, his siblings often believed he received special treatment.

Joseph snapped out of his reverie at the sound of Simon calling from atop the beams.

"If Yeshua were here, he could have used his special powers to lift these beams into place. Oh, I forgot ... he chooses not to use his power—at least for his family."

Simon laughed caustically, then stretched out his arms and leaned toward Jose to direct the newly hoisted beam, which was swinging just inches from Simon's left shoulder.

"Simon!" Jose's scream echoed throughout the jobsite as the massive cedar swung back then thudded into Simon. He slouched to the right, his hands flailing for a grip.

Simon's bellowing scream cut into Joseph's heart as Simon tumbled toward the ground, his body slamming from board to board of the scaffolding, shattering the boards, and plummeting to the ground in a limp free fall. The scaffolding swayed in a death dance before collapsing in a heap on Simon's bloodied body.

Jose clattered down the emergency ladder built against the wall for such occasions, screaming his brother's name over and over.

Within moments Joseph, Jose, and the day workers were scrambling through the rubble toward the location where Simon's body had slammed to the ground. Removing boards one by one, they worked their way toward the sound of moaning.

Joseph focused on each board, refusing to acknowledge the panic that tore at his chest. Simon was all right. Simon had to be all right. But Joseph understood Yahweh did not promise escape from pain—His plan for the universe extended beyond what His people could see or understand. Joseph could not allow himself to think of bringing an injured son home to Mary.

Just in front of him, a day worker threw boards furiously.

"He is here! Be careful. I will clear the boards before you approach. They are too heavy, and causing further collapse is too dangerous."

Excruciating moments passed as Joseph waited for beams to be cleared. The worker gave a signal, and Joseph picked his way through the rubble, Jose following behind.

Simon lay twisted, bleeding, and writhing in pain. His low, guttural moans frightened Joseph. Even Matthan had not made such sounds of pain. His leg was broken, and the bone was exposed. Deep cuts had laid open Simon's flesh from the thigh to below his knee. Exposed bone meant a risk of deadly infection that could cost Simon his leg.

Joseph discarded his mantle and tore a strip from the hem of his white linen tunic. He tied it firmly around Simon's upper thigh to stop the bleeding. Simon screamed, his face turned ashen, and he began to sweat. Joseph's son needed his help quickly.

"Should we pray?" Jose sneered. "Perhaps Yeshua will appear. He has always been quick to help in the past." Suspicion of Yeshi's credential let his brothers to question God's demands on their lives.

The words seared Joseph's heart. His rebuke would be useless, and his silence would be seen as weakness. Jose would have to find his own way to faith—his father could not help him. Joseph could only be faithful and do what he believed best.

Joseph directed Jose to prepare a splint from the broken boards scattered around them. He wrapped the board with linen cloth from one of the worker's tunics and bound it against Simon's leg with a strip of cord from a goatskin bedcover. Several men ran back to the worksite to gather food and drink. Other workers constructed a litter made from lumber from the building site and covered it with the remaining goatskin blanket. Four men hoisted it to their shoulders, and Joseph, Simon, Jose, and a few workers set out from Sepphoris to Nazareth. Carrying their load, they hoped to have Simon home by midday.

Joseph led the group, his pace deliberate and his route the most direct. Jose followed close behind him, occasionally starting a sentence, then stopping. The men carrying the litter talked among themselves, recalling each detail of the accident over and over—the sway of the beam, the blow, Simon's struggle to regain balance, the sound of Simon's body hitting the ground.

Joseph fought not to scream and cover his ears. Thoughts pounded through his brain like a hammer on rock.

If only I had offered better supervision …

If only I had insisted on hiring skilled workers to set the beams …

If only I been well enough to …

Regret clung to his every thought on the long journey home. He could only imagine that Jose, who had been sitting beside Simon during the accident, was also blaming himself. Joseph's mind told him the fault was not his, but his father's heart refused to listen. His eyes stared blankly at rocks, weeds, and obscure details in the road as time passed in a still void.

I must get Simon home, I must get Simon home, I must get Simon home …

They stopped for rest and refreshment, but Joseph ate nothing. He swallowed a few sips from the waterskin Jose forced into his hands.

"Abba, you must drink, or you will collapse. Simon and Ima will need you when you get home."

Yes, Ima, whose son would be laid at her feet mangled, bleeding, at the edge of death. Joseph flung his head back in a shriek and tore his mantle.

He took the waterskin from Jose's hands, drank, and wiped his mouth with the back of his hand. Then he rose and set out again toward Nazareth.

* * * * *

When the group reached the outskirts of Nazareth, Joseph insisted on going ahead. The family needed to prepare for what they would see. He placed Jose in charge.

Joseph set off as fast as his weary legs and crushed spirit would allow. Mary answered his call at the door and read the sorrow he was fighting to hide. He described Simon's fall, and before he could describe the injuries, she had called the girls to gather medical supplies and prepare Simon's bed. Then she took Joseph's face in her hands.

"We cannot undo his injuries, Joseph. Jose is not at fault, and neither are you. Do not waste your time accusing yourself. Simon needs you. I need you. You can start by getting water and heating it on the fire." Mary pulled his face toward hers and kissed him lightly. "Now go."

Joseph hurried toward the kitchen and busied himself warming water. Mary's words were true, but they did not feel true for him. Was Simon's fall yet another sign of his failure as an abba?

A call came at the door, and Rebecca quickly answered. Jose stepped into the gathering room, followed by the day workers who bore Simon on the litter. The rigors of the trip had caused the wounds to bleed and crust, and Simon had fallen into a deep and dangerous sleep.

Mary stared, trembling, at her son's blood-soaked body. She swallowed repeatedly as she fought back tears. Tenderly, she unwrapped the makeshift splints and cleaned the bloody, dirty wounds with the warm henna-soaked cloths Joseph had prepared.

She flinched and paused at the sight of exposed bone but continued.

"Joseph, these wounds are beyond my skills," she whispered. "He needs an *uman* to perform surgery and a rophe to medicate him."

Joseph's heart sank. He knew the implication of her words. The break and additional fractures were so severe that the leg might require amputation. If so, Simon would never work again.

Even worse, amputation often brought death,

Oh heavenly Av, please help us.

Joseph watched Mary's every move—calm, deliberate, compassionate. While she was obviously shaken, she was also focused on Simon's needs. She turned to Jude, the youngest.

"Hurry to the clinic at the synagogue and bring the priest-uman. Tell him Simon has a badly broken leg and will need surgery."

With the command from Ima, Jude disappeared through the door.

For the next two hours Simon's fever rose and his pain escalated as the family waited in frustration for Jude's return. Yeshua sat and prayed as his mother and sisters applied cleansing poultices to the wounds and cold cloths to bring down his fever.

When Jose returned with the physician, the family learned he had been at the home of another patient in critical need, and Jose had been forced to wait.

Neighbors and friends heard word of the accident and gathered to pray in the meeting room. By late afternoon, James received word from a neighbor from Nazareth who had taken the news to the Galilee fishermen. James was told the moment he returned from his fishing run.

Standing in the shadows near the back of the kitchen, Joseph noted James's sullen expression the moment he entered the door. Not coming would have been hurtful, and he would never have done something so disrespectful to his ima. But James had always felt that Yahweh owed his family the responses to life *he* envisioned. If the Jews were Yahweh's special people, He should protect them. And if Yeshua was a special gift from Yahweh, he was a failure or a fake. He'd never done anything extraordinary to help his family. James had always believed his ima and abba had treated Yeshua like he was better than his brothers and sisters and had resented Yeshi for it.

James went to his ima's side, ignoring the prayer group in the gathering room. But moments later, the prayer time ended, and Joseph watched as Yeshua drew his brother aside.

"We are glad you have come, James. We will tell Simon you are here."

James sneered. "And why are *you* here, Yeshua?" James's more recent sympathetic feelings toward his brother seemed to have faded in light of the new circumstances. "Are you just another carpenter? A rabbi with the same message we have been told for centuries? Or are you a deceiver? Have you tricked Ima and Abba into believing you are someone you are not—the great Messiah?"

The final word hung in the room with a venomous hiss as James leaned toward Yeshua's face. Joseph clenched his fists and forced himself to remain in the shadows.

"The Holy Book says the Messiah will heal sickness and do miracles. Have we *ever* seen a miracle from you? Can you heal your sick and brokenhearted mother, or are you not willing? Will you once again stand like stone and watch a member of your family suffer and perhaps die?

James whirled and walked out the door, as Yeshua silently watched his departure.

A hand touched Joseph's sleeve.

"The surgeon is about to begin. We need you."

* * * * *

Simon lay sleeping in a nest of clean blankets. The rophe had given him wine boiled with myrrh, frankincense, and some herbs to ease his pain and induce a deep slumber. Joseph held his breath as the uman made an incision with a sharp knife and forced Simon's bone back into place, aligning the jagged edges as best he could. Then he wrapped the open wound with a linen cloth that had been boiled in hot water and henna to help keep the injury clean. Bowing his head, the uman repeated two blessings, one for the tragedy and one for healing.

"Blessed is He who is the true judge. Blessed is He who does good to the undeserving and has rendered kindness to us."

Joseph stepped out of the room and moved again into the shadows of the kitchen. Yeshua still stood motionless in the place where James had unleashed his fury. Joseph could see that Yeshi was hurting more than anyone to see Simon in pain. None of his brothers and sisters could understand the price of his obedience to Yahweh, his rejection by his own family, his isolation and abandonment by those who should love him most.

Joseph walked to Yeshua's side, unable to find words, but Yeshua turned and looked into his abba's eyes.

"You have no need to ask, Abba. To heal Simon because he is my brother, because he is in pain, is to ignore the most important question: what does Yahweh ask of me in this crisis? If I heal to satisfy earthly understanding and desires, I forfeit the eternal heavenly mission for which I was sent. I must leave Simon in the hands of our heavenly Av, who knows what is best. Trusting Him when we believe we know a better way will always be the biggest battle. James believes he knows a better way, and he must find his way through anger to faith or unbelief."

Joseph and Yeshua stood side by side in silence. Both Simon's fate and James's were in Yahweh's hand now.

Fifty-nine

Death Casts Long Shadows

Simon's accident sent cold ripples of doom into motion. Or so it felt to Joseph, as he clung to his faith.

Simon's recovery from his injuries was slow and brutal, and work on the Sepphoris administration building slowed. Roman officials threatened to revoke the contract, and in spite of his failing health, Joseph had taken on extra hours that wracked his body with fatigue and pain. He fought continual tightness in his neck and arm, like a coiled snake squeezing the life from his body. Sometimes he awoke at night sweating, sipping shallow breaths as he prayed to endure crushing heaviness in his chest.

Despite months of rest and family prayer, Simon had been forced to face the truth that his leg would never function normally again. He walked with a limp, battled continual pain, and tired easily. Joseph had put him to work supervising laborers, securing building materials, and negotiating with the Romans, which Simon took on with great skill and near diabolical pleasure.

Summer settled over the land with suffocating heat. With each passing day, Joseph's strength faded and his sensibilities diminished. But he would not stop working until he had earned all he could to provide for Mary in widowhood, as was spelled out in the ketubah.

Once again Joseph awoke with the familiar pain that overshadowed his days. He picked at the porridge Mary had prepared, eating less than half, then spread the remains around the inside of the bowl. His appetite had faded in recent months. Mary would scold him if she noticed he had not eaten everything she had prepared.

The summer heat further diminished his appetite and strength. Several times of late on the walk to the jobsite in Sepphoris, he had grown lightheaded and had been forced to sit down to rest in the shade. Unfortunately, Jose left early that morning to organize work materials before the day laborers arrived, and Joseph set out to walk to the site alone, but for his prayers and fellowship with Yahweh. In recent days, Joseph's prayer time had grown sweeter and Yahweh's voice more clear.

He was ready, but was Mary?

Again, the voice whispered reassurance.

Those who live in the shelter of the Most High will find rest in the shadow of the Almighty. This I declare about the Lord: He alone is my refuge, my place *of safety; He is my God, and I trust Him.*[100]

* * * * *

The late morning wind had stilled, and breath came in searing sips. Marcus was the first to spot Joseph half collapsed behind a pile of dressed stones that had been prepared for laying. One hand was drawn to Joseph's chest. The other was extended, as if reaching for someone else's hand. Marcus raced to his side through the blazing sand.

"Joseph! Are you all right? I am Marcus, a day laborer. You need water and shade."

He lifted Joseph into his arms, but Joseph's eyes, which had sunken deep into his face, remained fixed and staring. Marcus forced down the panic that rose in his chest. It was not uncommon for workers to be struck down by heat and die. He had to move quickly.

He reached for his waterskin, lifted it to Joseph's lips, and forced a few drops into his mouth. Then he trickled water over Joseph's head and stroked it over his brow. Words slurred from Joseph's lips, but they were senseless. His left arm hung limp as Marcus shifted his weight, stood, and carried Joseph to the shade of the awning made of palm leaves and lattice where he had last seen Jose directing workers.

As Marcus had raced to Joseph's side, he caught sight of Jose and Simon standing nearby, frozen in shock. Their abba's collapse registered first as stunned silence, followed by a flurry of preparation for transporting him home for medical attention. Simon directed the litter construction with fervent intensity, yelling orders at workers and shaking his cane in frustration as the men worked. Jose hastily gathered water for the litter carriers, Abba, Simon, and himself, and placed his senior mason in charge of the work. Marcus, having been assigned the task of rear litter carrier, hurried off to find someone to take over his tasks on the job in his absence.

The group soon set out on the route back to Nazareth. Simon led, setting a slow pace that accommodated both Joseph's perilous condition and his injured leg. Occasionally his defective leg let him stumble, and muttered curses spilled from Simon's lips.

Marcus struggled to keep the litter level and his pace smooth, but every step stirred moans of agony from Joseph and increased Simon's agitation. He beat the path with his cane as if striking out at an unseen adversary.

But by the time the group reached the outskirts of Nazareth, Joseph's moans had ceased. His ragged breathing was marked by a deep rattle, and he had fallen into a deep sleep.

* * * * *

Mary tried to mask her terror as Joseph was carried through the door. His breathing and ashen skin told her he was clinging to life. She busied herself with his care to keep from thinking beyond the next moment, the next breath. Life without her beloved was beyond comprehension.

The family gathered as soon as they received word. Jose shared details, and family members took turns sitting at Abba's side, praying and encouraging him. Mary refused to leave his side, bathing his forehead in cool compresses and stroking his hands and face.

But he remained asleep and unresponsive, even as neighbors gathered in Nazareth's synagogue and at Mary and Joseph's house to pray for his healing.

As the evening passed, Joseph's breathing weakened, and he no longer attempted to talk. Mary called the children into the tiny bedroom where her beloved lay.

"Yahweh holds your abba's healing in his hands. The rophe is God's instrument. Our job is to pray and to trust." Mary pulled her prayer shawl over her head and raised her hands.

Why, Yahweh, have you struck Joseph when we need him, when he has been so faithful to you? Please restore him. Please. Our children are struggling to trust You—especially James and Simon, who are so angry. They need their abba.

Mary glanced up. James had been glaring at Yeshua from the moment he had entered the house, his expression haughty and hateful. His voice exploded through the house.

"Do something, Yeshua ben Joseph! Or will you be silent and watch him suffer, like you did when Simon had his accident?"

Yeshua gazed back at James, his eyes never leaving his younger brother's face as James's words lashed through the air. Yeshua responded softly, yet his voice filled the room.

"My time has not yet come. My heavenly Av has appointed my mission, and I do His bidding."

"And Yahweh's will is that you stand by and watch our abba die."

Mary winced at James's poisonous response. Sobs rose from the bench in the gathering room where the girls sat together. Rebecca's shoulders were shaking as tears streamed down her face.

"Stop it, James! How dare you disgrace Abba at a time like this? If you cared so much about our family, you wouldn't have run off to sea because of your selfishness. How dare you raise a voice to Yeshua, who remained home to work with Abba to care for our family. Put your childish jealousy aside and have respect for Abba, Yeshua, and Yahweh who grants you breath to speak. Behave like the adult you are supposed to be."

Mary watched in shock and pride as Rebecca straightened her back and strode to her father's room.

James turned toward his mother. "Ima, your daughter needs to be taught her proper place. She has been given too much liberty, thinking she can speak to men in such a manner."

James whirled on his heel and stormed out the door, muttering profanities.

Please, Yahweh, I cannot bear this dissension. Joseph may well die, the children are arguing among themselves, and I may become a widow by daybreak. Yahweh, be my strength, for I am not strong enough for this discord.

Mary sighed and turned toward the remaining children in the gathering room. "Your abba needs us to care for each other now more than ever."

Rebecca released a guttural sob and pressed her face into her hands.

* * * * *

The family sat in silence in the gathering room for excruciating hours as Mary worked to ease Joseph's discomfort, applying cold compresses, stroking his hands, retelling stories of their life together, and whispering words of love. She spoke of the olive grove, the difficult days of their betrothal, the arduous trip to Bethlehem, and their first steps of faith with Yahweh.

Near daybreak Joseph roused from his deep sleep, his eyes still closed, and whispered a single question: "Was I a good husband and abba? Will Yahweh be pleased?"

A sob caught in Mary's throat, and she squeezed Joseph's hand.

"Yahweh chose *you*, Joseph. He knew you weren't perfect—no man is—but that you would be the best abba for Yeshua. You were a wonderful abba to all of our children. Yahweh is pleased. We can never be good enough, yet Yahweh provides a way because of His great love. Be at peace."

"Yahweh provides a way." A smile worked its way across Joseph's lips as his fingers relaxed in Mary's.

He was gone.

* * * * *

Mary sat beside Joseph, praying, weeping, and stroking his arms and face one more time before she faced the children. A pressing weight of helplessness fell over her like a blanket drawn from water. For a moment she feared she could not speak, but she made her way from the sleeping room and told the children their abba had died.

Ruth tore the right side of her clothing, and Rebecca covered her upper lip with her head scarf to show her grief.[101]

Mary could not be consoled and sat silently, speaking as little as possible. She watched Yeshua. His eyes revealed his deep grief—he *could see* what was happening on a supernatural level and in the hearts of everyone in the room. He placed his arms around Mary to comfort her, but comfort would not come. She was not angry at Yeshua. She was numb with grief, overwhelmed with questions beyond the wisdom of this world, brokenhearted by her children, and afraid to think about the moment when Joseph's body would be taken from the house forever.

And for the first time since she could remember, she was angry with Yahweh. Yes, Yeshua was His Son, and Yahweh was in control of all things, but she was angry.

"What have I done to deserve this? Your abba and I did all Yahweh asked. We loved each other deeply. He stood by me before we were married, when most men would have turned their backs. When I was pregnant with you, the village people criticized him for marrying a *sharmoot*. Your youngest brother and sister are still dependent upon my care. How will we survive?"

Mary's voice rose as she spoke, and she fought not to lose control. "Yeshua, why has this happen to your abba now of all times when we need him so much?"

Yeshua put his arms around his ima and pulled her head to his shoulder.

"You feel abandoned. Your pain is real, and Yahweh suffers with you in the same way you suffer for your children. I promise you that even now Yahweh is caring for your needs in unseen ways. You need not fear. He knows every hair on your head, and He will provide for you.

"Abba was in great pain for a long time, and he prayed for release."

Mary drew her head back in surprise.

"Ima, I am grateful for every moment I had with Abba. I am privileged that Yahweh chose Joseph to be my earthly abba and mentor. He provided all the earthly wisdom I need to fulfill my ministry, and Av will provide all you need for the future."

Mary was silent as tears streamed down her cheeks. Then she stood and stepped toward Yeshua and laid her head upon his shoulder.

"I know all that is true about Yahweh and His goodness and faithfulness. I also trust that He is not angered by my questions and that He wants me to bring them to Him.

"I will be all right. Deep down I have confidence of this because I have seen His mercy and His goodness, and I know those things more deeply than I have ever known them because I see Him when I look at You."

Sixty
Mary Confronts Her Sorrow

Mary sat on a pile of hay in the corner of the stable watching dust motes drift through the rays of light that pierced the windows. Members of the housing community shared the common stable that sat behind the long rows of apartments where a crowd had gathered on Mary's rooftop to mourn.

She had meticulously prepared Joseph's body for burial according to tradition, then escaped to the privacy of the stable to be alone. She found the animals comforting companions—silent, yet present. Her many children were her greatest blessing, but she could not find a space in her small home that was not occupied with a hovering loved one. She needed time just to be, to cry or not to cry without concerned eyes watching. She needed to be in a stable where it all began and remember who Joseph and Yahweh had been in those moments—who they had always been.

She needed to remember and trust, no matter her feelings.

Yeshua would join her soon. She had asked him to come to sit with her and talk. His voice was the only one she needed.

A shadow darkened the doorway.

"Come in, Yeshua, before anyone sees you."

Yeshua moved from the doorway into the stable and settled beside her.

Mary's face flashed a wistful smile. "Your abba's first glimpse of you was in a stable. I wrapped you in blankets and made your bed in a nest of clean straw. We couldn't take our eyes off of you, our child of wonder, whose conception and birth made no sense. But none of it made sense—angels, my pregnancy, that your abba would marry me under such circumstances, that we would find our way to Bethlehem as the angel had spoken."

Mary picked up a handful of straw and plucked pieces from the clump. "We didn't understand that obedience would break our hearts and our family. But I wouldn't have chosen anything but the life I have lived. I regret nothing. I promised Yahweh my all, and I have always tried to give it to Him."

She leaned back against the wall of the stable.

"I'm sorry for my unrestrained emotions at your abba's bedside. Everything happened so suddenly … Abba went to work, and before I had time to prepare dough for tomorrow's baking, he was brought home with the pallor of death on his face.

"Yeshua, you speak to Yahweh and say He speaks to you. Where is He when we hurt and ask for help? Right now I feel like He has abandoned me, that I must have displeased Him for Him to have taken my Joseph, although I cannot think what I could have done that would merit this pain."

Mary turned to face her son. "I dare not speak these words to anyone but you, but I am upset with my heavenly Father. I know I am not the first of His servants to feel angry. Gideon asked, 'Sir, if the Lord is with us, why has all this happened to us? And where are all the miracles our ancestors told us about?'[102] 'I cry out, "Help!" but no one answers me.'"[103]

Yeshua took her hand. "The justice you seek will come, but until creation is transformed, God will not intervene in every heartache or disaster. For now, creation groans as in the pains of Childbirth and operates under God's creative laws, which sin has influenced.[104] But one day creation will be liberated."

Yeshua explained, "Tragedy teaches us through our response to suffering. Questioning the cause is pointless because humans cannot understand the complexities of the eternal.

"Yahweh taught you of Himself through the delights of your marriage to Abba. He also teaches us when our hearts cry out to Him. Listen. Be still. You are angry with Him because your heart knows He is there and that He is good."

Yeshua paused letting his words sink in.

"The pain and suffering that has crushed this world for centuries has crushed your heart. Yahweh seems unjust because the ultimate price of sin—death—has touched your home and loved ones. This is why our people offer sacrifices—there is no escape from sin. Even nature bears witness. Storms, earthquakes, floods, and droughts are sin's curse upon creation's orderly design."

A sheep had wandered to his side, and Yeshua ran his fingers through the animal's wool. "The people who daily pour sin into the world blindly ask, 'Why? Where is God? Why doesn't He stop evil? Doesn't He care?'"

Yeshua shook his head knowingly.

"He cares so much that He allows people to have their own way—to choose destruction when He offers life. But then, Ima, why is there so much good in the world? Do we attribute that to God? The world is in an obvious battle between good and evil. God is not the author of evil, but our ever-present help in our trouble."

A wave of shame swept over Mary's heart. Her motives had been laid bare. She accused God of being unfair because He allowed pain to touch *her* life and the lives of those she loved. And she had seen Yeshua, God's Son, suffer through the same pain—illness, grief, rejection, abandonment.

If a messiah is needed because God's people and the

world need a savior, then I also need a savior. Why should I be excused from suffering?

Mary's anger stilled. Death had not come for Joseph. Death was an ever-present reality in the world that would come for everyone. Every person who ever lived faced sickness, disasters, and death

Yeshua continued speaking in the third as if quoting scripture, "Ima, you may not understand now, but God's Word tells us of suffering and pain that His own Son must experience. He will be despised and rejected by humankind, a man of suffering familiar with pain. Surely He will take up our pain and bear our suffering, but He will be pierced for humanity's transgressions. He will be crushed for their iniquities. The punishment that brings humankind peace will be placed on Him, and by His wounds they will be healed. After He has suffered, He will see the light of life and be satisfied."[105]

Mary tilted her head, deep in thought.

"God loves His creation, but He wants a relationship with His children. All have sinned and fallen short of God's glory and must undergo transformation. Tragedy provides a place for renewal.

"You must choose, Ima, like anyone who has suffered. You can turn to Av during this time of grief, or you can turn away. He offers you freedom of choice, and He is waiting for you."

With those words, Yeshua left the stable and rejoined the mourners. Mary followed him soon after, his words pounding through her head: "You can turn to Av or turn away. He is waiting for you."

Sixty-one
Mary and Levirate marriage

Mary soothed her aching heart during the months of Avelut with hard work, friendship, and routine. The twelve months of mourning passed more quickly than she had imagined. She busied herself baking bread and other foods Joseph delighted in eating and sold them in Nazareth's market. She sought the company of other widows, many of whom had been left near destitute. They gathered in her home to bake, spin, and make items to sell at a profit. By the time the year had ended, Mary found she was making a modest sum each month and gaining skill as a businesswoman.

With Ima settling into a routine, Yeshua expanded his teaching ministry—traveling farther and staying away for longer periods of time. His message was simple: prepare his people for the coming Messiah.

Mary was surprised to find Joseph's brother Nathan at the door one evening, asking to talk with Yeshua, now the presumed head of the family. Mary had placed the evening meal on the table: cooked lentils, savory stew, baked bread, stewed fruits, and assorted nuts. Yeshua happened to be home at the time. Nathan and Joseph had been close over the years, and Mary had grown to appreciate Nathan's sense of humor and support for their family. He and Yeshua exited the house for the privacy of Joseph's workroom to talk alone. When they returned sometime later, Yeshua called Mary into the gathering room to join them.

"Ima, Nathan has come to ask for your hand in marriage. He understands that his request does not fully meet the standards of Levirate marriage which would provide an heir for the deceased."

Yeshua smiled, and Mary quaked. She'd had no idea Nathan had taken an interest in her. Her beloved, Joseph, had consumed her love for so long that she had no intentions of remarrying. Her only desire was to care for her family, now adults, and to enjoy the grandchildren that would soon be added to their homes. She did not need or want a second husband.

Like a schoolboy, Nathan spoke humbly and earnestly, obviously hoping to be persuasive.

"Mary, we have known each other for many years, and I admire your devotion to Joseph. I could never take his place, but do you think we could be happy together?"

Mary saw the genuine intent of his heart, and she softened at his words.

"Nathan, Joseph and I often talked about your friendship and loyalty."

Mary's words emboldened Nathan.

"You know you will have my full love and attention, and I will be the best provider I can be to your children."

Mary thought his words sweet. However, Nathan's attention embarrassed her.

Brushing back a lock of hair under her scarf, her respectful words flowed gently. "I am honored that you think me worthy of your affection ..."

Her apologetic, noncommittal words did not offer Nathan much hope. His countenance fell as he waited for a glimmer of positive response.

"Nathan, I am humbled by your proposal. You would make a wonderful husband and provider."

He hung on every word she spoke, and Mary's heart flooded with guilt. She respected Nathan beyond measure.

He had been a worthy, godly mentor to Yeshua in the fields and a close, loyal brother to Joseph.

Mary continued, "Nathan, God gave me a life partner in Joseph and the love of a man few women ever experience. I have joyfully committed myself to my heavenly Av to meet my earthly needs—and my wonderful children are here for me as well."

Mary poured a glass of her finest wine in honor of Nathan's visit.

"I am honored you have asked me. You have been a wonderful friend to our family. If ever I were to consider marrying again, you would be my choice. But ..."

Nathan murmured under his breath as he awaited Mary's next words.

"But despite the fact that you are a wonderful, godly man I respect and care about, I cannot. Joseph will always be my only husband. I hope you can understand."

His disappointment hurts my heart, Yahweh. He is a good man. Please help him understand that I have not rejected him, although that is certainly what he must feel.

Mary smiled. "I am grateful for you, Nathan."

"I will be here for you as a friend, Mary. Joseph would want that. He would want to ensure that you are safe and cared for. I assure you that you can turn to me if you need anything."

A deep tension released in Mary's body and spirit, and tears suddenly pooled in her eyes. "You are Yahweh's gift to our family, Nathan. Thank you for understanding. I do not have words to express my appreciation. May God's blessing follow you all the days of your life, and may He bless our households and our friendship."

"Our households and our friendship," Nathan echoed. "To the glory and the praise of Yahweh."

With Nathan's words ringing in her ears, Mary closed the door behind Nathan as he exited, and then she returned to the tasks of caring for her family.

Sixty-two

A Refuge for Rebels

Mary sat on a low stone wall, shivering in the tiny courtyard where she and Joseph had retreated after dark to talk alone. She drank in the sight of snowcapped Mount Hermon to the north and the shadowed, craggy hills of western Batanea. Low-lying hills stretched west of Nazareth to the Mediterranean Sea, and to the south, mountains overshadowed the Jezreel Valley, sending sunlight and shadow spinning in a dance of darkness and glimmer. To the east, the Sea of Galilee and Mount Tabor vaunted their beauty.

Joseph's death had ended not only his earthly life but also the future she had envisioned for herself—growing old beside the man she loved as they poured their lives into their children and grandbabies. But Joseph's death brought loss far beyond grief for a husband or abba.

Mary was more aware of her sons' bitterness toward Yeshua, as well as the hardness of Jewish hearts to his message. Self-interest, pride, and complacency ran deep through the hearts of Jewish leadership and common people. Most were driven by curiosity about what Yeshua might do for them, how he might make their lives easier, or how he could solve political problems with Rome. Few were drawn to him by spiritual thirst.

Mary saw the world with new eyes, and she was troubled. Rejecting God's message and His messenger would only bring His chosen people more pain and suffering. Mary's family also worried her. James and Simon still held deep anger against Yeshua and rejected Yahweh. She sighed and pulled her blanket tightly around her shoulders as she rose to return to her empty bed, praying with a heavy heart.

Dear Av, have patience with me and with Your people. Forgive the selfishness that blinds our hearts to You. I desire greater passion to be about Your work, to speak Your words, and to bring Your truth and light into the world. Be my strength when I am weak and my hope when I am discouraged. Help me take each breath with gratitude, knowing I depend on You alone.

* * * * *

Pounding echoed in the distance, and Mary rolled over in bed and moaned. *How often have I told the boys they are past the age of wrestling?*

Another thud. And another. Mary forced herself to semiconsciousness in the darkness.

It must be near the last watch of the night. The noise is coming from the front door.

Panic gripped her throat. No one had called out at the door to identify themselves, which was the custom. She fought down the fear that Romans were coming to threaten Simon and Jose regarding Joseph's contract in Sepphoris. But she had no choice but to answer, lest the children go to the door first. She refused to have them protect her like a child.

Mary rose, pulled a tunic over her head, and took the candle she kept burning at night from a niche in the wall. Then she walked toward the door as she prayed for protection.

She eased the door open a crack. The flicker of her candle revealed two bloodied, wounded men clutching each other as they leaned against a wall of the small portico. They were severely injured.

Why are these men at my door? Who are they? Criminals?

Rebels? Whoever, they cannot last long without help, and as a widow, I cannot let them in.

She then jerked opened the door, and the men stumbled through, collapsing into a heap on the floor. The sound of voices screamed behind her as Mary's children rushed into the gathering room behind her.

A quick glance told her that the men had been wounded in battle or were the victims of a beating. The younger of the two men had managed to stand and spoke first.

"I am Simon Cananeus from Cana. Our forces attacked and attempted to take the strategic Roman position at Sepphoris. We believed their military was weakened and were confident we would conquer the city. Unbeknown to us, a large Roman force was waiting to ambush us. We didn't have a chance."

Simon gasped for life-giving air, and Mary's heart froze. The men were Zealot rebels!

"We need medical attention. We are asking for your help, and then will be on our way. Our men scattered to the wind when we saw the Roman garrison was too much for our meager forces."

Simon hesitated, recognizing the risk.

Did they desert the Zealots? How did they come here? Was Yeshua at risk?

Mary scanned the men for identification, but their faces were bloodied and bruised. The older man crumpled on the floor showed obvious signs of torture, evidence of abuse in a Roman prison, which granted him immediate status in Mary's eyes. He moaned and tried to lift his head. Perhaps he knew Matthan or possessed information about how he died. Mary knelt and, with Rebecca's help, rolled the man to his back and lifted his head.

He whispered.

"Sir, I cannot hear you," Mary said as she leaned closer.

"I am Matthan ben Jacob from Nazareth."

Mary gasped, and her hands flew to her mouth.

"Matthan … it cannot be you! Please, sir, do not deceive me. My husband's brother died in the prison in Tiberias."

The man gave a weak smile. "But I did not, Mary, wife of Joseph, mother of Yeshua. I did not die. You, of all women, must understand that many things we are told to be true are not true. Sometimes we must wait for the truth."

Mary's heart pounded in her chest. If only Joseph had known Matthan was alive before he died! Tears filled her eyes, and she brushed them away. She reached for Matthan's hand.

"Rebecca, get him fresh water. Jose can help you tend his wounds. And bring warm water and clean rags."

Rebecca and Jose headed for the kitchen.

"Mary, I did not want to bring trouble on you or your family. It was best no one had knowledge that I was alive." Matthan struggled for each word. "I joined the rebels again after escaping prison—I cannot tell the details. Our group joined Judas Iscariot and his Sicarii, who attempted to take Sepphoris."

Mary noticed that Jude was listening intently as his dod spoke, his eyes brightening with each added detail.

"You are my dod Matthan!" he blurted out, as if meeting a childhood hero.

Matthan nodded. "And you must be Jude. I never expected to see your family again."

He winced as Mary washed a wound with warm water mixed with medicinal herbs. Mary lifted a second cloth to his mouth when he coughed, and it came away stained with blood.

"Joseph's time with me was not wasted. Prison's greatest opportunity is time—time to think about life and death. After so much time battling alongside the Zealots, I longed to locate and to know the Messiah who would fight for us. For years our people have debated whether the Messiah will come and destroy the hated Romans. The Essene Messiah is called the Teacher of Righteousness. Perhaps he is the

Messiah, or is there another? Do you have an answer for me, Mary?"

Mary smiled. Yes, she had an answer.

"We will speak further about this, Matthan. You have just arrived, and both you and your friend need medical attention, food, and rest. But be at peace. God brought you here for more than physical help. He brought you here to find the answers you have been searching for."

* * * * *

Early the next morning Anna and Jude hurried to the guest room where Matthan and his friend Simon were being nursed. Jude was eager to talk to Matthan.

"Dod Matthan, we thought you were dead. What happened?"

Matthan winced with pain as he tried to turn to face his visitors.

"While I was in prison your abba visited me. He risked his life to care for me and encourage me, even though he was certain I would be executed or die at the hands of my torturers. Still, he hired a young Jewess to bring me food and clean clothing.

"I was desperate and believed the end was near, so I planned my escape. I had no intention of being crucified or dying in prison. But I feared my actions in fleeing might endanger my guardian angel Susanna, so I devised a plan that would protect her."

Jude sat spellbound and Anna's eyes sparkled with excitement as Matthan haltingly related his daring escape from Galilee's most notorious prison: Tiberias.

"So, what did you do?"

Matthan continued. "I was beaten daily. My hands had become swollen and gnarled, and my arms became crooked from the many broken bones. Guards tried to force me to reveal the names of other Zealots. Eating was difficult, so I asked my little angel, Susanna, who was attending me to bring me a utensil to assist my eating and our escape. I'm not sure how she hid it from the guards, but they were convinced that I was on the brink of death, and they had turned their attention to stronger prisoners."

Mary entered and held warm wine with herbs to his lips. He sipped several times, then nodded, and she left the cup on a small table near the bed before exiting the room.

"Just a few more minutes. He needs rest," she called over her shoulder.

"I think the wine potion will take care of that," Matthan whispered to Anna and Jude.

"We were all in pitiful condition, and the guards often left the prison doors open. We were restrained only by chains. My fellow Zealot Barabbas and I worked on each other's chains with the sharpened utensil smuggled into us until we loosened each other. His young, strong body was in much better shape than mine. He waited for the opportunity, and when one presented, he overpowered the guard.

"Barabbas did it too enthusiastically for my conscience. He strangled him, then stripped him of his uniform and put on his clothing."

Matthan stopped. The room went silent as he stared at something on the wall, something unseen to Anna and Jude. Then just as suddenly as he had stopped, he began again.

"The prison administration decided to make examples of all of us to the remaining rebels. Torturers came en masse. The screaming still haunts me. Prisoners were crucified or buried alive at the whim of the Romans. In the chaos, Barabbas carried me as we went undetected past guard after guard. Perhaps they thought Barabbas was taking me to be dumped in the open grave. It is as if we had become invisible to our enemies and as though angels escorted us into the streets of Tiberias as free men."

Matthan's eyes had grown heavy, and he drifted between slumber and wakefulness. His voice had become a whisper.

"Those who survived torture were crucified. The rest were thrown into open graves after their bodies were desecrated. Word was sent out to all of Galilee that not a prisoner survived. Barabbas and I were happy that the Romans believed us to be dead. This provided us an opportunity to attack their forces incognito as soon as we recuperated."

Matthan struggled to raise his head. "Did any other Zealots find their way here?"

Mary heard the tension Matthean created and rushed into the room. She gently but forcefully pushed Matthan back to the mattress. Brushing his hair gently he became calm again.

"No, we have seen no other rebel forces. Are you saying we should expect more?"

Jose noted the look of alarm that crossed his ima's face. Even Matthan and Simon's presence placed them all in great danger. More rebel soldiers converging on their house would draw unwanted attention. But Matthan did not appear to have heard her question.

"Mary, where is my brother? I have not seen Joseph."

Jose saw the sudden fear in Matthan's eyes and the stricken look that flickered over his ima's surprised expression.

Mary took a deep breath. "He is gone, Matthan. It has not been long. I only wish he could have been here today to see you." She brushed a tear quickly from her cheek. "Yeshua is the head of the family. I am cared for, and Joseph is greatly missed."

Matthan turned his face to the wall. "I'm sorry. I caused you and Joseph much pain. If Joseph were here, I would tell him he was right. The Zealot cause is hopeless. The defeat at Sepphoris hopelessly scattered our troops. Most of us are too old and beaten up to carry on. We need a messiah to overthrow the Romans.

"Simon and I will leave your home as soon as night falls tonight so we do not further endanger your family."

Mary sighed. "Matthan, we live and move under Yahweh's protection. Yes, we do need a messiah, but not to save us from Romans. We need a messiah to save us from our continual rebellion against God. Our Messiah will come to save us from ourselves. And the sad thing is that when He comes, we—the people who should be devoted to Him and love Him—will turn away."

Matthan looked into Mary's eyes and reached for her hand.

"Not I. If Yahweh chooses to spare my life, my only wish is that I might be in the presence of this Messiah and serve him until the end of my days."

Sixty-three

The Desert Crier

Caleb was frustrated by the inconveniences of leading a large caravan. More people meant more stops, more time on the road, more breakdowns, and more conflicts between frustrated travelers.

But more people also meant more pay. He chewed on a piece of hay as he scanned the caravanners milling about a small shopping and refreshment area on the outskirts of Jericho, a city strategically built between the wilderness of the Judean desert and the rich, fertile plain of the Jordan Valley.

A loud voice drew Caleb out of his reverie, and he surveyed the crowd of shoppers and those who were resting or eating. A strange-looking man stood in their midst, his hair long and unkempt. He was brandishing a staff above his head to emphasize his words.

The travelers were frightened by his unconventional appearance and passionate communication. They listened and watched amid the sounds of early evening caravan exhaustion: the bleats and cries of weary animals, children released from confinement or complaining about endless walking, women unloading carts and preparing evening meals, arguments among weary and short-tempered travelers. But however frightened they might have been, they were also held spellbound by the man who spoke with the fervor of the old prophets.

Moved by the travelers' obvious interest, Caleb summoned his caravanners to gather around the lead wagon, and he was pleased to see that he had sparked their curiosity. Within a few moments everyone had gathered.

"This eccentric man is well-known in this region as a *spiritual rebel*. In fact, Roman's newly appointed Judean prefect, Pontius Pilate, is as fearful of spiritual influences as political. This rebel has rejected his God-given birthright to be a practicing priest in the prestigious Jerusalem temple to preach the coming of the Messiah. He can often be found speaking to crowds in this area."

The travelers kept turning to stare at the man while listening as the wagoner explained.

"He is known as John the Essene. He studied for months under the rigors of Essene life at Qumran, where he learned their practice of ritual baptism. After leaving the community, he began a ministry with a different message. He emphasizes what he calls 'baptism with repentance' and announces the coming Messiah and the kingdom of God. We are not sure of his intent, but he preaches with great vigor and authority."

The caravanners listened, spellbound.

"Because the Qumran community requires members to give up all their worldly goods and live a communal life, the man you see before you left the sect without means to support himself."

Most serious Jews knew about the sect inhabiting the cave area of Qumran. But most often, those who lived at Qumran were dismissed as curious fools who rejected traditional Judaism and practiced legalistic, heretical principles.

Without taking a breath, the wagoner continued. "This man now lives in the wilderness wearing simple clothes and living on locusts and wild honey. His message encourages holiness of living and repentance from evil."

The wagoner knew John's ministry well and had often listened to him preach while on his travels. John's hard life in the blazing Judean desert had toughened his lean body. Even on the hottest days, he dressed in a one-piece garment of camel's hair girded with a leather belt. John's unkempt and tousled long hair and beard gave him the appearance of a deranged man, and his weather-beaten face aged him beyond his years. That he seemed unaware of his strange appearance and zealous passion for his message made him even more frightening to strangers.

But Caleb was acquainted with him as a gentle man committed to his message—a message he found to be worthy of consideration.

* * * * *

Caleb had learned much about the strange man whose name was John. He believed he was preparing the way for the Messiah. Until such time as He would come, he was preaching the righteousness taught in scripture, not the watered-down "good works" version taught by the Pharisees, Sadducees, and temple priests—and Essenes. John's message focused on personal sin and the need for all to repent. He was not concerned if his message condemned kings, rulers, or sacred teachers. He was devoted to teaching the words of the ancient prophets. John was searching for the Messiah, as well as carrying out what he believed to be his role in announcing the coming Messiah to the world. Nothing else mattered to him.

Caleb addressed his travelers and explained John's life and mission—at least what he understood it to be. Some who listened murmured in pity. John was a man to be respected, a man certain of his purpose, unlike most men Caleb had met. But some people in the crowd listened and drifted closer to John with what appeared to be newfound respect.

A voice called out from the back of the crowd. "Don't pity or fear this man."

The voice, with a Galilean accent, came from an inconspicuous rabbi who had joined the caravan at Nazareth.

Heads turned in curiosity to identify the man who seemed to be familiar with the man Caleb had identified as John.

"Truly, I tell you, among those born of women there has not risen one greater than John the Baptizer."

"This cannot be true," a voice challenged from the crowd. "How can this man be greater than our prophets Elijah, Elisha, Daniel, Isaiah, Jeremiah, or Ezekiel? Who are you to make such a claim about him? Are you one of the Essenes?"

Caleb rubbed his chin.

John the Baptizer. A better name than John the Essene. It describes this man who preaches with power and brings a new message announcing the coming Messiah.

The rabbi's eyes met his and held his gaze, as if he had read Caleb's thoughts. Peace washed over him like a cool rain after a searing drought.

The crowd dissipated and chose their places to bed down for the night. But Caleb knew he would not sleep. His thoughts had been captivated by the teacher from Galilee. Who was this man who spoke with such power?

Sixty-four

Messiah's Forerunner

The next morning John watched the caravan depart at first light, taking the remaining caravanners to the Feast of Tabernacles. One man had remained behind: Yeshua ben Joseph of Nazareth, his cousin.

The moment John heard Yeshi's voice, he recognized his beloved childhood friend. He felt Yahweh had brought Yeshua to him in answer to his prayers.

John needed Yeshua's wisdom. He had long been searching for the Messiah, and the time he had spent at Qumran with the Essenes had not solved the mystery of his father's prophecy that he would serve as the Messiah's forerunner.

John suggested the solitude of the desert as a place where he and Yeshua could retreat to pray and talk about spiritual matters. He had waited since his youth for this time with Yeshua, rabbi, son of Joseph the carpenter, and friend knit to his heart.

Together they set out into the harsh desert, sharing conversation about their lives and their families as they walked, then retreating to the freshwater springs of En Gedi, the largest oasis along the western shore of the Dead Sea. Abundant springs and a year-round temperate climate provided perfect conditions for a short retreat. The men experienced Yahweh's presence in the place that had served as David's refuge when he fled from King Saul.

Hours and days passed as John poured out question

after question. The men shared stories of their families, their childhoods, their disappointments, and their faith. Sometimes they sat in silence; sometimes they fell so deep into conversation that they forgot to eat. Their laughter rang through the oasis like the sound of the *rimonim* and gold bells that hung from the high priest's garment.[106] As Yeshua spoke about his siblings' rejection, about his special relationship with Yahweh, John trembled.

Is it possible? The circumstances of our births were remarkable. Ima told me I leaped in her womb in the presence of the preborn Yeshua. But why? Could my spirit have recognized his nature even before my birth?

As the idea tumbled through John's brain like rocks in a landslide, Yeshua smiled.

"Just speak, John, what your spirit is telling you."

John leaned back on a boulder as the sounds of a freshwater spring gurgled behind him. He took a deep breath to quiet his pounding heart, knowing his destiny and the destiny of his people rested in Yeshua's answer.

"Yeshua ben Joseph, the writings of the sages at Qumran state that two Messiahs are coming: one from the kingly line of David and one from the priestly line of Aaron. I learned much my first year with the Essenes as an initiate before I was asked to join. Many things within the community challenged my desire to serve Yahweh. The Essenes wanted reform for the corrupt Judaism practiced in the Holy City. They believed they needed to withdraw from the beliefs and practices of a wicked world.

"The goal was for members of the Essene sect to enter a covenant relationship with God founded on inward spiritual obedience in response to God's mercy and forgiveness."

"Go on," Yeshua encouraged.

"When I met with the Essene leaders, they explained the requirements of full membership. If a member who had lived with them proved worthy of their principles, that person would be admitted into their society. But before anyone can participate in the Essene banquet feast, they must take a lifetime oath. That oath is a public commitment to exercise piety toward God and a promise to do no harm to anyone, either of your own accord or by the command of others. It is an oath to always hate the wicked and strive on the side of the righteous. It is also an oath to show faithfulness to all men at all times, especially those in authority, because no one gains government office without God's assistance. And if you are in authority, you will at no time abuse your authority, nor endeavor to stand above your subjects either in conduct, in attitude, or in the wearing of garments or finery.

"You must perpetually be a lover of truth and purpose to yourself to reprove those who tell lies. You will keep your hands from theft and your soul from unlawful gain. You will neither conceal anything from those of your sect nor reveal their documents to others, even though someone should compel you so to do at the hazard of your life.

"You can see, Yeshua, the Essenes are serious about being faithful to God. However, things still troubled me about the way they exercise their faith. The Essene belief system is exclusive and places restrictions on potential candidates. This troubled me. I was offended when the restrictions required that if a Gentile or Samaritan wished to be a covenanter, they must first become a Jew and follow celibacy laws."

John took a quick drink of water from his waterskin and continued.

"If worshipping God is important to Him, why would devotion to Him be so restrictive and limited to a specific group of people? Would it be more like God to invite everyone to enjoy the riches of His goodness?"

Yeshua nodded. "I understand." Yeshua waited for John to complete the summary of his teaching at Qumran.

John continued, "The Manual of Discipline, the document that explains the Essenes' religious and moral ideals, catechetical discourses, and organizational and disciplinary rules, seems to teach that a forerunner and prophet will announce the priestly Messiah. I questioned whether perhaps that might be me.

"However, while I was supervising the Essene library, I read the Damascus Document of the Essenes, and it suggested the Messiah would come at the end of the present age. But, in fact, there would be not one Messiah but two: one priestly Messiah from the tribe of Aaron who is superior in authority, and one kingly Messiah from the line of David who must consult the Aaronic Messiah for decisions. The words were 'the Messiah of Aaron and Israel.' These two Messiahs represent the king and priest in the future. However, the Community Rule scroll adds a third Messiah as a prophet, but perhaps, a prophet of the Messiah rather than a Messiah prophet. This sounds like a *forerunner* to the priestly Messiah."

John took a deep breath and raised a hand. "I am giving much detail, but it is all important to my question.

"The Manual of Discipline doesn't mention the Messiah of Israel except in conjunction with the prophet of the Messiah and the Messiah of Aaron. The Damascus Document mentions the 'arising of the teacher of righteousness at the end of days.'"

John leaned forward. "Does all of this mean," he queried, "that the Teacher returns at the end of time as the Messiah? And if I am to be a forerunner to the Messiah, which one?"

John took a deep breath and waited. Perhaps Yeshua did not have the answer. And if he did not? John wasn't sure he could bear that response. He looked at Yeshua, but not into his eyes.

Yeshua opened his mouth to answer, but another thought flickered through John's mind.

"Some even believe the Teacher of Righteousness is the priestly Messiah and that he would return later with the king Messiah. Abba prophesied that I was the forerunner of the Messiah. Perhaps because I am in the priestly line of

Aaron, *I am* the priestly Messiah and the forerunner for the kingly Messiah.

"I studied with the Essenes to learn the truth, but I found myself even more confused. I need your wisdom."

John could see that Yeshua was holding his tongue and waiting for him to pause. He had also wanted to ask about the Essenes' ritual baptismal bath. A probationer would bathe daily before meals by total immersion as a ritual symbolic act. Most of the neophytes, however, assumed the procedure purified them from their sins. To the community, the observance signified deep purification and required strict observance. But John held his tongue and waited.

Yeshua's silence was agonizing. Suddenly John burst into details of the Essene "sacred meal" and ritual baptism and his respect for the symbolic significance that reflected personal commitment.

"For the Essenes the sacred meal is the final ritual that signifies induction into membership. It is a time when the new member demonstrates a commitment in all areas of life to the Essene belief system."

Yeshua listened, then smiled and clarified John's understanding of the cultural intent of the sacred meal.

"A sacred meal is a traditional ceremony that confirms an initiate's commitment to belief," Yeshua stated. "The act of sitting at a table to eat together is a pledge to treat those who share the meal as true brothers in a mutual covenant.[107] While the practice is commendable in a group setting, the Essenes restrict the practice beyond a cultural expression and make it an intricate part of their sect's teaching."

John concurred that Yeshua's assessment was accurate, so accurate that his confidence in Yeshua's insight multiplied.

"Likewise," Yeshua continued, "Essene baptism is a symbol of cleansing from past *ritual impurities*. John, your ministry of baptism is *for repentance* and *forgiveness*."[108]

Clarification came to John in one explosive moment.

His message aligned perfectly with Yeshua's. Yeshua had confirmed the message he had been preaching.

But what did that mean? And what did that tell him about Yeshua's message—and his identity?

Sixty-five

Yeshua's Identity Unmasked

John's back was tired, and pain was shooting down his legs. He had been sitting far too long on an uneven rock. But just as he was preparing to rise, Yeshua enthusiastically jumped into the conversation with *his* thoughts.

"John, no forerunner and prophet announce the coming of a lone *priestly* Messiah."

"No forerunner?" John stammered. "I don't understand ..." He leaned forward to listen as Yeshua continued, drinking in every word.

"There is only one Messiah, John. He will unite all the messianic offices: prophet, priest, and king."

The pain in his body disappeared as he waited for Yeshua's next words, but not before asking a question: "Where does the scripture teach this?"

Yeshua's answer made sense, but the ultimate test was understanding the text that taught this position. John's faith had always relied on the authority of scripture.

"A prophet both proclaims a divine message and prophesies future events as the Lord God reveals them," Yeshua replied. "Prophets are reformers who deliver God's message to the people and challenge them to serve the Lord."

Yeshua looked into John's eyes as if he could see his soul.

"John, you are a prophet in the sense that you have a message to proclaim that prepares the way for the Messiah."

Yes, I understand my call, but who is the Messiah? Whom am I preparing the way for?

In the distance, the sound of bleating wafted on the breeze. Small herds of goats dotted the steep rocky escarpments as they grazed in the crevices of the rocks. Several young ibexes had come to the stream behind them and were drinking from the fresh, inviting spring waters. John furrowed his brow in impatience for the interruption.

Yeshua spoke again. "Scriptures often call a prophet a 'man of God' or a 'seer.'[109] The Messiah will both proclaim God's message and prophesy the future."

John chided himself. "I should have known that. Our prophets taught this."

"John, you have given your life to seeking the truth. Yahweh knows your heart.

"God told Moses, 'I will raise up a prophet like you from among their fellow Israelites. I will put my words in his mouth, and he will tell the people everything I command him. I will personally deal with anyone who will not listen to the messages the prophet proclaims on my behalf.'[110] The Messiah is the fulfillment of these words."

Yeshua's eyes and face brightened.

"John, I tell you the truth that one day the magnificent temple in Jerusalem will be destroyed, not one stone will be left on another, and every stone will be thrown down. Messiah will establish His kingdom forever.

"The Messiah is not from the tribe of Levi but is a priest after the order of Melchizedek. As a priest-Messiah, He will offer Himself as a sacrifice. He is both the priest who offers and the sacrifice as the 'Lamb of God.' He is not as Aaron, who must offer a sacrifice for himself, but He will be God's sacrifice for the sins of humankind."

John recoiled and folded his arms across his chest. *A Messiah who would be offered as a sacrifice for the sins of humankind? The idea is beyond comprehension.*

"We won't need to offer blood sacrifices for forgiveness ... ever again?"

Even asking the question seemed strange, almost heretical, to a man raised in the home of a priest whose life was given to offering animal sacrifices in ritual atonement.

"The Messiah's sacrifice is once for all, and then He will take His rightful place at the right hand of the throne of God.

"Humankind does not have a high priest who is unable to empathize with their weaknesses, but they have one who has been tempted in every way, just as every man, woman, and child—yet He does not sin. This will enable humankind to approach God's throne of grace with confidence, so they may receive mercy and find grace to help in their time of need."

The conversation was not another of the boring lectures John had experienced at Qumran, but an intense *conversation* between two men seeking Yahweh's will.

"One day after the Holy One's sacrifice, everyone will serve as a priest before God and approach His throne boldly, knowing that they have an advocate before the Father in the Messiah."

John thanked Yahweh. But Yeshua wasn't finished. He was enjoying at long last the opportunity to talk to someone about God's plan of redemption.

"The covenant God made with King David declared that his house and kingdom would be established forever. The Messiah would be in David's line (Judah). Scriptures say the following." Then Yeshua quoted:

> For a child is born to us, a son is given to us.
> The government will rest on his shoulders.
> And he will be called:
>   Wonderful Counselor, Mighty God,
>   Everlasting Father, Prince of Peace.
>   His government and its peace
>   will never end.

He will rule with fairness and justice
from the throne of his ancestor David
for all eternity.
The passionate commitment of the Lord of Heaven's
Armies will make this happen![111]

John didn't fully understand the significance of the promise, but he tried to put the pieces together. While the covenants promised a kingdom here on earth, the prophets described the glories that extended beyond a mere political earthly kingdom. Through David's line, the Messiah would bring peace, righteousness, and prosperity to the nation. He would come as a Savior to redeem fallen humankind and as a Sovereign to reign upon the earth. Messiah, from David's line, would fulfill God's promise by sitting on David's throne and ruling His people. The kingdom of God is both a spiritual heavenly kingdom and an earthly kingdom. One enters the earthly kingdom by physical birth and the spiritual kingdom by new birth from above.

John stood, walked to the river and knelt, then cupped his hands and scooped a drink of fresh spring water.

"Your ima told mine that she would conceive and give birth to a son, and she was to call him Yeshua. An angel told her he would be great and would be called the Son of the Most High. The Lord God will give Him the throne of His father David, and He will reign over Israel forever; His kingdom will never end."[112]

John gazed across the wilderness as his mind raced and the truth came clear.

The Messiah would be from the seed of a woman, virgin born, in the line of Jacob, from the tribe of Judah, of the house of David, and born in Bethlehem. Is it possible that Yeshua is the Messiah? He fits the description, and he speaks with authority from Yahweh.

Could it be possible? I dare not ask. If he wanted me to know, he would have told me.

The question pounded through John's mind the rest of that day and through a sleepless night.

The next morning Yeshua prepared to continue on to Jerusalem and the Feast of Tabernacles. John would remain at the oasis communing with God and waiting for the next caravan back to Jericho. But he could wait no longer to ask Yeshua about his identity. He approached Yeshi as he was dousing their fire.

"Yeshua, I must ask you a question that I cannot get out of my mind. Are you the Messiah, or should I look for another?"

His cousin smiled and placed a hand upon his shoulder.

"John, you will know when the time comes. Messiah will be revealed in due time. For now, preach His message."

John's heart sank. Yeshua's answer was no answer at all.

Or was it? He had not laughed, reacted with disdain, or said no. He had replied that Messiah's identity would be revealed in due time. Messiah *could* be Yeshua. The facts of his birth and heritage fulfilled the prophecies of scripture. John's head spun as he helped Yeshua prepare for the long walk back to Jericho, where he would join a caravan that would take him on to Jerusalem. Moments later, John bid farewell to his cousin, certain that Yahweh had spoken to him in the wilderness of Judea and revealed Himself through the heart of Yeshua.

As Yeshua disappeared on the horizon, John's mission grew clear. The Word of the Lord had energized his body, mind, and soul. He was to preach, baptizing men and women in flowing living water for repentance from their sins and to proclaim the coming of the kingdom of God.

Over the following months, John traveled up and down the Jordan River, along the coast of the Dead Sea, and through the wasteland of the Negev, preaching that the kingdom of God was near and baptizing believers. Hundreds came to the banks of the Jordan to hear him speak about the coming Messiah who would take away the sin of the world.

Still the question burned John's heart: Was Yeshua, the cousin whom he had known from birth, the soon-to-be-revealed Messiah? Could it be possible that a simple carpenter would fulfill God's plan for the world?

If the answer was yes, it would seem that, before the foundation of the world, Yahweh created a plan to lay down His glory and become a God-man who walked the earth. But what would this mean for Yeshua's future—and for the future of the world?

Act 5

Resolution: Faith Endures (ca. 29–30)

(Hebrew Calendar ca. 3790–3791)

Sixty-six

Encounter at the Jordan River

Word reached Mary that John would be teaching and baptizing on the far side of the Jordan River. James agreed to accompany her to ensure her safety, and Mary was delighted that he would hear John's message for himself. Perhaps, after Mary's many years of prayer, James might trust Yahweh again and accept Yeshua as His son.

For days before their scheduled departure, Mary thought of little else but the trip. Something inside her longed to see Elizabeth's son. She gathered a small group of widows who seldom traveled to join her in the adventure, and their group set out on the trip from Nazareth to the Jordan River near the Wadi el-Kharrar (Hajiah ford), just five milla passuum north from the Dead Sea and five milla passuum from Jericho. They arrived the day before John would speak and spent the night in Jericho with the family of one of the widows in the group. James good-naturedly hovered over the women and seemed to find an awkward satisfaction in overseeing the trip.

The group departed for the Jordan River early in the morning to find a shaded site where they could watch and listen. They chose a small shaded knoll near the river. Sitting under a sycamore tree, the women and James pulled their tunics over their heads to further shield them from the burning desert sun.

A crowd soon gathered, and before long, John appeared

in the distance, walked through the crowd, and entered the river. Conversations hushed, and all eyes focused on the bearded man standing in the swirling water. John's ministry had become widely known, and the crowd included Roman officials, Jerusalem Pharisees, Jewish farmers and tradesmen, eager baptismal candidates, seekers, and the curious. All waited in anticipation to see what would unfold.

Please, Yahweh, protect him from being arrested. Silence those who have come to protest or to provoke. Use this day for Your glory.

Mary had long known that John disdained the hypocrisy of the priestly class, and he had refused to attend the feast in Jerusalem. Earlier in his life, family assumed he would become a priest, following in his father's footsteps. But he was repulsed by the corruption he observed. As a result, he kept as far from Jerusalem as possible. His time at Qumran had fortified his resolve to oppose the corrupt priesthood. Instead of becoming a part of the priestly establishment, he devoted himself to his ministry proclaiming the coming of the Messiah.

John's beliefs and practices had brought great controversy, particularly his substitution of baptism for repentance in place of the Jewish ritual of self-cleansing in a mikvah. He had encountered the practice of baptism at Qumran, and it had seemed symbolically purposeful.

Despite controversy, people from all over Jerusalem and Judea came to listen to his simple message: "Repent and be baptized for the kingdom of heaven is at hand."

* * * * *

John's message had become clear during his visit with Yeshua in the wilderness. His ministry was now empowered under the full authority of God, and John was confident of his message.

From his location standing in the river, John spotted a large group of Pharisees and Sadducees joining the crowd.

His blood boiled. They had not come seeking truth, but to disrupt. He took aim at their hypocrisy and yelled above the soft murmuring of the waiting truth seekers.

"You brood of snakes! Who warned you to flee the coming wrath? Prove by the way you live that you have repented of your sins and turned to God. Don't just say to each other, 'We're safe, for we are descendants of Abraham.' That means nothing, for I tell you, God can create children of Abraham from these very stones."[113]

His vibrant oratory continued: "I baptize with water those who repent of their sins and turn to God. But someone is coming soon who is greater than I am—so much greater that I'm not worthy even to be His slave and carry His sandals. He will baptize you with the Holy Spirit and with fire."[114]

Rage registered on the faces of the religious leaders. John's words had hit their mark.

And John knew that, apart from Yahweh's grace, he had made himself a target for execution.

* * * * *

Mary squirmed at John's condemning words that challenged the hypocrisy of the Pharisees and Sadducees. His comments would infuriate the powerful religious elite, who had the power to destroy him. No sooner had the thought passed through her mind than a Pharisee shouted, "This is a dangerous man. He threatens our way of life and all we stand for. If Herod won't do something about this rebellion, perhaps we should!"

Mary turned to one of her traveling companions. "I am worried that John challenges these powerful men. Does he not know better than to aggravate those who have the power of life and death over people they believe to be their enemies?"

Mary glanced at James, whose views of Yeshua had become more tolerant. He sat listening. His world had been filled with turmoil in the past months, and Mary could see that her son was growing weary of his battles with Yahweh and Yeshi.

She adjusted her head covering around her neck and shoulders. The sun could creep in from any angle, leaving a painful burn.

I hope John's teaching will help James recognize who Yeshua truly is.

James placed a hand on Mary's shoulder, as if he had overheard her silent prayer.

"Ima, is John saying he is the herald for the Messiah, that Yahweh sent him with a message to prepare our hearts? Do you think the Messiah is with him today? Could he also have been a member of the Qumran? I am aware that Bo John spent a short time with the Essenes, and he was confused about whether there were one or two messiahs. But then, John is from the priestly line himself."

Mary could see that James was confused, but for the first time in several years he was searching for answers.

James continued, "We are from the tribe of Judah, the kingly line, not the Aaronic line. Could Yeshua be the kingly messiah and John the priestly messiah? This seems to be what the Essenes taught. Is this what you and Abba have known since Yeshua's birth?"

Mary recognized James's words, but her mind was straining to listen to John, who was continuing to insult religious authorities.

Why is he so careless? Is he inviting their wrath?

Mary dropped her head, asking wisdom for her response to James and protection for John in his boldness.

James sat wrapped in thought.

"The thirsty crowd here today suggests John is offering answers not offered by temple priests," Mary insisted.

James froze as the color drained from his face, then turned his head, as if looking for a familiar voice.

Mary took his hand. "What is it, James? Are you sick?"

She tried to focus on John's words, but concern pulled her attention back to her son.

James bent toward her and whispered in her ear, "I heard a voice, Ima, a voice that has spoken to me before, evil and seductive. It said to me, 'James, do not believe that Yeshua is the Messiah. John the Baptizer is a pretender, a bitter Levite. Both are imposters who will be destroyed.'

"I know this voice, Ima. It was the voice described to me by Mary Magdalene, the voice that spoke to her and through her in her darkest days. When she was in her times of greatest despair, I heard the voice myself. It is a deluder and liar and is not to be trusted. It is telling me to mistrust the authority and words of John and Yeshua, but I refuse to allow this dark enemy to deceive me."

Mary sat speechless.

Did James just say he is trusting in Yeshua as the Messiah? It can't be true.

She shook her head, and her eye glimpsed a silhouette standing on a rise behind the crowd. She blinked and shaded her eyes against the bright sunlight. It appeared to be an elderly man whose movements indicated he wanted to remain unseen. As the figure moved into the shadow of a tree, Mary noted the man's limp, the line of his shoulders, the details of his form. Her hands flew to her mouth to keep from screaming, and tears poured from her eyes. She jumped up and pushed her way through the crowd, half walking, half running, so as not to call attention to her approach.

Her friends called after her, but her tears would not allow her to respond. She ran at full pace across the final space of open grass and threw herself into the arms of the rugged-featured man she had recognized from a distance.

"Matthan, Matthan, is it you? We didn't think we would ever see you again, but you are here!"

Mary cupped Matthan's face in her hands as tears poured down her face.

"You have recovered. You are well, you are well."

Mary's words poured out like the banks of Jordan at harvest flood stage. "I know Joseph would be proud of you for being here."

"How often I have longed to see Joseph and to thank him for placing his life at risk for me. I have missed my brother." Matthan paused. "Mary, after the Zealots' foolish attack on Sepphoris and your words of encouragement, I thought deeply about my life as a rebel. My actions brought our nation no closer to freedom than before I became involved. I only hurt my family."

Mary read the deep sorrow and sincerity in Matthan's eyes.

"I am here because my life has meant nothing, and I want to spend my remaining, although short, days seeking the true King and Messiah. Many people have told me that John is preaching a coming kingdom, and I wanted to hear his message for myself because I want to be part of that work."

Mary tried to offer a prayer of gratitude, but words were inadequate to express her joy. She would have to trust that Yahweh heard her heart and that He was working and had always been working in ways far beyond what she could see or imagine.

* * * * *

Donae had felt uncomfortable about taking duty at the Jordan River, but Roman soldiers were not given choices. He had taken his place with other soldiers patrolling the gathering there. They had been ordered to look for signs of insurrection among the crowd. A large group of Jews always presented the possibility of riots. Roman authorities distrusted public gatherings, and any threat of popularity by a Jewish teacher who might threaten the authority of Governor Pilate in Judea or Herod Antipas in Galilee would be met with force.

So Donae was not surprised when he overheard soldiers talking among themselves.

"This John the Baptizer is trouble."

"The crowd is large, and his message is captivating."

"He is certain to find more followers. And he preaches a coming king. Should we notify Pilate?"

Many years prior, Donae had refused to participate in the slaughter of infants in Bethlehem who purportedly threatened Roman rule. He quickly responded.

"No, he is a Galilean and is Antipas's problem."

He hoped his words would protect the zealous baptizer and the Messiah he spoke of who offered hope for a hate-filled world.

But in the distance Donae spotted a small contingent of soldiers from Galilee who were known for their loyalty to Herod Antipas. They were headed in the direction of his commanding officer.

Herod would soon know that a Messiah was reportedly on the horizon, and the monarch would no doubt feel threatened.

* * * * *

Simon Cananeus and Judas Iscariot had accepted the risk, knowing a seemingly harmless choice could cost them their lives. But few choices in their adult lives had been harmless. As leaders of the Zealots and Sicarii, they were despised by the powerful Pharisees and pursued by Antipas's soldiers. They had heard much about the enigmatic John and wanted to listen for themselves and decide whether his message was blasphemy or offered hope for their people. Astute in military tactics, the two men had planned a route for a quick escape, should it become necessary. They had located a position in a dense stand of poplar trees that screened them from view of the crowd and patrolling soldiers. They sat, motionless, hoping they would not be spotted by keen-eyed soldiers whose job was to search out rebels such as themselves.

Judas scanned the crowd. A group of angry Pharisees stood on the fringe of the group, waiting for an opportunity to challenge John's authority. Among them was a young man known to be outspoken in his skepticism: Saul of Tarsus, a student of Rabbi Gamaliel, who had traveled from Jerusalem with the Pharisees. Saul's voice was fearless for one so young and could be clearly understood from a distance.

"This John the Baptizer is dangerous, and his message is contrary to Rabbi Gamaliel's teaching of the Torah. We cannot tolerate this rebel heretic gaining influence!"

Saul glanced around at the crowd, searching for supporting voices of outrage at John's "heresy." He believed it was his mission to rid the country of the Baptizer's teaching, and he was looking for recruits.

Simon and Judas shook their heads at the chutzpah of the bold young Pharisee.

Judas crossed his arms. "The Baptizer and his Messiah would be wise to remain far from the reach of young Saul from Tarsus."

* * * * *

Bo John arrived at the Jordan after visiting his saba during the Feast of Passover. He always enjoyed this special holiday with his saba Aaron, who was a temple priest and accompanied him in his duties on the Temple Mount—except for restricted areas. He had become familiar with the priests and the forbidden areas, as well as those areas where he was permitted. The priests enjoyed joking with him and explaining the significance of the rituals and ceremonies.

As soon as he reached the Jordan, Bo John searched for Mary and her friends. He soon found them seated on their blankets under a tree, shaded from the heat of the sun. He seated himself with them and accepted Mary's offering of wine, bread, nuts, figs, and dried fish.

Invigorated by the food and drink, Bo John took a deep breath.

"Mary, I need to tell you something. Perhaps this is a good time. I see that John the Baptizer is resting in the shade to eat his midday meal."

Mary smiled. "Of course, Bo John. I sense your urgency. What is it?"

"I followed Yeshua into the city the other day. He was heading toward the center of the city by way of the Beautiful Gate."

"I am quite familiar with that location." Mary nodded.

"Beggars and pilgrims crowded the gate, making it difficult for him to pass. Many of the people were wracked by disease, deformed by accidents or birth. Some were lacking limbs, or blind, or sick of mind, but all were outcasts—many forced to live outside the city walls."

Mary looked down. "Their plight tears at my heart. I always give alms when I pass."

"Although many passed by without looking, Yeshua stopped and took a seat among them. He sat in the filth of the gate, where animals walk and ... and ... the stench was indescribable. Yeshua *joined* them. He sat *with* them as brothers as sisters, the same in dignity, as if saying, 'You, too, are Yahweh's children, with the same dignity and beauty as all who pass through this gate. Although others turn their faces away, I see you as *beautiful*.'"

Mary drew her hands to her heart. The picture of her son, of God's Son, seated among the least of these overcame her heart with the force of a maelstrom.

But that was not all to the story. Bo John continued, "Yeshua told them stories from scripture: Noah's faithfulness in following God's commands, Abraham traveling to an unknown land while facing a questionable future, blind

Samson's strength in destroying his enemies, and the bravery of the boy David facing a giant foe.

"Most of the outcasts sitting with Yeshua had received little instruction in scripture. They crept closer in any way they could to listen to the teacher who cared enough to stop what he was doing to sit among them and teach them. They even stopped begging to draw closer, quietly enthralled, while crowds stumbled past them.

"Then Yeshua looked directly into their faces and told them, 'There will be no more sorrow, no more deformities, and no more suffering. Messiah will heal all diseases and repair all broken hearts. God's people will dwell in mansions and bathe in the glorious light of the eternal God.'

"One beggar seemed overcome by Yeshua's words and cried out, 'Who is this man of gentle spirit from whom we are hearing words of love and compassion?'

"A woman who had only one leg and was leaning on her crutch also spoke. 'This man's words are spoken with authority.'

"Others called out—the blind, the lame. Until several cried out, 'Hosanna in the highest.'"

Mary listened, tears streaming down her face.

His time is near.

"An hour passed before Yeshua stood. He drew his purse from inside his mantle, took out a handful of coins, and distributed them. Then he told his listeners, 'I have given each of you what is needed for your "daily bread." God will provide again when you are in need again.'

"While they were expressing amazement among themselves at the gift, Yeshua disappeared into the crowd."

Bo John waited for Mary's response.

"Mary, it is clear to me that Yeshua is more than a simple rabbi."

Mary nodded. "Dear Bo John, you are right. And perhaps today will be the day Yahweh will reveal who Yeshua is. But I believe you already have full knowledge of the truth in your heart."

Bo John's eyes grew wide as the words of John the Baptizer echoed over the waters of the Jordan.

* * * * *

James stood and scanned the crowd. No sign of Yeshua.

The crowd had grown excited and buzzed with whispers of speculation that the Baptizer might be the Messiah. This very thought had been James's suspicion until hearing about what Yeshua had done at the Beautiful Gate.

John the Baptizer was now preaching to the hearts of the Pharisees and the multitudes. He was also baptizing those who desired to confess their faith in John's teaching regarding the Messiah. James made his way into the waters of the Jordan and expressed his desire to be baptized. John pressed him below the waters of the Jordan and raised him again, sputtering and dripping.

But as the water washed over James's body, he prepared to wade back to shore when he noted John's gaze had shifted. He was staring at a man standing on a hill, the sun glowing red and framing his radiant image in the afternoon sunlight. The moment froze in time. The sun paid homage, the winds seemed to bow, the world was about to change forever. A look of recognition washed over John's face, and his arms stretched out in welcome.

"Look! *The Lamb of God*, who takes away the sin of the world! Yeshua, Son of God."

An audible gasp came from the crowd as Yeshua descended the hill and walked through the crowd to the water's edge. The people hushed as He passed, and Mary rested on her knees in reverence, her hands raised in the air.

Yeshua's words rung through the silence. "John, baptize Me."

James watched, bewildered, from the place in the grass where he had rested after his baptism.

John's thoughts embraced his growing conviction. *Yeshua is the Messiah I have waited for, for so long. He is the prophet, priest, and king.*[115] *I am not the Messiah; I am a witness to the Messiah. He is the Lamb of God.*

"I am the one who needs to be baptized by You, so why are you coming to me?" John replied humbly.

"It should be done, for we must carry out all that God requires,"[116] Yeshua responded.

The crowd of witnesses watched silently as John consented. With a new awareness of the significance of his actions, he grasped Yeshua by the shoulders and reverently lowered his Messiah into the waters of the Jordan River.

The crowd stretched to see the action as they watched in rapt attention as Yeshua disappeared beneath the water.

James heard a gasp and turned. Mary's hands covered her mouth, and tears streamed down her face. James placed his hand on her arm. For thirty years his ima had watched Yeshua grow from an infant in her arms to a man intent on fulfilling His heavenly Av's mission. He knew her heart was fighting, knowing Yeshua was prepared to give His life to carry out His mission. But she was also proud. Her beloved son was stepping into His divine destiny.

As John lifted Yeshua out of the Jordan waters, the heavens rumbled with the sounds of a host of fluttering wings stirring the clouds in the heavens. In view of all present, a white dove descended and landed on Yeshua's shoulder—the Spirit of God, descended to anoint the Messiah. The babe born in a manger who grew in wisdom and stature was God's Messiah.

Then Yahweh's echoing voice thundered from heaven with the authority of the universe, "This is my dearly loved Son, who brings me great joy."

* * * * *

God's words introduced a new world hope. From this time, *they called Him Jesus*, the Christ, Messiah, a name that one day *all humankind* will confess.

"Therefore, God elevated Him to the place of highest honor and gave Him the name above all other names, that at the name of Jesus every knee should bow, in heaven and on earth and under the earth, and every tongue declare that Jesus Christ is Lord, to the glory of God the Father" (Philippians 2:9–11).

"Amazing grace, how sweet the sound, that saved a wretch like me."[117]

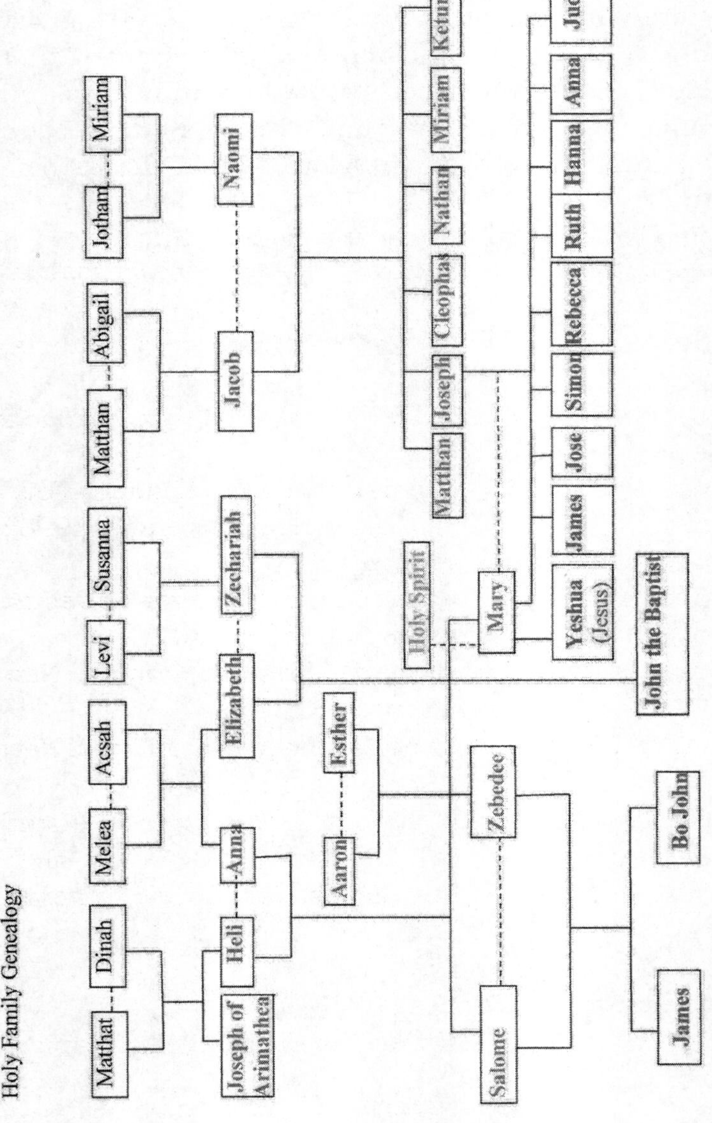

Holy Family Genealogy

Bibliography

Bahat, Dan. *Carta's Historical Atlas of Jerusalem.* Jerusalem: Carta, 1973.

Batey, Richard A. *Jesus and the Forgotten City.* Pasadena, CA: Century One Media, 2000.

———. "Sepphoris—an Urban Picture of Jesus." *Biblical Archaeology Review* (1992): 50.

Ben-Yehuda, Nachman. "Where Masada's Defenders Fell." *Biblical Archaeology Review* (November/December 1998): 32–39.

Bivin, David. *New Light on the Difficult Words of Jesus.* Holland, MI: En-Gedi Resource Center, 2007.

Black, Matthew. *The Scrolls and Christian Origins.* New York: Charles Scribner's Sons, 1961.

Bouquet, A. C. *Everyday Life in New Testament Times.* New York: Charles Scribner's Sons, 1953.

Brake, Donald L. Sr., with Todd Bolen. *Jesus, a Visual History.* Grand Rapids, MI: Zondervan, 2014.

Burrows, Millar. *The Dead Sea Scrolls.* New York: Gramercy, 1955.

Connolly, Peter. *Living in the Time of Jesus of Nazareth.* Jerusalem: Steimatzky Ltd., 1983.

DeHaan, M. R. *The Chemistry of the Blood.* Grand Rapids, MI: Zondervan, 1974.

Gaster, Theodor H. *The Dead Sea Scripture in English Translation.* Garden City, NY: Doubleday and Co., 1964.

Hoehner, Harold. *Chronological Aspects of the Life of Christ.* Grand Rapids, MI: Zondervan, 1977.

———. *Herod Antipas.* Cambridge, England: Cambridge University, 1972.

Jeremias, Joachim. *Jerusalem in the Time of Jesus.* Philadelphia: The Fortress Press, 1969.

Kauffmann, Joel. *The Nazareth Jesus Knew.* Nazareth: Nazareth Village, 2005.

Klausner, Joseph. *Jesus of Nazareth.* Revised edition 1979. Translated by Herbert Danby. New York: Menorah, 1925.

Kotker, Norman. *The Holy Land in the Time of Jesus.* Edited by Horizon Magazine. New York: American Heritage. Distributed by Harper and Row, 1967.

Levine, Lee I, ed. *Ancient Synagogues Revealed.* Jerusalem: Israel Exploration Society, 1981.

Lewis, C. S. *The Problem of Pain.* New York: Macmillan, 1962.

Loffreda, Stanislao. *Recovering Capharnaum.* Gerusalemme: Edizioni Custodia Terra Santa P, 1985.

Mackowski, Richard M. *Jerusalem: City of Jesus.* Grand Rapids, MI: William B. Eerdmans, 1980.

Maier, Paul L. *In the Fullness of Time.* Grand Rapids, MI: Kregel Publications, 1991.

———. *Pontius Pilate.* Wheaton: Tyndale Publishers, 1968.

———, ed. *The New Complete Works of Josephus.* Translated by William Whiston. Grand Rapids, MI: Kregel Publications, 1999.

Mazar, Eilat. *The Complete Guide to the Temple Mount Excavations.* Jerusalem: Shoham Academic Research and Publication, 2002.

Miller, Madeleine S., and J. Lane Miller. *Encyclopedia of Bible Life.* New York: Harper and Brothers, 1955.

Moldenke, Harold N., and Alma L. Moldenke. *Plants of the Bible.* New York: Dover, 1952.

Morgan, Barbara J., ed. *Illustrated Dictionary of Bible Life and Times.* Pleasantville, NY: Reader's Digest, 1997.

NIV Archaeological Study Bible. Grand Rapids, MI: Zondervan, 2005.

Nun, Mendel. *Gergesa (Kursi): Site of a Miracle Church and Fishing Village.* Ein Gev, Israel: Kibbutz Ein Gev, 1989.

———. *The Sea of Galilee and Its Fishermen in the New Testament.* Ein Gev, Israel: Kibbutz Ein Gev, 1989.

Pelikan, Jaroslav. *Mary through the Centuries.* New Haven, CT: Yale University Press, 1996.

Pentecost, J. Dwight. *The Words and Works of Jesus Christ.* Grand Rapids, MI: Zondervan, 1981.

Perowne, Stewart. *The Life and Times of Herod the Great.* New York: Abingdon Press, 1956.

Raney, Anson F., and R. Steven Notley. *The Sacred Bridge.* Jerusalem: Carta, 2006.

Richman, Chaim. *The Holy Temple of Jerusalem.* Jerusalem: The Temple Institute and Carta, 1997.

Ritmeyer, Kathleen, and Leen Ritmeyer. *Secrets of Jerusalem's Temple Mount.* Washington, DC: Biblical Archaeology Society, 1998.

Rousseau, John J., and Rami Arav. *Jesus and His World.* Minneapolis: Fortress Press, 1995.

Schlegel, William. *Satellite Bible Atlas: Historical Geography of the Bible.* Jerusalem: William Schlegel, 2012.

Shanks, Hershel, ed. *Understanding the Dead Sea Scrolls.* New York: Random House, 1992.

Spangler, Ann, and Lois Tverberg. *Sitting at the Feet of Rabbi Jesus.* Grand Rapids, MI: Zondervan, 2009.

Tenney, Merrill C. *New Testament Times.* Grand Rapids, MI: Wm. B. Eerdmans, 1965.

Thiede, Carsten Peter. *The Dead Sea Scrolls.* New York: Palgrave, 2001.

Trever, John C. *The Untold Story of Qumran.* Westwood, NJ: Fleming H. Revell, 1952.

Ward, Kaari, ed. *Jesus and His Times.* Pleasantville, NY: The Reader's Digest Association, 1987.

Werblowsky, R. J. Zwi, and Geoffrey Wigoder, eds. *The Oxford Dictionary of the Jewish Religion.* New York: Oxford University Press, 1997.

Wright, Paul H. *Greatness, Grace, and Glory.* Jerusalem: Carta, 2008.

Yadin, Yigael. *The Story of Masada.* New York: Random House, 1966.

———. *The Temple Scroll.* Jerusalem: Steimatzky Ltd., 1985.

Websites

Jewish Encyclopedia. www.jewishencyclopedia.com.

Jerusalem Perspective. www.jerusalemperspective.com.

Wikipedia. www.wikipedia.org.

Acknowledgments

A novel is unlike writing an academic or historical book. It requires the author to enter into an unknown world and let his mind create the story. A novel sensitive to the cultural, historical and geographical context of the first century while incorporating unrecorded fictional events in Jesus's life posed many challenges. No one has dared to speak fully to the thirty missing years simply because one must confront the mystery of the incarnation of the God/man. To put words in Jesus's mouth could cause readers to believe that is actually what God said. I pray that I have given justice to both His deity and humanity without wandering from scriptural principles. It is my hope that the subject of this novel will be glorified.

My time at the Institute of Holy Land Studies (now Jerusalem University College) and the teaching of Jim Monson and Bill Schlegel fueled my love for Jesus in His homeland and created an appetite for writing a historical novel about Jesus's missing years.

Those who made a direct contribution, I will mention here:

Mesa Andrews, who encouraged me to write and gave me early help in the literary formula for fiction—point of view, character development, plot, and structure.

Dr. Latayne C. Scott, Dr. Diana Severance, Carol Trumbold, Mike Petersen, Stu Weber, David Sanford and Mesu Andrews, for their suggestions and kind words.

My wife, Carol, for insights and editing.

Carol Trumbold, for editing the manuscript and making helpful suggestions.

Ron Waalkes, professional artist, for willingness to do an original oil painting for the cover, and art for the city of Jerusalem and first-century compound.

Shelly Beach, for her writing gifts, skills, and biblical knowledge which are deeply entrenched in the entire work. Shelly seemed to be imbedded in my mind as she edited, rewrote, and constructed dialogue with the skill of a professional.

The editors and designers at Archway Publishers, for their expertise in production.

Endnotes

1 Hebrew Calendar 3761 begins year one of Roman Calendar.
2 Josephus records the turmoil in the Holy Land during this period of history. Rebels sought any excuse to harass the Roman occupiers. Galilee was a known hotspot for rebellious activity.
3 It is normally assumed that the Zealots began with Judas of Gamla in reaction to Quirinius's tax census of AD 6. However, the origins of these rebels were earlier.
4 A *mohar* in ancient Israel was the price the father of the groom paid to the father of the bride.
5 Luke 1:46–55.
6 There are some interpretive issues with whether or not Mary remained at Elizabeth's until John was born (Luke 56–57).
7 In 6 BC, the Feast of Tabernacles occurred September 27–October 3. The Jewish calendar:
Tishri, September/October; Succoth (Tabernacles); Yom Kippur, Simchat Torah, Rosh Hashanah (New Year) (Feast of Trumpets); only post Old Testament did rabbis move the feast from spring to the fall.
Cheshvan, October/November; harvest green olives
Kislev, November/December; Hanukkah (Feast of Lights); plowing, harvest black olives
Tevet, December/January; sowing grain
Shevat, January/February; winter rains fill cisterns
Adar, February/March; Purim; almonds in bloom
Nisan, March/April: Passover (Pesach); barley
Iyar, April/May; wheat
Sivan, May/June: Shavuot (Pentecost)
Tammuz, June/July; heavy (dew no rain) fruit trees

Av, July/August; harvest grapes; Sirocco winds bring transitional seasons in winter and fall

Elul, August/September; harvest pomegranates and figs

8 Simon was a known rebel fighting with the Zealots. Josephus, *War*, 4.514–520.

9 There has been a theory that the "eye of the needle" referred to a small opening in a huge gate. Others say such an interpretation is unwarranted. The Greek expression "eye of the needle" when joined with "camel" refers to the smallest thing and largest object (William F. Arndt and F. Wilbur Gingrich, *A Greek-English Lexicon of the New Testament* (Chicago: The University of Chicago Press, 1952), 402. The expression could simply mean it is impossible to put a rope through the eye of a sewing needle.

10 Five English miles.

11 Leviticus 23:40–43.

12 Luke 1:31–33.

13 Luke 1:68.

14 The fourth watch in the first century was 3:00 a.m. to sunrise.

15 It was not until much later that writers would refer to his Greek name, Jesus.

16 Luke 2:10–11.

17 Matthew 1:25 strongly suggests Mary and Joseph had natural, intimate marital relations after the birth of Jesus. But Joseph did not have sexual relations with her until her son was born and Mary was cleansed at the temple.

18 The magi's ethnic origins are unclear. They seemed to know the scriptures.

19 Numbers 24:17.

20 The trip was about 810 miles or 744 milla passuum.

21 The Bible does not say much about Jesus's brothers and sisters, only that He had them (Matthew 13:55–56).

22 Some traditions suggest James was the son of Joseph from a previous marriage; others see Jesus's brothers and sisters as cousins. This would require both Joseph and Mary to have remained celibate. But Matthew 13:55–56 suggests natural children, half-brothers of Jesus: "Then they scoffed, 'He's just the carpenter's son, and we know Mary, his mother, and his brothers—James, Joseph, Simon, and Judas. All his sisters

live right here among us'" (also Mark 6:3). The name James is historically the English spelling of Hebrew *Jacob.*

23 Matthew 2:20.

24 4 BC.

25 Josephus wrote about the battle in great detail. Josephus, *Jewish Antiquities,* 17:260–98.

26 Many scholars believe Joseph and his son Jesus worked in Sepphoris during this time in Jesus's life.

27 Died ca. 69 BC.

28 R. J. Zwi Werblowsky and Geoffrey Wigoder, eds., *Oxford Dictionary of the Jewish Religion* (New York: Oxford University Press, 1997), 215. Jewish education was a well-established practice among early Jewish communities but was often ignored because of financial concerns and household duties. Some assume the Jewish education was in Aramaic or Greek because it was the lingua franca of the land. However, it is likely studies for Jewish children came from the Hebrew Torah and so they spoke Hebrew along with Greek and Aramaic.

29 The Hebrew has twenty-two letters, but another five have different forms when ending a word.

30 Jesus was a human boy and no doubt had a normal childhood—laughing, playing, crying, etc. Those emotions are not sin in themselves.

31 Kaari Ward, ed., *Jesus and His Times* (Pleasantville, NY: Reader's Digest Association, 1987), 151.

32 Scholars really don't know how long the family stayed in Egypt, but Joseph probably had access to its libraries.

33 Job 9:9.

34 These were common board games played and the kind of figures enjoyed by Jewish youths.

35 The pseudepigraphal gospel *Infancy Gospel of Thomas* (paragraph 2) written in the second century records childhood miracles of Jesus before He was twelve years old. No doubt it was an attempt to satisfy the hunger for information about the formative years of Jesus while avoiding the mystery of the Incarnation.

36 Jesus often used illustrations from the characteristics of sheep. He must have had personal knowledge of sheep.

37 Jesus, in His later ministry, used parables and illustrations from agricultural features. Perhaps He gained His knowledge from interaction with His farmer saba.
38 Breeding mules in Israel was forbidden (Leviticus 19:19). Mules were probably imported from Egypt.
39 A Roman *mille passuus* (plural, *milla passuum*) equals 0.919 miles, and one *pes* (plural, *pedes*) equals 0.971 feet (English 15 miles and 2,510 feet, respectively).
40 Psalm 122:1–2.
41 63 BC.
42 37 BC.
43 20–19 BC.
44 Bar mitzvah is not a term used in the scriptures, but a similar event took place in Israel.
45 Jesus seems to be a family friend of Lazarus, Mary, and Martha. He spent his last week of life with them. He may have been introduced to them at an earlier time. See John 11:3, 11.
46 Story in Exodus 11–12.
47 The "ten days of awe" lead to Yom Kippur on Tishrei 10, the Day of Atonement.
48 Gamaliel, a well-known character in the apostle Paul's life, no doubt was a prominent figure in Jerusalem. Acts 5:33–35: "When they heard this, the high council was furious and decided to kill them. But one member, a Pharisee named Gamaliel, who was an expert in religious law and respected by all the people, stood up and ordered that the men be sent outside the council chamber for a while. Then he said to his colleagues, 'Men of Israel, take care what you are planning to do to these men!'"
49 There is no real evidence that Joseph was related to Jesus. The inference comes from the fact that he boldly asked for Jesus's body after His crucifixion. It is asserted that he was of the family of Nathan and so of royal blood. Tradition has maintained the family relationship with Jesus.
50 Zechariah 9:9.
51 Taken from Daniel 9:24–27.
52 This name of God means "all-seeing, watching" (Genesis 16:13).

53 First-century parents were not as strict in having hour-by-hour supervision of their children. The children often "ran wild."

54 Some traditions suggest John's parents Elizabeth and Zachariah had passed away while John was still quite young. Perhaps Joseph of Arimathea had taken him in as his nearest relative.

55 Those in the New Testament who had their first encounters with Jesus, seem to indicate many recognized Him as a teacher, but others question His credentials—He is just a carpenter from Nazareth (John 3:2; Mark 6:2–3).

56 Isaiah 11:1; Bargil Pixner, *With Jesus through Galilee according to the Fifth Gospel* (Rosh Pina, Israel: Corazin, 1992), 16.

57 Matthew 2:23; Ray A. Pritz, *Nazarene Jewish Christianity* (Jerusalem: Magnes Press, 1988), 11–18. Pritz's book argues convincingly of this relationship between "Nazarenes" and *nezer.*

58 Writings from the Essenes, living near the Dead Sea in a community called Qumran, referred to these family ties: "Netzer shoot planted by God." The term *Nazarene* referred to Yeshua's Davidic lineage as the branch or netzer. He was the netzer shoot, the name of Nazareth.

59 Leviticus 27:1–8.

60 The description of Nazareth homes comes from *The Nazareth Jesus Knew*, 26.

61 English, 229 feet long and 262 feet wide.

62 Leviticus 16:17.

63 Leviticus 16:4.

64 Exodus 28:9–10.

65 Exodus 28:30.

66 Hebrews 6:20 – 7:1–3.

67 Leviticus 16:5–8.

68 First Esdras (Apocrypha book) 1:54 reads, "And all the holy vessels of the Lord, great and small, and the treasure chests of the Lord, and the royal stores, they took and carried away to Babylon" (Revised Standard Version).

69 Leviticus 16:13.

70 Leviticus 16:18–19.

71 Leviticus 4:7.

72 Many books and stories suggest Jesus was married, and the usual prospect is Mary Magdalene. While the evidence for such a union is lacking, His relationship to Mary and Martha could have developed an environment that gave Mary and Martha's father the freedom to hope that such a mutually beneficial arrangement was possible.

73 There is no evidence that Jesus was ever married. His life was totally dedicated to His mission. No doubt, because Hebrew culture strongly urged marriage, Jesus would have been considered a prime candidate for marriage. Even Joseph may have discussed the issue with Jesus.

74 First Corinthians 7:8–9.

75 First Corinthians 7:1.

76 Jesus is known as a master teacher. Where did He get His ability in oratory? What about the structure of His messages? Perhaps His innate ability was supported by His contacts with the theater in Sepphoris.

77 Matthew 6:28–34.

78 It is perhaps a false notion that Jesus never suffered sickness or pain. The scriptures demonstrate that He did have pain and suffered—beatings and suffering on the cross are just an example.

79 Isaiah 52:13–53:12.

80 Hebrews 4:15.

81 Deuteronomy 23:3–7.

82 Matthew 5:48.

83 The tzitzit (tassels) and the tallit (cloak) are of postbiblical rabbinic origin and vary among various Jewish groups. However, Yeshua had a unique tallit that identified Him as a teacher.

84 Matthew 5:27–30.

85 Matthew 5:33–37.

86 Matthew 6:1–4.

87 The question is often asked if Jesus's wilderness temptation was His first encounter with Satan. Given the nature of Satan's wiles, undoubtedly he would not wait for his victim to reach the age of adulthood—he doesn't operate that way.

88 While Jesus's confrontation in the wilderness after His baptism was Satan's temptation for Jesus to thwart the kingdom of God, it seems probable that Jesus faced Satan's attacks before His three-year ministry.

89 The description of a beautiful and sexy woman comes from the book Song of Solomon.

90 Matthew 5:27–28.

91 First Corinthians 7:1–7.

92 Exodus 13:1–10; Deuteronomy 6:4–9, 11:13–21.

93 The region of Batanea (Bashan) became known as the Golan Heights after the Six-Day War in 1967.

94 Jeremiah 31:31, 33–34.

95 The long ending of Mark (16:9) and Luke 8:2 say Mary Magdalene was a woman with seven demons. In the Middle Ages, Mary Magdalene was conflated in Western tradition with Mary the "sinful woman" who anointed Jesus's feet in Luke 7:36–50. It resulted in a widespread erroneous belief that Mary Magdalene was the same prostitute. This novel does not identify Mary Magdalene with the sinful woman Mary. Most associate Mary's "sin" with prostitution, although the Bible does not directly say this. Mary Magdalene had seven demons. We don't know what or who they were. It is generally believed demons enter through the weaknesses or portals because of sin, depression, or illicit sexual behavior. This novel portrays Mary as being abused and forced into sexual misconduct (resulting in entry or result of seven demons), not of her own volition, but because of Silas's unspeakable mistreatment, which led to deep, dark depression.

96 A denarii was the first century agricultural wages for one day (Matthew 20:2).

97 The name Iscariot comes from the name Sicarii, meaning "assassin." Some historians prefer to find the name Iscariot from his hometown, Kerioth-hezron.

98 English, 38 miles by first-century foot travel.

99 Josephus later records that Antipas forced Jewish settlers to inhabit an area repulsive to them: "Strangers came and inhabited this city, a great number of the inhabitants were Galileans also; and many were necessitated by Herod to come there out of the country belonging to him; and were by force compelled to be its inhabitants; some of them were persons of condition. He also admitted poor people, such as those that were collected from all parts, to dwell in it. Nay, some of them not quite freemen. ... [Herod] built them very good houses at his own expense and by giving the land also, for

he was sensible, that to make this place a habitation was to transgress the Jewish ancient laws, because many sepulchers were to be here taken away, in order to make room for the city Tiberias whereas our laws pronounce that such inhabitants are unclean for seven days" (Josephus, *Antiquities*, 18.37, 38).

100 Psalm 91:1.

101 Ezekiel 24:17, 22.

102 Judges 6:13.

103 Job 19:7.

104 Romans 8:22.

105 Isaiah 52:13–53:11.

106 Exodus 28:31–35.

107 There is no evidence that Jesus modeled the Last Supper after the Qumran ritual. The cultural significance of eating together representing a mutual commitment is most likely a common occurrence.

108 John's baptism is not for regeneration, but as Josephus says, "...for that the washing [baptism] would be acceptable to him [God], if they made use of it, not in order to the putting away [remission] of some sins, but for the purification of the body; supposing still that the soul was thoroughly purified beforehand by righteousness." *Antiquities* 18:5.2.

109 Second Kings 1:9, 17:13.

110 Deuteronomy 18:18, 19.

111 Isaiah 6:2–3.

112 Luke 1:31–33.

113 Matthew 3:7–9.

114 Matthew 3:11.

115 While in prison waiting to be beheaded, John asked if Jesus was the Messiah or if there was another to come (John 7:18). Could he be asking because of the Essene teaching on multiple messiahs?

116 Matthew 3:13–15.

117 John Newton, "Amazing Grace," original hymn published in 1779.

About the Authors

Donald L. Brake Sr., PhD, Dallas Theological Seminary; Dean Emeritus, Multnomah Biblical Seminary of Multnomah University.

The author's experience as president of the Jerusalem University College (previously Institute of Holy Land Studies) has given him insight into the historical and geographical background of Israel and the life of Christ.

Dr. Brake has led tours to the Holy Land and has taught the life of Christ and the Bible's historical/cultural backgrounds for more than thirty-five years.

Dr. Brake has written fifteen articles for the *St. Louis Metro Voice*, has published the *Wycliffe New Testament*, and has written various mission articles for magazines. His book *A Visual History of the English Bible* was published in 2008 (a 2009 Evangelical Christian Publishers Association Christian Book Award finalist); *A Monarch's Majestic Translation*, in 2017; and *A Visual History of the King James Bible*, in 2011 (with Shelly Beach; also translated into Portuguese as *Uma Historia Visual Da Biblia King James*), a commemorative edition celebrating four hundred years of the King James Version. His major article "Versions, English" was published in *The Interpreters Dictionary of the Bible*, vol.

5, and he wrote *Jesus, a Visual History* with Todd Bolen, published in 2014.

Shelly Beach, MRE, Grand Rapids Theological Seminary

Shelly is an award-winning author of eight books of both fiction and nonfiction. She served as managing editor of Zondervan's *Hope in the Mourning Bible* (Fall 2013) and was one of three writers of Zondervan's *NIV Stewardship Bible,* as well as a contributor to *Tyndale's Mosaic Bible.* She is cofounder of the Breathe Writer's Conference and the Cedar Falls Christian Writer's Workshop and speaks nationally on a wide variety of issues and presents seminars for Daughters of Destiny, a national women's prison ministry. She is cofounder of PTSD Perspectives and presents educational seminars on posttraumatic stress disorder to medical and mental health professionals, counselors, social workers, law enforcement officers, child advocates, educators, and other professionals.

Printed and bound by PG in the USA